An Intimate history of the Greater Kingdom

LOVERS & BELOVEDS

This work is published by:
Sans Culotte Press
4110 SE Hawthorne Blvd #428
Portland, OR 97214

Cover illustration and design by Alice Fox: http://www.alicefox.net/
Book design by MCM: http://1889.ca/
Editing by Annetta Ribken: http://www.wordwebbing.com/
They are all brilliant, and you should hire them right now.

Go to http://www.meilinmiranda.com/ for information, discussions, stories, artwork and more.

Printed in the United States of America
First printing: October 2010
ISBN: 978-0-9813071-7-6

To the forty-eight people who funded the production of this book,
expecting nothing but the finished story…
But mostly, to the man whose love I work every day to justify.

An Intimate history of the Greater Kingdom
LOVERS & BELOVEDS

BY
MEILIN MIRANDA

ONE

In the stable yards of Whithorse Estate, two lanterns burned. They shone up at their owners, who sat on a straw bale against a brick wall. The low light transformed the rangy, blue-eyed one's fair hair into a burnished bronze, and turned the shorter, stockier one's eyes near-black. Both wore battered old tweed caps, and coats just heavy enough for the early spring night. The shorter one held a flask of wuisc, full at the start of the evening, and as its level dropped, they listed into one another more and more.

"Say, d'you plan on drinking that whole thing yourself?" said the tall one.

The shorter one passed the flask over. "Be careful, Tem, you're not used to this stuff."

"And you are?" said Temmin. "If I'm going to the Keep, I have to learn to drink." He took a choking swallow, and pulled a face. "Where did you get this stuff? Besides, it's our last night to do this sort of thing. Any sort of thing." Temmin sighed and bumped his head against the bricks. "Why do I have to go, Alvy? Why can't I stay here in Whithorse? Breed horses for the family or something?"

"Don't gulp it, sip it," said Alvo. "The King needs just so many horses, and you're his only son."

"Sedra should be the Heir. She's smarter, and she's the oldest."

Alvo took the flask back, sipped, and snorted. "A woman will rule when Nerr gets the Heir. For that matter," he added, "this wuisc will be drinkable when Nerr gets the Heir. I told you I couldn't get the good stuff. Crokker would've given you some if you'd just asked."

"And let Mama find out? I don't think so." Temmin sat up straighter. "Here's a thought. You go to the Keep and be the Heir and I'll take your job."

"You could pass for a groom in that cap, but somehow I don't think His Majesty would mistake me for you."

"And why won't he let me take you with me?" said Temmin. "You're my best friend, and the best groom I know. What will I do without you? What will Jebby do without you?"

"They have grooms at the Keep who'll keep your horse in trim. You spoil him, y'know."

"Jebby deserves all the sugar lumps in the world, if I could get them away from Elly. She shouldn't eat 'em all, anyway. T'ain't fair to the horses, and gives her the headache. Sisters—between her and Sedra…"

They fell silent as the sky faded from deep indigo to black. "Turning eighteen is awful," Temmin resumed. "They make you do things you don't want to do, like study, and have tea with old baronesses that smell like heliotrope soap."

Alvo took his friend's hand. "I don't want you to go, either, but you gotta." He looked down on their joined hands, both short-nailed and tan from the sun, his own rougher and the nails much dirtier. "I need to tell you something." He pressed his lips together and licked them. "I love you."

Temmin gave his friend a bright, unsteady smile. "I love you too, Alvy." He resumed staring into a wobbly middle distance.

"No, I mean I *love* you—"

"Ssh!" Temmin blared. "I hear someone!" He rose to his feet, listening. Floating from the hedge alley came the sounds of a young woman's light laughter, ending in a soft groan.

Alvo took up a lantern, rising more surefooted. "You don't know who's there!"

"That's the point!" Temmin lurched on tiptoe toward the alley and barged through a gap in the hedge, Alvo on his heels.

Two young lovers appeared in the lamplight. A footman pressed a maid up against the hedge, his arousal poking from his unbuttoned fly; her breast shone white and rose against the dark green of her open bodice. The footman jumped back, fumbling with his trousers. "Who would you two be—my Gran's, judging by the livery," said Temmin, tipping on his heels as he stared. The footman hid his face in his coat, and ran down the alley toward Meadow House, the smaller of the two great houses now barely visible against the night sky. "Hey! Did you see who that was?" he said to Alvo, who shook his head.

Temmin turned toward the girl. She hid halfway in the hedge and tried to cover her breasts, but her fingers shook too much to do up the fastenings. "It's all right—no, let me see," said Temmin, staying her hand. "Alvy, hold the lantern. I haven't ever seen a woman undressed. You're very pretty. What's your name?"

"Temmin, leave her alone," coaxed Alvo. "Let's go back, we haven't finished the flask." He tugged at the Prince's sleeve, but obediently held up the lantern.

Temmin shook him off. "So you serve the Dowager Duchess at Meadow House?" he said to the girl. "What's your name?"

"Mattisanis Dunley, Your Highness, but everyone calls me Mattie," said the girl. "Please, sir, I need my job. Please don't tell Mr Crokker!"

"Why would I tell the butler one of the maids has pretty tits? Alvy, how come none of the maids at the Great House have pretty tits?"

"Tem, *come on!*" said Alvo.

"No, it's true! All the maids at the Great House are old women—at least 35 if they're a day—and they're as homely as ever a woman was." Temmin's hand still rested over hers, and his thoughtless thumb stroked the bare skin above her breast. "You really are very pretty. Mattie, is it? Was that your sweetheart? Not a very amiable fellow, if you ask me."

"Please, sir! Don't tell Mr Crokker!" she said. Tears dampened her heart-shaped face, and Temmin fuzzily followed one off the point of her chin, past her collarbone, and down between her breasts.

"Now, there, don't cry!" said Temmin, patting her cheek in drunken concern. "Pretty girls shouldn't cry. If he's really your sweetheart, he'll come back." He handed her a handkerchief. Mattie wiped her eyes, but when she moved to close her bodice, Temmin stopped her again. "I'm not done looking, and you obviously don't mind or you wouldn't have been out here with that footman. In fact, I should really like to touch them. May I touch them? You seemed to like it."

"Tem!" hissed Alvo. "You're *drunk!*"

"Pagg's own balls! Why would I be drunk just to want to touch a pretty girl's tits! Don't you want to?"

"No!"

"Just don't tell Mr Crokker, sir, please don't tell, I need my job, you can touch all you like, just please don't!" Mattie pleaded. She opened her bodice further.

"See?" said Temmin. "I told you she liked it! Now," he said to Mattie, "do stop crying, and stop asking me not to tell Crokker, I'm going to do no such thing!" He stumbled, steadying himself on her breasts. "Oh, that's so nice! I've always wanted to feel one. Alvy, you sure you don't want to have a go? She ha two of 'em, and she doesn't mind, do you?"

"No, I don't want to *have a go*, I want to get out of here and leave her alone!" said Alvo.

"Then go," said Temmin. "But leave the lantern." Alvo stomped away, leaving the lantern on the ground; it lit one side of Mattie's face and threw the rest into shadow.

Temmin pressed closer; she turned her face away, but he brushed it back toward the light. "Does your sweetheart kiss you? D'you like that? Never kissed a girl a-tall—don't tell anyone. May I have a kiss? Just one." She nodded, tucking her chin into her neck.

He kissed her, sloppy, inexpert and fumbling; she alternately squirmed and turned rigid, until Temmin broke it off. "Don't you like this?" he asked. "You said you did."

His eyes grew wide, his stomach lurched, and he stumbled back. "Alvy?" he called. "Dammit! Not now! Alvy!" Alvo ran back, just in time for Temmin to drop to his knees and vomit.

"I told you to sip it!" said Alvo. He turned to Mattie; she held her bodice closed with one hand, the other over her mouth. "He doesn't know much about girls except his sisters, and he's pretty drunk. I'm sorry about this whole thing. Nothing will happen to you, I swear. Just go and don't be stupid again—you were lucky it was us and not someone else!" Mattie nodded and ran down the dark hedge alley toward Meadow House.

Temmin heaved a few times more before he sat back on his heels, gasping. "Are you done?" said Alvo.

Temmin nodded. "I think so. Oh, gods." Alvo moved to help him up, but Temmin held up one hand and stood on his own. He swiveled a bleary gaze round the alley. "Where's the girl?"

"She's gone. I sent her home."

"What did you do that for? She might've let me kiss her some more!"

"Go wash your face and rinse your mouth out. You stink." Alvo stalked back to the straw bale and plunked himself down again. "Tem, that was not right," said Alvo.

Temmin stuck his head in the horse trough and came up dripping and spitting."She said yes, and she let that footman do a lot more to her than I did. Where's the flask gotten to?"

"No. No, no, and no."

Temmin sighed, sat down, and adjusted himself. "Pagg damn it, why'd you send that girl away?"

"You wouldn't know what to do anyway."

"I might've found out! And like you know anything about girls, either."

"I'm not interested in knowing anything. Tem, what if that had been Elly or Seddy?"

"That's disgusting!"

"I don't mean one of your sisters literally! She's probably someone's sister, and I know how I'd feel if someone tried that with my sister. What if someone tried that with one of yours?"

"Never happen," declared Temmin. "Can't see either of 'em hiding in the hedges with a footman."

"Oh, gods, I give up."

Temmin adjusted himself again. "Doesn't matter anyway. She's gone, and I'm left with this."

Alvo looked at the ground. "Tem," he began. "I've been trying to tell you something tonight. Wasn't brave enough before now, but I'm out of time—listen," he said, taking his friend's arm. "Chances are we won't ever see each other again."

"Don't be stupid, I'll come home at some point."

"I don't think they'll let you. Not till you've forgotten me and your whole life here. We've been best friends 'most all our lives—"

"We'll always be best friends, no one can stop that."

"They're gonna try! I think that's why I can't come with you—I'm just a groom, and you're the Heir, we can't be friends forever, they won't let us. And I think that's why you won't be coming home any time soon. Maybe never. I think this is our last night."

"Who's 'they?'" said Temmin.

Alvo shook his head. "If this is the last time, I have to tell you—I love you."

"Y'already said that, Alvy, I love you too."

"Would you listen!" Alvo crouched down on the ground before Temmin and put his hands on his friend's knees. Tears streamed down his broad face. "I love you! I don't love anyone else in this world like I love you! You're all I've ever thought about, since we were ten! I feel like I'm gonna die when you go, you understand? I love you!"

Temmin leaned forward in alarm. "What are you talking about?"

Alvo put one calloused hand up to Temmin's face. "I just love you." He came up off his heels, and kissed Temmin on the mouth. "I love you."

Temmin moved his friend's hand away from his cheek, but kept hold of it. "Alvo…"

"I know you don't feel the same way, I know you like girls more than boys, I know all that! Can't you pretend, just for now? Can't you let me have this little bit? Please. Tomorrow you'll be gone, and you'll get a new best friend, and you'll get married, and become King some day, and forget about me." Alvo's voice broke. "Please, Tem. Please."

Temmin stared down into his friend's pleading eyes, tears forming in his own. Alvo was his best friend; he'd never thought of anything else.

When they were younger, they'd kissed a few times. It was fun, but he'd always thought of it as practice for girls. He loved Alvo, but this—he didn't have time to think, he was going away tomorrow morning, he was drunk, why now? Alvo sobbed, great, heartbreaking waves of tears.

Frustration and grief rose in Temmin's throat. "Why didn't you—why now? Dammit!" he said aloud. He pulled Alvo close, and tried to comfort him, pulling him back onto the straw bale. When Alvo kissed him again, Temmin didn't pull away.

They kissed until they gasped. Alvo fumbled with Temmin's clothes, finding the trouser buttons. "I know this isn't for me, but let me just touch you," Alvo whispered. He took Temmin's erection in his hand.

Temmin groaned and slumped back against the bricks. He'd touched himself, many, many times. Nothing like this, nothing so emotional, or so pleasurable; the sensation left him as dizzy as if he'd been knocked over the head. Alvo slipped down from the bale to kneel between Temmin's legs, stroking him. "Just let me—" He licked at it, then took it in his mouth.

No one had touched Temmin like this before. The heat, the wetness, the friction, the anticipation—all of it new, ecstatic, and terrifying. He held his breath as his orgasm built faster than he could control. He came without a sound, eyes wide and astonished, hands resting on Alvo's head. He gulped in air; his brain, already muzzy, refused to work at all, and he slumped against the wall in a stupor.

Alvo jumped to his feet. "I have to go now."

"Alvy, wait!" Temmin tried to get up, but his friend was faster.

"I just have to go! I have to go!" Alvo ran, leaving his lantern behind.

Temmin watched his friend disappear into the darkness. He leaned back against the bricks, the lamplight reflecting on his still-wet cheeks. He fastened himself up. Wiping his face on his coat sleeve, he picked up his lantern and wobbled up the alley toward the courtyard and the Great House beyond, leaving Alvo's lantern to burn itself out.

The next day hurt. "It's called a 'hangover,'" said Jenks as he bustled around the room packing Temmin's last things. "The first one's the hardest. Come on, Your Highness, ass out of bed. Serves you out for drinking in the first place."

"Go away, Jenks. I'm not going," said Temmin.

"Balls to that, and up you go, young sir. I've only got two hours to get you into a state fit to be seen by your mother, let alone smelled. Drink this," he ordered, thrusting a glass filled with a viscous, malodorous liquid in Temmin's direction.

Temmin took the glass. He gave the big man a dubious eye, the glass an even more dubious eye, and downed it. "My gods! That's foul!" he spat.

"Aids the head and the stomach. Take it from one who knows. Into the tub. No sympathy from this corner. You did it to yourself. What did you two drink last night?"

"Was supposed to be wuisc," mumbled Temmin through the washcloth over his mouth.

"Horse piss, more like," said the valet, his solid bulk filling the doorway. "Tell Alvo next time to come see me. If you two are set on drunkenness, I don't want blindness following on its heels."

Temmin dunked his head and blew water out his nose; if Alvo was right, there wouldn't be a next time. And what would he say if there were?

Temmin found his mother already waiting in the grand entrance hall. Queen Ansella had given Temmin his blue eyes and golden blond hair, and this morning the smooth blond plaits framing her face shone in the light from the wide, round window over the great doors. How pretty she was in blue! Only her children would recognize the unhappy cast to her eyes, an unhappiness Temmin shared. They had both been born at Whithorse. Temmin had lived there his entire life. He wanted to be cheerful for her sake, and though the hangover remedy helped, it didn't help enough, and he glumly shook hands and said goodbye to his grandmother the Dowager Duchess and the Great House staff. Every last servant cried, even the fierce Crokker; the butler shook his hand with such emotion Temmin blushed for him.

Temmin waved out the window until the Great House disappeared and they were well on the road to Reggiston. Once out of sight, he slumped into a groaning heap. "Pagg's own, my head."

"Don't swear, Temmy," said his mother. "And if you're going to get drunk, you should expect a headache."

Temmin sat up. "Who told you I got drunk last night?"

"You did, this very second." Ansella smiled. "I was guessing, sweetheart."

Temmin closed his eyes in queasiness and consternation, but opened them again. "Say, where's Sister Ibbit?"

"She's leaving from the Healer's House. I suspect she wanted to give us this last moment to ourselves."

"That's strangely thoughtful of her."

"Respect for clergy, please, Temmy." Ansella stared out the window at the rolling pastures, dotted with horses and sheep. "We won't get much time alone from now on. Your father will be getting the most of you. But promise me you'll spend a little time with me, and with your sisters. We won't have them much longer. In fact, it won't be long until you'll be my only baby left."

Temmin opened his eyes again. "Mama, I'm not sure about anything in my life right now but you. Things and people I thought I knew—everything's upside down."

"You'll be rightside up before you know it, my sweetheart. Listen a little while longer, and I'll leave you to your headache," she smiled. A pause, and she turned serious. "You will be around women a great deal in the City, many of them...notorious," she forced out. "I want you to be careful."

"Notorious women?" he said hopefully. This was not the first time his mother had gone on about notorious women, to the point that Temmin was extremely curious to meet one and find out what made them so notorious.

"You'll be tempted to make...make wrong decisions. I don't want you falling into some hussy's clutches, or worse, led into spending time at...oh, at houses of ill-repute!"

Temmin had no idea what a house of ill-repute was, and said so.

"This is your father's office, but he would never give you good advice!" murmured his mother in agitation. "It's a house where women sell themselves, a horrible, horrible place! Nothing more infamous!"

"I'm sorry, Mama, but d'you mean a whorehouse?"

His mother winced. "It pains me to hear the word."

"Pains me to say it to you, but you would ask! Never worry," he said. "I won't go to one." In fact, his mother had spent many years arming him against hussies and loose women, whatever they were; he had no clear idea what went on in a whorehouse, but he knew the men who went to them should be staying at home, or at worst going to the Lovers' Temple and renewing their faith, though he had no clear idea what happened in the Temple, either.

The rolling pastures and woods turned to new-plowed fields. At the outskirts of Reggiston, the Station stood in its proud new cast iron and gilded glory. Waving crowds stood in little knots around the station. On the tracks, the royal train awaited, a great black locomotive at its head, its details picked out in gold, the platform round it and its coal tender behind painted the deep red called Tremontine red: the color of garnet, of pomegranate, of a thick pool of blood. On each side of the handrail at the very front of the engine flew small Tremontine flags in that same red, three golden triangles grouped in the middle.

Temmin settled into the resplendent, wood-paneled car that belonged to his father, the salon car sandwiched between it and his mother's coach. Beyond that rolled the royal dining car, and at train's end trailed the kitchen. The remaining entourage traveled closer to the engine and its noise and smoke.

By the time the train left Reggiston behind, he felt a little better and asked for a small lunch. "Meaning one chicken, not two?" said Jenks on his way to the kitchens. But once the plate sat before him, Temmin picked at it. "Now you have me worried, young sir. You should be over the worst of it by now."

Temmin shook his head, and ran his fingers through his locks; Jenks winced in dismay at the ruination of the royal hair style. "No, I'm all right. A little headachy, but whatever you gave me did the trick." He furrowed the mashed potatoes with his fork. "Jenks, what if I can't do this?"

"Do what, Your Highness?"

"Be what they expect me to be. Be the Heir. Be King in my turn." He knocked the fork against the plate's rim. "I mean, I think I know what's going on, and then I don't. I don't want to go to the City."

"So you've said about two dozen times today, the day before, the day before that, and all of Winter's End. But you're on the train to Tremont City, and when you get there, that's where you're staying."

"I'm the Viscount of Prunedale, and I don't have to go there," said Temmin. "Though I do like prunes."

Jenks ignored this. "Besides, you haven't seen Miss Sedra in three years, and it's been a year and a half since Miss Ellika left."

"Oh, I'll be very glad to see them, and Papa, too. I haven't seen him since he came to fetch Ellika." Temmin stopped sculpting the potatoes. "It's funny. I've hardly seen him apart from a visit or two every year, but Mama always insists we call him Papa."

"Her Majesty wanted you to feel close to your father despite the intervening miles, I believe. She has certain ideas about raising healthy children. Are you through?"

"No, I'm just thinking." He took a few mouthfuls. "Jenks, do you know why Alvo wasn't allowed to come with me? I wanted him to be my groom."

Jenks stopped brushing Temmin's dinner coat. "Oh, young sir. You know the answer to that yourself."

Temmin remembered Alvo's words: *We can't be friends forever, they won't let us.* What were they now, he wondered? He decided not to think on it, and ate another chicken leg.

To Temmin's dismay, his mother's religious advisor joined the royal party at dinner. At Whithorse, Sister Ibbit lived at the Temple of Venna in Reggiston and never dined with them, but tonight Ansella seated the priestess to her left and Temmin to her right. Looking up from the soup, he caught Ibbit staring at him in contempt, and wondered if he'd have to endure her half-hearted religious instruction at the Keep. He'd managed to out-and-out skip most of it, with Ibbit's approval; her open hostility led him to avoid her as much from personal dislike as boredom, and she seemed to share his feeling.

After dinner, he and his mother were to play cards in the salon car, but before he could follow her there, Ibbit blocked his way. "A word with you," she said. "We will not be taking up our lessons in the City, Your Highness. I am sure you will have too many other demands on your time."

"Oh," said Temmin, trying to contain his glee. "I shall be very... sorry...to miss our times together."

She examined him down the length of her forbidding nose, and cocked her head. "Our *understanding* cannot be continued at the Keep. You will be watched too closely for that comfortable relationship to continue."

Temmin thought to himself there had never been anything comfortable about their relationship, but said nothing.

"I'm sure they'll give you a Brother to pretend to instruct you while giving you a good beating," she continued, "though I don't know what kind of religious instruction a priest of Farr could possibly impart. Furthermore, I have always felt religious instruction wasted upon men. I will be happy to end the connection." She turned and left the dining car, holding her gray robes clear of the platform gates.

That answered that question, thought Temmin.

Over the next two days, Temmin watched the scenery change from Whithorse's beloved rolling grasslands and forests to the foothills of the Altenne Mountains, rising high and snowy above the valley. Many small cities and towns dotted the landscape, often built up the sides of the lower foothills each with their Temples clustered at the top in the ancient style. The train passed through several, slowing down as it approached the stations but never stopping, though Temmin wished they would; he'd seen none of the country outside Whithorse, and the mountains looked like the borders of the world.

They came to a small town tucked in a little valley, its thick bands of orchards so covered in blossom they looked more like clouds than trees. It was Temmin's holding of Prunedale, and he chuckled as they passed; he'd had to go there after all.

Up and up, through the dusky foothills, into the pines as the track switched back through the Sella Gap and up above the treeline, the track cutting through the snow in thick, blue-white walls on each side. They crawled down the Altennes into the Feather River valley. The long, fat ribbon of trees and settlements along its banks got closer and closer until the train plunged into the valley, tracing the river itself. Their progress slowed as the train passed through countless villages and towns, but again did not stop.

All along the way, especially here by the river, people gathered along the tracks to watch the train pass, though Temmin wondered why they cared. Didn't this train come through at least once a week? The tracks followed the Feather west and south toward its confluence with the Shadow River, leaving the countryside around the City behind; it slowed near the city, and crowds packed beside the tracks. "Why is everyone so glad to see the train?" said Temmin.

"They're glad to see you, young sir," answered Jenks. "Now. Out of that dirty shirt—how you manage to drop sausages down your front at your age I'll never know." Jenks coaxed his charge into clean linen, a formal gray suit, Tremontine red brocade waistcoat, black cravat and his grandfather's amber studs and cufflinks. "I shall not have you reflect badly on Whithorse, Your Highness."

"You mean, you."

"And your mother would kill me if you weren't properly turned out," rumbled Jenks in his gravelly baritone, putting an end to any argument.

"Ugh. I feel like one of Elly's old dolls." Temmin moved to run a hand through his golden hair, but at a look from Jenks, he checked himself and put his hat on his head with a sigh lost in the hiss of the train's brakes; they had arrived at the River Street Grand Railway Station.

Red and gold banners fluttered from the empty railway station's high ceiling, and crowds thronged the streets all around for a glimpse over the shoulders of the Royal Guard. Around the platform itself, Brothers stood guard; the spring breeze rushed through the open station, picking up the long strands of the Tremontine red horsehair tassels atop their bright silver helmets. He wondered how the Brothers could stand the strands tickling their faces, but then, the priests of Farr were cut from stone, the saying went.

His father and sisters stood alone on the platform. The gray in King Harsin's dark hair and beard had increased, but otherwise he looked the same: a serious, handsome face with a slight, sardonic twist to it; powerful; tall. Temmin wondered if he were still shorter than the King, and tugged his waistcoat down.

His sisters looked like women now; Sedra was just turned twenty-one and Ellika was halfway between nineteen and twenty. In her elegantly tailored, sober gray coat, Sedra resembled the King, tall, dark and serious; her face bore a twist as well, but one less cynical and more humorous. Merry little Ellika dressed in rose, their mother's twin but for their father's dark eyes. Ellika rose up on her toes in excitement, until Sedra put a quelling hand on her shoulder.

Temmin and the Queen stepped onto the platform. A roar went up. It shook his bones; he had never heard so many voices cheering at once, nor seen so many people. Hundreds? Thousands? He thought he heard his name among the cheers. The King greeted his wife with a kiss on each cheek; he took his son's hand in a too-strong grip. His sisters each offered a cheek to be kissed, and Ellika whispered, "I've missed you! I'm so glad you're finally here!"

Ansella's daughters both forgot their dignity and threw themselves into their mother's arms. "There, my girls," she laughed. "I'm not going anywhere. We're in public! Behave!"

Greetings exchanged, the crowds acknowledged, the royal family left the station. As the royal carriage rolled away, Temmin saw his horse Jebby taken off the train and thought of Alvo. Why couldn't he have come? And why had he ruined everything?

"Temmy, are you listening?" said Ellika, whacking his knee with her fan. He started, and glanced out the window; they had crossed the Feather at Kingsbridge, and were approaching the great gates leading to the parklands around the base of the cliff that held Tremont Keep.

"We're having a ball for your birthday," said Sedra.

"A ball? Who wants a ball?"

"You do," said the King.

"Me? I hate balls, they're boring!" He'd been dragged to many a small dance, filled with pimply cousins and dowdy girls from the local gentry who couldn't do more than giggle, but then Ibbit arrived and the dances stopped—one of the few benefits of the Sister's presence.

"I did tell you about it, Temmy," murmured his mother.

"You will not be bored," said Harsin. "You will smile, you will dance, and you will celebrate your coming of age with your people. We will not discuss this." His father had not changed. "You will enjoy yourself more than you suspect, son," Harsin amended. "I know you're used to doing as you please, mucking about with the stable hands—" here he gave his wife a sharp look— "but you're an adult now. I expect you to take up your studies in all seriousness. My own tutor will be taking you in hand. Your childhood is over, son."

The gates closed with a thunk. The carriage rolled down the long drive, toward the ancient fortress castle on the cliff.

Temmin woke the next morning from a dream of Alvy with breasts, to find his brown bedcurtains had turned red. He sat up, puzzled, before remembering he wasn't in bed at home. The curtains parted, and Jenks stuck his head in. "Ah, we're awake, are we?"

"I want to go home, Jenks," said Temmin as he rubbed sleep from one eye.

"We are home, young sir. Moping won't change it, and I for one am tired of your complaining."

"How you talk to me! If you were anyone but you, I should have you horsewhipped."

"If you were anyone but you, I'd've taken you over my knee by now." Jenks opened the window shades to reveal rosy clouds in the pre-dawn sky. "But you are you, and I am me. You wouldn't whip a horse anyway. Now—" He waggled a pair of riding boots. "I suggest you keep your old habits in this new home, and be at the stables before breakfast."

"Jebby! He must be scared stiff!" Temmin walked into the wardrobe, and stopped short. "Where are my riding clothes in this warehouse?"

"On the dressing stand, Your Highness."

Temmin surveyed the immaculate riding coat and breeches. "A cravat? A *hat*? Jenks, these are not riding clothes. These are *formal* riding clothes. Where's my cap?"

"I got rid of that rag before we left. It's high time you do as the Cavalry does, if you have any aspirations to it. Clothes make the officer."

"If clothes make the officer, why were you a corporal?" grumped Temmin.

A clean and exquisitely dressed Temmin stumped down to the stables, a small flask of sweet wine and a prayer written on birch bark in his pocket for his offering to Amma. Bath before riding, what nonsense. He'd just get dirty again. At least Jenks allowed his old boots, though shined to an unaccustomed polish. When Jenks could no longer see him, he stashed his smart topper in a secluded bush, fished the disreputable, ancient tweed cap he'd filched from Jenks back home from his pocket, and slapped it on his head.

The stables at the Keep made the Estate's yards look small, and he looked forward to a heady array of horses. Surely, with all this room, he'd be allowed to breed stock as he had at home. Once in the stableyard, though, he groaned; they'd seen him coming. Every groom, every stableman, even the boys still clutching their polish rags stood in ragged lines awaiting him, caps in hand. A grizzled old man in riding master's boots bowed. "Welcome, Yer Highness," he said in a thick Far Isles accent. The workers all put knuckles to foreheads.

Indoors, Temmin was used to a modicum of deference, but not in stables. He mucked out stalls, toted hay bales, polished tack, and curried Jebby himself; he'd always been one of the men, since he'd been a tiny boy darting among the horse's legs and bothering everyone. "If you'd like t'inspect the stables now, sir?" said the old man. "I yam the riding master, by name Cappel, sir." The hands looked to Temmin, faces nervous and expectant.

After an astonished pause to gather his wits, Temmin said, "I'm just here to ride my horse. I do want to see the stables, but not this morning." The men and boys deflated. "Unless—unless you've gone to some effort?"

"Aye, well, sir," murmured Cappel, "they been cleanin' fer the last week, sir."

"Ah," Temmin murmured in return. He spoke up louder. "Ehm...I'll take a turn round these fine-looking stables after all." The stablemen brightened. "But one thing." They leaned forward, waiting as if for a command. "I'm just here to take care of the horses, and you're just here to take care of the horses, so let's all take care of the horses, yes?" No one moved until Temmin thought to say, "Ehm, dismissed?" Satisfied, the men and boys touched their knuckles to their foreheads again, put their caps on their heads, and stumped off to their chores.

They stopped first at Amma's shrine in the main courtyard. Temmin poured the sweet wine he'd brought over the altar stone and made Her sign: he touched his head, heart and groin, and murmured "Merciful Amma, keep me from harm," then tucked the birch bark prayer under the stone. Proper obeisance to the Lady of Cattle made, he let Cappel hustle him through the huge complex, the men's eyes following them; Temmin made sure to exclaim at how clean it all was.

In the royal family's personal stable, Jebby filled the last stall. The chestnut gelding whickered. Temmin pulled a sugar cube from his pocket and held it up for the big horse, who lipped it into his mouth. Jebby turned his head sideways and stared, one-eyed, until Temmin took an apple from his other pocket and cut it in half. "Greedy guts," said Temmin as the horse munched.

He turned to see Cappel lugging an immaculate saddle from the tack room. "Ah, I'll take that!" said Temmin, reaching for it.

"I yam not s'old as all that," said Cappel. "And that's no work for such as you, sir."

Cappel's age had not occurred to the young Prince. "I'm used to doing for myself, though," said Temmin.

The riding master squinted at him. "That's as may be, but my men and I have our pride, sir. Let us do our jobs, and you do yours. Our jobs is carin for the horses, and yours is bein a prince, sir. But," he amended, observing Temmin's dumbfounded expression, "why don't you, just this once." He leaned against the stable wall, and watched as Temmin displayed his mastery of tack. "Eh, aye," he admitted, "you know your way around a horse. T'will be our pleasure to look after you, sir."

Look after him? Temmin looked after himself in stables, he huffed to himself as he rode Jebby out of the yard. He didn't order people around. If he did, they paid no attention. What was the point? Stablehands treating him like an outsider. He didn't like the Keep.

He and Jebby came to the great War Road leading into the King's Woods; six men could ride abreast down it, and had done so when Tremont's military campaigns departed from the Keep long ago. Jebby danced in place, until Temmin stuffed his cap back in his pocket, tapped his heels into the big horse's sides, and yelled "Gidyap, Jeb!" The chestnut took off down the Road, ecstatic to stretch his legs.

For Temmin, this was pure delight—the fresh morning, the sturdy horse moving beneath him, the wind whipping his hair back. This would not be taken from him. This belonged to him. Temmin leaned down over Jebby's neck and let him run.

When Temmin returned, he got no further than the Keep's mud room when Jenks pounced. He traded his mucky boots for carpet slippers, and once upstairs, his dusty riding clothes for more elegant attire. "Do you need a shave this morning, young sir? You rushed out before I could get a good look at you," called Jenks from the wardrobe.

Temmin examined his chin in the mirror; still not enough beard to grow out, though his plentiful sideburns and moustache left little to be desired. "No. Why can't I just change my boots?" he said, scrubbing his face with a wet flannel.

"This is court, Your Highness, you cannot go to breakfast smelling like a horse."

"I've washed my face and hands! Oh, really, Jenks, a tie? At breakfast?"

"Just a soft one. The dark blue suits you. And do try to keep egg yolk off it, Your Highness, silk is the Bloody One's Own to clean."

"Explain to me some time why clothes are such an obsession in the Cavalry," said Temmin, fastening the unwanted cravat with a simple horseshoe stickpin.

"That's too casual, young sir!" said Jenks as Temmin escaped.

"That's too bad, Jenks!" replied Temmin over his shoulder.

Downstairs, most of his family waited for him outside the morning room. "Where's Elly?" said Temmin.

"She stayed up half the night playing cards with friends in the Little Salon," Sedra sniffed. "She almost never wakes up in time for breakfast."

"Really?" said Ansella, taking her son's arm. "That will change."

Indirect sunlight from many high windows flooded the morning room. It was painted robin's egg blue, its longest wall lined with tall mirrors that brightened the room even more. The morning room was a Whithorse innovation, transplanted to the Keep at the insistence of the

Queen, and Temmin immediately felt more at home. Strong coffee, cocoa, sausages and newsprint scented the informal room's air. Even the King's face softened as his family gathered round the table, together for the first time in nearly two years.

"I'm very happy to have you here, Temmin," Harsin said.

"I'm very happy to be here, Papa," he replied. Affton appeared at his elbow and poured him a cup, half coffee and half cocoa—Temmin's favorite. He liked a well-briefed butler.

"Tomorrow is your birthday—a man at last," said Harsin. "We shall meet tomorrow morning with Teacher. He was my tutor as well, you know."

He must be ancient, Temmin said to himself, and added aloud, "What's his name, sir?"

"Name? Just Teacher." Harsin tapped one finger on the cream damask table cloth. "Tomorrow night is your birthday ball. Everyone of any note in the empire will be attending—most of the major nobility, the high priests and Embodiments of all the Temples but Harla's, of course." Temmin shivered inwardly; who would want Death at one's birthday? "Inchari princelings, ambassadors from the Vakale'le Confederacy nations, and Sairland, too," his father continued. "I trust you are prepared for diplomatic occasions?"

"Do I have to go? I don't care to dance, and I'm not very good at it," said Temmin. He'd never been to an actual ball, only little parties to practice dancing with his sisters and a few friends.

"It's in your honor, of course you have to go," said Sedra.

"You will brush up your dancing with Ellika, then," said Harsin. "The servants are already preparing the ballroom, and the music master is planning out the program this afternoon. That should give you music for practice. I shall have my secretary send Ellika to you whenever she graces us with her presence. You'll acquit yourself just fine—you have your mother's light feet. I've seen you dance myself," he added.

"You have? When?" said Temmin.

"Newspapers, Your Highness?" murmured Affton at Temmin's elbow.

"Ehm, no." He eyed the salver stacked with the morning's news. "I don't read 'em."

"Very good, young sir." The butler moved on to Sedra. He deposited a large stack of papers at her right hand, a stack almost as high next to Harsin, and a single magazine next to Ansella.

"You really should read the papers, Temmy," said Sedra, rattling open the top one on the stack with an emphatic flourish. "Rulers must know what is being said."

"Why are *you* bothering, then," he snickered. To his surprise, her offended face appeared over the drooping paper; she'd always dismissed his needling with a "Pfft!" and a toss of her head before. "What's wrong, Seddy?"

She set her jaw, her sharp resemblance to their father strengthening. "Nothing. I've simply forgotten your style of humor."

Temmin looked down at his plate. She'd always been proud, but she never rose to his bait. Everything and everyone was different here, and he hated it.

Temmin spent the morning in etiquette drills with Jenks. "Tell me again how one would address the chief wife of the ambassador for the Vakale'le Confederacy."

"This is pointless—I already know!"

"Then tell me again."

By afternoon, he wanted nothing more than a nap on the green velvet couch in his study—the one near the fire. Perhaps a little lunch beforehand. A nicely roasted chicken, a glass of wine, some spring greens in vinaigrette. Soup would also be good. And bread with a bit of cheese and some pickle. And a pudding. Nothing too substantial.

Ellika found him two hours later, stretched out on the couch sound asleep with the napkin still tucked in his collar and crumbs in his moustache. "Wake up!" She dropped his carpet-slippered feet to the floor, and sat down next to him in a pale green froth of silk flounces.

Temmin opened one eye. "You look like a cabbage. A very large, very pretty cabbage. Go away." He put his feet in her lap and closed his eye again.

"I said, wake up, Sir No-Beard!" Ellika poked him in the ribs and bounced on the couch. "Wake up wake up wake up!"

"I am awake! And I'll have you know I counted ten whiskers this morning," grumbled Temmin.

"I'm less interested in the condition of your chin than I am in the condition of your feet." She dumped his feet from her lap and stood up. "On with your dancing shoes, young man, I intend to make sure you don't embarrass me or yourself at your birthday party."

"I don't see where my skill as a dancer has anything to do with you," he said as he removed his carpet slippers.

"I am widely held to be the best dancer in the City, Temmy, and it will not do to have my little brother stepping on feet and stumbling into people. Come on, up up up!"

Servants already filled the grand ballroom. Tables and chairs ringed the floor's edges; a small army of boys on ladders polished the gilt-framed mirrors covering the longest wall, their shape echoing the graceful arches of the red-curtained windows they faced. As soon as the Prince and Princess entered the room, the bustle came to a halt; the footmen and maids bowed deep and curtsied deeper, and the boys almost fell off their ladders in their attempts to show respect. Then, as one, the servants turned their faces to the walls.

"Oh, turn around!" said Temmin. "I despise that custom, and we don't stand for it at the Estate. Affton," he called to the butler, "please instruct the staff not to do that around me." The butler bowed, the smallest of frowns around his eyes. The servants turned to face the room again, timid and surprised.

Ellika stared. "Seddy and I have been asking them not to do it for ages and ages, but no one listens to us."

On the stage at the end of the long, gleaming floor stood two tall, thin men with identical black mops of hair, thick moustaches and emphatic eyebrows; the two were busily directing the arrangement of the orchestra's chairs, each contradicting the other. Ellika marched her brother to the stage and clapped her hands for attention. The two men turned in bemusement, and bowed.

"Master Sullo! Mister Sullo!" she called. "We require practice music. Indulge us, please."

The musicians blew out their moustaches like hairy little curtains; the music master took up his violin, and his brother flexed his long fingers above the piano. They struck up a tune, a simple dobla. Ellika gave a deep curtsey, and Temmin stumbled a bow. "Feet together, Temmy," Ellika murmured.

Temmin took his sister's hand and let her lead him through the dobla's repeating figures: step, point, switch hands and again, step step step step. A child's dance, the traditional opening of uncouth country barn romps or the most formal ball—cheerful, simple and innocent.

"It's like sitting a horse," said Ellika. "Balance and posture and keeping your joints loose! Now, see, this isn't so bad!"

Temmin took her hand in the turn. "It's just been such a long time— we haven't had a dance at the Estate since you left, you know."

"Whyever not?"

"Why d'you suppose? Sister Ibbit disapproves of dancing."

"Oh, pooh. She would. Now, pay attention to what you're doing!" Ellika's sweet, sly smile and quick feet made it more than a children's dance. She added a little snap to the turns, sending her blond curls flirting over first one shoulder, then the other. To Temmin's irritation, she mesmerized every onlooker, especially the junior footmen. He tightened his grasp on her hand, and took her back up the floor away from the servants.

"Temmy, you dance well!" she crowed when the music ended.

"I s'pose I do! At least the dobla. I don't know if I remember anything more complicated. And we don't have any other dancers to practice with. So we're done?" he added.

"Nonsense. We shall practice the quarta." She ran a critical eye over the servants, still standing in an astonished clump at the floor's edge. "Dannikson! Wallek! I know you two can dance—I've caught you at it, and Affton, you are forbidden to punish them," she called up at the butler, who gave a frosty bow.

A freckled young footman with the brightest red hair Temmin had ever seen and an even younger maid shuffled out from the gaggle. The maid's turned-up nose and wide hazel eyes reminded him of the girl in the hedges at Whithorse, but prettier. A dark, shiny corkscrew curl escaped from her starched white cap; he suppressed an impulse to brush it from her blushing cheek, and smiled at her instead.

"You take Dannikson, and I'll take Wallek, Temmy," said Ellika. She took the footman's hand in hers, gazing up at him through her lashes. It set Temmin's teeth on edge. Was she flirting with a footman? Wallek held his head up, flushing beneath his freckles, but didn't meet the prince's gaze until Temmin took the maid's hand; his eyes met Temmin's in a clear flash of possessiveness, and Dannikson ducked her head.

Ellika cleared her throat and Wallek returned his attention. "Shall we dance?" she said. The four placed themselves in the pattern for the quarta, and the music began.

The steps came back to Temmin faster than he'd expected. He steered Dannikson more than led her, but soon her light, pliant step sent them gliding through the forms: twirling, changing partners, dancing in a ring, beginning again. The girl laughed, nerves forgotten, her cap's red ribbons flying; more curly tendrils slipped out to flutter at her nape. Temmin pulled her closer by degrees. She smelled of hay and tea, and he wanted to bury his nose in her neck. Her quick pulse beat at her wrist beneath his fingers, her corset bones stiff beneath his hand at her back; he wondered how soft her breasts were, whether her nipples were the same sweet, rosy color as those of the girl in the hedge, and he grew impossibly, uncomfortably hard.

The dance ended. He came to himself and realized she'd sensed his interest, her downcast face mixing pleasure and fear. On a sudden impulse, he bowed over her hand, and released it with an intimate smile. Dannikson burst into a nervous titter, bobbed a curtsey, and ran to hide herself in the knot of maidservants. Temmin fastened his coat, and hoped it hid his arousal enough.

Ellika dismissed Wallek with a nod and a smile, and slipped her arm through her brother's as they left the ballroom. "I don't care for you flirting with footmen," said Temmin as soon as they were out of earshot.

"*You* were flirting. I was making my partner comfortable," said Ellika with a dismissive wave. "Dannikson and Wallek are sweethearts. Everyone knows. Don't let Mama see you flirting with the help, or you'll get the poor girl fired."

*   *   *

Temmin found his tea laid out on the small table in his study. "Oh thank Amma, I'm starving," he said as Jenks poured him a cup.

"When are you not starving, young sir? How did your dancing practice go?"

"Very well, actually!" said Temmin around a mouthful of ham sandwich. He swallowed. "I remember more of my dancing than I expected to, and I rather enjoyed it. And I danced with the prettiest maid."

"Stop dunking biscuits in your tea, you turn eighteen tomorrow. Miss Ellika is very lovely indeed, young sir," said Jenks as he walked back to the bedchamber.

"No, no, not Elly, though she's a very pretty maid, if you want to put it all poetically. Jenks, she was flirting with a footman!"

"Miss Ellika flirts with lampposts, Your Highness," the valet's voice floated from the other room.

"She needs to stop. She's a princess. No, I mean an actual maid, a very pretty little thing named Dannikson."

"Oh?"

"She reminds me very much of a girl I kissed at the Estate, the night before we left."

The valet's head appeared in the doorway. "You kissed a girl?"

"That's what I said, isn't it!" said Temmin, pleased with himself.

"You just surprised me, that's all," said Jenks, returning to his side. "I thought you were out drinking with Alvo that night. Who was this girl, young sir?"

"Don't know, really. Just a maid," said Temmin. "Never saw her before. I think she works at Meadow House. Quite pretty. I would have noticed if she'd been among the old biddies we have for maids."

"Meadow House," said Jenks, leaning against the couch. "What was her name?"

Temmin slurped his tea. "Mmpf—Matti-something. Said they called her Mattie."

"Mattisanis Dunley, perhaps?"

"D'you know her?"

"I know *of* her," said Jenks, face closed. "So, what happened, young sir? Did we become a man earlier than our birthday?"

"Oh, no such luck. Though she did let me kiss her. Let me touch her breasts, too, before I threw up. Gods, I was drunk as Farr. Jenks, did you know, breasts are incredibly beautiful."

"Yes, they are" said Jenks, his voice abstracted. "Temmin, promise me something." Temmin looked up; Jenks seldom called him by name. "Promise me you'll leave Miss Dannikson and the other maids alone. That's my hunting ground, not yours. D'you understand?"

"Bit young for you, old man, wouldn't you say?"

"Be careful. You're unused to court life and young women. You're not a boy. You're eighteen tomorrow. Even if you weren't young and handsome, you'd dazzle a princess let alone a downstairs maid—you're the Heir. You may find yourself entangled before you know it."

"I'm not going to get my heart broken by a maidservant," snorted Temmin.

"Yours isn't the heart I'm worried about," said Jenks. Temmin furrowed his brow, puzzled. Jenks sighed. "Your Highness, just be careful. Leave the maids to me. You're sure her name was Mattie?"

"Positive! You're not going to go look her up too, are you?" said Temmin in irritation.

"Oh, no, not at all." Jenks walked back to the wardrobe, hands clamped behind him. "I'm fairly sure I know who she is."

TWO

The first thing Temmin saw when he looked into the bathroom mirror on his birthday was a man. He was eighteen; that was that, he was an adult now. "And I still can't grow a proper beard," he said aloud, rubbing his chin.

"What, sir?" called Jenks.

"Nothing!"

The second thing he saw when he looked in the bathroom mirror was a face not his own.

Underneath his own reflection lay a faint tracing—a smooth face, a paler, thinner face with precise features, odd silver eyes, and iron-colored hair pulled back in an old-fashioned tail. He blinked, and it disappeared.

"Jenks? Insanity doesn't run in the family, does it?"

"Not to my knowledge, sir," said Jenks.

It happened again when he came back to the stable yard from his ride with Jebby. They went to the trough, and Temmin leaned down to splash himself. The water's smooth surface reflected his face: flushed, sweaty, happy, and a little dusty. But as he watched, the strange figure reappeared, its cold, intense eyes staring. For some reason, Temmin thought of the wardrobe in Nurse's room, back in the nursery at the Estate. How convinced he had been that the Black Man lived in there—why would he think of that?

The impatient Jebby stuck his nose in the trough and took a slurp; ripples broke the water's surface, and the reflections vanished. "Here, Your Highness," said a groom, taking Jebby's bridle, "I'll see to 'im, go off to your birthday breakfast. You look a bit pinched, if I may be so bold!"

"I am hungry, thank you," he murmured. "That explains a great deal."

Even Ellika, pink and yawning with sleep, attended the breakfast table that morning. He accepted everyone's congratulations, and sat with his back to the morning room's mirrors. Why were there so many mirrors in this place?

Sedra was polite but formal, and said nothing to him about newspapers even though he took *The Daily Voice of Tremont* from the pile atop Affton's salver. "You don't want that," said his father. "Read *The Morning Capital* first—a proper newspaper—then you can read that radical nonsense." Temmin nodded, put both papers beside his plate, and opened neither.

"I have meetings this morning, Temmin," said Harsin at meal's end, "but after lunch I shall expect you in my study to meet Teacher."

"I'm going back to bed," said Ellika, still yawning. "No amount of coffee can wake me up."

"Oh dear, I hoped we'd go through my jewel case, to see if there's anything you'd like to wear tonight," smiled her mother as she rose. "I suppose it can wait."

"Mama, wait!" said Ellika, following Ansella from the table. "I'm suddenly feeling much more awake!"

Sedra tucked her remaining newspapers under her arm, and rose herself. Now, Temmin decided, was the time to patch things up. "Seddy," he said, catching up with her at the door. "Do you still like to walk after breakfast?"

"I'm sorry?"

"It's just that it's been so long," he said, keeping pace as she strode through the halls. "You always used to take walks after breakfast, and sometimes you'd let me come with you. D'you still do that? Would it be all right if I walked with you? I've missed you," he said. "I feel as if we don't know one another any more, and I thought perhaps we could...catch up?"

"I still know *you*," she said, stopping at the foot of the stairs. "You're trying to get out of something."

"Only this rock pile. I'm going to be cooped up here the rest of the day, and it's a nice morning. Seddy," he wheedled, "let's go for a walk."

"You don't need me to go walking, Temmy," she said, climbing the stairs.

"No, but I want to walk with you."

She looked down where he stood on the bottom step; he put on his best little brother smile. She softened. "All right," she said. "Meet me on the terrace in twenty minutes."

Jenks insisted on yet another wardrobe change: "You can't go wandering around in the woods in your nice day suit!" The ensuing, futile argument and inexorable swap of the day suit for a tweed walking suit and sturdy boots meant it took the full twenty minutes for Temmin to run back downstairs. Sedra waited, dressed in a sensible blue walking dress cut short enough to show the tops of her black boots. On her head sat an equally sensible blue felt bonnet, lined in a flattering rose silk. Her only other concession to fashion was a voluminous fine wool Inchari shawl, beautiful but practical on a brisk spring morning.

"How many sets of clothes does one go through in a day around here, Seddy?" said Temmin, offering his arm.

"Let's see," she said as she took it. "Rising dress—I suppose for you that's riding clothes—then morning dress, then if you have visitors that day there's afternoon dress, and then dinner dress. More if one goes walking or riding during the day, or goes to a Temple or the Promenade, or out after dinner—theater, dancing, card parties. Or if you're Elly," she finished with a grin.

"And how are you and Elly getting along these days?" he said, letting Sedra choose which path they took through the gardens.

Sedra sighed. "I'm only a year and a half older, and I feel as if I'm her mother."

"You have been, in a way. Mama's been at the Estate with me."

"I suppose you're right. Elly is so unwise sometimes, and she won't listen to a thing I say! She flirts shamelessly with anyone she pleases, no matter his rank or position—I've even caught her flirting with girls. She's escaped harm so far, but I worry. The Beloved watches over Elly, but one of these days, Blessed Neya won't be watching." She kicked out her skirts as they stepped onto the wide green lawn, first-cut for the season the day before. In the distance, a reflecting pool lay before a little marble pavilion ringed with cedars, and Sedra led him toward it. "What worries me the most," she continued, "is that Elly is determined to make a love match."

Temmin considered. "I can't say I blame her. I should very much like to love whoever I end up marrying, wouldn't you?"

"Oh, to be sure," retorted Sedra. "It would be lovely."

"Well, it would, wouldn't it?"

"Temmy, whatever Ellika and I would like has absolutely no bearing on what will be. If I fall in love with a fine and respectable gentleman—let's say, the Earl of Random—but Papa wants me to marry the horrible old Duke of Accident for political reasons, off I go to become Duchess Accident no matter how much I hate Accident or love Random."

"You've never loved anything random, Seddy, you're the most methodical person I know."

"Stop it," she laughed. "You know exactly what I mean." Her smile faded, and her brow grew darker still. "It'll be the Grace of Amma if I'm paired with anyone I can stand, let alone love. I'm twenty-one, and it's already getting late. This time next year I'll very probably be the Duchess of Accident, or something like." Temmin squeezed her arm.

They sat on the benches inside the ridiculous little folly; on its columns, walls and ceilings, a profusion of inlays and exotic carvings strove to imitate Inchari temples. It failed, utterly and charmingly. "You, on the other hand," she continued, "will very probably have some say in who you marry—at least a choice among several eligible Ladies Accident and Random. But then, you have the advantage over us in several ways."

"I don't see how," said Temmin. "I don't get much more choice than you or Elly. I still have to study things I don't want to study, and do things I don't want to do—"

"Tem, you'll be king some day," she cut in. "And when you're king, you can do what you want to do, and no one will ever tell you otherwise. Well…mostly," she amended.

"The one choice I don't have is whether to be king or not. I'm sure I don't know why any sensible person would want the job, though there are times I think *you* do. Which makes me wonder how sensible you really are."

Sedra glanced at him from the depths of her bonnet, her deep brown eyes brimming with a passion that stoppered his mouth. "I was born to rule in every way but my sex. I know it, you know it, Papa knows it. But I'm not even allowed to study any more, apart from my own reading."

Temmin faltered, then said, "You can study with me if you'd like. Papa doesn't have to know. I've always said you were smarter than Ellika and me put together. You even look the most like Papa," he said, trying to jolly her out of her anger. "I'm meeting with Papa and this Teacher person this afternoon—perhaps—"

"I've been forbidden to learn from Teacher," she said, her voice turning flat.

"But Papa doesn't have to know—"

"He'll know."

Temmin considered the set of her jaw. "So you've studied with Teacher? What's he like? He has to be as old as the Keep if he tutored Papa. Can he even stand up?"

"I don't want to talk about it," said Sedra.

"But I only—"

"Please, Tem, I don't want to." She laid a firm hand on his arm. "Please?"

"All right," he said. "Perhaps it's best anyway. If you were there, I'd have to work harder!"

She turned on him. "If you're going to be king, Temmin, you have to start taking things more seriously! Will you ever stop being such a child?"

"At least I *was* a child!" he said, dropping her arm. "You were born with your nose in a book! Do you ever have fun?"

"The kind of fun I have, real entertainment that engages the mind, you wouldn't understand in the least!"

"And another thing!" he said as she stood. "I am sick and tired of everyone telling me how stupid I am!"

"Then stop being stupid!" she cried, face mottled and mouth contorted. He watched her stomp off, a skirt-blue and petticoat-white froth around her legs, and snorted in the clear, cedar-scented air. Why was she so upset? What had he said but the truth? More sincerely than ever, he wished they were all back at the Estate, where she had been more amiable, and he hadn't needed half so many clothes.

When she walked out of sight, he drifted to the reflecting pool. He picked up a perfect rock, lying among the gravel, and drew his arm back to skip it. On an impulse, he looked down into the water; he saw his own bad-tempered face, superimposed over the cold, smooth face of another. "Who are you!" he shouted. "No—you're no one, you're something I've made up, just go away! I have enough to worry about without worrying about my sanity—!"

A hand reached out of the pond, followed by an arm, a shoulder, and a head. "Do be quiet," said the head. The hand closed on Temmin's ankle, and yanked him into the pond.

He closed his eyes and held his breath, struggling against the tenacious grip on his ankle in panic; he would drown. His stomach turned inside out.

When it stopped, he opened his mouth and gulped in spite of himself. To his surprise, he took in air, not water; he patted himself in confused agitation and found his clothes were dry. Temmin opened his eyes and found himself in an unfamiliar room—round, as if in a tower. The face in the mirror stood before him; it belonged to a slight figure dressed in black robes over a severe black suit and Tremontine red cravat, sharp against the white of the shirt; a pair of gold pinch-nose glasses dangled from a matching red ribbon. If this were the Black Man, he was a more meticulous dresser than Temmin would have suspected.

"The first time through can be difficult. Next time, do not hold your breath. Do you need to vomit?" said the stranger.

"No," said Temmin, hands on knees. "Well, maybe...no, I'll be all right. Harla's Hill, what just happened?" He looked around. A large mirror hung on the curving wall, a long library table stooped under heaped-up books and scrolls, heaps that spilled onto the only stool in the room, and a lectern stood in one corner, holding an aged red leather-bound book.

"You saw me," said the stranger. A restrained excitement threaded through the silvery voice. "You may deny you have seen my face in reflections today, but I know better. I thought it best to sort things out on our own, you and I."

"Yes, well, you and I don't know each other," said Temmin, standing up to his full height—half a head taller than his captor, if he were held captive — "Who are you, where am I, and how did I get here?"

"I am your father's counselor. I go by the name of Teacher. You are in my library. And I pulled you through a reflection."

Temmin found his voice and said, "You pulled me through a reflection. I have no idea what that means."

"Shall I do it again?" said Teacher, plunging an arm up to the elbow into the mirror.

"No, no!" said Temmin, holding up his hands. "Not again! Don't do it again! I don't know if this is real, but my stomach thinks it is!"

"It is quite real. If there is a reflection near what or who I wish to see, I can go anywhere or see anything in the Kingdom unobserved."

"I'm just going to pretend this makes sense, shall I?" said Temmin. "You've been popping up in reflections all day. If no one can see you, why can I see you?"

"Apparently, you are 'no one,'" said Teacher in a paper-thin voice.

Temmin wiped his face with his handkerchief. "Why now? Why did this start today? Did you just start watching me?"

"You have come of age," said Teacher, "When the men in your family had this power themselves, it fully revealed itself at eighteen. But no Tremont has shown signs of it in more than three centuries."

"Hang on, *we* could do this? You said your name is Teacher—you're my new tutor?"

"Yes."

"And you were my father's tutor." Temmin examined the smooth face for signs of advanced age. "You don't even look as old as my father. I mean, you're old, but not *that* old. How old are you—twenty-five? Thirty-five?"

"Many times that," said Teacher.

"Impossible."

"So is traveling through reflections. I suggest you go eat your luncheon and ready yourself to meet with the King. He will explain my importance to the royal family, most likely in different terms than I would use."

"Are you going to tell him I can see you?" said Temmin.

"Do you want me to?" asked Teacher.

"I'm not sure—no," said Temmin. "Don't. Everyone thinks I'm stupid as it is. Adding crazy doesn't help, and I'm sure in the end this will all turn out to be some sort of…something."

"As you wish. Would you like me to take you to your rooms?" Teacher murmured at the mirror; it wavered, settling into a view of Temmin's study, where Jenks was setting the little table by the window for lunch.

"No!" said Temmin. "No. I'll walk. Thank you."

Teacher bowed, and showed Temmin the door. "Happy birthday, Your Highness."

Temmin half-bowed in acknowledgement as the door closed. He looked around; he didn't know where he was. He thought of knocking on the door and asking, but the less he saw of Teacher, the better. He was inside a tower—an ancient one, judging by the stonework. He took to the stairs, a near-endless flight; when he made it to the bottom, he realized it had to be the Keep's central tower—part of the original fortress, built on the highest point of the rock overlooking the City. He found his way back to his rooms only after taking several wrong turns and amusing innumerable footmen as he asked for directions.

"The Prince is here, Your Majesty," said Harsin's secretary with a bow.

"Very good, Winmer, give us a moment and then show him in," said Harsin. "What have you observed of Temmin so far, Teacher?" he continued, turning toward the fireplace.

Teacher considered. "'Callow' is not too strong a word, Your Majesty."

"I agree. I admit to disappointment," said Harsin, shaking his head.

"I should not be disappointed," said Teacher. "eighteen is still quite young. Remember yourself at that age—I caned you for fourteen days straight. I am surprised you can sit down to this day."

"I was hoping he would be more prepared than this."

Teacher leaned against the mantel. "You are still young yourself, Harsin. You have many years to prepare Temmin for ruling."

"Even so," said the King, "more and more I feel raising him at Whithorse was a mistake."

"His prophecy—"

"I know what it says. We may have interpreted it wrong." Winmer ushered Temmin into the room. "Well, son!" said Harsin. "A glass of something, perhaps—Winmer—" Two glasses of pale red wine appeared, and Winmer disappeared through the door, his last bow more of a little bounce on his toes.

"Thank you," said Temmin; a faint tremor shook his hand as he accepted the glass, and Harsin swallowed a lump of dismay. The boy had no spine, no spirit.

"May I introduce Teacher, my own tutor and this family's counselor for many years," said Harsin. Teacher bowed.

"And you are to be my tutor, now, sir," said Temmin.

"Please do not call me 'sir,'" muttered Teacher.

"Teacher has his ways, Temmin. Pay attention, or it's the cane. Trust me on this. Now," Harsin said, shifting in his chair, "there is much to discuss. The matter at hand is your coming of age. It's time you heard your birth prophecy."

"My what?" said Temmin.

"At birth, every male child is taken to the Queen of the Travelers, who gives him his prophecy," said Teacher.

"The Travelers? You took me to a bunch of vagabond thieves and actors, well-known frauds—for a prophecy," said Temmin. "I hope you didn't pay for it."

That was more the spirit, thought Harsin. Aloud, he said, "A little more respect, please."

"Think what you will of the Travelers, Your Highness," said Teacher, "but their Queen can see the future—reliably when it comes to the royal family. Hers is a true gift, not play-acting."

"All right, then," said Temmin as he squared his shoulders. "Let's hear it." Teacher recited:

> *Love to bear him, love to raise him, love to send him on his way*
> *Son in sorrow, son in joy, brings darkness or the brightest day*
> *Two the consorts, two the paths, two the deaths for him to rule*
> *One will be the trusting child and three will be the rivals cruel*

Thirst and hunger, sleep and death will come to strike a trusted one
And stones will shatter, stones will stand when might reclaims the rising sun

"That's conveniently cryptic!" said Temmin. "I have no idea what it means."

Harsin took a long draught of his wine, and studied the glass in his hand. "We can make fair guesses about much of it. Some lines are quite clear. 'Two the consorts'—you'll marry twice. And one of the deaths for you to rule will, of course, be my own. Now, stop, Temmin. You wouldn't become king if I were still alive, would you? Regent, perhaps, should I be unable to rule, but not king. And it's likely you'll have one son, the 'trusting child.' We thought the first line meant you should be raised at Whithorse, with your mother." Harsin gave Teacher a hard look from the corner of his eye. "I would have preferred to send you to Parkdale, where I went to school, and I'm still not convinced we did the right thing. You will start your studies with Teacher on Ammaday, to account for the hangover I'm sure you'll set yourself up for tonight." He rose, and Temmin rose with him. "One last thing: I have asked the son of a very good friend to be your companion, to help you adjust to life here in the City."

"I had a companion, at Whithorse," grumbled Temmin.

"That groom? He wasn't a companion, he was a servant," said Harsin. "It's time you kept company with your own class. Percet Sandopint is the oldest son of my good friend, the Duke of Corland. He's styled Lord Fennows. He'll be at the ball tonight."

"I know him, a little," said Temmin, failing to stifle a grimace. "He visited us one winter for a spoke." Almost seven weeks of incredible boredom, he added to himself.

"Well, then. Go have your tea, son. I'm glad we had this chance to talk."

Once Temmin left them, Harsin said, "More pluck than I'd feared. He's spent far too much time chumming around with commoners. I'm hoping Fennows will properly introduce him to City life—show him things about his place in the world he can't learn from you or me—things he should have learned by now."

"Lord Fennows has an indifferent reputation."

"But he's hardly a wild terror. Ansella sheltered Temmin far too much. Wouldn't surprise me if the boy were still a virgin. Ha! That's going a bit far, but he is still quite the wide-eyed child." He finished his glass and added, "I shall be very amused to see his face when we show him the magic."

"Yes," said Teacher. "I am sure it will be quite comical."

Jenks had gone through every combination of black and white clothing in the room, considered them, and discarded them, until he'd made the only possible conclusion and assembled it on the dressing stand. "It's a ball!" said Temmin. "One wears a black dress suit, a white shirt and stock, and a white waistcoat. All of the men will be dressed identically!"

"You are so, so wrong, Your Highness," said the valet, surveying the tidily ransacked wardrobe. "There are subtleties to the male wardrobe only a connoisseur may perceive, and while you are not yet a connoisseur, you shall be when I'm through with you. In the meantime, you will look the part." Temmin rolled his eyes. "It's for the pride of Whithorse, sir, think of it that way."

"Your pride'll be the death of me," grumbled Temmin.

"My pride will be the making of you, sir, depend on it."

Once dressed, Temmin had to admit Jenks was right. The suit fit him just so; the rich yet subtle pattern of the white waistcoat relieved its formality without vulgarity; just the right amount of lace edged his stock. The royal rubies glowed at his cuffs and the fob of his watch, neither ostentatious nor inconsequential. His hair even behaved, arranging itself into golden waves. "Well done, Jenks, I must say! I look as elegant as a portrait, and about as stiff."

"The elegance is mine, the stiffness is yours. Take Miss Ellika's example to heart and go have fun, sir," beamed Jenks, walking his charge to the door.

"D'you know, I just noticed something—you've started calling me 'sir,'" said Temmin.

Jenks gave him a fond smile. "You're a man now, Temmin, not a boy, and you're due that much respect." He put his big hands on Temmin's shoulders. "And you're within half an inch of my height now. Another year and you'll be past me entirely. The older you get, the more you remind me of your uncle."

"D'you think Uncle Pat would be proud of me, Jenks?" said Temmin, ducking his head.

"Lord Patrin loved you very much, sir, and I'm sure he would be exceedingly proud of you," said Jenks, his eyes turning watery. "Off to your birthday celebration. Go."

"Well, aren't we looking sleek!" came Ellika's voice as soon as Temmin stepped into the hall; her bright head peeped out from her doorway. "Come in!"

"Isn't it time to go down?" he said.

"Don't be ridiculous! The thing's just started. We can't go down for another fifteen minutes at the earliest. Now, come in and tell me how splendid I look!"

He walked into Ellika's sitting room, and blurted, "You look like a riot in a lacemaker's shop!"

"Temmin, you have no taste at all. You should thank the Beloved for Jenks."

If one row of lace pleased Ellika, twelve rows pleased her more. Its exuberance suited her. A sapphire and pearl necklace set off her bare shoulders, which rose creamy and pink from her sky blue silk dress. Though Ansella dressed more conservatively, Temmin couldn't help but see his mother mirrored in his sister's face.

"Shall we see if Sedra's ready?" he said.

"She's probably already gone down. She hates balls, always wants to get them over with. We're not allowed to leave until Papa does, but he usually doesn't last much past the second set of dances after dinner. He has other engagements," she added, thinning her lips. "Put your gloves on, Temmy, and don't embarrass me."

"Yes, well, don't call me Temmy downstairs and I'll see what I can do." He stopped before Sedra's study to knock, but the door swung open. Sedra started back from the threshold in surprise. "Merciful Amma, Temmy, you scared me to death!"

"I'm sorry, Seddy," he said, red-faced. "I—we're going downstairs—I thought—"

"Sedra!" exclaimed Ellika over his shoulder. "You look splendid! I don't know how you manage to wear off-season colors so well, but it's perfect."

In contrast to her sister, Sedra's dress avoided all frills, relying on the deep Tremontine red satin and cut for its elegance. Pearls and rubies encircled her neck, and plaits encircled her head in the classical style, dark roses forming a crown along their curve.

In her hands, Sedra held a little knot of white roses, trailing blue ribbons. "For you," she said, pinning it to Ellika's sash; her sister let out a tiny, delighted squeak, and kissed her on the cheek. "And," she said to Temmin, "for you." She produced a rose of the same deep red as those in her hair, and pinned it in Temmin's buttonhole. "Happy birthday," she added, giving his shoulder a tender, tentative pat.

Temmin gathered her into his arms. "Thank you, very much."

"I'm sorry," she murmured in his ear.

"Don't be, it was my fault." He hugged her close and kissed her on the forehead. "*Now* is it time to go down, Elly?" Ellika pulled out his pocket watch, consulted it, and gave a nod. Temmin took a sister on each arm, and the three headed downstairs.

The music stopped as the high doors to the ballroom opened and the siblings descended the broad staircase. The dancers turned, and the orchestra struck up a patriotic fanfare; Temmin flinched before a wave of deafening cheers and applause. On his right, Ellika reflected the adulation back onto the throng, glittering and happy, and on his left, Sedra grew taller and even more regal, her head held proud and high.

A thought crept in on him: no matter how beautiful and intelligent his sisters were, all this was for him—the Heir—not them. His hands held the reins to the crowd; he could feel them. Whenever he acknowledged the cheers, they redoubled. This must be what power felt like. He straightened his shoulders and let the energy fill him.

He led his sisters onto the emptied floor, they saluted the crowd, and the orchestra began a tripla. Dancers took the floor in threes behind them —a woman with two men, a man with two women, and so on down the rows. Tonight, the eyes on him gave him paradoxical strength; they cleared his head, and made his feet sure.

He turned to the buxom young woman behind him and took her hand; their eyes met, and her heated glance brought him up short. No girl had ever given him a look like that before, ever, and his pleased smile made her blush and simper. If being the Heir came with this, he would enjoy it a great deal indeed, he decided. Every girl he danced with presented some variation on the same theme, some shy and admiring, some sly and inviting, and one girl who pressed herself close to him every chance she got.

Dance after dance, and Temmin began to tire of it despite endless beautiful women fawning over him. When the dancing paused he'd have to socialize, and that would never do. Near the end of the first set, Temmin escaped from the floor to find somewhere quiet and something to drink more quenching than sparkling wine. "Does no one drink beer in this place?" he muttered to himself.

Poking around the ballroom's edges, he peered into the many attached salons, small and large, excusing himself from one—"Terribly sorry, didn't know anyone was here," he said to the fumbling couple in the corner—until he came into a long, deserted corner; a swaying curtain hid an oddly angled spot. Two little black boot toes peeped from its hem, moving in time. Temmin watched, curious, until a curly head in a maid's cap peeked out, spotted Temmin, gave a tiny squeak, and retreated behind the curtain. Temmin followed into a wide, hidden service hall, and caught the retreating maid by the arm.

"I thought it was you," he smiled. "You're the maid I danced with, Dannikson, yes?" Gods, what a beautiful girl, as lovely as any he'd danced with that night—lovelier, her little form trim and straight in the severe black and white household livery, her lace cap crisp and its red ribbons dangling down to her waist. Her uncooperative hair looked ready to burst from the cap again. He wondered if she still smelled as good as she had the last time they met.

"I'm so very sorry, Your Highness," the girl said. She blushed, and her voice shook. "It's just I love dancing and they didn' need me at the moment, I just wanted to look—oh!" She put her hands over her mouth, and her wide hazel eyes filled with tears. "I shouldn' even be speakin to you! Oh, Mr Affton will send me packin!"

"Now, now, don't worry about that!" said Temmin. "Why does everyone seem to think I'll tell on them!" He dropped her arm, and pondered her for a moment. He wondered if he would ever get used to the staff quailing at the sight of him; he didn't care for it at all. "What's your name?" he coaxed.

"Dannikson, sir," she said, blinking hard.

"No, your first name."

"Arta?" she quavered.

"Arta? Are you not sure?"

"Of course I'm sure, sir," she laughed, flicking away a tear. "My name is Arta."

Caution was called for, thought Temmin. How might he set her at ease, at least a little? "Well, then, Miss Arta," he said aloud, "let's not waste the music." He held out his hands. "Shall we?"

"...Shall we what, sir?" she said, turning white.

"Dance! Shall we dance! You like to dance, and I'm discovering I like to dance, and you won't get to dance tonight otherwise. So dance with me!"

Arta glanced around. "Well—this hall really isn' in use tonight—but if someone were to catch me…"

"I will make sure nothing happens to you. I'm trying my best to dance with the prettiest girls in the room, and if I don't dance with you, I shall miss the prettiest of them all."

Arta turned a bright crimson, and hesitantly took his hands; before long they were looping up and down the hallway. Temmin found himself eager to make her comfortable. He'd never thought about it before; he behaved how he behaved and didn't wonder about the comfort of others. Why would he think about that in the stables? Everyone was comfortable there already. No one on the Estate treated him differently—respectfully, but no differently, not really. If they were comfortable together, he and Arta, perhaps something more might come of it? Something pleasant? It seemed possible, especially after the girl in the hedge.

He watched with increasing relish as the little maid relaxed, her trusting, mischievous face with its pointed chin losing its pinched anxiety with each turn. She forgot herself and danced in earnest, her smile enough light for the dim corridor. "Truth be known, sir, I hear music and I must look! I had to hear the music proper, and see the girls in all their dresses, and wish I was one of 'em."

"Oh, you don't want to be one of *them*," said Temmin. "You're much prettier, and a better dancer in the bargain." She tittered and withdrew into herself, until the music coaxed her back out again.

Arta was far better company than any of the simpering misses thrown at Temmin in the ballroom. He slipped his hand to her waist and pulled her close; it would have been splendid were she in a ballgown like the ladies after all, to see her shoulders, and perhaps the tops of her breasts. Did she have freckles on her shoulders? He knew women considered freckles a fault, but he found them charming, especially the faint gold dust on Arta's cheeks where the sun had last kissed her. The dance came to an end. Temmin spun her around until her skirts flared out in a bell, and then bowed to her. She curtsied low, and he kissed her little work-roughened hand as he brought her to her feet. Should he kiss her now? No, that hadn't worked well the last time. Best not to frighten her. "Now, Miss Arta, do you know where I might find something proper to drink? Not sparkling wine? I'm positively parched!"

"Oh!" she said. She shook herself, as if waking up from a pleasant nap, folded her hands, and dipped a servile curtsey. "Yes, sir, there's punch and lemonade in the Grand Salon."

"No beer? Or cider?"

"At a ball in the Keep? No, sir!" she said, scandalized.

"Water, perhaps."

"Water? You'd drink water? Well, sir, we have a tap here for the servants," she said, and watched astonished as he drank five ladles from the basin, for lack of a glass.

"Much, much better! Thank you, Miss Arta, we have had a fair exchange! Now, off with you before someone catches you!" He watched her scamper back down the hall and disappear into the realm of the servants.

Being with Arta felt easy; she was more like the people he'd grown up with at Whithorse, uncomplicated and honest. He would watch for her, especially now that they shared a secret. He turned and slipped back to the dance, missing a figure hidden in the drapes—a dapper little man whose eyes appeared to take in everything, and who wrote down every detail somewhere inside his skull. The little man tilted his head to one side, bounced once on his toes, and strolled down the hall after the maid.

Temmin, meanwhile, had rejoined the party just in time for the break he'd hoped to avoid. His thirst slaked, he took up a glass of sparkling wine. He had nothing against it, but a thirsty man wanted something more substantial. He'd worried about making small talk with strangers, but found he had to say little as a steady stream of well-wishers were presented to him one by one, just long enough for a "So pleased to meet you" before being pushed out of the way by the next one in line.

When the music began again, he'd had three glasses of sparkling wine without even noticing, and sparkled himself as he took up a plump, lively girl—the Earl of Something's daughter, he hadn't caught it—and started the second set of dances. Near its end, he found himself with a familiar blonde: his sister. He gave Ellika an extra twirl, and she giggled. "Doesn't Seddy ever dance?" he asked her.

"Not if she can sit in a corner with her nose in the air," said Ellika. "But tell me, are you having fun? You look as if you are!"

"The girls here are *much* prettier than they are at home, Elly!" he said, thinking still of blushing Arta more than the sly daughters of the nobility.

"That's because the prettiest girls are sent to the City, silly, in hopes of snaring someone like you. Especially you."

"I can only marry one of 'em!"

"Oh, Temmy," said Ellika, shaking her curls. They twirled apart, and he found himself face to face with his last partner for this dance.

He met eyes green as leaves, in the face of a woman so stunning Temmin lost his place in the dance and stumbled. When he recovered his feet, all he could manage to get out of his disobedient throat was, "Hullo."

"Hello, Your Highness," she answered in a low, honeyed voice like nothing he'd ever heard. Nor was she like any woman he'd ever seen, so much a classical Tremontine beauty that she might have stepped out of a painting of Neya the Beloved.

Temmin said nothing more and danced automatically, paying no attention to anything but the woman on his arm. When the dance ended, he demanded the next one, the last in the set. "Happily," she said, and he took her up in his arms again, oblivious to the presence at the floor's edge of an outraged man in a blue honor sash who'd sworn he'd already asked the lady for that dance.

Among the onlookers, another young lady peered through her magnifying glass. "Oh dear me," she said. "It seems Neya's Embodiment has made another conquest."

Sedra took a sip of lemonade and laughed. "That's not even worth remarking on, Despie."

"This time it is," said the lady, nodding over Sedra's shoulder. Sedra followed the nod, and choked; Temmin was dancing with Allis Obby, looking for all the world like a gasping fish on the beach, hook still in mouth.

Oh, Weeping Amma! thought Sedra. "The last I knew, he never showed an interest in any female who didn't have four hooves and a tail, but that was three years ago. He would have to start at the top, wouldn't he."

"Don't worry over him so, Seddy, you're not his mother," said her friend.

"I'm not worried," Sedra lied. "He's a grown man. Temmy just doesn't have much experience with girls, if I know Mama. I've learned Elly can manage herself—mostly. I'm not so sure about him yet. Where *is* Ellika?"

As it happened, Ellika twirled in the arms of Percet, Lord Fennows. "I shall be spending a great deal of time with your brother soon," he said as they looped round and round. "I am hoping that means I might have the pleasure of your company more often."

"How charming your sister looks this evening, Fennows!" said Ellika, looking over his shoulder. "Rose is such a flattering color on one of her complexion. I must ask after her dressmaker!"

"To be sure, Despilla looks very well tonight," said Fennows. "What I mean to say is, I should very much like to spend more time with you—"

"And how lovely Allis Obby is tonight, but then, there isn't anything unusual about that! Have you danced with her yet tonight, sir?"

"Yes, but—" The music ended and the assembly applauded, cutting Fennows off.

"Thank you for a *lovely* dance!" said Ellika. "Oh, yes, of course you may walk me in to dinner, I would never break with tradition! I'm so terribly sorry to be up on the dais when all of you are on the floor, but these silly state occasions!"

"Of course, but—"

"Here, take me over to Miss Obby and my brother please, Fennows, dear, I need to make introductions." The unhappy Fennows offered his arm and did as he was told, Ellika chattering all the while to friends they passed along the way.

Meanwhile, Allis curtsied to the floor, and as Temmin lifted her up by the hand, he couldn't help staring into her bodice. The familiar low twitch began; he swore to himself, and tried to think of everything other than her breasts—Jenks in his underwear, that usually did it. He started at the sound of Ellika's voice. "Prince Temmin, Heir of Tremont, may I make known to you the Embodiment of Neya, Miss Allis Obby of the Lovers' Temple."

The Embodiment of Neya? How was he supposed to make small talk with the personification of a Goddess? He took Allis's hand and bowed low over it to hide his astonishment. His shock must have made it past his moustache, for Miss Obby came to his rescue and so deftly steered the conversation that by the time they'd made it in to dinner he'd invited her to go riding with him. "I should love to, Your Highness!" she exclaimed, as if Temmin had given her a longed-for gift. "I will await your invitation."

"May we dance after dinner?"

"Oh," she said, dropping her eyes. "I'm afraid my card is filled."

"Oh," said Temmin, drooping. "I would imagine so."

"But I promise I shall save a dance for you at the next ball. Will you be attending the Duke of Litta's ball on Nerrday next?"

"Yes, of course!" said Temmin, with no idea if he'd even received an invitation. "Please, Miss Obby, I would be very grateful if you'd save me an entire set!" She laughed; he pulled out her chair, seated her, and walked down the rows of tables in a haze of green eyes, black hair and sweet, pink breasts. *Blessed Mother, help me,* he thought. *Miss Allis Obby.*

He took his place next to Harsin, Ellika on his right. "Oh dear," she said. "You do realize who Allis is."

"You told me!" snapped Temmin. "Ah, I'm sorry, Elly, but it was completely unexpected. I didn't even show proper respect—I should have called her Holy One! I had no idea an Embodiment would look like her."

"Don't be a goose. The Lovers' Embodiments are always beautiful, Temmy, and as much like twins as possible," said Ellika. "The two before the Obbys—they're here somewhere, just in from Kellen for a week— stunning. Blondes, unrelated but very well matched, could easily pass for twins. Of course, Allis really *is* a twin. Her brother, Issak, embodies Nerr. There he is, just down the right-hand side at the table with that annoying Lord Fennows. Gods, what a bore, I couldn't shut him up the whole time we were dancing!"

Ellika kept chattering, her voice a soft chirp as she pointed out various luminaries. Temmin paid little attention. He sorted through the bobbing heads, people nodding and making small talk around the tables, until he saw a man with the same silken black hair as Allis. He had to be Issak Obby.

As Allis represented the unattainable Tremontine ideal for women, so did Issak for men: tall, broad but not barrel-shaped, slim of waist and hip, all his gestures great and small as perfect as his form. The smooth incline of his back as he kissed his dinner partner's hand; the light touch of his long fingers as he held his wine glass; the summoning of a footman, called over without so much as a word or a nod—

He looked up at Temmin. Issak's eyes were the same deep green as his sister's, but while her gaze invited, his gaze commanded. The Embodiment smiled up at him, unblinking, until Temmin colored and averted his gaze. He realized the air beside his right ear had stilled. Ellika no longer prattled but studied his face, amused and sympathetic. "Gently, Tem, gently," she murmured, putting her hand over his. "Go gently, little brother."

THREE

Temmin danced every dance until the Obbys went home, even though Allis had no spots on her card left; most of the dances involved changing partners, and he made sure he danced in her group. He racked his brain for clever things to say when they partnered, failed, and settled for staring at her every chance he got over the shoulders of his partners. More than one young lady told her maid later that though the Heir was handsome, he was unpardonably rude; you'd think he'd never seen an Embodiment of Neya before!

Temmin himself remained oblivious; the only person he saw was Allis, though he noticed her brother more and more. While Issak usually danced in different sets than his sister, he sometimes ended up next to Temmin, or even dancing with him in the figures where the sexes broke apart. Each time they met in the dance, Issak's effect on Temmin grew, and Issak seemed to sense it. A close pass brought their faces within inches, and Temmin swore Issak nearly kissed him. It should have displeased him, and he wondered why it didn't.

Halfway through the ball, Allis and Issak partnered for the traditional dance between brothers and sisters, and Temmin dragged Sedra onto the floor. "Do stop gawping, Temmy," Sedra murmured as his head whipped around to keep the Obbys in view. "You're embarrassing yourself."

"Am I?" said Temmin, turning his face to hers. "I thought everyone was watching them." In fact, the crowd had pulled back to form a clear circle around the twins. *They're perfectly matched,* he thought, *like carriage horses—no, that's a horrid thought, like—well, like two beautiful things that look alike!* He sighed to himself; love poetry was out of the question.

He let Sedra steer them out of sight of the Obbys. "You don't know what you're getting into when it comes to them," she said.

"Probably not," he agreed, "but I should very much like to find out."

Temmin's new best friend Fennows buttonholed him time and again, and wouldn't stop pestering him about Ellika. Temmin found this irritating, as it cut into his questions about Allis. He found the only way to shut Fennows up was to suggest a bumper of sparkling wine, and soon the two sat before the fire in an unoccupied salon off the ballroom proper, empty wine bottles in an untidy pile under a table.

"So, in the City two days, eh?" said Fennows, refilling Temmin's glass. "Someone like you, I should like to know how many tasty bits you left behind in Whithorse!"

"Tasty bits?" said Temmin. "The only thing I left behind in Whithorse was my freedom. And my best friend," he added, glowering at the pimply young man across from him.

"You'll have plenty of good hunting here, my friend. You—*you* can have any girl you please! Good-looking, the Heir—" Fennows burped. "Excuse me. No girl'd turn *you* down, not even the daughters of the nobility if you wanted 'em. My position gets me plenty, I assure you, but— say, are you sure you can't put in a good word with your father on my behalf? Corland is important to the empire, and Papa pays a good deal of tribute. Past time for the ties between us to get stronger. Matrimonial, I should think."

"I don't think Elly is in the marriage market," said Temmin. "At least she hasn't said."

"She's not the one who decides whether she is or not, now, is she!" said Fennows. "I'd treat her like a precious—a precious—*thing*, I dunno, statue, gem, some such, I should think. All she'd have to do is stand in the middle of the room, just stand there and listen, and I'd make her appreciate the life of the mind, like poetry—I write poetry, d'you know—and I know she'd come to love it, if she'd just give it a chance! I'd protect her from all that is coarse and impure, from those stupid, handsome things she likes to dance with—I tell you what it is, old man," he added, wobbling forward in his chair. "I tell you what it is. I've done a great deal of thinking on this. Women are a separate species. They're not like you and me a-tall."

"They're not?" said Temmin.

"No, no!" said Fennows, settling back in his chair. "Not a-tall. Think of your sisters, eh? Not like us, I should think, not a-tall. No appreciation of the real things in life, of the life of the mind. No appreciation. They're all clothes and simpering."

"I'd like to see Sedra simper, that'd be a sight," said Temmin, blinking.

"And then!" Fennows said, leaning forward again. "And then, there are species in the species!"

"I don't get—get your meaning," said Temmin, dribbling from his glass. He scrubbed at his waistcoat, relieved the wine was white; he'd catch it from Jenks otherwise.

"Well!" said Fennows. "Can't say a merchant's daughter is the same species as our sisters, I should think! And then there're maids! And then the ladies of a house, d'you know!"

"What makes 'em species in the species?"

Fennows laid out his philosophy, a neat deck of cards kept in his head: "You can keep a merchant's daughter, but you can't just tumble 'er. You can tumble a maid any time without keepin' 'er, but if you get 'er in the family way you have to pay 'er a bit and support the brat at a Mother's House. Else she'll go to the Father's Temple for justice, didn't she, and then there's a fuss. Justice for a housemaid, feh." Fennows considered his glass, then said, "And ladies of a house—different species altogether. More like us. They'll do anything with anyone, and they're business-like and friendly. Don't expect anything from you but your coin. No pretending, just fucking. Know how to treat a man. Oh, you can make an appointment with a Beloved at the Lovers' Temple, but then they make you think about it! Gods, I'd keep any number of merchants' daughters to stay out of that pink marble heap, but for Neya's Day! Now, that's a sight worth seeing, I should think! Ah, Farr hang it, dead soldier," he finished, shaking the last drops from the current wine bottle.

"Hang on," said Temmin, "hang on, it's a ranking? Women like our sisters, then merchants' daughters, then maidservants, then…ladies of a… house? What ladies?"

"I mean whores, old man, what d'you think I mean!" hooted Fennows.

Temmin frowned. "Whores? Wouldn't do. Hussies. Dishonorable. Wouldn't like 'em."

"That's what's so good about them! They have no honor! No, rank women all you'd like, they're none of 'em like you and me," Fennows said. "Not properly people, are they? Don't understand 'em a-tall."

"I understand my sisters—mostly. They're certainly people! Sedra has a—what d'you say?—a life of the mind. That's *all* she has! I don't know any merchants' daughters—"

"Yet."

"—And I've never met a—a whore—what house are you talking about, anyway? As for maids, all the maids I know are people," said Temmin, thinking of the pleasant, motherly women who attended the Queen and his sisters—the last women in the world he'd "give a tumble." Aloud, he said, "What else would they be?"

"A different species!" declared his companion. "You can't say you treat 'em the same as your sisters?"

Temmin's thoughts turned from from the ladies' maids to Mattie, whose soft breasts had until that night been the focus of his daydreams, and little Arta, whose happy face and trim figure caught his interest on sight. Allis Obby had supplanted both, but oh, they were different from the ladies' maids he'd known since childhood. "No," he said, "I can't say as how I do."

Temmin woke late the next morning hungover for the second time in a week, and cursed Fennows. When the room appeared more level, he gingerly stepped out of bed. "Jenks!" he called, then louder, "Jenks!" to no reply. He shambled into his study, hanging onto the furniture and the doorframe, but Jenks was nowhere. He tugged on the bell rope, and a pink-faced footman entered. "Bring me some sort of—something. Tea. Toast. And something for my head. Find Jenks! He'll know what." Pagg damn that Jenks, he grumbled to himself. Always under foot until you needed him.

"Very good, gentlemen," said Harsin to the table full of ministers. "You know our concerns, and we are aware of yours, so let's be at it. We will be busy the rest of the morning, and so we will resume tomorrow." With that, Harsin left his conference room, his secretary trailing behind him.

"The Queen is waiting in your study for the discussion of the Prince's further education, Your Majesty," said Winmer.

"Alone?"

"Yes, sir."

"Where is Teacher? Where's the Colonel? I thought they would wish to participate in this."

"They are elsewhere," said Winmer.

"I don't want them elsewhere, I want them here," said Harsin. "See to it, Winmer."

"I will try, sir, but I'm not sure either of them is within reach."

Harsin raised a brow at this, but said nothing. He walked into his study, to find only his wife waiting for him. Her face was blotchy, and the cameo pinned to her breast rose and fell in time with her rapid breathing. "A by-blow!" shouted Ansella.

"You've been at the Keep all of three days, and your dramatics are already boring me! What now?"

"A by-blow, a bastard," she said. "You promised me! You promised me no child would come out of all your whoring!"

"I prefer the term 'engagements,'" said Harsin. "And no child has come of any of them."

"That you knew, apparently!"

"Annie, you attack me in my ignorance," said Harsin, sitting down. "Please enlighten me."

Ansella trembled, her fair brows low. "Do you perhaps remember in all your 'engagements' a maid at Whithorse named Tellis Ambler?"

"Tellis Ambler? Tellis…" said Harsin, rolling the name around his mouth as if calling up the memory of a wine.

Ansella let out a disgusted breath. "It would have been about the time Temmin was born."

"Ah!" he said. "Oh, yes. I remember her."

"You have a daughter. Her name is Mattisanis."

"Do I!" said Harsin with a surprised smile. "Is she as pretty as her mother was? What's she like?"

"She's a maidservant, is what she's like!" said Ansella. "Until this morning, she worked at Meadow House for my mother!"

"Until this morning—Annie, what have you done?" said Harsin. "You will not harm this girl."

"I haven't done anything to hurt her," said Ansella, turning away. "I know the girl, and her mother, and I'm clever enough to know who's really to blame. I sent Teacher and the Colonel to deal with it."

"Without consulting me? Whatever for? I'll have Winmer arrange a stroke of good luck for her, and there's an end to it."

"Don't bother. They went by mirror early this morning. She has to be out of the way as soon as possible, out of the province if they can manage it!"

"How did you discover all this?"

Ansella paused, considering. "The Colonel has known all this time, and didn't tell me to spare my feelings until circumstances required it. He's always been very considerate of me. Unlike you!"

Harsin shrugged. "Tellis was a maid, of no consequence whatsoever. I didn't even remember her name until you told me."

"She was of consequence to me! You—*had* her when I was in labor with our son!"

"Just the once, not an ongoing affair, unlikely to result in any sort of child—an impulse."

"An impulse like your father's many 'impulses' that litter the countryside? I'd think you have enough ongoing affairs not to need 'impulses.' Do you intend to leave Temmin with bastards to deal with as well? This House has enough trouble with *your* half-brothers. How many have you sired on your little 'impulses?'"

She leaned forward as she spoke, shaking with effort; she was as close to dissolving into pure rage as Harsin had seen her in years. "Don't agitate yourself, Ansella, if I had a son other than Temmin, we'd know. This is a girl," said Harsin, "a girl I had no idea existed until today. She's no threat whatsoever to Temmin." Ansella laughed. "D'you see some threat I'm not seeing, wife?" he demanded.

"Harsin, your son kissed her."

"So?" said Harsin.

"He found her with a young man and she let him—*touch*—her in exchange for keeping her job."

Harsin's brows rose, and he pursed his lips. "Interesting! He threatened her?"

"No," admitted Ansella. "But apparently she was quite frightened."

"Sad for him it was his half-sister. Ah, well, Teacher will sort it out. He didn't leave her pregnant, I hope? I suppose Teacher can take care of that, if it comes to it—take her to one of the better Mother's Houses, perhaps even arrange a quiet marriage," he said. He dropped into his favorite chair, a tufted leather wingback near the hearth. "Will you sit?"

"Pregnant?" said Ansella, white-faced. "How can you be so cavalier about such a disturbing possibility!"

"I'm not *cavalier*, I am pragmatic," he snorted. "I find the prospect mildly unsettling myself. Is she?"

"No, she is not. Temmin is still innocent."

"As far as you know."

"I made sure of it," Ansella said, staring him down. "I made sure he had absolutely no opportunities to turn out like his father and grandfather. I raised him in accordance with Venna's Way. He's a virtuous boy!"

"He's an unnatural boy, you mean!" said Harsin. "What does the Sister's Way have to do with it? The girls have to pass Her test, but he certainly doesn't have to! How could you do something like that to him?"

"I've done nothing but keep him safe. That's all I've ever done, is keep my children safe!"

"He's safer here than anywhere, and his virginity is no one's business but his own!" boomed Harsin, rising from the chair. "And that's the last word on the subject!"

Ansella closed her mouth. Her trembling stopped, but the rims of her eyes showed red around the blue. She searched for words. "You may not believe it, but your whoring endangers your children," she finally said.

"Annie," he said, opening his hands in conciliation, "this is nothing new. We were not a love match, as you're so very fond of reminding everyone, and we both have lovers. Why are you so angry?"

Ansella's face mottled, red and white. "Don't you dare paint my one— my *one*—relationship in the same light as all your mistresses!"

"I've never shamed you, nor have I ever put a one of them above you!"

"You've never had to! I've been a thousand miles to the west all this time!"

"And whose choice was that!"

"As far as I'm aware, it was mutual!" She marched through the door and slammed it behind her. Harsin heard her slam the door to his receiving room as well, but knew that once she made it to the hallway, she would be composed enough to avoid strong emotion in front of the servants. He sighed.

"Winmer," he called, "As soon as Teacher and Colonel Jenks return from Whithorse, bring them in. And I don't care how fucking early it is, I'm in need of a brandy."

Teacher and Colonel Jenks—for Jenks was no corporal—arrived before the brandy. The Colonel let Teacher give the details of their trip, standing back from the King in what anyone else would see as respect, but which Harsin knew was something less. "Thank you. Teacher, please stay. Colonel, you're dismissed." Jenks tapped his heels, bowed, and left, his manner stiff and formal; Harsin wondered if the man would ever forgive him for the past, and wondered again why he cared. He turned to the pale figure by the fireplace. "I want you to show her to me. My daughter."

"Very well." Teacher faced the great mirror over the mantel. "Show me Mattisanis Dunley of Reggiston."

The reflection rippled once and reformed into the kitchens of the Whithorse Estate's Great House. The servants ranged around a long table with Crokker at its head. The perspective narrowed more, onto a girl with Harsin's own dark hair and her mother's heart-shaped face. Easy smiles flashed over her open, sweet face as she passed dishes and drank her tea, until a footman entered the room. Her eyes hardened, and Harsin's own implacable nature flashed across her face before she turned her back on the young man. In spite of his mercenary words to his wife, the King's heart twisted. "Another spirited daughter," he murmured. "Another child I don't know."

"There you are, Jenks!" exclaimed Temmin. "I've been calling and calling!"

"I'm very sorry, sir," said Jenks, walking through the study to the bedchamber. "I was unavoidably detained. I'll draw your bath, shall I?"

"I woke up and you weren't there," said Temmin, following him. "I hate that! I've been up for a couple of hours, had to call a footman for some sort of breakfast!"

"I'm glad you got something to eat, then, sir," said Jenks, turning on the taps.

Temmin sat on the closed commode and winced at the sound of the falling water. "Pagg damn, my head! You can't have been a very good orderly for Uncle Pat if you were in the habit of just—*disappearing* whenever you felt like it!"

"My service with Lord Patrin is not yours to criticize nor speculate upon, Your Highness." The big man stalked from the room, and Temmin followed, the belt of his robe trailing behind him.

"It's not my fault you never made officer! I'm sorry, Jenks, but my head is pounding—oh, is this the same stuff as last time? Thank the gods!" Temmin drank off the contents of an offered glass in one gulp. "Merciful Amma, that Fennows is a pain!"

"You thought Lord Fennows interesting enough to get drunk as Farr with him last night," said Jenks as he took the empty glass.

"What else was I supposed to do with him! He wouldn't leave me alone, and kept prattling on about Ellika—I think he wants to marry her, Jenks."

"So I've heard from a number of sources, sir."

"Can't let that happen," said Temmin. "I'll go straight to Harla's Hill before I'll have that man as my brother-in-law." Jenks said nothing; he put Temmin's picked-at breakfast outside the door to be taken to the kitchens, and returned to the bathroom. "Oh, don't be like this! I'm sorry, Jenks! I feel horrid, and I'm acting horrid, and I can't help it!"

"Yes, sir, you can," said Jenks. "More will be expected of you now you're an adult. Adults do not take out their petty illnesses and complaints on others, no matter how poorly they're feeling."

"Yes, they do," said Temmin. "They do it all the time!"

"Well, they shouldn't."

Temmin slipped out of his nightclothes and into the tub. "Thank you, Jenks, this feels good. You aren't going to stay mad all day, are you?" he called, but Jenks was gone. Temmin sighed; he wobbled his head, and discovered both his spirits and his headache had lifted, if only a little. Potent stuff in that glass, whatever it was. As the throbbing in his temples receded, the night before came flooding back. Not the drunken episode with that detestable spotted lordling, but dancing with Allis Obby. The beautiful Obbys, both of them, dancing round and round and somehow always gazing into his eyes as if the three of them were the only ones in the room. He shivered, and slid his head under the water.

"Gods, I hope he gets his drinking phase out of the way soon," groaned Jenks at tea. "I swear, Annie, I'll thrash him otherwise."

"I seem to recall another young man whose 'drinking phase' lasted well into his twenties," said Ansella.

"That's different. I was an officer—"

"—And you had to keep up with my brother. I know." Ansella considered her reflection in the silver tea service. "How did it go, Standfast? How did you manage to explain things to her?"

"I didn't," said Jenks. "I talked to Tellis, instead—her name is Dunley now. I gave her a thousand gold, with a guarantee of two thousand more as Mattie's portion, told her to bring her daughter home and why, thanked her for her discretion and left it to her to explain the money away, though I made some suggestions—including a very strong one about leaving Whithorse and moving where no one knew them."

"What did her husband say?"

"He's dead."

Ansella sighed. "She was a nice girl, Mattie. So was her mother. Tellis was very, very pretty. She left service rather abruptly, and I remember wondering why."

"She seemed to expect me—extremely nervous. I think she thought I was there to kill them."

"It wouldn't be the first time someone killed an inconvenient lover, though I don't think Harsin's ever done it," she said. "What did Teacher do?"

"Ferried me back and forth. Stood behind me looking disturbing—it's no wonder poor Tellis thought we were there to murder her. It was overkill, you know, Annie, Winmer could have handled this easily."

"I know. I know. I just didn't want Temmin calling her up to the City, and I didn't want to tell him why he can't. I don't want this place to change him, Standfast. He is the sweetest boy imaginable, and I want him to stay that way!"

"He won't stay a child forever. This whole incident is proof of that."

A discreet knuckle rapped on the door; it opened a crack. Ansella's chief maid and dresser pushed her grizzled head through it. "Begging pardon, Your Majesty, but Sister Ibbit is here."

Ansella brightened. "Send her right in, please, Hanston!"

Jenks sighed and rose from the table. "Then I'd better absent myself, even though I had more to discuss with you. I know the Sisters of Venna generally don't care for men, but Ibbit—" He shook his head. "Don't worry, Annie, my dear," he added. "I'm always watching over him, body and soul."

"As his mother's religious advisor, his soul has always been *my* province, Mr Jenks, not yours," came Sister Ibbit's frosty voice.

Jenks bestowed a sour look on her. He turned back to Ansella, raised her hand to his lips, and kissed the air above it. "Good day, ma'am," he said. As he passed Ibbit, he gave her one last disdainful glance, which she ignored.

"Do sit down, Sister," said Ansella, rising herself. Once the door closed behind Hanston, she took Ibbit's hands and kissed them. "Oh, Ibbit," she said, holding them against her cheek. She burst into tears. "Such a day I've had! Such a terrible day!"

"I shouldn't wonder, if you've been taking tea with *him*," Ibbit said. She stroked Ansella's flushed face. "But it's all right, I'm here now." Ibbit kissed Ansella's tear-stained lips, and Ansella clung to her solid form like a tender vine. "I'm here now, sweetheart."

FOUR

"All right, I'm not angry anymore! Please, stop, sir," laughed Jenks.

Temmin groveled at his feet. "You're sure you forgive me?" he said.

"Yes!"

"I can cringe even better than this, you know, if need be."

"Get up, you ridiculous boy."

"Ridiculous *man*, thank you," huffed Temmin, rising to his feet. "I am sorry, though, Jenks. I shouldn't tease you about being Uncle Pat's orderly. It must have been disappointing to retire a corporal, but I know how proud you are of your service."

Jenks smiled. "It's quite all right, sir. Serving Lord Patrin was an honor even without high rank. Now that you're in better spirits, and my greater chores are done, tell me, how did you enjoy your birthday—apart from Lord Fennows?"

Temmin's eyes went wide, and he plunked down on the green velvet couch. "Jenks, I saw the most amazing girl I have ever seen in my life." At the valet's inquiring look, he continued, "I can't get her out of my mind, she's perfect, she's even prettier than Elly! Nothing like the other girls—no fiddle-faddle. She even wore her hair loose instead of all fussy on top of her head! Her name is Allis Obby."

"Not the Embodiment of Neya?" said Jenks.

"Yes! D'you know her?" said Temmin.

"Your Highness, everyone knows her," said Jenks. "And did you dance with her?"

"Twice! And I walked her in to dinner. Oh, Jenks," he said, throwing himself down on his back, "I can't stop thinking about her!" Or her brother, he said to himself.

"Oh, dear," said Jenks. "Have you made any commitments, or did you have time to speak with her at length?"

"She was very charming to talk to, though I didn't have much to say—I was speechless! But somehow, and I swear I hadn't meant to, I ended up inviting her to go riding. I don't know how I managed to get her to agree!"

Jenks sat down on the back of the couch and looked down at his rapturous charge, still in his pajamas and robe. "You do realize she's an Embodiment, and what that means."

"Well, it means she's possessed by the Goddess Neya now and again, on Neya's Day, certainly, and I think Nerr's Day, too. And everyone knows what goes on at the Lovers' Temple."

"You have no idea what goes on in that Temple, sir, you've just come of age and you're still innocent, unless there's something you haven't told me."

"Oh, no, nothing's changed in the last week," said Temmin with a touch of lemon in his voice. "You're probably the only one I'd tell in any event, old man. But why are you so ominous all the sudden? I invited a beautiful girl who happens to be a religious figure to go on a ride. Her vows certainly don't keep her from going riding, do they?"

"Sir, if I'm not mistaken on the nature of your infatuation—"

"It's not an infatuation!"

"—Of your *interest* in Miss Obby, you'd like a great deal more than a pleasant afternoon on horseback with her at some point."

"Well—" said Temmin, flushing, "—certainly! I can't think of many things I'd like more! I'd very much doubt you wouldn't want the same if you were in my place. In fact, it'd be really the most ideal way in the world for me to—to become more *experienced* in life. Don't you think?"

"Ideal? Perhaps," said Jenks. "How much did Sister Ibbit manage to get into that brain of yours about religious orders?"

"Not much," mumbled Temmin, running his fingers up and down the nap of the upholstery and watching it turn from leaf green to moss green.

"Not much," repeated Jenks. "Well, let me fill in a little gap in your knowledge she wouldn't have wanted to discuss with you even if you'd bothered to show up for your lessons, which we both know you didn't. If you want to 'become more experienced' with Miss Obby, you either have to lose your innocence beforehand, or take orders in the Temple—very specific orders. What you're proposing is Supplication." Jenks squirmed, and Temmin looked up. "I hate discussing these sorts of things with you," said Jenks. "If the Embodiments wish to take an...*experienced*...person as a lover, nothing stands in the way; they simply pursue a normal courtship. But inexperienced people are a different issue." He cleared his throat and blushed—he never blushed, thought Temmin—and continued, "If Lovers' Temple clergy take the virginity of a petitioner, it makes for a bond between the petitioner and the cleric. The cleric becomes responsible in a way for the spiritual development of the petitioner—it's not done lightly. In the case of the Embodiments, the only time they take a virginity is when they've accepted a petitioner as a Supplicant."

"So if I wanted her to...I'd have to become a Supplicant, if I wanted to...what does being a Supplicant mean?"

"Did Ibbit teach you nothing?"

"If I could possibly help it."

"Supplicants are like Postulants—fledgling priests—except more so. They're chosen because they have displayed a gift that sets them apart from the other Postulants—an especially talented warrior at the Brother's Temple, for instance, or an insightful intellect at the Wise One's Temple."

"I'm glad one of us is devout, and that it's not me," said Temmin, crossing his long legs at the ankles.

"You'd do well to take your devotionals more seriously, sir," Jenks said, frowning. "The King leads his people by example, and your father has always made his devotionals with great fastidiousness. And your mother is openly devout, and not just at the Sister's Temple. At any rate, what I'm trying to say is, if you want the Holy One that badly, and if you want her to be your first—your first *experience*," he grimaced, his face a light green, "you'd have to become a Lovers' Temple Supplicant. And they'd have to accept you. It's called the Chase, after Nerr's pursuit of Neya. You chase, and they either let you catch them or not."

"'They?'" said Temmin, sitting up.

"The Embodiments are a pair, sir. If you chase one, you chase both."

"Oh," said Temmin, blinking. His mind turned to his only reading of the Lovers' Saga. "Jenks, Allis and Issak Embody Neya and Nerr, yes?"

"Yes," said Jenks.

"Does that mean they're…lovers like the, ehm, Lovers?"

Jenks flushed again, turning his green pallor into an odd shade of gray. "At Spectacles, yes, in a manner of speaking. When the Gods take them, They re-enact the Chase. To witness it is considered very good luck. People from all over come to the City, some from as far away as Sairland. He chases Her, and when He catches Her, They…"

"Yes, yes, I know, I was speaking about the Obbys in particular."

"As far as what happens in the Embodiments' private lives, I couldn't say, sir."

Temmin flushed himself. "So, if I understand you correctly, I have to devote myself to the Lovers' Temple and take a form of religious orders if I'm going to…and Mr Obby as well?"

"You understand me entirely, sir."

"And…have you seen Nerr catch Neya?" he said.

"I have, sir, but not in the persons of Mr and Miss Obby. Well," sighed Jenks as he stood up, "I'm glad we had this little talk." And, his sweating forehead seemed to say, glad it was over.

"Yes, thank you, Jenks," said Temmin as he watched Jenks disappear into the bedchamber and the wardrobe beyond. "I think. This puts things in a different light." He let his head fall back against the couch. A different light, he repeated to himself. All he had thought about, between bouts of nausea and headache, was Allis—and, truthfully, her brother.

They had sex? Together? In front of other people? He'd been looking forward to the Neya's Day Spectacle since his voice dropped. The one in Reggiston, or anywhere else but the City, didn't have the Embodiments in it, but he'd heard something of what went on, and to a young man with a vivid imagination… Still, the idea of watching Allis and Issak make love was both horrifying and highly arousing.

But Allis, oh, Allis. How could he get a woman like Allis out of his mind? Very odd to feel that way about someone he hardly knew. Mattie had been pretty, yes, and more than once he'd fantasized about somehow getting her into service at the Keep. But now, she barely crossed his mind, though she had been the focus of his cross-eyed imagination every time he'd satisfied himself since touching her five days before.

Everything about Allis radiated sex. But more, when he looked in her eyes, he felt—he *knew* he could trust her with every secret his body contained, every awkward touch and shameful thought, every tender part of him. And then, her beauty—the long black hair in thick waves down her back, the flare of her hips and the swell of her breasts... The low twitch began again, swelling into a full twinge. He adjusted himself and contemplated taking care of things, but Jenks was in the next room.

He sighed and worked out his options. He could find a girl, any girl, and "tumble 'er," as that prat Fennows put it, and then he'd be free to pursue Allis like anyone else. Or, he could 'chase' both Allis and Issak, and enter service at the Lovers' Temple. Why was he even considering this?

He thought of Issak. When they'd met in the dance, Issak's hands were strong, reassuring. His mouth seemed hard and soft at the same time, and the near-kiss—he'd leaned into it, as if he wanted it, as if Issak compelled him to. He thought of Alvo, kneeling between his legs. Did that count as losing his virginity? Who could he ask? No, he was fairly certain losing one's virginity involved a woman.

Temmin groaned. He missed Alvo, or at least he missed the friendship he thought they'd had. He wished Alvo were there to talk to. He always had been. At this rate, he'd lose his virginity when Nerr got the Heir. Perhaps, he thought as he closed his eyes for another hangover-induced nap, he should follow Fennows's advice. He was a prat, but he seemed to know more about this stuff than Temmin did.

Temmin spent Paggday at the stables after a long ride, gradually coaxing the men into trusting him. He thought he might even have picked out a matched pair of horses for his curricle, sleek grays with just enough Inchari stock in them to impart the breed's fine heads and high-held tails, without their characteristic skittishness. He would have to consult his mother; her judgment of horses surpassed that of everyone he knew. He'd needed that relaxing day, for today, Ammaday, he began lessons with Teacher.

At breakfast, two members of the family were animated and talkative, two were sullen and withdrawn, and Temmin stood alone in the middle, looking anxiously round the table. Harsin and Ellika were both in fine spirits. The King beamed at Temmin, a mildly unnerving development. Ellika remained her usual ebullient self, even when she burned her tongue on her coffee. Sedra and Ansella, on the other hand, were not; Sedra looked alternately glum and resentful, stealing glances at both Temmin and her father over the top of a resolutely isolating newspaper, and Ansella kept her eyes down, answering questions with a frozen smile and as few words as possible. Temmin thought he would never understand his family.

He covered his own nerves about the upcoming lesson, and stalled for time, by eating as much and as slowly as possible. True, he was hungry—he was always hungry—but eventually he'd eaten all the soft-boiled egg and toast even he could hold, along with a great deal of bacon, tomatoes, and coffee cut with cocoa. Nothing for it but to return to his study, and face Teacher. "Don't worry, son, you might even enjoy yourself," said his father as he rose from the table. Temmin gave a weak smile, and dragged himself up the stairs.

His tutor waited for him, back to the door and gazing out over the great expanse of lawn outside the windows. "I see you have covered up all your mirrors," said Teacher. "I do wonder how you shave in the morning."

"Jenks insists on shaving me. I don't want you spying," said Temmin, spreading himself out on the couch.

"I do not 'spy' on you. I observe you from time to time, nothing more."

"Really? Every time I looked in the mirror on my birthday, there you were," said Temmin.

Teacher smiled. "It was your birthday. I was curious to see whether you could see me. I spend much of every Heir's eighteenth birthday that way, and this is the first time in 358 years I have not been disappointed."

"Three hundred—really, I wish you'd stop that immortal nonsense. Next you'll be telling me you're the Black Man."

"There are people who believe I am, though I do try to discourage the belief. And I am not immortal. At least I hope not."

"Why wouldn't you wish that? I should like to live forever, I think."

"You are eighteen. You already think you are going to live forever, and that nothing can hurt you." Teacher looked down. "An abnormally long life is not as enjoyable as you might think. That aside, it is time to see what you know. I have heard you have spent more time in the stables than the schoolroom."

"Speaking of which!" said Temmin, brightening.

"Unlike your past tutors, I cannot be bribed," said Teacher. "There is nothing you have that I want."

"Nothing?" said Temmin, face falling.

"Nothing but your attention, which may be considered a rare and elusive commodity."

"I don't know why you want to bother," grumbled Temmin. "Everyone knows I'm the dull one."

"You are much brighter than you think you are," said Teacher.

"How would you know?"

Teacher considered. "I said I did not spy on you—and I did not. But your father and I watched your progress in reflections over the years. You are quite bright, and quite inventive."

"Sedra is the smart one," said Temmin.

"Do not compare yourself to your sister," said Teacher. "Few compare to her. She is more intelligent than your father, and that is a high standard. Let us survey what you know."

They spent the morning touching on everything from trade routes to exports to classical Old Sairish. It surprised Temmin how much he actually knew, though the main passages he had memorized were two vulgar love poems and several tongue twisters. "Nevertheless," said Teacher, "rattling off the tongue twisters without hesitation shows me your pronunciation is quite good."

"If I ever find myself in ancient Sairland, I'll count myself lucky."

"Old Sairish is the universal, civilized tongue of the West, Your Highness, and to know it is to understand our own language. Should you come across an educated person whose language you do not speak, the chances are good you will both have at least a smattering of it, and so can communicate. It is also convenient for speaking privately amongst less educated people."

Jenks came in, signaling luncheon. "I confess Sedra and I used to do it all the time, usually when we were arguing and didn't want the servants to know and tell Mama," said Temmin in classical Sairish.

"Do what all the time, sir?" said Jenks in the same language.

Teacher smiled at Temmin's astonished face, and said, in Tremontine, "We will resume after lunch."

"Jenks, damn you!" said Temmin after his tutor left the study, "all this time! Why didn't you tell me you spoke it!"

"Because it was more entertaining to listen to you and Miss Sedra concocting mischief. Now, it's lamb chops and spring greens. I suggest eating while it's hot," he said, effectively distracting his charge from an unfortunate line of questioning.

Temmin woke up with a start. Something had just whacked him on the nose.

"Get up, sir," said Teacher, brandishing a rolled-up newspaper.

"You hit me!" squawked Temmin.

"I usually use a cane on the bottom. Be grateful for a newspaper on the nose," retorted Teacher. "I beat your father for two weeks straight before he got his head on the right way round, and he would be the first person to say it made him a better ruler."

"How do I avoid his fate?" said the Prince, rising from the green velvet couch and pulling on his suit coat.

"It's simple, really. Do not misbehave. Be awake when I return from now on or I really will beat you."

Temmin drew his eyebrows together. "You are nothing like my other tutors."

"You have no idea how true that is."

"All right, then, I'll do my best to behave. Can we get on with it? What next?" said Temmin. "Geography? Trigonometry? What do you want me to recite?"

"Perhaps history."

Temmin groaned. "I hate history. I know it all, anyway. I can recite the kings from Temmin the First onward. Temmin the First, called Great, Gethin the First, Hildin the First, Temmin the Second, Andrin the First, Temmin the Third, called Bastard, Andrin the Second, Harsin the First, Warin the First, Gethin the Second, called Sad, Warin the Second, called Wise—"

"What about Hildin the Second, called Usurper, between Gethin the Sad and Warin the Wise?"

"No one counts him," said Temmin. "We don't even use the name any more. Bad luck."

"What do you know about him?"

Temmin shrugged. "He was king for a day. He wasn't supposed to be. The end."

"He was directly responsible for the unification of Tremont and Litta, though it was called Leute then."

"Ah, now you're trying to trick me—the only child of the last king of Litta married Hildin's brother, Warin the Wise, and their son Gethin the Third, called Uniter, inherited both kingdoms. See? I told you I knew my kings."

"I am sure you do, Your Highness," said Teacher, "but there is much about the story you do not know—much that is not written in the official histories, or even the unofficial histories."

"What kinds of things?" said Temmin, curious. "What could you possibly tell me other than the names and dates? That's all anyone seems to care about."

"I can tell you what kind of men your ancestors were, because I knew them. And I can tell you the stories of the women."

"Who cares about that?" said Temmin. "Women have nothing to do with the running of the kingdom and never have—I'm sure Mama doesn't!"

"Even if you believe the women of your family truly had nothing to do with ruling, they still influenced their men, and how their men treated them speaks volumes about who those men were."

"If the women were so important, why aren't they in the histories?"

Teacher gave a thin smile, and slid an ancient-looking book across the table, neither large nor small, covered in leather dyed Tremontine red; it was the old book from the lectern in Teacher's library. In dull gilt lettering on its front and spine were the words, *An Intimate History of the Greater Kingdom.*

"They are in this one," said Teacher.

Temmin opened the book. "It's blank," he said.

"Once upon a time," intoned Teacher. Words blossomed on the page. Temmin pulled his hands away from the book in astonishment, and the words vanished. He looked up at Teacher, who said, "It is all right. It cannot hurt you." Temmin hesitantly took up the book, and Teacher began again:

> *Once upon a time, in the old Kingdom of Leute, there was a Princess named Edmerka. She was as beautiful as her name was dissonant. When Edmerka was still quite young, her mother died, leaving her as King Frederik's only child. The King paid little attention to her, and she grew up desperately lonely. Though Frederik loved his daughter, he spent most of his time with his new wife, trying to produce a son and heir.*

As Teacher spoke, words scrolled out into the empty book, faster and faster, until the pages spilled over. The words continued to flow, growing larger, taking form, turning into pictures, then pictures that moved. Temmin saw as if from a great height, higher than a tower; below him spread rivers and mountains, rushing closer as if he were falling, and though he wanted to cry out, he couldn't make a sound. He swooped over a forest, flying over villages and what must have been considered a city, its houses mostly of wattle-and-daub and rough, thatched roofs not much more sophisticated than the villages. An imposing stone castle stood apart from the little city, an actual moat encircling it. It must have been a very long time ago, thought Temmin dimly. Teacher continued:

Instead, the servants raised her, and they spoiled her. Though she was by nature a kind and loving child, her loneliness overwhelmed her. Soon she was as arrogant and haughty as she was beautiful.

A portrait of a breathtaking young woman appeared, dressed in rich clothing from long ago like a princess in Ellika's illustrated book of Corrish fairy tales. Her soft mouth and strong brows drew into a frown, but her blue eyes were more sad than sulky. Teacher's voice began to fade. "Her story," said Teacher, "is called 'The Curse of the Traveler Queen.'"

The room fell away, and Temmin fell into the distant past, caught in the pages of the book.

The Princess Edmerka raged in her room, throwing anything within reach at anyone within range. "Why must I do *anything* he wants me to! He doesn't care in the least about me, so why should I care what he wants!"

"I'm sure I don't know, miss, don't blame me!" cried her nurse. "The King merely said it's time for you to come talk to him and 'face your future,' I think is how he put it!"

"I don't want his future, Olka! I don't want to marry this week's favorite, I don't want to enter the Sister's Temple—I want *out* of this place! I want to be left alone! *Go away!*"

The sound of broken crockery followed Olka down the hall as she ran to Edmerka's father and prostrated herself: an oversized, gray dumpling dropped on the floor at his feet. "Begging your pardon, Your Majesty, but the Princess is in a rage again. Nothing satisfies her. We bring her your presents, and she throws them at our heads! Now she says she wants to be left alone. Please tell me what to do, sire."

King Frederik pinched the bridge of his aquiline nose, and glanced at his young wife, demurely embroidering at his side. She dropped her needle long enough to brush her long fingers across his hand, until he returned her intimate smile. "What does she intend to do," he said to Olka, "move to a cottage in the woods by herself? Amma bless me, she's a Princess! She can marry or go into the Sister's service, and I'd rather she marry. Without an Heir of my own, I must depend upon her to have a son, and soon, if I can find the right husband for her. Who'd take such a shrew!"

"It's only a matter of time until you have an Heir yourself, my lord," said the Queen, taking his hand in hers. "Perhaps if your daughter gives us some peace, we might...strive toward that goal."

Frederik gave a short-lived grin. "Edmerka hasn't given me a moment's peace since her mother died. What do you suggest, my love?"

"I have three brothers, you know," she said, stroking his palm deftly. "It would please me greatly should Edmerka become my sister as well as my daughter. Perhaps an extended visit to my family?"

Frederik shivered in delight. "Olka, pack Her Highness's trunks."

And so the Princess found herself bundled off far to the west to her stepmother's family, strangers all. "At least she's only sulking," Olka said to the captain of Edmerka's escort. "How much longer?"

"We should finish the journey late tomorrow," he answered.

But as they approached their destination the next day, the Princess caught sight of a Traveler encampment, its bright caravans in a half-moon to one side of the road. She cried, "Stop! I wish..." To roam the world like that, she thought. Free, stopping where you wished when you wished and moving on in your own time, never bowing to anyone else's demands. With that kind of freedom, it wouldn't matter whether anyone loved you or not. The caravans spoke of all that. "I wish to have my fortune told," she said.

"Oh, Your Highness, whatever for? They're frauds and liars. You won't learn a thing," said Olka. "Besides, we're almost to your mother's people."

"She is not my mother, and you will stop!" said Edmerka. The captain called a general halt. Edmerka climbed down from the carriage, and marched into the camp, Olka and the captain trailing reluctantly behind. "I wish to have my fortune told," she announced to the raggle-taggle band by the fire.

An otherwise handsome young man with rusty hair and one wandering eye separated himself from the rest; the captain put his hand on the hilt of his sword. The Traveler men instantly pulled their own steel and took a step forward, tense at the young man's back. "Travelers never ask for trouble, sir," he said, "but when it finds us, we're more than able to send it on its way." The captain frowned; he moved his hand, but gestured minutely for his men to come up a pace toward the camp. The young man signaled his own men; they sheathed their swords, but never let down their guard. "Now, then, my lady," the young man resumed as he fixed the Princess with his good eye, "a fortune, is it?"

"Are you very sure that's what you want?" said a creaky voice. In the doorway of a red caravan stood the oldest crone the Princess had ever seen, bent and gnarled.

"Yes, of course I'm sure," snapped Edmerka. The old woman beckoned her into the murky caravan, and shut the door. Edmerka stooped to keep her head from hitting the low, curved ceiling; she gathered her skirts close to her, though the caravan appeared to be well-ordered and clean. The crone folded out a tiny table attached to the caravan's side, its legs barely held together with wooden pegs, and offered her a seat on a barrel.

"Now, my dear," said the old woman, "let's see what the cards say about you, eh?" She spread the cards out one by one on the little table; it trembled precariously under the weight of each one. "Ah, how fitting. The Princess of the Flames, reversed—d'you see? Wrong-side round. Bad-tempered, easily provoked to foolishness, spoiled, bored and spiteful."

"And who is she?" said Edmerka, thinking of her stepmother.

"Oh, she's you, miss," said the old woman with an empty-mouthed grin.

"How dare you!" said Edmerka.

"Travelers dare often, and easily, miss," cackled the woman. "What stands in your way—my, my. Farr the Warrior, reversed. Uncontrollable impulses and ruthless lust." She clacked her tongue. "And such a nice girl you are. Who'd've suspected?"

Edmerka's face grew blotchy, but she held onto her temper. "Go on."

"Your enemy's card is the Prince of the Winds, reversed—untrustworthy, violent, selfish, ruthless, and reckless."

"Who is he?" said Edmerka, wondering which of her stepmother's brothers he might be.

"I can't see everything, just most things," said the crone. "Help will come from the King of the Winds, reversed. Goodness, many people in your fortune, dear, and so many reversed. Troubles, troubles."

"And who is this King of the Winds?"

"A wise man, an honest man—but a man out of place, and blind to it. He will need help himself, I don't doubt. The path before you is the Bloody One, reversed—goodness, goodness. Choices taken from you, compulsion, confinement. You have two choices of action. The Nine of the Winds, reversed, is despair and submission."

"And the second?"

"The Courage card," said the old woman. "I should think that would be self-evident even to you."

"Finish the fortune," scowled Edmerka.

"Very well. Your outcome is the Lovers. Ha! Not reversed, at least. With all these people wandering through your cards, I should think that means a marriage. But with which man is anyone's guess. A bumpy road, in any event!"

Confinement, choices taken from her—a marriage. It couldn't possibly mean anything else but a forced marriage to one of her stepmother's brothers. "I don't like this fortune!" said Edmerka. She stood up; the little table finally gave up and folded itself into the wall, scattering the cards.

"Like it or not, it's what I see, my girl," said the crone. "I'll have my silver now."

"Silver?" said Edmerka as she climbed down from the caravan. "I wouldn't give you half a copper for that! And I won't!"

"You won't pay me?" cried the old woman, clambering after her.

"No. Captain! We'll be on our way now!" The visit had become an ill omen, the caravans no longer symbols of freedom, and she hurried toward her carriage.

"Stop!" ordered the old woman. She threw something acrid on the fire; a silver smoke rose from the flames, and ghosted its way through Edmerka's escort. One by one, the guards dropped their weapons and stared stupidly at one another. The coachman let go the horses' leads, and Olka, who'd been sitting on a little fold-up stool, stood up and looked around as if she'd woken up in a start.

Low chuckling broke out among the Travelers, who advanced on the Princess. She moved backward toward her carriage, until she ran up against a Traveler man; he shoved her toward the old woman. "What's the matter with you all!" Edmerka shouted at her guards.

"Will you pay me?" said the old woman.

Edmerka set her stubborn chin, raised her head high and said, "No!"

"All right, if you won't pay me in coin, then pay me in kind. Kiss my son, and I'll consider the debt paid." The young man with the wandering eye smiled, one tooth shy of a leer.

"Certainly not!" said Edmerka.

The old crone chuckled. "Oh, Princess Edmerka, you've insulted the wrong Traveler." The men rose from their places round the fire.

"I don't recall telling you my name," the Princess answered, her voice trembling though she kept up as brave a facade as she could manage.

"Of course I know who you are, child," said the woman. "You're stubborn, and courageous in your way. It's your downfall now, but it will be your salvation later. I am Maeve, the Queen of the Travelers, and I am your fate." Her aspect changed; the grizzled, withered crone flickered into a dark-haired, implacable young woman and back, over and over until Edmerka grew dizzy. The Traveler Queen spit in her hand, cupped it to her mouth, and shouted gibberish through it. The captain of the guards awoke from his stupor, wild-eyed.

"Captain!" cried the Princess. "Draw your sword, defend me!"

"Draw my sword? Who are you?" said the captain. "Where is this place? I remember nothing…no, this is not home—that's all I remember— I have to go home!" He stumbled back in terror, and fled. The rest of the guard panicked and plunged after him into the woods. Even Olka ran away, fat legs flying. Edmerka faced the Travelers alone.

"Your fate has found you, whether you like it or not, Your Highness," said the Traveler Queen.

The Travelers took the carriage, the horses, and Edmerka's trunks. They took the clothes from her back, down to her stockings and hairpins as she struggled to cover herself with her hair and hands. She longed to fight, to rage, to throw things, but she had nothing to throw. She was one girl against a dozen or more, but she'd let Harla take her to the Hill before she'd show them how frightened she was. "Take everything," she said. "They're only things. Kill me, and my father will hang your heads above our castle gates!"

"Brave and foolish in equal measure, just as the cards said," sighed the Traveler Queen. "Very well." She threw another handful of herbs on the fire. Silvery threads wove themselves around Edmerka; her skin drank it up. She felt it slink through her, as if it seeped into her very bones. Edmerka's joints loosened, and she stumbled. She burned from the inside. Her cheeks flushed, and her nipples grew hard and dark. "I foresaw this long ago, girl, and its necessity made me uneasy. I had no idea you'd be quite this disagreeable, though. Thank you. That makes it much easier," said the old woman. "From now on, you'll give a kiss to anyone who wants one—more, you'll give your body to anyone who wants you. You shall not only be powerless to resist, you'll return their desire. And now it's cast, not even I can lift it. The only way to end the curse is to bathe in the blood of a king."

Edmerka's brave front crumbled as the curse bore down on her. Thin threads of lust trickled into her, twining themselves together as the smoke had, until they formed binding ropes of arousal. She knew who among the Travelers wanted her, and how badly; they burned candle-bright to her, and to her shock, she wanted them with a passion just at the edges of her control. "I'd rather die," she sobbed. "I'd rather die than live my life out like this! Kill me!"

"Killing you seems a bit harsh for refusing to pay us," said the wall-eyed young man.

"Be quiet, son," said the Queen. "It's more than that, and you know it."

"What will happen to me? What will I do?" Edmerka sank to the ground, sobbing and clutching her knees. If she held on tight enough, she reasoned through the red and silver haze blanketing her mind, she wouldn't pull the nearest man to her, though her body ached for him.

She rocked back and forth and wailed, until the Traveler Queen took pity and said, "I cannot lift the curse, but I can ease it." Edmerka looked up in unwilling hope. "Give your maiden blood to my son, and I will make you forget who you are. It won't change anything, but perhaps remembering no other life will make this new one easier to bear."

The more she turned it over in her mind, the more Edmerka realized it was the only kindness she would get. "Very well, I agree," she said in a small voice. She let the Traveler Prince pull her gently to her feet. His mother licked a finger and traced a sigil on Edmerka's left hip, to her disgust; it glowed silver until the spit dried. The Queen's son led the Princess to his caravan as the Travelers hooted. To Edmerka's surprise, the Queen scolded them: "Hush! It's difficult enough for her."

Standing naked in the autumn chill left Edmerka grateful to be inside. The tiny caravan had the same barrel ceiling as the Queen's, and the same fold-out table. An elaborately carved and painted lintel framed a bigger bed built into the back atop low cabinets, a thick, surprisingly luxurious eiderdown covered the mattress. She sat down hard on it, sniveling, her arms crossed to hide her breasts; she felt his eyes, his hands, his breathing. The Princess kept her eyes on the floor. "Well?" she said.

"My name is Connin. I won't hurt you," he said.

She scoffed. "You won't hurt me. What do you think you're doing?"

"I think I'm doing you a kindness. Better I should do this than the first stranger you meet."

"You *are* a stranger!" she said.

He sat down on the bed next to her and coaxed her arms down. His passion swelled in her, and her breasts ached. "I am a stranger who won't beat you, or keep you in a brothel, or kill you," he said, his bad eye swiveling wildly. He slid a rough, thrilling hand up her thigh. "I'm a stranger who will take this one gift from your body and give you forgetfulness in return. I know you feel how much I want you—you're shivering."

"It's cold," she said, shifting on the bed.

"Then let me warm you."

Her pulse fluttered as his hand traced the curve of her hip. Fingers brushed her thick hair back over her shoulders, and traced feather-light along her collarbone. She wanted him to crush her in his strong hands, she wanted to strip his clothes away and lie skin to skin, she wanted to feel his mouth on her breasts—his desire had become hers. "How willing must I be?"

"Willing enough," he said.

"Then get it over with," she whimpered, squeezing her eyes tight. "Just be about it, get it over with!" She felt his hot breath on her face, and then he kissed her. No man had ever kissed her before; his lips were softer than she expected, and she leaned into him, his hands cradling her head.

"Your cheeks are on fire," Connin murmured between kisses. "They will burn through my palms."

"I'm so ashamed," she wept.

He pulled her closer, and moved his mouth to her neck. He bit her gently, and she moaned aloud as he sucked at her skin. "The only shame in your life is the way you've behaved until now," he said, pushing her down on his bed. "Perhaps this will teach you some overdue humility, but there's no shame in being enchanted, Edmerka."

"Don't call me by name!" she said. "Please, don't call me by name!"

Connin stopped her pleading with his tongue; it slid deliciously across the roof of her mouth. He covered her body with his, her nipples rubbing against the coarse linen of his tunic. She brushed them against him over and over, unable to fend off the impulse. He rolled briefly to one side, unfastened his leggings, and tugged his tunic over his head; his skin felt cool against her, and she pulled him to her, unwilling but desperate for whatever would end this burning. "What do you know about lying with a man?" he said.

"Nothing," she gasped. "I've never even seen a man's body."

"Give me your hand." He wrapped her fingers around his length. "That's what a man feels like." Edmerka clutched at it, thrilled and terrified at the hardness under the soft, loose skin. He licked and sucked at her nipples, and she cried out as each tug sent exquisite jolts through her body. He smelled of salty musk, dry wood, campfire smoke, and leather, his beard brushed the underside of her breasts: overwhelming, foreign maleness, all of it. She felt lascivious, helpless, and horribly alive. When his fingers slipped between her legs, she cried out in need and humiliation.

"Do you feel that? I do. You're dripping for me. Have you ever touched yourself there? No? Here." His thumb brushed against her clitoris, and suddenly all emotion and sensation condensed into that one little spot. He brushed it again as she clutched at him, at the coverlet, at the air. He chuckled low in his chest and latched onto her nipple, still stroking her. The sensation grew, and she cried out to Amma for help. "Don't be afraid," he whispered against her breast. "Give in."

"What's going to happen? I'm going to die!" Connin's thumb moved faster and faster, and he pushed a single finger into her; she screamed, thrashing in his arms. Blackness gathered at the corners of her eyes until it darkened her vision completely, then flashed into hot, hot white.

When sight returned, sweat covered her. She panted, limbs loose and trembling. "You're alive, never more," smiled Connin. "That is called spending, sweetheart." He centered himself between her legs, forcing them roughly apart, and she groaned in shame and anticipation. She had lost, she couldn't fight it, she didn't want it, she wanted it. "It will hurt, but only a moment." He pushed, breaking past her maidenhead before she completely realized he'd entered her.

He hadn't lied. She felt a sharp pain, but the unfamiliar, uncomfortable stretching faded horrifically into pleasure. "Mine, Princess. Just this once, you're mine," he whispered in her ear. "And then you'll be anyone's." He pinned her to the bed, thrusting deeply into her as she bucked and sobbed; he took her cries into his mouth.

She fought within herself as she struggled against him, but she could no longer tell between struggle and complicity; every attempt to fight resulted in pulling him closer, until she followed his every movement, her hips fixed to his. She cried out, "Please! Please!"

"Please, what, little wanton?"

"I don't know!" she sobbed.

She broke, and the spell drove an ecstatic pulse through her, stronger than before. The only thing she cared about was the man crushing her down onto the bed, plunging into her. As the pulse left her, so did consciousness; her war against the man and the curse had exhausted her.

Connin pounded into her for his final thrusts until he collapsed atop her limp body. He recovered his breath, and sat up. The princess lay sprawled on the bed, breathing deeply in unnatural sleep. He reached to a shelf above the bed in its alcove, and took up a tiny vial; he knelt between Edmerka's legs, and gently scraped her maiden blood into it, corked it, and replaced it on the shelf. He stroked her cheek tenderly, his wild eye calm for once. "I'm sorry, truly," he said, though she couldn't hear him. "But we cannot escape our fates. And you have given me a greater gift than you know."

He fastened his leggings, and jumped down from the caravan. "It's done," he told his mother.

"The horses are hitched," she answered. "Let's go."

The Travelers took the road leading away from the stepmother's family until they came to a fork. One side led back to King Frederik; the other led over the Leute River's western branch into Tremont. They crossed the river at a shallow ford and kept going until they were well inside Tremont's borders, stopping at a clearing near the only cottage for miles. There they left the Princess Edmerka, naked and sleeping in the moonlight.

Temmin released the book. His shaking hands still felt Connin's skin; the Princess's terror and arousal coursed through him, as if the smoke of the Traveler Queen's spell had seeped through the book into him as well. Was he male or female? He consulted the stiffness between his legs: male. It had happened to someone else, it had happened to a character in a story, not to him.

Shafts of gold and white light slanted low onto the lawn outside the windows; three or four hours had passed. "What in Harla's Name does this fiction have to do with anything?" he said.

"You did not like it?" Teacher said mildly. "I thought you would at least be interested."

In fact, Temmin was afraid to stand up. "I don't see how this connects at all to history," he muttered.

"This is the story of your family," Teacher replied.

"We have nothing to do with fairy tales about Travelers."

Teacher smiled sardonically. "Travelers are intimately entwined with your family."

"I've studied my family's history. There are no Travelers in it!" said Temmin more emphatically.

"The Intimate History contains all the untold stories of your ancestors, excised from official and unofficial chronicles."

Temmin was flushed and irritated, and dearly wanted Teacher to leave. "If they've been excised from the chronicles, then they're not relevant. I don't see what this unfortunate girl's story has to do with me, even if it is true, which I doubt."

"You feel this girl's situation was unfortunate?"

"Of course it was!"

"How so?" said Teacher. "She was unpleasant and spoiled. Did she not get what she deserved?"

"I don't know," said Temmin, suddenly confused. "But—she was forced into—something!"

"Was she? She seemed willing to me."

Temmin gaped. "What kind of man are you! How can you be willing when you're enchanted?"

"Interesting. I am surprised you came to that conclusion. It happens every day, you know, without enchantments."

"What does?"

"Many of us are confronted with choices that aren't choices at all."

"Oh!" said Temmin, leaving the story behind. "That's certain! Look at me—I'm stuck here when I'd rather be back home on the Estate! But what choice do I have?"

"To be sure," murmured Teacher. "But truthfully, Your Highness, you were the last person I was thinking of."

Long after Teacher left, Temmin considered the story, and Teacher's last stinging remark; he repeated it to Jenks, leaving out the whole magic book part. "What could he have meant, Jenks?" he asked as he dressed for dinner. "As if I had any say in anything! If I did, I certainly wouldn't be studying with *him*, the old crow." Choices that aren't choices—he could come up with several examples from his own life, if he squinted hard.

"Your Highness," said Jenks, "I suggest you grow up."

"How'm I supposed to grow up when I'm not allowed to do anything?" said Temmin. "And stop rolling your eyes!" When they'd gone walking, Sedra hadn't been terribly sympathetic either, now that he thought about it. He gave an aggrieved, inward sigh; sympathy was in short supply in the City.

After dinner, his father invited him for a brandy—not an invitation one refused, and thus a new resentment for Temmin to mark on his lengthening list. "Why am I studying fairy tales, Papa?" said Temmin as he accepted the snifter.

"Do sit down, son, join me. Fairy tales? What fairy tales?" said Harsin.

Temmin colored and looked away. "Some sort of story about…about an enchanted princess," he mumbled.

"Ah," smiled Harsin. "You don't like that story?"

"He told it to you? You're not saying it's true, are you?"

"Oh, yes. It was the only one from the book I listened to, though. I didn't pay much attention to anything else, and Teacher gave up and focused on teaching me statecraft. And the managing of magic."

Temmin fumbled with his brandy. "I'm sorry?" he said.

"You haven't wondered how Teacher does the trick with the book?"

"That's exactly it. I had it pegged as some sort of trick!"

"Oh, no. It's quite real, I assure you. Has Teacher not taken you through a mirror by now? That would surprise me."

"Oh, yes," said Temmin weakly. "He has." He kept seeing Teacher in the mirror to himself.

"I imagine it must seem strange to find out magic is real, even though your mother raised you up with bumpkins. Country people still believe in magic and superstition, don't they?"

"To be sure," said Temmin, warming instantly. "In fact! The grooms insisted one too many times on taking a new mare widdershins round the entire stables before bringing her inside the first time, and I said, 'You're ridiculous, the lot of you,' and just brought 'er in directly. One of the grooms fainted dead away!"

"I believe it," chuckled Harsin. "And then I imagine the rest ran to the little shrine of Amma in the barnyard and made an offering to keep the horses from dying, yes? Here, all the servants think Teacher is the Black Man. They make the Sign of Amma every time he passes."

"Is he?" said Temmin.

Harsin considered. "I suppose he's how the myth started. But I'm not talking about superstitions and stories to frighten children into being good, Temmin. Teacher is power, real power that has kept us an unbroken dynasty for the last thousand years. Even though the men of this family lost our own magic more than 350 years ago, Teacher holds it for us, along with a great deal more—oh yes, he's really that old, older than that. He served Gethin the First. With Teacher's magic behind us, we will always be stronger than any outside enemy, though our nobles must still be managed with a deft hand. Statecraft. When you become king, you will control

Teacher. He will teach you what the magic can and cannot do. As long as the land recognizes us, and as long as we have Teacher, our family will rule."

"How did Teacher end up with our magic? And what does this girl have to do with it?" Temmin demanded.

"It's not her story," said Harsin. "I like that part too, you should understand. I like it very much, in fact, and I've remembered it fondly many times over the years. But Teacher misses the actual point, as far as I'm concerned. This leads me to something. I had a conversation with your mother yesterday, and I'm very curious as to your side of the story."

"My side of which story?"

"Something about a maidservant at the Estate, if memory serves."

Temmin's dinner curdled. Who could have told his mother? Was it Jenks? No, never! Someone else at the Estate must have found out and told her. He wondered if he could send a letter to Alvo to find out who—Gods, it wasn't *Alvo*, surely? "What did Mama say?"

"That you kissed a maidservant under somewhat coercive circumstances."

"Coercive? She said yes."

"Temmin, we both know she said yes because she was afraid of losing her job." She'd certainly begged him not to tell Crokker, but he'd never considered she really might lose her job. Why would she lose her job? "There's nothing wrong with that," the King smiled, his teeth white against the dark of his beard and moustaches. "I've always found something rather arousing about holding that over them. Apparently you are of my mind."

"But I didn't hold it over her," said Temmin, appalled.

Harsin shrugged. "You don't have to justify yourself to me, son. Take a maidservant if you wish—take several. I've heard you're behind your peers on that score. I've left off the Keep's maids for your mother's sake—promised her I'd never have a mistress in the house—so the field is quite clear."

"You have mistresses?" said Temmin.

"No, Temmin," said his father. "I've been celibate for the last eighteen years. Of course I have mistresses."

"But what about Mama? You're a married man!"

"When your mother said she sheltered you, I had no idea how serious she was." Harsin's voice softened. "You must understand the deep affection and love I have for your mother. Ansella and I may not have been a love match, but I could not have asked for a better Queen and mother for my children. I hold her in the highest esteem—she is an excellent, if frustrating, woman."

"Then why take mistresses?" Temmin muttered.

"The question isn't why *I* have mistresses. The real question is why haven't you taken one by now. Your mother says you haven't."

"I don't really think that's a proper conversation to have with one's father."

"No," said Harsin, eyeing his son's burning cheeks. "You wouldn't. Is it a question of preferring men? To think on it, it's high time I found you a Mentor."

"No, no, sir. Men don't disgust me, but women are..." Temmin trailed off.

"Just so," chuckled his father. "In any event, your mother was concerned you might try to call this maid up to the City from Meadow House. Don't."

"I hadn't really thought about it," Temmin lied.

"Of course you have. Any red-blooded man would, if he fancied the girl enough."

"There's someone else I fancy a great deal more, actually," said Temmin, brightening.

"Fortunate, because this girl is out of the question," answered his father.

"I thought you wanted me to tumble a few maids."

"I want you to do as you please in that regard, is what I want. But not with her." Harsin sighed deep in his chest. "When you were born at the Estate, I was there, you know. So was a very pretty little thing in livery named Tellis Ambler. Beautiful hazel eyes, sweet rosy cheeks. Quite a beauty. Are you attending me, Temmin?"

"You don't want me repeating your mistakes, perhaps?"

"No, I don't want you having sex with your half-sister. Do mind the brandy, son, you're about to spill."

Temmin sat back in the wing chair, his brandy dangling from his fingers. "You're telling me Mattie is your daughter?"

"Yes."

"I kissed my sister."

"Half-sister, actually."

Temmin swallowed hard, his face gone from cherry to chalk, and he broke out in a cold sweat. "Does she know?"

"She has no idea. Her mother knows, your mother knows, and now you and I know. And Teacher knows—Teacher took care of things, along with your manservant."

"Took care of things how? You didn't hurt her?"

"Do you think I would hurt my own daughter? No, we gave her mother some money—a great deal of money, actually—and strongly encouraged them to take up residence as far away from Whithorse as possible. Mattisanis has a nice dowry now, and she'll find herself a nice squire in Alzeh, or Kellen, or wherever they end up."

"May Amma forgive me," Temmin said, his voice breaking.

"For what? You didn't know. I've taken a look at young Mattie through the mirror. Don't feel too badly, Temmin, if I hadn't known, I'd have done it myself. Not as pretty as her mother, but that's a hard standard to meet. No, don't worry about her. She's well taken care of. I may even acknowledge her, if I need to shore up a minor alliance. But tell me," said Harsin, switching tacks, "who's captured your eye? Anyone I know?"

Temmin was still lost in uncomfortable thoughts—sisters, breasts, threats, infidelity, enchantments, sex, Travelers, magic—but said, "Who'm I interested in? Allis Obby."

Harsin burst out laughing. "Allis, the Embodiment of Neya? That Allis? Well, you're the Heir. You won't have to do any persuading or tithing —just make an appointment!"

"That's odd. I've been told I'd have to chase her—her and Issak Obby."

Harsin instantly grew serious. "Chase them—you're not seriously thinking of becoming a Supplicant?"

"Is there a reason I shouldn't?" said Temmin in surprise.

"I thought you'd planned on lay dedication to Farr the Warrior, not the Lovers. No Heir has ever been a Lovers' Temple Supplicant."

Temmin gaped. "Are you forbidding it?"

Harsin's brow darkened. "That would be impiety. Despite my reputation, I believe in the Gods. I've seen too much not to believe. I don't want you taking Supplicancy in any of the Temples, but this one in particular. In fact, I object in the strongest terms."

"But why would it be such a terrible thing?"

"You've heard the saying, 'When Nerr gets the Heir,' I gather? Of course you have—we all say it whenever we think something's never going to happen. Few remember what it means. It was once a prophecy. When an Heir becomes a Supplicant of the Lovers—when Nerr gets him, in essence—it foretells good times for the common people."

"What's wrong with that? It sounds as if I should go right now, if it means luck for our people."

Harsin shook his head. "At Eddin's Temple, the Scholars believe the saying means the common people will gain this luck at the expense of the nobility. Everything balances, Tem. If they go up too far, it follows that we go down."

"But it doesn't have to be that way, surely. Wouldn't their prosperity lead to ours?"

"Too much prosperity for the people generally leads to unrest, even more so than not enough prosperity. The just-desperate-enough are easier to control. I wouldn't take the risk."

Temmin tensed and leaned forward, propping his elbows on his knees. "So what are you telling me, sir? That I can't do this?"

"I am saying my strong, strong preference would be for you to lose your virginity to anyone other than Allis Obby, and then you can spend as much time with her as you want. You can even become a devotee of the Lovers' Temple if you absolutely have to. If you can't find someone yourself —" Harsin's lip twitched, and Temmin colored further— "I'm sure we can acquire someone for you. The City is full of women, some of whom are almost as beautiful as Allis. I'd even hire you a girl if you'd like, though I don't care for professionals myself. Dirty, and not in the good way. All covered in pawprints. How do your tastes run? Dark hair? Light hair? I'd suppose dark, considering Mattie and Allis, large-breasted, too. Tell Winmer, and we'll arrange something. He tells me there's a girl here at the Keep you seem to like—little thing with curly hair, downstairs maid. Take her for your first. She won't deny you, I guarantee it."

"How'd you know about her?" demanded Temmin. "And I haven't touched her—well, I've touched her, I suppose, but not like that—"

"I encourage you to touch her all you'd like, any way you'd like, but don't go to the Temple a virgin. Am I clear? I can't forbid it, but I can say I am completely opposed."

"Very clear, Father," Temmin said, ice in his voice. He left his brandy on the side table, untouched.

"Jenks!" he called when he returned to his rooms. "Jenks, Pagg damn you! You—Caid," he said, sticking his head out the door and hailing the nearest footman, "off you go. I want a bottle of apple brandy, quickly, please."

Jenks found him after an hour, staring into the fire through the rosy amber in his glass. "Did you know that girl was my sister—half-sister?" Temmin asked him.

"Yes, sir," said Jenks gently. "And as I'm sure you're sitting there suspecting terrible things, I'll come straight to it: I told your mother. If I hadn't known the parentage of the girl in question, I would never have said a thing."

"No, I know you wouldn't. I'm not drunk, if you're wondering. I'm just tired of feeling how unfair everything is. Something's not right in this place."

"There's always something not right, sir, and life isn't fair," said Jenks. "These are the great secrets of adulthood."

FIVE

The royal carriage rolled through the streets of the City on the night of Lord Litta's ball. Temmin sat within on the Tremontine red velvet cushions, drumming his fingers on the window; Ellika sat opposite in a swansdown-trimmed hood that gave her the look of a fluffy white kitten. "Why isn't Seddy coming?" said Temmin.

"She never does," Ellika sniffed. "She only came to yours because it was in the Keep. Oh, she's not as bad as all that. The season is winding down, is all, not even two spokes left, and I don't understand why anyone would want to miss out on what little fun is left. After Nerr's Day there won't be any balls or theater at all, just a few small dances, dinners, card parties, outdoor concerts—little entertainments, no more than a few hundred people at most and usually half that. And then we'll be at High Haven for the whole of Summer's Ending, and it's boring as anything up there. Though it is nice and cool, and the City is so very hot in the summer. But I do miss the grand balls!"

Temmin let Ellika's voice flow over him as he watched the streets and squares glide past the window. Would Allis be happy to see him? And what about Issak?

What about him, indeed. Temmin hadn't considered men much, apart from observing his older cousins and their Mentors, and some adolescent groping with the stable boys. The former filled him with apprehension more than desire, and the latter seemed like so much play—practice for when they could get girls. It had stopped a couple of years ago, anyway, until Alvo. Thinking of Alvo made his eyes smart.

His mind returned to his destination. It's just a dance, he told himself. Why did it feel like so much more?

His father had made his wishes quite clear, but why should he listen to him? Harsin didn't even know how many children he had. Temmin thought of Mattie, and winced. Perhaps he hadn't behaved well towards her, and not just because she was his half-sister. Had he done the right thing with Alvo? Possibly not, but what could he have done? Alvo had run off without saying anything. He resolutely turned his mind back to the ball, and thoughts of the Obbys. They alternated his mood between elation and apprehension. He didn't have to become a Supplicant to see them. That would certainly please his father, but doing so both cheered and irritated Temmin himself. Perhaps he'd seek out that little maid after all, the one with the curly hair—

"—I'm sure, though, we'll make our own fun in the mountains— Are you even listening to me, Temmy?" Ellika said. "Do stop brooding. If I wanted brooding I would have stayed home with Seddy and discussed the Inchari Problem, or the philosophy behind postage stamp portraits: left profile or right profile. Neya bless me, am I the only one in this family who's any fun whatsoever?"

"You're entertaining enough for the three of us, Elly," smiled Temmin. Ellika bounced on the red-cushioned seat, and he glanced out the window: they had arrived.

The Duke of Litta's townhouse stood in one of the most fashionable yet conservative districts in the City. During the day, its white-painted brick and polished brass gave off a formal, rather stuffy air. Tonight, light and gaiety poured from every window, and the reception hall glittered.

As did Ellika. Amethysts circled her neck and wrists, and winked from her ears. Her dress was almost subdued, for her. Not a scrap of lace, sashed, simple, full-skirted, purple and white shot silk that shimmered in the gaslight: a fairy princess.

"Tem, look around," she whispered as he offered her a proud arm and they proceeded through the genuflecting crowd. "Notice anything?"

"What am I supposed to be noticing?" he whispered back.

"The young men! Look at them. They're all trimming their beards to look like you—moustaches and sideburns and no chin whiskers!"

Temmin looked around. Every third man under the age of 30 had trimmed his beard to look like his, unintentional though it was. "Isn't it hilarious?" giggled Ellika. "They're calling the style 'The Heir.'"

"Jenks makes me shave my chin to keep from looking scraggly until it fills in more," grumbled Temmin. "Maybe I'll just shave it *all* off."

As they entered the ballroom, the crowd broke out into thunderous applause and cheers, and his transitory bad mood lifted. This enthusiastic reception, from the stable hands to the crowd at a grand ball, increasingly felt natural, as if he might gather the energy in his hands and mold it if he could only learn how. He greeted the Duke of Litta, trying hard not to stare at the lurid scar slashed through His Grace's left brow.

All the acclamation almost made him forget why he came, until he looked out into the crowd and caught not one but two pairs of languid green eyes. Allis once again wore her thick, black hair loose to her waist. No one else in the room wore their hair loose but Issak. All of the women had their hair in great piles on their heads. Those men who wore their hair in the conservative longer style had it tied neatly back. The loose hair gave the twins a wild elegance; everyone else looked contrived.

Ellika nudged him. "Temmy, you're staring again. Oh, do get it over with! Find out when your dance is!"

Temmin walked through the parting crowd to the twins. He passed unseeing over most of the faces, though he did spot Fennows, who gave him a knowing wink, the prat.

He held out his hand. Allis took it and curtsied low, and Issak bowed. "Holy Ones," bowed Temmin, his voice much stronger than his nerve. "Miss Obby, I do hope you've saved a dance for me."

Allis looked up at him through her dark lashes and smiled; his soul lit up. "You asked for a whole set of dances, Your Highness," she said. "Do you still wish it?"

"Oh, yes," he said, stunned and happy. He offered his arm, and they took to the floor with the others.

This time, Issak stayed near. Temmin said little to Allis, and she said little to him; words seemed unnecessary. He never knew what to say at these things, but with her, awkwardness didn't apply. She made him comfortable, even though in the back of his mind he knew everyone in the room was staring at them, and some of the stares were not friendly ones.

When the set of dances ended, the revelers began milling about in gossiping clumps. The men escorted their partners to seats, and hurried off to fetch ices, tidbits, sweets, drinks. "May I get you some lemonade, Miss Obby? Wine, perhaps? Are you hungry?" said Temmin.

"I should prefer to see the gardens—I haven't been in Lord Litta's townhouse in too long. Would you fetch my shawl, Your Highness?" said Allis.

"Yes, of course," said Temmin.

The lanky Heir raised several eyebrows as he hurried through the crowd to the cloak room. "Didn't take long for His Highness to sniff out Allis Obby," smirked the Duke of Corland.

"Jealousy is unbecoming, Borney," smiled Lord Litta. "Make an appointment."

"An appointment?" Corland barked with laughter, shaking his chins. "I don't think so. Too complicated, those Lovers. Fennows tells me the Prince is a virgin."

Litta frowned, puckering the saber slash through his left brow. "A virgin, at his age? Is he a lover of men?"

"Damned if I know. Only been here a few days. He'll find his fancy, or have one thrust upon him. Thrust! Ha!"

"I'm not sure it's a joking matter, Corland," said Litta, eyes following Temmin through the ballroom.

"Eh, I'm not much for prophecies. Encouraging Fennows to get the boy laid as quickly as possible, all the same."

When Temmin returned with her shawl, Allis said, "There is a small but lovely garden here. I thought perhaps we could show it to you. Issak has disappeared somewhere to bring us all some wine, but he'll catch up.

My, but the terrace is crowded. It's a warm night, isn't it? And I'm surprised they have the garden lanterns lit, the moon is bright tonight," she murmured as she guided him down stairs and pathways to the arbor, where fragrant, drooping wisteria glowed pale among wrought iron trellises and marble classical columns. "Come, sit," she said.

Temmin cleared his throat, groping for an opening gambit, but Allis spared him. "Shall we speak freely, Your Highness?"

"You may always speak freely to me, Holy One," said Temmin.

"Please, call me Allis."

"It would feel strange, then, to have you call me anything but Temmin," he smiled.

"Tell me, then, Temmin, do you observe people?"

"I beg your pardon? I'm not sure what you mean."

"I mean, can you learn something about who people are by watching them?"

Temmin started. Had his staring been so very much? He searched her face for signs of displeasure, but her luminous green eyes showed nothing but an absorbing interest in him. "I suppose so," he said. "I've never really thought about it. I don't do it of a purpose, I can tell you that much."

"Are your eyes used to the lower light yet? Very well. Do you see the man strolling with the young woman in the pathway toward the rose garden? They've stopped below a lantern. You should be able to see them clearly now. Tell me, what is happening between them?"

"I don't know. I can't hear them."

"No, I want you to tell me based solely on observation."

"Is that possible? They're not touching or anything."

"Even so."

"All right, I'll try," he said doubtfully. He shifted on the bench as the couple sauntered down the path. "Well, the man's lying to her, I can see that much."

Allis inclined her head toward him. "How do you know?"

"He looks just like the horse traders trying to slip one over on you at a fair," said Temmin, nodding. "See how he strokes his cheek? Dead giveaway, though he's trying to hide it."

"And the girl?"

Temmin frowned, concentrating. "No," he said. "I can't tell a thing. I just don't know many girls."

"You have two sisters," said Allis.

"I can tell you what *they'd* be thinking, but I have no idea what *she's* thinking!"

"Pretend she's one of your sisters. Or your mother."

"Oh," he said. He examined the woman anew, doing his best to ignore the warmth of Allis's arm in his. "As it happens, she's acting just like my mother does around Sister Ibbit."

"How so?"

"Well, watch. She's facing him. He's not looking at her, but she's looking at him. She has her hands clasped, low, in front of her. Mama does it all the time around Ibbit."

"What does it mean, do you think?"

Temmin shook his head. "That he's teaching her something? Or at least she thinks he's teaching her something? I don't know, I don't pay any attention to Sister Ibbit if I can help it. He's lying, though. I do know that."

"Reasonable, for a beginner," said Issak from behind them, his sudden appearance nearly unseating the Prince. Issak handed round three empty glasses and filled them from a bottle he'd tucked under his arm. "Do you want to know what she's thinking? She desperately wants to believe him. Her hands are clasped before her—she wants reassuring. And she's watching his face for signs she can believe him. She's going to fool herself into believing him, whatever it is he's telling her."

"You can see all that?" said Temmin.

The twins nodded. "And a great deal more," said Allis.

"I hate to think what you see when you look at me!" said Temmin, taking a light-hearted sip of his wine. He looked up from the glass at their silence; their faces were both amused and grave. "Do you see things when you look at me?"

"Of course," they said, almost in unison. "Lovers' Temple training teaches us a great deal about someone just from the way they hold their heads, let alone the rest of their bodies," continued Allis; self-conscious, Temmin brought his head up high and stiff on his neck. "All Lovers and

Beloveds know it, to some degree," she continued. "We look for those who have natural talent."

"You show signs of having it, Temmin," said Issak.

"I do?"

"You're very observant, when you wish to be, which I think is not very often. That's hardly damning—most young men your age don't wish to be, either," said Issak.

"Oh, come now!" said Temmin. "Talking like an old man—you can't be more than two or three years older than me!"

"We turn twenty-one in Summer's Ending," said Allis, "but we've been training for our positions informally since birth, formally since age ten—not in the Temple, to be sure, we didn't come to live in the Temple until we turned eighteen. But we've been studying people since we could stand."

"So—why…why would you be interested in seeing this talent in me?" said Temmin rather nervously. "I certainly can't become a Lover."

"No, Your Highness," smiled Allis. "Most certainly not."

"The dancing will resume shortly," said Issak. "We should go back in soon."

"Oh, well, if you want to go in," hastened Temmin, "please do, Issak! I should like to stay out a little longer." He gave Allis a hopeful smile.

"If you want to kiss her, kiss her," said Issak, adding gently, "and if you want to kiss me as well, kiss me."

Temmin realized how close they all sat on the bench. Allis pressed against his right, her hand light on his thigh; Issak boxed him in on his left, one hand soothing up his back before resting on his shoulder. "Just—kiss you?" he squeaked. "*Both* of you?"

"Have you never kissed a woman?" said Allis.

"Not this sober, no."

"Lesson number one," said Allis, turning his face to hers. She kissed him, soft and slow.

The tender pressure of her lips, the scent of her hair: something floral, sweet incense, clean skin underneath. Heady. Only his lips touched hers, but the kiss resounded through his body, sending minute shocks along his skin; they set his hair on end.

His eyes drifted closed. When they opened at the end of the kiss, she moved from a distant object of beauty and desire, static as a statue, to a woman; amusement, compassion, pleasure and hesitancy moved across her face, and to his surprise, he caught each look and understood them all.

A different hand turned his face the other way. "Lesson number two," said Issak. His firm kiss hardened; Issak's insistent tongue opened Temmin's mouth, and left him whimpering as it explored inside. Allis's fingers trailed across the taut front of his trousers. He fell out of the kiss with a gasp, leaning his head against Issak's broad shoulder. Was it intentional? Did he care? He did not. Such a small touch to leave such a great ache behind it. Another touch from the other side, more deliberate, and he pushed out, groaning.

"Sshh," soothed Allis, kissing him again. "Quietly, Temmin. We wish no more attention than we've already gathered. We should go back now, before we're missed. Listen, the music's started, the dancers are beginning to assemble again."

"I—I can't go in just yet," Temmin said, dazed and uncomfortable.

"Stay outside if you wish," said Allis, wrapping her shawl around her shoulders. "We have dances bespoken in this set."

Temmin gripped the bench, as the twins stood before him arm in arm. "What just happened?" he said.

"We will see you inside, Your Highness," said Issak.

The Obbys returned to the ballroom. Temmin took to pacing the little arbor in agitation. Jenks in his underwear, he recited to himself, Jenks in his underwear, Pagg-damned Jenks in his Pagg-damned underwear, to no avail. He strode down the paths leading deeper into the garden, hoping to walk off his arousal, but the paths left by fingers and lips refused to fade. He stopped in frustration under a tree whose low, spreading canopy sheltered him from sight. The party noise seemed tinny, and bright, and quite far away. He braced himself against the trunk with one hand, while he worked himself with the other one.

Kisses. Touches. He imagined where they might have gone, how Allis might have opened his trousers and caressed him, how Issak might have bent his head back and kissed him, how Allis might have knelt between his legs as Alvo had, how her mouth might have felt, how she might have looked up at him just when—

Temmin came in a longing spurt against the tree trunk. He rested his forehead on the smooth bark until his breath came more easily, then cleaned up what hadn't hit the tree with his handkerchief, thinking he must wash it out before putting it in the laundry. He checked himself all over for signs of impropriety, and stepped out from the tree's shelter toward the house.

A man he didn't recognize approached, still far down the path. Temmin took his hands from his pockets and straightened his shoulders. He was just reassuring himself that the stranger had been far enough away during his interlude under the tree, when the man drew a long dagger and ran at him.

Time slowed down, as it sometimes does in dangerous moments.

The man came between Temmin and the safety of the house. Only the King wore a ceremonial dagger at balls now; Temmin had no weapon. He cast about for anything nearby he could use to defend himself, found a palm-sized rock in a decorative grouping beside the path, and pitched it hard, scoring a solid hit on his attacker's temple. A cut opened; the man checked his stride, but only for a moment.

No more rocks, nothing to use as a shield or as a weapon. Nothing else for it: Temmin set himself in a defensive stance and sent up a prayer to Farr. "I'll send a case of the best wuisc I can find to Your temple, Warrior, if You get me through this," he muttered.

Several dark figures rose out of the nearby greenery. Accomplices? Three of them raised small crossbows and let fly; Temmin's attacker dropped, a bolt placed neatly between the eyes up to its fletching and two more in his ribs.

Another figure stepped into the path. "Your Highness!" said the figure, dropping to one knee and opening his arms. "I'm a Brother. We're Brothers. You're safe."

Temmin's heart beat so hard he could feel it in the tips of his ears. The Brother got to his feet, and said, "I'm Senior Brother Mardus. Are you hurt at all?"

"No, Brother, just—" scared, he admitted to himself. Aloud, he said, "Startled. Who was that? What in Harla's name just happened?"

"Another assassin, sir, though not a very good one. Hard to find professionals nowadays outside our service. I assume he was sent by your uncles."

"An assassin? Who'd want to kill me? I only have one uncle, and he's dead!"

Mardus clamped his mouth closed. "You had best ask your father about them, sir. It's not my place."

Time had returned to its usual flow, but Temmin's nerves still jangled and rang; he put his hands in his pockets to hide their shaking. He looked back at the dead assassin, whose eyes still stared up into the low light from the paper lanterns. The fletching bristled between the man's eyebrows. He was young, rough-looking; his formal apparel didn't fit well, as if it were borrowed. One eye had filled with blood; it trickled down the side of his face onto the gravel path.

Up came Temmin's dinner.

He retched into the grass, Mardus and another Brother standing respectfully to one side. When he'd finished, Mardus handed him a large bandana with a discreet, "Your Highness"; Temmin wiped his mouth. "I collect you've never seen a dead man before, sir?" said Mardus.

"Not like this, no," said Temmin.

"Don't be embarrassed," Mardus murmured. "Every man here has done the same, at least once." He took the bandana from Temmin's shaking hands, and folded it into a pouch hanging across his chest.

"What happens now?"

"You go back into the ball, sir, and we sweep the grounds. You will stay in the same dancing set the rest of the night, please, though you may choose different partners. The men in the set will be ours."

"Brothers dance?" said Temmin with a little smile.

"The dancers are officers from the Royal Guard. They've been among the dancers the entire time, sir." Mardus grinned. "Spares us Brothers the indignity of dancing with women." He shooed Temmin back to the house.

Ellika waited on the terrace; when she saw him, she ran up and took his arm. "I've been looking for you—you look terrible—you *smell* terrible! Did you throw up? Here—rinse your mouth with this lemonade and spit over the terrace, no one is looking. Did you have a fight with Allis already? That didn't take long!"

"No, and I'm not in the mood to be teased."

Ellika took a second look at his ashen, serious face, and said, "I'm sorry. No teasing. What happened?"

"Do you know anything about us having uncles on Papa's side?"

"Uncles? Papa didn't have any brothers, just Aunt Sofalla and Aunt Tessia. What's this about?"

"I don't know," said Temmin.

When they returned to the Keep, much earlier than Ellika would have liked, Temmin found himself summoned to the King's study, despite the late hour. Teacher stood leaning against the mantelpiece, such a habitual position that Temmin wondered if the advisor weren't glued to it by the elbow.

"You're all right?" said Harsin. "A glass of wine? No? Very well. I've received a preliminary report from Brother Mardus. Needless to say, the Royal Guard will be under extreme scrutiny for this security breach. Mardus says in his note you acquitted yourself well."

Temmin shrugged, embarrassed. "I winged him with a rock. Nothing else for it. I'm just glad Alvo and I used to practice hitting old bottles."

"You've had archery lessons, surely," said his father.

"Arrows aren't rocks. Listen, Papa, who are these brothers Mardus mentioned? The only uncle I know about is Uncle Pat."

Harsin sighed and sipped his wine; he looked tired, and the fire picked out the gray in his hair and beard. "I'm the youngest of four brothers, and the only legitimate one," answered his father. "Their names are Perin, Tallin and Ruvin. All of us are half-brothers—different mothers."

"Temmin the Fifth was a ladies' man, let us say," observed Teacher. Harsin rolled a quelling eye toward the mantelpiece, but Teacher continued. "Your father was something of a last-minute surprise. Your grandfather's first wife died in childbirth, and the baby not long after. The

King took his time remarrying. His three illegitimate sons were recognized and brought into the Keep."

"Then my father remarried," said Harsin, "and here I am, and my sisters, too. Perin never forgave me for removing him from the succession —he was fifteen when I was born, and fully expected to ascend to the throne."

"Worse," said Teacher, "Temmin the Fifth sent all three brothers away from the Keep into the countryside as soon as your father was born, against my advice. Tallin was twelve, and Ruvin was just five."

"No wonder they were upset," said Temmin. Unexpected homesickness struck him behind the eyes; he blinked hard and looked away.

"Don't waste too much pity on them," said Harsin. "They left the Keep lords, all of them, with substantial holdings. They had respect, influence and wealth enough for anyone, but they began plotting against me. Several assassination attempts."

"To be fair, Ruvin was a cat's paw until he reached his majority," said Teacher.

"When our father lay on his deathbed, Perin led an open rebellion against the throne. Tallin and Ruvin joined him—why not? It isn't as if any of them had any brotherly feeling toward me. None of them really knew me. We put the rebellion down, but they escaped. They're in exile, and still attempting through proxies to kill me—and you, Temmin. If I die, you become king. But if we both die, my oldest remaining brother takes the throne. Perin is 56 now, Tallin's 53 and Ruvin's 46. They're running out of time, and when you have a son, the odds are completely against them or their children ever becoming King. Your mother is at the end of her childbearing years. Unless I set her aside and take another wife, which I will not do, you will remain my only son. You've been their main target since you were born, and we've stopped many, many attempts on your life. It's the main reason you were kept in Whithorse. You were safer there. Every man and woman at the Estate would gladly die for you, and some did."

"People died for me?" said Temmin, stepping forward. "Who?"

His father waved his hand. "It doesn't matter. You're safe here in the Keep, and in the King's Woods. No one can get in from the far side of it but the Travelers."

"I'll explain later, Your Highness," murmured Teacher. "It has to do with the story we're studying."

Temmin moved closer to the fire, chilled. "Where are they—your brothers?"

"I cannot find them," said Teacher, "which means they are either extremely careful about reflections, or they are not within the Kingdom's boundaries."

"That's how it works, eh?"

"Outside Tremont and its territories, I have no power at all. It is tied to the land."

"We have agents looking for them outside the kingdom, as well as Teacher's regular searches," said Harsin.

"All right, so no one knows where they are. Why does no one talk about them?" said Temmin.

"Their names were wiped from the family rolls," said Teacher, "and it is generally believed best not to speak of them. The former princes were recognized, and their training for leadership begun, but their places in the succession were never announced, and they were rarely spoken of outside the Keep except as the King's bastards."

Temmin supposed Mattie was a bastard. He didn't like thinking of her that way; he didn't really know her, but it didn't sound right. "Mattie was a surprise," he said aloud. "How do you know I don't have a brother?"

"I know," said Teacher. "If a potential Heir is conceived, I know immediately. I knew the moment you were conceived. Your father may have countless daughters—I never know about the daughters—but you are the only son."

"Thank you for the explanation, Teacher," said Harsin, with a stern glance that Teacher ignored. Harsin turned to Temmin. "You look exhausted, son. Go to bed." Temmin nodded, gravely shook his father's hand, and took his leave.

Once in his room, he let Jenks prepare him for bed. "Papa said people died for me at the Estate. Why wasn't I told?"

"You were a child," said Jenks, shaking out his nightshirt. "It was better that way. It's better now." Temmin began to speak, but Jenks stopped him. "You're a Prince, sir. Many people have died and will die for your sake. And that's all you'll get from me."

As Temmin drifted off to sleep that night, his last thoughts were of the dead assassin, blood pooling in his unseeing eye.

Temmin slept late the next day, but went out on his usual ride; while he had no marketing of his own to do this Paggday, he had the day off with everyone else. "No hangover, Jebby! There's a rare thing after a party. I wouldn't even have minded one today, what a night," Temmin said to his horse. The gelding snorted. They walked at a leisurely pace through the King's Woods, down a tributary path of the War Road. He knew the Woods were safe, but he still half-expected to see Brothers secreted in the underbrush.

The morning chill lifted. Mist rose thready from the meadows he glimpsed through the trees; birdsong and the murmur of streams rushing down to the Shadow River were the only sounds. A beautiful day, the kind of day that made him wish to ride until dark, and sleep where he stopped. He certainly hadn't slept well the night before. He knew the assassination attempt was political, but in his young heart he could not get over it: why would anyone want to kill him?

Into this green restfulness came a discordant sob. Temmin pulled Jebby up short, listening. It came from just ahead on the trail; he urged Jebby toward it, until they came to a downed log just off the path, and a girl sitting atop it, crying tears enough to join the Shadow in their own little salty stream.

Temmin dismounted. "Miss? Are you all right? Miss?" He crept forward, wary of frightening her.

The girl hid in her bonnet, but at his voice, she lifted her tear-stained face. "Your Highness?" she said. It was the pretty maid with the curly hair: Arta Dannikson, he remembered. His father's advice came to mind—"She won't deny you, I guarantee it"—and he flushed. "Why are you here?" she quavered.

"Why are *you* here? These are the King's Woods."

"I know," she said miserably. "I know I shouldn't be here. I sneak off sometimes to be by myself, and I needed to be by myself. Please don't tell Mr Affton!"

"For the last time, Dannikson, I'm not going to tell anyone! That's twice I've had to rescue you from the wrath of Affton, you antic girl," said Temmin. He handed her his handkerchief; she hesitated, took it, and wiped her turned-up nose. "Now, what's amiss?" he said. "Why would a pretty girl come out here, against the rules, to cry her eyes out?"

"It's nothing to concern yourself over, sir," she said to her boots.

"I choose to concern myself," he said, sinking down onto the log.

She scooted self-consciously to one end. "There's really nowhere else to go to have a good cry. I share my room with three other girls, and there's no privacy anywhere at the Keep."

"Don't I know it," Temmin grumbled.

"It's just a beautiful wood. Even when I'm sad I feel better here."

"Why are you sad? Come on, out with it, Arta."

"My sweetheart ain' my sweetheart any more," she wailed, lapsing fully into a mid-Valmouth accent. "He says he don' love me!" Arta buried her face in the borrowed handkerchief.

"A pretty girl like you? Why would he say that? Your sweetheart's the redheaded footman with all the freckles—Wallek, is it?"

"Fen Wallek, yes, sir," she said into the handkerchief.

"What did you fight about?" She closed her eyes tightly and shook her head, sending the curls around her forehead bobbing in an uneasy dance. "Come now," he said. He gently pried the used handkerchief from her hand and gave her a fresh one, silently thanking Jenks for making him carry two at all times. "You can tell me," he coaxed, keeping hold of her hand. "I should think by now you'd trust me a little."

"I can," she sniffled. "I'm afraid to."

"It's all right. Nothing will happen to you, I promise."

She wiped her nose again, and glanced blearily from under her plain straw bonnet. "We fought over you, sir. Miss Ellika, too, but he started it."

"Elly? *Me*?" said Temmin.

"Someone saw us in the service hallway, sir. Word got around we were alone, an now people think—*things*—about me an you." Arta noticed her hand clasped in Temmin's, and slipped it free.

"What sort of things?"

She gazed at him in disbelief. "What sorta things d'you think? Oh!" She clapped her hands over her mouth.

"We only danced."

She dropped her hands. "Sir, that was enough! An the gossip ain'—isn't —" she hastily corrected as she remembered her training— "about us dancin. No one saw that, or I'd've gotten the boot. Bein seen alone was enough! It's never good when the family notices one of us—whatever family we're with."

"No," he said, thinking of Tellis, and Mattie. "I imagine not. What happened with Wallek?"

She bit her lower lip, looking off into the forest. "Fen asked me about the gossip. I told him there was nothin to gossip about, but he said he didn' believe me, and no one else did, either. I said, everyone knows about you danglin after Miss Ellika, as if a redheaded junior footman would come to her notice. But he has, sir," she said, turning to Temmin, her face wretched. "We were to go today to get our promise rings in town, and instead he told me the princess asked him to move furniture for her. I said, let the on-duty men do it. An he said, no, she asked for me by name, an I can' say no. An I said, of course you can say no!"

She warmed to the memory, the wretched look giving way to wrath. Words came rushing out, angry and hurt. "He's always goin on about how beautiful she is, she's so graceful a dancer, she's a fairytale princess, his ideal, and on and on! An she is, she's all that, but really! He's a junior footman, not the Duke of Valmouth! I said, who d'you think you are, Fen Wallek, that a princess would pay you any mind? An he said, you're just jealous because she's prettier than you! An I said, if you're stupid enough to dangle after a princess, you git, then don' expect me to declare for you! An then he said—he said—why would—I want you to!" She broke down in sobs again.

Temmin took her hand again, and this time she didn't pull it away. "Now, then, you know you're a very fetching girl! He's a lucky man, that you love him!"

"I don' know I do any more," she sniffed through the last of her tears. She looked sideways at him. "You really think I'm pretty?"

"I can't imagine anyone who'd think you weren't," he said. He thought of her in his arms, her light steps as they danced, the scent of her hair, and her happy, eager face turned up to his. He slipped an arm around her, and stole closer to her along the log. Maybe his father was right. Maybe this would be for the best. She wouldn't say no. And then he'd go to Allis and not think about the rest. He put a tentative finger under her chin, tipped her face until their eyes met. She looked so serious, lips parted. He could kiss her right now, and she wouldn't say no. He slipped his hand round her neck, fingers tangled in the hair at her nape, drew her close, and kissed her.

Her lips were so soft; her small hands rested against his chest, and without opening his eyes he kissed her again, groaning into her mouth. The feel of her mouth against his went straight down his body; he pulled her closer, but her back tensed under his touch, and he realized her hands on his chest meekly pressed him away.

Jenks came to his unwilling mind: "Promise me you'll leave Miss Dannikson and the other maids alone." But then, there was Fennows: "You can tumble a maid any time." Fennows was a prat.

And then there was Allis.

He looked down into Arta's flushed face and saw Edmerka, aroused and horrified at the same time. He let Arta go.

Arta slumped in relief, and brought a hand to her throat. "I'm very sorry, sir," she whispered. "This is all my fault. I'm so sorry!"

"Ask me not to tell Affton and I swear I will," said Temmin in a false, jolly tone; she gave a rueful laugh. "This is no one's fault," he added.

"I s'pose. I just needed to know that even if Fen doesn' think I'm pretty any more, *someone* did. And then, everyone thinks you an me—already—"

"I'm sure Fen still thinks you're the most beautiful girl in the world. I've told you a dozen times now how beautiful you are."

"Oh, sir, you can't mean that, not with you an the Holy Ones—oh, I've gone too far again!" she fretted.

"What do you know about that?"

"Servants see things, sir," she murmured.

Temmin threw his hands up in exasperation. "Privacy. I have none!"

"But sir, we're all so very happy about it! I mean, assuming you qualify," she stammered. "But I'm sure a handsome young man as you—"

"Don't tell anyone, Arta, but I do qualify. I'm serious. Don't tell."

"Oh, I never should, sir! Such good luck for the common folk it'd be—well, it's just an expression as far as I know, but my gran used to say, when Nerr gets the Heir, our fortunes really will change, an my gran was always right about those things!"

"You really believe that?"

"I do, sir," she declared.

"So does Jenks," he said, "and he's always right about those things, too." He glanced at her face, nearly restored to its usual open cheerfulness. "Arta, you are a prize, and if your Fen doesn't come to his senses, I'll beat some sense into him for you."

"Oh, please don' do that," she said, alarmed and delighted in equal measure.

"For your sake, I won't. Let me walk you back to the Keep," he said, helping her stand.

"No, sir, oh, please don'! If anyone sees us alone together again—especially coming out of the Woods—!"

"Listen," he said. "You hold your head up high against the gossip. You and I know it's not true." Yet, said a tiny, insinuating voice in his head. "If I can help dispel any rumors, I shall."

"If you chase the Lovers, no one'd believe you an I had any dealings a-tall, sir!"

"But we will have dealings, Arta." She gazed up at him anxiously, head turned to one side. "I want you to consider me a friend."

"I could never do that, sir!"

"Nevertheless, you will come to me when you need me. I command you," he grinned.

She drew her eyebrows together, happy but puzzled. "Yes, Your Highness!" she curtsied, answering his grin.

"Now, off with you. Go back to the Keep and make up with your young man." She curtsied again, and ran down the path to the Keep.

Temmin watched her go with regret. He knew where to find her if he changed his mind, he supposed, but more and more, his path seemed to lead to the Lovers' Temple.

As it happened, Temmin was the topic of a pressing conversation at the Lovers' Temple among the senior staff at that very moment. "The Heir?" said High Lover Gan, shifting to find a more comfortable position on the pillows of his low couch; his old body seemed to complain the loudest in the spring. "Are you sure that's wise?"

Issak and Allis stood before the couch, nodding. "Teacher has promoted his candidacy to us, and now that we've observed him twice, I am inclined to agree," said Allis, "though we will learn more about him before we decide. The signs are subtle, but we see them."

The High Lover shook his white head. "I don't know. There has never been an Heir of Tremont accepted as a Supplicant in the thousand year history of this Temple. Is he willing?"

Issak smiled. "Oh, yes, he's willing. He doesn't understand what it entails, but even once he does I'm sure he'll be quite willing."

"I don't know," Gan repeated. "Usually we don't even look for Supplicants at this time of year—they've been chosen by now. We thought we'd give you a chance to settle in, let you pick one next year."

"Royal patronage is always good for a Temple," said High Beloved Malla beside him, patting his knee with her wizened hand. "Princess Finnia was a Supplicant."

"Finnia's been dead some 700 years, sweetheart," said Gan.

"Ah, but she became High Beloved. It was this Temple's golden age," Malla said. "Even without a royal Supplicant, our most influential times have been when members of the royal family have joined our clergy."

"It's true," said Gan reluctantly. "But should we aim so high, then? The prophecy—the nobility are bound to object, the fools. Why not pursue Princess Ellika? She's already a devotee, isn't she?"

"Nominal at best," said Issak, shaking his head. "I fear the Princess is not the most serious of ladies. She hasn't even taken her training."

"What's this young man like?" said Gan, flexing his aching hands. "He can't possibly qualify. A virgin nobleman, at age eighteen? I find it extremely hard to believe."

"You wouldn't if you'd met him," said Issak. "For some reason, he's been quite sheltered growing up—innocent as a puppy."

"Puppies have teeth, no matter how innocent," said Gan. He sighed. "Old age is making me suspicious and cranky." Malla brought his hand to her lips and kissed his bony fingers, and he gave a happier sigh. "Well, we will see, eh, dear? Has he declared chase?"

"I'm to go riding with him soon, and I expect it then," said Allis. "At the least I'm sure I can persuade him to tour the Temple."

"And that should be that," said Issak.

"Hm. What do you think?" Gan asked his partner.

"I am of two minds," said Malla. "The sacred mind says, I trust the Embodiments to make this decision on the Temple's behalf. The secular mind says, I must encourage acquiring the Heir as a Supplicant at all costs for the benefit of this Temple, regardless whether he is a good candidate."

"And which mind is winning?" said Gan.

Malla raised a wispy eyebrow. "The secular mind says, now that I have planted the thought, let the sacred mind prevail."

Gan laughed and kissed her. "You are still the same girl who seduced me in Kennerton."

"You seduced me!" she said demurely.

"No, you only let me think I had," said Gan. "Took me a few years to realize it, but we've had a few years, haven't we?" Gan turned to the twins. "Examine him thoroughly and make your best decision, keeping all we have spoken of here in mind. Now," he added, lying his head in Malla's lap. "Your Most Highs are tired. This Most High is, at any rate. Off with you, pretty children. It's time for our nap."

Every Lover and Beloved the twins passed in the hallway murmured greetings and bowed, but Allis paid no more than polite attention. "You look disturbed, sister," said Issak. "Are you unsure?"

Allis shook her head. "No, not exactly. The Prince is qualified. He shows the beginnings of talent in observation. His effect on people is immediate and rather startling, and it's more than just his being the Heir. He has presence. And he's completely unaware of it."

"Your hesitation?"

"His lack of awareness. It's been some time since we've dealt with a man so young, let alone one so…"

"Innocent?"

"Easily led!"

Issak laughed. "Come in, we shouldn't be talking about this in the hallway." He escorted her through the red door leading to his apartments, and addressed the plump young woman inside. "Anda, tea, please. Now," he said, once they were settled and alone in his sitting room, "d'you really think he's so easily led?"

"I feel as if I have a puppy on a leash, trotting along behind me!"

"That's infatuation. You've seen it a thousand times, with the old and battle-scarred as well as the young and inexperienced. Remember the Duchess of Barle?"

"This is different." The tea things arrived, and Anda bowed herself out.

"Here, now, drink your tea, steady yourself," said Issak. "It's not any different at all. He'll come to, and then we'll see what we'll see."

"But is it fair to lead him to Supplicancy when he's like this? Ah, it's hot!" she said, putting the cup down and shaking her hand. "Once he's taken his vows, he'll wake from his little spell and find he's bound for two years. What then?"

"He'll find himself bound in very pleasant ways. Difficult ways at times," he conceded. "But he won't have any regrets. I'm sure of it."

"So you have no qualms at all?"

"None."

Allis let her hair fall around her face, and breathed in the fragrant steam from her cup. "I worry we're being mercenary about this—that between Teacher's wishes and the advantage for the Temple, we're convincing ourselves he'll be a good Supplicant."

"Allis, I face a Master, just as you face a Mistress. If we make this choice for the wrong reasons, we will be held responsible when They take us on Neya's Day, and a long while after. I don't want to risk Their displeasure any more than you do. It hurts enough when They're pleased with us. Ah, the post. Thank you," he said, dismissing the servant. "For you."

Allis took the crisp, little white packet and broke the seal. "As expected," she said, "an invitation from His Highness to go riding this coming Neyaday."

"He's convinced himself already."

"Possibly," said Allis, running a finger along the lines of exuberant handwriting—the Prince's own, she thought. "Perhaps he'll convince me as well."

As Temmin walked to the Keep's mudroom from the stables, he saw Ellika in the gardens, cutting carefully chosen roses in fastidious little snips. She wore a dress of tiny pink and white stripes, with a neckline that would have gained their mother's strong disapproval without a modest lace fichu tucked into it. Atop Ellika's pile of blond hair balanced a wide straw hat covered in a ridiculous mound of silk roses, tied under her chin with trailing pink ribbons. Trotting after her in nervous, guilty adoration came the redheaded footman, Fen Wallek, holding a rose-filled trug basket.

"Temmy!" she called. "How d'you do! Isn't it lovely out? You'd hardly know Neya's Day hadn't come yet!"

Temmin ducked under the avalanche of silk roses and kissed each cheek. "How about giving me an early tea? I rode through lunch and I'm famished. And I'm hoping you can tell me more about—about someone we both know."

"Allis Obby, perhaps?"

"Behave, Elly," he said in an unsuccessful attempt at severity.

"Oh, I never behave," she answered, winking at Fen. The poor footman turned crimson under his freckles. He glared at Temmin, who returned the glare with interest. Fen dropped his eyes to the trug basket and kept them there.

"Somehow I can believe it," said Temmin, offering his sister an arm. She laid her shears in the basket full of roses, and sent Fen into the Keep with instructions to take the flowers up to her rooms and give them to her maid with instructions to expect His Highness at tea; Fen bowed, eyes worshipful, and sprinted into the mudroom. Temmin scowled.

Once safely in Ellika's sitting room, he said, "You really shouldn't torment the footmen, you know."

"Oh, nonsense," she said. "They like to look at me, and I like to be looked at, and there's an end to it. Thank you, Iddie, we'll have tea in here, please," she said to her maid as she sailed into her private sitting room. She perched herself on a spindly gilt chair at her spindly gilt tea table. "Wallek's attached to little Dannikson in any event, or so Iddie tells me. Don't they make a sweet pair? I'm hoping he declares for her soon so we can throw a little wedding party for them. Servants' weddings can be so diverting and sweet! And then perhaps we'll have little ones with curly red hair come of it, how charming! I shall take one as a page!"

"You're not breeding lap dogs."

"You shouldn't scold me if you want to hear more about Allis," she said.

"Miss Obby isn't the subject, though I wouldn't mind hearing more about her. We're going riding this Neyaday—do take off that hat, I feel as if I'm talking to a centerpiece—thank you. No, I actually came to talk to you about this footman, Wallek. Don't lead him on," he said, ignoring her tiny grimace. "He has a sweetheart, you know."

"I'm the one who told you about them!"

"You need to start acting as if *you* know about them. He's starting to take you seriously."

"He couldn't possibly!" exclaimed Ellika.

"He broke up with Dannikson over you." A partial fib, no more, he told himself. "They were to buy their promise rings in town today, but he stayed behind to move your furniture."

"How d'you know all this?"

Temmin paused, and said, "I heard it from Dannikson herself. I found her crying in the woods."

"You did, did you," she said, eyes narrowed. "You realize there's servants' gossip about the two of you."

He closed his eyes in consternation. "I swear on our mother's head there's nothing to it, and I'd hope you would pass that knowledge along—

especially not as coming from me! I've only talked with her once or twice, and it was completely innocent."

"Oh dear. Dear, dear," murmured Ellika. "Wallek is a dunderhead, but he's an endearing dunderhead. One of my favorites. And little Dannikson is adorable. Well! We can't let this state of affairs stand, especially if we're partially to blame."

"You, not we," he grumbled.

"Leave it to me, Temmy, this is the kind of project I love. I'll have them back together in no time! Now that I've satisfied you, you must satisfy me," she continued. "Have you made up your mind about the Temple? Do you intend to see Her Holiness before—or after?"

"Before or after what?" he said uneasily. Ellika leveled a gaze at him until he shifted in his chair and blurted, "I don't know yet. Papa says after. Jenks seems to think before, but I haven't talked with him directly about it. And don't really want to."

"What does Mama say?"

"I'm not going to ask Mama! It's bad enough having this conversation with you!" he said.

"Pfft. I worry about you, either way."

"Why? Is there something wrong with Allis?"

"Oh, not at all! I'm the highest-ranking patroness of the Lovers' Temple, and I've gotten to know both Embodiments very well. Allis and her brother are the most amiable, sympathetic pair in the world," she declared. "I dare say you could tell them anything. Well, you *can*—they've taken vows of confidentiality, haven't they? Allis loves to ride almost as much as she loves to dance, so you could not have invited her to anything she would enjoy more. Now, tell me you love me, and pass me one of those butter cakes before you eat them all." He did so, and snagged the last lobster roll in passing. "I'm very glad I warned Iddie you were coming," said his sister. "Speaking of warnings! What happened last night? You never said, and I was half asleep on the ride home or I would have asked you then."

"It's a bad business, Elly. I don't really want to talk about it."

Ellika cocked her head at him. "I asked Mama this morning about any spare uncles I might have. She said something about Grandpapa scattering children across the country. I suppose we have a few bastard uncles we don't know about?"

"You'll have to ask Papa about it. No, don't cajole me—girls shouldn't ask about such things. Besides," he added, "I don't like the word 'bastard.' It's not the baby's fault, is it?"

The Sign of the Owl was one of Reggiston's best inns, and certainly its best post house. For the quality, the Owl kept a neat set of rooms, and a neater set of post-horses and chaises for hire. The one leaving this morning for the northwest was hired by a young woman and her mother, a woman who seemed to be in a tearing hurry.

"I don't understand, Mama," said the daughter. "I don't want to leave! Why are we moving so far away, so suddenly—to Corland of all places? How can we afford to go post instead of on the mail, or even the stage— new clothes—where did all this money come from?"

"Don't ask questions, Mattie, just get in," said Tellis, shooing Mattie into the carriage. Tellis looked over her shoulder, let the ostler hand her in, and sighed as the door closed behind her.

Tellis Dunley was not given to nerves, and her only child settled into the unfamiliar plush seats, disturbed. "Something *must* be wrong, Mama. Are you ill? Is there some sort of healer in Arren? I can't believe we're moving to Arren, it's right on the border. We'll freeze! And the Corrish sound so funny!"

"They think *we* sound funny, and you'll be used to it soon enough. And I'm not ill, I'm fine—for the time being. Now be quiet! We can talk once we're under way!"

The horses took off from the Owl's courtyard at a smart trot. Mattie stared mournfully out the window as the streets of home slipped away, and they turned onto the main road north to Corland. "Now, Mama," she said, "now we can talk. Please tell me true: it's because of me, isn't it. It's because of me and His Highness. I'm sorry, Mama, I didn't want his attention, but I didn't try to stop him, either! That groom Nollson promised me I wouldn't get sacked, but…"

Tellis pursed her lips until they paled; she turned her wedding ring round on her finger. "You didn't get sacked. Mr Crokker never said a word to me. I know I lied to you when I fetched you from Meadow House, but it's nothing to do with any of that. We came into a small inheritance. A stroke of luck. No one's to know for fear they'd try to take advantage. We can't stay in Reggiston if we're going to get on in life. A fresh start is what we need, dearest, a fresh start among people who don't know us. Mattie," she said, leaning forward and emphasizing every word, "a fresh start is what we need. And so we are changing our name."

"Whatever for!"

"We are to take my maiden name, Ambler—no, Ambleson. Ambleson, that's better. No argument, missy. We must not be known in Arren, or anywhere, as Dunleys from Reggiston. No one must know we're from Reggiston, nor that we're anything other than genteel. We must put goose grease on our hands at night with gloves over all until they soften—no going anywhere or doing anything without gloves until then, but we must keep to ourselves in any event. And remember your school lessons—no cant language—the King's Tremontine at all times, even between ourselves. Thank Blessed Eddin for Lady Ansella's school," she muttered to herself.

"Well, then, where are we from?" said the astounded Mattie.

"I don't know yet," fretted Tellis. "I'll know where we're from when we get where we're going."

SIX

Temmin spent a restless night dreaming again of the assassin. Next time, he thought when he awoke, he would be better prepared. "Jenks!" he called as he came in after breakfast. "I know you weren't an officer, but have you ever trained with the Brothers?"

The balding head appeared in the bedchamber doorway. "The Brothers?" he said cautiously. "Why d'you ask?"

"I'm just wondering if Papa might let me have one as a fighting teacher. I'm sure Brother Mardus could show me more than the pudding bags I had at the Estate."

"Those men were not 'pudding bags,' sir, and Mardus isn't available. He's the head of your security detail. We can continue our sparring in the interim, and you can ask your father about training with the Brothers."

"I'm thinking he might like it if I did. Perhaps make up for the last time we talked. We rather argued about religion."

Jenks walked into the room. "I can't imagine the two of you in a theological dispute. What did you argue about?"

"My seeing Allis, about my going to them—her—inexperienced."

"Ah," said Jenks. He turned on his heel and went back into the bedchamber.

"You don't disapprove, too, do you?" said Temmin, following behind.

"No! No, not at all!" said Jenks hastily. "I encourage you—in fact, it'd be a prime thing, for you to enter service at a Temple, any Temple! It's just…there are some things, sir, that I find it difficult to discuss with you."

"Such as?"

"Such as…sex, sir." The big man's face turned an unfamiliar shade of red.

"Since when!" said Temmin. "You're the one who explained it to me!"

"You were eight! I explained what the horses were doing!"

"Yes, but you told me it was the same with all creatures, even people."

"More or less," said Jenks, fiddling with a stack of neckcloths, newly starched, pressed and straight from the laundresses. He faced his young master. "I'll be blunt. Do you ever think of me in an intimate situation, sir?"

The whites of Temmin's eyes showed all round the blue. "Only when I don't—I—I should say not! That's the last thing I want to think of you doing!" Worse than thinking of his parents, he added to himself.

"And I don't want to think of you doing it either, trust me. If you need someone to talk to about this, we can talk about this. But I confess it makes me uncomfortable, sir."

"No, we don't have to talk about it," murmured Temmin. "But tell me, do you think it's the right thing to do, becoming a Supplicant? Or should I wait? I don't know what to do, and Papa is completely against it."

Jenks picked up the stack, and stood in the entrance to the wardrobe. "Sir, any discouragement of you is sacrilegious, and I must say I'm astonished your father would risk offending the Gods, even the Lovers, as powerless as they are these days. You know me to be a believer. I make regular rounds of the Temples, though I confess to favoring Farr. Your becoming a Supplicant at any of them would make me very proud, not that my pride has any bearing on it. But I can't make that decision for you. You will have to weigh whether pleasing your father or pleasing the Gods is the right thing to do and decide for yourself, sir. Who do you fear more?" he said, and proceeded into the wardrobe.

"Fear?" Temmin called after him. "Who says I'm afraid of my father?"

"A pleasant morning post, I take it?" said Teacher, coming through the door for once.

"Oh, very pleasant!" said Temmin, refolding a letter on elegant paper flecked with rose petals; Allis had accepted his invitation to ride on Neyaday, and her exquisite handwriting lifted his melancholy. He put it in his inner waistcoat pocket and settled back onto the green velvet couch.

"Good. Perhaps it will put you in the mood to work."

"I hate work," Temmin groaned, but he rose from the couch and walked to the library table.

"No, you don't," said Teacher, following him. "You love it. Look at your hands."

Temmin examined his callused palms. "Not this kind of work, then. Books are Sedra's work, just like dressing up and flitting around is Ellika's. Here, I don't know anyone, no one knows me—not even my family, except Mama, and I don't know where she's gotten to. I have no idea what's expected of me except in the stables, and they keep wanting to coddle me."

"Part of what I'm teaching you is what's expected of you, Your Highness."

Temmin squinted up at Teacher, framed dark against the bright light from the study's windows. He absently patted the crinkling letter in his pocket. "Do you know the Obbys at all?"

"The Embodiments of the Lovers?" said Teacher. "Yes, quite well. Why do you ask?"

"Nothing! Can we get on with it?"

"Certainly," said Teacher, passing the red-bound book to Temmin. He opened it and settled into his chair. Teacher's voice filled the book with words and swallowed Temmin up.

Warin woke from a light sleep to the sound of wagons in the distance. People rarely came down the road, other than the occasional smuggler, or a trapper who didn't know this was his territory; wagons hadn't passed by in some time, and he suspected he knew who drove them.

He folded his tall, lean frame through the low threshold; an autumn breeze played with the fallen leaves and the ends of his neat, dark braid.

He moved silently down the path toward the road, to the clearing the Travelers sometimes used on their way from Leute to Tremont. He slid up to peer through the foliage, expecting the bright caravans.

Instead, he found a girl, sound asleep in the cold and draped only in her long hair.

Warin abandoned stealth. Letting the leaves crackle underfoot, he stepped into the clearing and crouched beside her. It wouldn't be the first time a Traveler had left an enemy at the side of the road; was she dead? No, her breasts rose and fell, and she sighed in her sleep. Her breasts, rising and falling: it had been some time since Warin had seen any woman, and here was a perfect one. Hair shining in the moonlight, luminescent skin, lush curves. How could she be anyone's enemy? He brushed her hair away from her face, her rosy lips soft and open in sleep, and murmured, "What are you doing here?" She awoke with a small cry, louder as she stared about her; she scrambled away from him through the leaves and dead grass. "It's all right," he said, backing away with hands open before him. "I won't hurt you—I'm here to help you. My name's Warin."

She sat up and clutched her knees to her chest, pulling her hair around herself like a shawl, and said something in Leutish. He understood more than he could speak of the neighboring tongue; she was frightened, and wanted to know where she was. "*Understandish, yay—speakish na Leutish,*" he said in what he he hoped was Leutan but knew was probably gibberish; she looked at him quizzically. "You're cold," he resumed in Tremontine. "Here—" he removed his cloak, and tossed it to her, moving back again. She eyed him warily, but burrowed into the cloak as quickly as she could. "Who are you?" he said. "How did you come to be all the way out here like this?"

She shook her head; tears filled her brilliant eyes. To see such eyes, such beauty, so close after so long—a tremor of long-dormant lust shook him. To his surprise, she closed her eyes briefly, face flushed and slack in sensual concentration. Her features were fine; she had the look of gentility about her, and so he took a chance that she had some education. "How came you here?" he repeated in Old Sairish. He hadn't spoken it aloud since he'd left his studies behind; it sounded stilted and formal.

"I know not!" she answered in kind, bursting into tears. "I remember not!"

"You understand! Very well, we speak in Old Sairish. What is your name?" She didn't know that, either. She didn't know who her people were, where she was from, not a single thing. "Name or no," he said, "you cannot stay out in the cold any longer. Come with me to my home. Yes, this way. May I take your arm? No? Mind your step."

Once inside, he dug through the cupboard until he found a soft, threadbare linen smock long enough to cover her completely. He turned to stoke the fire, leaving her some small privacy though he longed to see her faultless body again. When he turned back to her, she wore the smock and sat on the little stool beside the hearth, warming herself with the cloak still round her shoulders; her lips showed blue in the firelight. "Do you hunger?" he said. "Here is stew, saved for breakfast, but you may eat it, if you would like."

He studied her face from his shadowy corner of the hearth as she ate ravenously. A strong brow, a fine nose, a round, obstinate chin beneath ripe lips. Nothing coarse or common about her: lustrous chestnut hair that had seen a brush and comb recently, clean, white skin…soft skin…sweet-smelling skin all over her…

Best to break this train of thought. "You must be from Leute, across the river to the east," he said.

"Ah?"

"You speak Leutish, not Tremontine."

"Ah? Tremontine—is that what you were babbling. I speak Leutish, you say."

"And you speak Old Sairish with an eastern accent."

She smiled briefly, dimples flashing in her cheeks. "I think that perhaps it is you who have the accent. No, thank you, I have eaten enough —thank you," she said. She gave him the bowl with soft, white hands— clearly unaccustomed to work. She sat straight and poised, as dignified as a queen. Not a peasant. Perhaps the daughter of a rich merchant.

She plucked at a strand of her long hair, drawing it over and over through her fingers as she thought. "What is to happen to me?" she said. "Where shall I go?"

"You have no memory of your home? You are welcome to stay here until you decide what to do. I can take you to the nearest village, if you would rather. You might find work there, until you remember or until your people find you."

"I know not how to do anything," she said, breaking into tears again. "I remember not what I did before you found me. I remember not a thing. Who will take care of me?"

"You may stay here as long as you need. I will teach you to care for yourself, do not cry. You will be all right, I promise." Warin took her hand, so soft in his callused palm. So long since he'd touched someone, anyone. The warmth of her small hand in his spread throughout him, and he wondered how she would feel in his arms. He thought of her lying naked in the clearing, her full breasts, the soft patch of dark hair below her belly. He felt a deep twinge before he could move his mind away from the image. When next he looked, her lips were wet and parted, eyes wide and dark; a flush covered her cheeks and neck, and her nipples showed hard beneath the smock, though he knew she was no longer cold. She averted her gaze, shivering, her natural dignity abandoned.

"Are you unwell?" he said.

"I know not! I know not anything, I know not what I am feeling, I understand not!" She clung to his hand and broke into Leutish. "*I'm frightened! Don't let go my hand!*"

The best he could do in Leutish was, "*I won't,*" and he folded her hands in his until she calmed. It had been some time since Warin had been with a woman, but not so very long that he'd forgotten the signs of a woman's desire; her fingers softly traced against his palms, and he closed his eyes. "Amma help me," he prayed.

"I feel your wishing," she said in trembling Old Sairish. "I feel your wishing to touch me, to do—things—with me—I know not the words in this tongue! And I wish these touchings, too! How is this? You are a stranger!"

Warin brushed her tears away with his thumb, and then kissed her; she opened her mouth to him with a moan approaching a wail. Perhaps she was a gift; perhaps the Lovers had given her to him for consolation. He pressed her close at the thought. She neither fought nor protested, but only followed, never leading. "Will you come to bed with me?" he said. She whimpered, head down, and nodded. Warin frowned. "You do not have to.

It is your choice." She nodded again, looking up at him through tears. He picked her up and carried her to his narrow bed, their clothes collecting in a heap beside it.

Warin buried his head between her plump breasts and breathed her in —fresh air, campfire smoke, warm girl—then ran his tongue over a nipple before suckling at it. She lay oddly passive beneath him, responding when he touched her, but never more; he found it troubling, but he set the thought aside as he ground against her belly. "Beautiful girl, Neya's gift, whoever you are—" he said in Tremontine, and slid inside her; nothing blocked his way. Someone's wife, or someone's mistress—the hazy thought jarred him, and he dismissed it as she wound her arms around his neck. He groaned, flexing his fingers into the ticking beneath them; she was thoroughly wet, burning with heat that could not be mistaken for anything but want.

His excitement mounted, and he closed his eyes, pausing to regain control. Moving inside her, her arms around him, her legs spread wide, one breast in his hand as he kissed her, his pace increasing. His thrusts shook the little bed. With each one she gave a cry laden with pleasure, and pushed up to meet him, until she thrashed beneath him, screaming something in Leutish, her head thrown back in ecstasy. Within her, she clutched at him, a pulsing ripple, until he gasped, "It's been too long—I'm not going to last—oh, you can't understand me—Gods, you're beautiful!" He came and came, her fingers digging into his arms, his forehead pressed into the ticking beside the crook of her neck. He gulped in air, feeling her pulse beat fast and hard within her.

She shook, Warin assumed from pleasure—he knew she had taken hers—but when he gazed down into her face, tears poured from her tightly shut eyes, down the sides of her face into her hair. He rolled off her, and she clutched the coverlet to her chest. "Did I hurt you?" he said. She shook her head. He reached out a hand to her cheek, but she flinched away. "Eddin's tits," he swore in Tremontine. "You did not have to be with me. Did you not want this?" he said to her in Old Sairish.

"I know not what I want! I wanted it and I wanted it not!"

"...I understand not."

"I understand not, as well!" she sobbed.

He remembered her strange passivity; comprehension wrapped cold fingers around his heart and squeezed. "Cry not. I will touch you not this way again until we understand," he soothed. He rose from the bed and tucked her into the thick blankets, alone. "I will sleep by the hearth tonight."

"No," she said, struggling up on one elbow. "This is your bed."

"If it is my bed, I shall give it to whomever I please," he answered, soothing her back down. She pulled the covers up again. "I wish I knew your name," he said.

"I have none," she said, staring at the ceiling. She turned her eyes to him. "Give me one."

"All right." Her hair shone with gold from the fire as Warin stroked it from her face. "An old Tremontine name, I think—Emmae." It meant, "worth loving."

"Emmae? That is pretty," she yawned. "It pleases me."

"Sleep now, Emmae."

She closed her eyes. Warin watched until her breathing came soft, deep and regular. He crossed to the hearth, and threw a log onto the sputtering fire. "Burn," he said. The flames revived; when a particularly bright one appeared, he snatched it from the fire. It flickered on his palm, waiting and obedient. He drew the flame into a wand, crossed to the bed, and drew golden patterns in the air above it. Warin murmured something in a language older than classical Sairish; the glowing figures changed, and reformed into a silver answer, floating silent in the air. Warin frowned. He slipped the blankets back from her hip, finding the faint silver mark he suspected she bore: a sigil against getting with child. He waved the wand away, and the shining patterns in the air dissolved.

An enchantment. He had suspected. But a girl, a beautiful girl, a willing girl, a naked girl, delivered to his doorstep after so many years— what should he have done? She said yes, gave every sign of enjoyment. He stroked his dark beard and watched the flames dart among the coals to lick at the log. No. He had suspected, and had failed.

As for the enchantment, men's magic could not break it. Only one person in the world could have cast it, and Warin had no easy way to contact her. His divining was inexact with women's magic, but the spell's intent seemed clear enough. She would need protection; he'd never be able to take her into the village, let alone a city. If he did, he'd as well take her straight to the nearest whorehouse. Her enchantment precluded even the Lovers' Temple, perhaps especially the Lovers' Temple. In the spring, when she could take care of herself alone, he would leave her and search for the Traveler Queen. The Queen would remove the spell, and then he would return Emmae to the rich Leutish merchant who must be her father—or husband. He winced, thinking of her in the arms of another. How odd—only one night to become jealous.

He fetched his bedroll from the cupboard. Should he tell her about her enchantment? No, it would frighten her, and make her even more frightened of him. Best not to say anything until he could find the Traveler Queen. He took one last look at the woman he considered a gift, however guilty it made him feel. Her arm pillowed her head. She'd pulled the blankets tight around her shoulders, and her mouth hung open; she should have looked ridiculous. He sighed once, and fell asleep.

Temmin sat silent for some time. The smoke of the fire still lingered in his nose, Emmae's skin smooth on his fingertips. He shook the feeling from his hands, and sneezed. If only he could shake Warin's shame off as easily; it clung tight to him, guilt mixed with erotic satisfaction. "I am Temmin of Tremont, not Warin the woodsman," he said to himself, "and I have not just finished making passionate love to a beautiful woman I've discovered is enchanted to desire me whether she wants me or not. A stunning woman I found naked in a clearing outside my lonely hut. A woman I want to make love to over and over and can't stop thinking about... Jenks in his underwear, Jenks in his underwear..." Aloud, he said, "Am I right in thinking this is Warin the Wise we're discussing?"

"You are," nodded Teacher.

Knowing the woodsman was his many times great-grandfather cut blessedly into the story's erotic effect, but as his arousal subsided, Warin's guilt nagged at him the more. "Warin was a good man, wasn't he?" said Temmin uneasily.

"What do you think, given what you know so far?"

"I know from the official histories that he was considered a fair and just ruler and the people loved him, but the histories say that about all the kings," said Temmin. "He didn't do much to extend the kingdom, and some historians fault him for this, though I think gaining Litta for his son without a drop of blood was a fair bit of statecraft. Ehm, strengthened trade relations with Corland, back when it was still independent—same with Alzeh. Defended Litta against the Northern Tribes, even before unification—oh, and he brought Litta into the Kingdom by marrying the...only daughter...of Fredrik the Last of Litta. Ah."

"Ah."

"Well! There's a happy ending on the way, at least!"

"Marriage is not always a happy ending. Your parents did not choose one another. Has it been a happy ending for them?"

"I hadn't really thought about their marriage," Temmin said, taken aback. "Why would I? They're my parents!"

"Your father lived here, and your mother lived with you and your sisters more than a thousand miles away, and you had not thought about it."

Temmin shrugged, disturbed. "That's how things were."

"It remains to be seen in the story whether there is a happy ending, even allowing that there are such things," Teacher continued. "The difference between fairy tales, as I hear you've described this, and reality, is this: In reality, there are no endings. Life goes on. When we return to Harla, life goes on without us. Fate can place such obstacles before a man that you would never believe he could have a happy life, no matter what he did. But even if fate is very cruel to him, a wise man can still live a good life, perhaps even a happy life. Tell me: were Warin's actions in this part of the story those of a good man?"

"He took in a stranger. That's a good thing. But then, taking in a beautiful, naked girl isn't that much of a sacrifice."

"What about giving in to his lust?"

"You can hardly blame him, she was willing as far as he knew."

"He suspected something."

"But she said yes! How is a man supposed to know a woman means no when she says yes!"

"You seem rather touchy on the subject."

"Listen," said Temmin, "if you're trying to make a point, just make it, all right? Then I'll parrot it back and we can both go to lunch." Teacher stared into his face. Temmin wondered if his own misreading of a girl showed; he blushed and looked away. "Just let me go to lunch," he said. "I'll come back and you can tell me more about Warin the Wise, though apparently this was before he gained the honorific."

Teacher swallowed a laugh, and Temmin retreated down the stairs to the dining room, grinning.

Temmin returned on surer footing; he'd half-buried the story with most of a cold chicken and a glass of newly vinted flosseling, still sweet but crisp. For him, a full stomach meant better emotional control. Sitting back down at the library table to wait for Teacher, his gaze fell upon the old red book, and the story emerged from under his lunch, back to the forefront of his mind.

Whatever spell the book wove made the story real. Everything Warin felt, he felt: the deep loneliness and need; the rough, lumpy ticking; Emmae's fevered kisses, her shining hair, her heartbeat pulsing against his length deep inside her. Strange to still be a virgin after experiencing all that. Warin's memories drew him toward the book; he wanted to see Emmae again, perhaps to touch her with Warin's hands. When Teacher returned, Temmin already had the book open and ready. Teacher resumed the story, and Temmin let himself fall into it.

The next day, Emmae kept her distance. When Warin served out fried salt pork and ash cakes, she wouldn't take the bowl from his hand; she made him set it on the hearthstones beside her little stool. He flushed and turned away. "Do you wish to leave now?" he said to the wall.

"Do you wish me to leave now?" she said.

He glanced down at her from where he sat in the room's only chair, her face so downturned he could only see the tip of her nose. If only she spoke Tremontine—how could he tell her all his regret, all his real remorse, if he had to say it in a language better suited for philosophers,

Eddinites and Sisters than lovers? Lovers—he had been alone far too long, if he already thought of her as his lover.

He faced the fire's warmth. "No, I wish you not to leave. But I swear on whatever God you choose, or all of them, that I will touch you not again."

She raised her head, eyes cautious. "And how shall I repay you, if not in that way?"

"A whore you are not," he said, his own vehemence surprising him. "Never. Never will I let that happen! You will help me in my work. I will teach you to speak Tremontine, and to earn your keep with honor." She nodded her agreement and gave him a tentative smile, and the chill around his heart began to lift.

They soon found she could do nothing. She didn't even know how to sweep, raising enough dust to make them both cough. He discovered her short temper and pride when she threw the broom against the wall in frustration. "This one is too tall for you," he said, easing her humiliation. "I will make you your own." Two nights later, he gave her a broom, its top carved into a little rabbit. She accepted it with dignity, said, "Now that I have a proper broom, I am sure I shall sweep properly."

When they turned to cooking, he discovered her stubbornness. She refused to listen to him, and burned herself on the crane holding the pot over the fire. He dragged her sobbing down the path to thrust her arm into the icy stream. He examined it and hissed. "It will not scar, but it will hurt for a while. You will listen to me now, headstrong girl, will you not?"

They hurried through the cold to the warm cottage; Warin dressed her arm with honey and wrapped it in scraps of linen. Emmae's tears redoubled. "You are so kind to me! Why? What kind of woman must I be, to be found naked in a forest?" she cried, still in Old Sairish.

"There's no need for me to be unkind," he answered in Tremontine. "And as for not knowing your past—take it as a gift. Whatever you were, it doesn't matter now."

"I understand your words now, but I can answer not."

"You will, soon." For she was not only proud, stubborn and hot-tempered, she was smart; she made rapid progress in Tremontine, and he began to pick out more words in Leutish himself.

Emmae had one talent: she could sew. Warin took a length of linen and one of wool from his cupboard, and clothes for them both soon filled her workbasket. She no longer sat by the hearth in the old smock, but in a gray wool dress, little sparrows embroidered in plain red thread round its neck, and was as pleased as any princess clothed in silk.

The spoke turned, and the snow fell. Warin set out his traplines; pelts made up most of his trade with the outside world, and often he ate what he caught. One afternoon, he led Emmae to a freshly killed brace of rabbits, hanging headless by their hind legs from a low branch. "Must I?" she said, her Tremontine now good enough to speak as well as understand.

"Do you want to eat?" he answered. "Watch." She winced but didn't turn away. He began on the nearest rabbit, deftly flaying the skin from its body.

She watched him work. "You're so quiet," she said.

He finished skinning, turned the pelt flesh-side out, and threw it into a nearby bucket of water. "This will make you a pair of mittens. Do a good job on the next one, and you'll have trim for a hood." He cut into the body. "Here. The liver. If you ever see spots, throw the whole carcass away. The meat's bad. No spots on this one," he said, holding it out. "It's good. Good eating, too." He worked in silence, then said, "This always reminds me of soldiering."

"You were a soldier?"

"Of sorts, when I was young. See here?" He aimed his knife between the rabbit's ribs. "Thrust here at a man—instant kill. Were we on the ground—" he drew along the inside of the rabbit's thigh— "I'd cut here. The blood just falls out. A quick, merciful death." He pulled the rabbit's innards out, and threw them onto the frozen ground. "I hated being a soldier."

She studied his bitter face, then said, "Is that why you came to the woods?"

"No." He wiped his knife in the snow and handed her the knife, hilt-first. Emmae fought down her nausea, and set about flaying the second rabbit.

The snow deepened, and still Warin kept his promise: he didn't touch her. He slept on the floor in his bedroll, and she slept in the narrow bed, alone. Even so, he could not help wanting her. Many nights, she'd wake from an erotic dream to realize it belonged to him, confused to sense his desire so acutely.

As the days passed, Warin's ache became hers, and she wavered in her determination to stay away from him. Her eyes lingered over his angular form, skin still tanned from the summer sun, his brown eyes softening whenever they met hers. She remembered his strong, work-hardened hands sliding over her body, coaxing, then demanding. She would wonder how those hands would feel around her waist, lifting her skirts, holding her down on the bed—how those long, rough fingers would feel against the soft skin of her breasts, or the inside of her thighs. A strand of his dark hair would fall across his face, and she would stop herself from tucking it behind his ear. His kindness, his patience, and his forbearance loosened the fear that had seized her the first night; she looked upon him, not with worry, but with tenderness, and more than tenderness.

For his part, Warin rejoiced to have Emmae near, though it caused him pain; he had been alone far too long, and she was far too beautiful. More than that, he admired her bravery. Once she realized that stubbornness and pride would teach her nothing, she faced her situation with intelligence, and without self-pity. She worked as hard at learning to clean pelts as she did at learning Tremontine, with a tenacity he would never have expected from the presumed daughter of a wealthy merchant. He loved watching her mend stockings or hem a shirt before the fire in the evenings, concentrating until the pink tip of her tongue peeked out. When she caught him gazing down at her, she'd smile up from the low stool, and his heart would swell with a love he knew he had no right to feel.

In this way, Winter's Beginning passed, and most of Winter's End, until one night not long before Pagg's Day. Warin's restlessness kept Emmae from sleep; he fairly shone in the dark with desire. Perhaps if he thought she slept he would finally doze off. She kept herself still, and made her breathing even, but still his thoughts caressed her, urgent and ghostly. His want swirled and pulsed through her, running in her veins, pounding in her heart, threatening to drown her.

"Emmae?" whispered Warin. "Are you asleep?" No answer. He groaned, almost inaudible, and his bedclothes rustled. She opened a slitted eye to see him silhouetted against the fire's coals; she could just make out his hand, moving down the length of his cock. His mouth formed her name. She opened both eyes and watched the banded muscles of his narrow hips flex, remembering their feel under her own hands. She sat up to watch him, moving silently, not wanting to startle him. She'd never seen or even heard him pleasure himself before, in all the weeks she'd lived there. His head lolled back, eyes shut tight. He stole a look in her direction, and froze, open-mouthed, to see her watching him. "Gods, I—"

"Don't stop," she said, her accent drawing out the words. Warin stared, stunned. "Go on," she urged. "I want to watch. You're thinking of me, yes?"

"I never stop thinking of you," he said hoarsely.

"I know. Don't look away." Their eyes locked, and he slowly pushed up into his hand. His breath grew ragged, and so did hers; it rose up into her head, threatening to carry her off. She finally stood up, stripped off her chemise, and sat down again, naked. "Come to bed."

He groaned. "Emmae, you don't have to—"

"I want to, I've wanted to," she answered. He joined her on the bed, sitting apart from her until she leaned into him, nuzzling his neck. His long hair was loose, and he smelled of clean dirt and leather. He pulled away, gazed down her body and then into her face; hope, hesitancy and desire shone in his eyes. She kissed him, unrestrained at last.

Kisses and kisses, weeks of wanting ending in an impatient sweetness. He traced his fingers down her arms, her back; any touch would have left her lightheaded, but together they sent her into a near-trance. Warin searched her face with bright, anxious eyes. "It's been so hard not to touch you—"

"Then touch me," she whimpered. "Please, please touch me." The dark red of his desire blossomed inside her, crowding out anything else that might have been in her mind. She took his hand and brought it to her breast, and he pushed her down onto the bed, just as she'd imagined, his hard body pressing her into the ticking. He kissed her over and over before he moved to her nipples, taking them one by one into his mouth; each suckle sent ripples through her, pooling between her legs. Her helpless pleasure magnified as his pleasure increased, and she clung to him.

He returned to her mouth; his hand slid down between her legs, the palm rough against the skin of her thighs as he pushed them apart. Warin slid a finger just past the swollen lips and into her wetness. He broke their deep kiss, gazing down on her, fierce and intent, almost smiling; another finger joined the first, slipping further inside her with no resistance, curving up with a gentle thrust, in and out as she moved with him. How had she denied herself this? She guided his hand with the movement of her hips, turning herself this way and that, showing him what she liked as his fingers ran over her slick inner lips, darting inside, brushing across the nub atop her opening—

The fingers withdrew; Emmae moaned in disappointment. She opened her eyes and watched him creep down her body, kissing and biting under her breasts, down her sides, across her belly, pushing her legs further apart. He brushed his hair over one shoulder, and then to her astonishment, he licked her. He ran his tongue over and over her thickened lips, circling closer, until he flicked the tip of his tongue over her clitoris. She brought her hands to his head and let out a short, surprised cry; he chuckled against her, and did it again, and again. He slid his fingers back inside her, concentrating all his attention on the little nub, sucking it in gentle rhythm to his fingers until she couldn't breathe. She heard her own voice give out an endless cry as she shook and bucked against his mouth.

Warin slid back up her body, and sank himself into her. His heavy hair fell around them, curtaining off the world outside the bed. Emmae could smell and taste herself on his mouth and in his beard. Each slow thrust left her open-mouthed and dazed, until her head rolled to one side. The fire on the hearth had awakened, bright and hot. How odd, she thought. Warin's pace quickened; she brought her eyes back to his face, the fire forgotten. He hooked an arm under her knee and pulled her leg up high over his shoulder, moving in earnest now, his face contorting. No gentleness now for either of them, only need suppressed, and need released. Emmae dug her fingers into him as he swelled inside her. With each thrust her mouth opened, and her sight grew unfocused until she couldn't see at all. Sight was unnecessary; she felt as one with Warin and somehow with the world. The ripples began again, spreading deep inside her and forcing her head back in a long, sighing scream. She contracted around him; he plunged deep, to the one place inside her he had not reached, knocking her back against the bedframe. He gave a growling shout, and came in shuddering spurts inside her. She released her hold on him, her strength gone, and lay shaking beneath him, both of them gasping for breath.

In time, Warin kissed her, voluptuous, satisfied, drowsy. "I love you," he said.

To her own surprise, she answered, "*I love you,*" but it came out in Leutish. It seemed he understood, though, and she kissed him in return. Little shudders shook them both; he stayed inside her until they fell asleep, tangled together.

Warin and Emmae made love and slept for three days, rising only when they had to, until they left the bed, dazed and happy. Emmae put wash water on to heat; Warin set to building a bigger bed.

The wheel turned to Spring's Beginning. The shed filled with pelts, and the cupboard emptied, until there was nothing for it but a trip to the village: "We're out of supplies, love," said Warin. "And no, you can't come with me."

"Why not?" said Emmae. "Oh, please! I want to see what a village is like. I don't remember going to one."

"I can't trade and take care of you at the same time," he said. "In fact, I'm going to leave you for one night on your own to see how you do before I leave for an entire week."

"You have so little confidence in me, and here I have every confidence in you," she laughed, and kissed him.

Warin left the cottage, took up his axe, and split logs for the fire; he could have split them all with a simple spell, but chose to do it by hand. As he worked, he considered the problem of Emmae. He imagined what might happen the first time they walked into a Paggday market; any man would see her beauty at once, and the enchantment might lead to the Gods knew what. *Thunk, thunk,* went the axe, splinters flying. The split wood under the eaves grew to be enough for three days. Still he chopped. With spring's arrival, it was time to look for the Traveler Queen. Perhaps he could persuade her to lift the spell. Why would the old woman do such a thing?

Warin left for a day and a night soon after to finish his last gatherings; rare mushrooms and mosses sometimes brought more in trade than even his beautiful pelts. Emmae decided it was better to be busy than sulky, and the day was bright, if cold. She took the bedding outside to air, draping the featherbed and ticking on low, bare branches in the sun. She finished the sweeping and cleaning, and turned to the cupboard for a full accounting of their supplies.

Out went the last of the wheatmeal, too lousy with worms to finish. If she washed off the wispy remains the meal moth cocoons left behind, they could still eat the oat groats. No oil remained, nor butter, nor dried fruit—barely enough of anything to scratch up a few more dinners, but she would manage. She'd learned to manage well, and looked proudly round the clean cottage. She set some oats on the hearth to soak and turned back to the cupboard.

As she sorted through the tanned pelts Warin had saved for their own use, she saw a dull gleam at the cupboard's very back—an ornate silver tray, black with tarnish. She eased it out of its hiding place. So fine a thing. Where had he gotten it? Why had he concealed it? She wondered once more about his past, and then her own. Who was she? Who were her people? Obviously from the east, in Leute. They should have found her by now. She wasn't sure she cared.

The sun vanished behind a cloud. She put the featherbed and ticking back on the bed and shut the windows, just in time; a rainstorm began pattering against the roof, and she threw another log on the fire. She ate her dinner alone, and spent the evening snugged by the hearth polishing the tarnished tray, though in the end she had to satisfy herself with a still-clouded shine.

Warin returned the next day to dinner and an avalanche of kisses. "I've been gone just one day!" he laughed. "Tomorrow I'll travel to the village and be gone the week. I did very well in my foraging. When I come back, I'll have some presents for you."

"What will you bring me!" she cajoled. "Tell me, tell me!"

"Linen for a summer dress, ribbons for your hair—and a ring for your finger. I can't marry you, Emmae—no, listen to me, don't look away like that. It's nothing to do with how I found you. I can't explain—I can't marry anyone. You'll always have to wear my ring on your right hand, not your left. But it will be you, only you, forever. Will you have me, even though we can't stand before Pagg?"

"Of course I'll have you, Warin, Pagg's blessing or no. I would have no one else, either." He kissed her, then, and their passion grew until Warin lifted her onto the table and made love to her, both too impatient to walk to the bed.

Leaning against the wall unnoticed, the tray reflected a murky image of their joined bodies in the firelight.

Far away, a Prince of Tremont sat before a mirror in Tremont Keep, contemplating not his own reflection, but the scene in the cottage. "Warin finally grew careless," he said. "With a wench—who'd have thought my brother the hermit would risk a woman, with his birth prophecy. Wine, boy."

"Yes, Your Highness." A blond young man just out of boyhood rose gracefully, filled the Prince's cup and returned to sitting on his knees at his master's feet. He followed his master's gaze into the mirror; a sort of haze obscured the image. Gian hadn't seen the man in the reflection for ten years, when he himself had been a boy of seven; just before he exiled himself, Warin had come to Casalaria, the seat of the Duke of Valleysmouth and Gian's childhood home. At the time, the Heir's close resemblance to Gian's master had shocked him.

The brothers still looked alike, he thought, looking up at Hildin: dark hair, deep brown eyes, the angular planes of their faces. While Warin's face was soft, intent on his woman, Hildin's was hard. He had all the dominance Gian himself lacked, and he'd obeyed his cousin as soon as he'd come to think of anything at all; Hildin was his master in everything.

Gian leaned into the Prince's side, returning his gaze to the mirror, and Hildin placed an absent hand on his fair head. "She's beautiful, isn't she? I wonder what backwater he found her in. Sit in my lap, Gian, I think you want a better view." Gian jumped up and took his place, nestling into the taller man. The nearness of the man he loved, and the couple's slow, sensuous movements in the mirror, brought him to hardness, a clear outline against the soft fabric of his tunic. "You're enjoying this, aren't you?" said Hildin in lazy amusement. The Prince's hand pressed against his length, and he closed his eyes.

"I'm sorry, Your Highness," he said in a low voice. "Should I not be?"

"Enjoy yourself all you'd like." Hildin reached under Gian's tunic and opened his hose. "Though I wish to see your need. Show me." He took Gian's cock in his hand and stroked it, slow and deliberate. "Tell me how much you want that woman. You do, don't you? You imagine yourself in my brother's place between her thighs."

"Yes, my Lord," said Gian, voice straining. "I want her. I want you to watch me take her, I want to suck at those tits."

"You always did like a good pair. We'll go and fetch her presently, as soon as he's left her alone. Perhaps I'll give her to you when I'm done with her." Hildin removed his hand. Gian groaned, and moved to touch himself, but the Prince stopped him. "I decide your satisfaction, and I say no." Gian groaned again, his cock twitching as it hardened even more. "She's more than a simple slut to him. See how they cling to one another?" said the Prince. Warin's movements quickened; the woman urged him on, crying out, though they could not hear her. Gian shifted in his master's lap, grinding against the erection he knew he'd find there. "Down," growled Hildin; Gian dropped to his knees, unfastened the Prince's leggings, and took his master in his mouth. "A pretty picture, my brother and his woman. I—intend—to alter it," said Hildin, the words catching as Gian began to suck. The Prince gripped Gian's head, fucking his mouth as he moaned in submission. Tears streaked down Gian's cheeks—they always did. Who could stand against him, thought Gian, and then he thought of nothing but his master thrusting down his throat.

Temmin left the book, desperately aroused. He couldn't say what provoked him more: Warin and Emmae's lovemaking, or the strange scene at the end. He gripped the table's edge and reached for quelling thoughts, anything to dull the book's effects. He turned to the story. "So it's Hildin the Usurper," he stammered.

"Still Prince Regent. King Gethin had slipped into senility by this time," answered Teacher.

"He had magic too? How many people held it?"

"Only the men of the royal bloodline. At this time, King Gethin still held most of it, though he could not use it. Warin held a considerable amount, then Hildin, and so on. The further from the throne, the less magic one possessed."

"Where did it go? How did we lose it?"

"Another story for another time."

Teacher said no more, and Temmin's thoughts drifted back to the two men at the end. Could one call that sex? The page focused so completely on pleasing the Prince, and Hildin didn't seem to care in the least; he expected it. It wasn't anything like what had happened with Alvo. "Why did Gian think of Hildin as his master? I mean, Hildin was his lord, yes, but 'master' seemed to mean more than that."

"Some people have a deep need to serve. Gian was one of them."

"Servants need to serve, certainly," said Temmin. "But none of 'em seem to want *that*!" The most disagreeable image of Mattie came to mind, and he flushed, fidgeting further in his chair.

"Servitude—true servitude—crosses the boundaries of class, wealth, power and gender," said Teacher. "Some are born with the need, some acquire it. If you decide to chase the Obbys, you will become quite familiar with the condition. The Temple deals with it all the time, though many seek private arrangements outside a religious framework."

Something in Issak's demeanor reminded Temmin of Hildin—not that Issak was cruel, as far as he knew, but he could see Issak commanding someone like Gian. He could see someone kneeling at Issak's feet, Issak's hand stroking a fair head, Issak sliding into a crying young man's willing mouth—

"I think I'm done with lessons for today," said Temmin.

"We are done when we are done, Your Highness," said Teacher. "I do not wonder that you are thinking on Hildin and Gian. You are due to be matched with a Mentor soon."

A Mentor. Temmin considered his older cousins and their Mentors. Sometimes their Mentors treated them with fatherly regard, sometimes with brotherly affection, and sometimes with open lust in the case of the handsome ones; most of his cousins tolerated it, and one or two of them reveled in being a more powerful older man's temporary confidant and bedmate. "Mentoring is rather like those two, isn't it? I mean, Mentors are older, and so was Hildin. Though not much older, was he. Ten years or so? And the Mentor has a great deal more experience and power than his Student, but then, that's rather the point, isn't it? To learn what the Mentor knows, to become friends with those in the Mentor's circle who can benefit him? It's that power thing you're always going on about." Temmin looked up at Teacher, too interested for bashfulness. "But what does the Mentor get out of it? Is it just the sex?"

"For some, it is the sex. For others, the service—teaching what one knows. For many, I suspect it is the chance to relive one's youth through another. Some Mentors and Students do not ever touch one another. Perhaps most."

"You'd never say that if you saw my cousins with their Mentors!"

"One wishes to keep up appearances," said Teacher. "The relationship between Mentor and Student is considered the most perfect, the most pure, a union of equals, at least in terms of class and education. Who would wish to proclaim himself a failure at that?"

"One of my cousins is still with his Mentor, and it's been years since they should have ended," mused Temmin. "I wonder who Papa is considering for me. I mean, I'm the Heir—no family is more powerful than ours. So I suppose I'd be matched with someone I can learn from—" He looked up, wide-eyed with a sudden thought: "It's not you, is it?" he said.

His tutor raised one elegant eyebrow. Temmin had never noticed the fineness of Teacher's face, the contrast of the soft mouth and sharp jaw, the smooth, pale skin betraying no sign of the years, the luminous, pale eyes— a face between handsome and beautiful, compelling in whispers. Teacher put two long, slender fingers under Temmin's chin. The unnerving, sensual mouth approached his own; his heart quivered, and he closed his eyes, unable to look into the intense silver. Teacher's cool, smooth cheek rested against his own.

He had nearly surrendered himself to a surprising swoon of anticipation, when a puff of breath hit his ear: "No," said Teacher in a laughing voice.

Temmin opened his eyes. "It's not funny."

Teacher pulled back, keeping hold of Temmin's chin. "Oh, I find it highly amusing."

"Don't make fun of me," he said, trying to wrench free.

Teacher gripped him tighter than Temmin could ever have guessed. "I am not making fun of you, Temmin. I am trying to get you to pay attention. You had no conception of or desire for anything between us, and yet I led you straight into it. You must learn to lead yourself, or at the least consciously choose to follow, instead of letting yourself be lulled along." Teacher let him go. "I do this with great fondness for you, whether you believe me or not."

Temmin gave a small, appalled shudder and looked away, composing himself. He schooled his face into something more poised, and said, "Has my father discussed Mentors with you?"

"To be sure. He wishes to match you with someone he needs to court politically, in the same manner as your sisters' marriages. There has been some talk of the Duke of Barle."

Temmin recoiled. "Barle? That hideous, boring old man? He can't even choose his carriage horses properly."

"It would be politically expedient. But if you go to the Temple, you will not receive a Mentor."

"Why not?"

"You would not have time. You are seeing Allis Obby this Neyaday?" said Teacher.

"Yes," said Temmin, surprised. "How'd you know?"

"She told me. But I assure you, anything private between you stays with her. I will never hear about it, even though Allis and Issak are dear to me—the closest I shall ever have to children, save one. If you want to understand these things, talk to them—study with them. The Lovers' Temple can teach you a great deal about 'these things.' Their tutelage would augment your studies of the History immensely—practical application of what you learn from the Book."

"She told you I'm considering chasing them, didn't she."

"Your Highness, your behavior has made it quite clear—she did not need to. It is all over the City. Everyone knows."

An icy spike at Temmin's groin killed any remaining, pleasant discomfort. "And does everyone know I...qualify?"

"Everyone has guessed by now," said Teacher in a gentle murmur.

"Pagg's own balls, I'll never live it down whether I go to the Temple or not! That damn Fennows—next time I see him, he'll be one big smirk!"

"Are you not getting along with your new companion?"

"Companion. Ha! I can't bear him. I've managed to avoid him since my ball."

"Strange. I heard you got quite drunk with him that night."

"I couldn't stand him any other way," said Temmin.

"Perhaps you might lay in a stock of wuisc, then," said Teacher. "I have been told he is staying at the Keep while his family retires to their seat at Maryakuspa on urgent business."

"When?"

"Tomorrow. I will be leaving you to attend to one another for the day, with or without inebriation, and shall see you on Eddinday."

A day alone with that wretch, thought Temmin. Well, perhaps he could ride.

SEVEN

In fact, Fennows could not ride. Fennows couldn't do anything. Temmin watched a groom trying, and failing, to give the spotty young man a foot-up onto his horse. Fennows abused the poor groom the whole time: did the groom know who he was—disrespectful cur—clumsiest groom in Tremont, he should think. And he got away with it! The groom didn't blink an eye. If Temmin had used that tone at home, he'd have found out what was what. But none of the grooms met Temmin's eyes this morning, merely pressing their knuckles to their foreheads or bowing, and all of them eyeing Fennows when they thought the Heir wasn't looking. It all conspired to deepen Temmin's already-sour mood.

"You will entertain Lord Fennows tomorrow, Temmin, and from time to time while he is with us as your studies permit," King Harsin had said the night before. "His father is important to me politically. Learn to like him. Is he really so bad?" he'd added at Temmin's sour face.

He was really that bad, thought Temmin now, watching Fennows jounce gracelessly into the Woods. Impatience got the better of him; he tapped Jebby in the sides, and galloped past His Lordship without so much as a glance behind him. Not long after, though, his conscience caught up, and he slowed to a walk; Fennows came puffing up at an awkward canter. "That really was unreasonable, I should think, Temmy!" he wheezed.

The unwarranted use of his nickname overrode any prickings at Temmin's conscience, however small. "It's unreasonable to waste the day," he snapped. "Keep up or go home! Gidyap, Jeb!" The big horse tore down the War Road, leaving the enraged Fennows gasping in the saddle.

Temmin didn't see Fennows until he returned to the stables for lunch, to be served in Temmin's study. They walked from the stables, through the mudroom—though Fennows disapproved of any door but the main one—and up the Residence Wing stairs in silence. Temmin knew he should apologize for his behavior, and disgorged a sort of one: "I'm sorry you couldn't keep up this morning."

Fennows immediately brightened. "Oh, that's all right, Temmy old thing," he said in an ingratiating tone that made Temmin regret the apology, as imperfect as it was. "I know you're quite the horseman, and riding isn't in my line."

"I really don't care for my childhood nickname any more, *Percy*," said Temmin as they entered his study.

"Oh, that's all right, you can call me Percy all you'd like—well! Hello!"

Standing near the bookshelves was Arta. She fumbled her feather duster in surprise, recovered herself, and turned her face to the wall.

"Arta—Dannikson, don't do that! You know I hate it," said Temmin in exasperation.

"I can see why. Want to see as much of that face as possible, I should think, though the back view ain't bad. A prime bit!" Fennows whispered, nudging Temmin and ignoring the Prince's answering glare.

Arta was in fine looks, a cluster of curls wisping at her nape, her hazel eyes clear and bright, if anxious. "I'm sorry, Your Highness, it's a habit," she quavered, turning to face them. "I was told to dust the upstairs studies, and I thought I'd be able to finish this one before you were due home, sir— I'm very sorry!"

"I'm not!" grinned Fennows. Arta blushed as red as her ribbons. "Spin round, my dear, let's get a good look at you!"

"No," said Temmin. He took Arta firmly by the elbow and escorted her through the door into the empty hall. "It's all right, you're not in trouble," he murmured. "Just stay away from Lord Fennows, or you'll be in trouble, and not with me or Affton."

"I'm sorry, sir, I didn't mean to bother—"

He stopped her, and gave a furtive glance up and down the hall. "Arta, you didn't bother me," he said. He ran his thumb along her cheek, and chewed on his lip. "I don't want him anywhere near you. If he bothers you, you tell me. Promise me."

"Sir, you don't need to worry about someone like me."

"Promise me."

She took his hand from her cheek, her face troubled. "I promise."

"All right, then. Go on."

She disappeared down the service stairs, and he stalked back into his study to the smirking young lord. "Ah, I see where things lie, I'm no dull wit, I should think!" said Fennows.

"I'm sure I don't understand you," said Temmin, throwing his coat over the back of the green velvet couch.

Fennows chuckled. "You don't have to play coy with me, old thing! Last person in the world you have to play coy with when it comes to a little love! When did you land her? I should have snapped her up the minute I saw her, too! Those eyes—and nice tits under the livery, I'd wager, hey?"

Temmin advanced on him, his jaw tight; Fennows shrank, but held his ground. "You stay away from her, Percet Lord Fennows," he spat. "She is to be left alone, by you and everyone else, d'you understand me?"

"Never worry, never worry," said Fennows, hands before him. "She's your little bit, I shouldn't *dream* of poaching 'er."

"She's not my 'little bit,'" said Temmin.

"Eh?" blinked Fennows.

Just then, Jenks entered with lunch. Temmin's every glance pleaded, "Don't leave me alone with this idiot," but Jenks returned his mute entreaties with flinty unconcern and left once he'd set the meal on the little table by the window.

Fennows pounced on the wine. He finished off a glass in two gulps and poured himself another. He regarded Temmin across the table, as the Heir piled his plate with ham and cold chicken. "D'you mean to tell me you haven't bedded that little darling?"

Temmin's hand paused over the bread basket. He blushed, but said, "It's none of your concern, Fennows," and fished out a roll.

Fennows squinted at him, malice playing around the corners of his mouth. "Touchy! It's true, isn't it? You do qualify for Supplicancy. And at your age, tsk."

"I said, it's none of your concern," said Temmin. He took a fierce bite from a chicken leg.

"Dear me," said Fennows. "I'd be grumpy if I were a virgin, too, I should think. What is it, old thing? Don't like girls? One would assume you do, the way you stare at Allis Obby, but then, perhaps it's Issak Obby who's your ultimate goal? Well, they're a package deal, ain't they."

Temmin wiped his mouth. "I like girls just fine, thank you."

"But you're eighteen, and you haven't fucked one."

"I haven't had the opportunity," Temmin said. He plucked the decanter off the table and filled his glass to the rim.

"Haven't had the— You have plenty of opportunity with that maid. She's right here, and five dozen more just like her under this roof alone! It's clear you want her, if you're this jealous of me."

Temmin stopped himself from retorting that he was hardly jealous of a prat like Percet Sandopint, and said instead, "I leave the maids alone." He picked up his glass, found he'd managed to empty it somehow, and poured another.

"Then let me have a go at her. Oh, see there!" cried Fennows. "Look at that face! Never worry, I'll stay well clear of her. Nerr bless my prick, to be so inflamed over a maidservant, and then not fuck her! Are you worried about your lack of experience? Is that it? I tell you what. I'll take you to the best house in the City—and that's saying a great deal. The City has it all over Maryakuspa when it comes to houses, I should think, and we have some fine ones. I know a girl at this one, a fine girl. Plump and happy, thighs like marble. They say she washed out of the Lovers' Temple, but before she left, she learned this trick with her tongue…"

"You do realize if I accept Supplicancy, I'll be practically living at the Temple among hundreds of Beloveds who've forgotten more tricks than that girl remembers."

"And you do realize, old thing, that the Obbys' only interest is in snaring you as a royal patron for the Temple, don't you?"

Temmin stopped short, glass halfway to his lips in surprise. "They have one," he said. "Ellika's a devotee."

"For now," snorted Fennows. "Harla take me straight to the Hill if I'd let a wife of mine serve at the Lovers' Temple! Pay respects, of course, I should think—wouldn't do to miss Neya's Day, hey? But let Elly serve there? Out of the question."

"You have no right to call her 'Elly,' for starters, and for seconds, she's not your wife," said Temmin.

"Well, really, Temmy, I'm trying to help you out here before you make a horrible blunder! You do know what those two Obbys get up to when they pretend to be 'possessed,' don't you? Gods know what they do in private!" Fennows leaned toward him, face avid and wolfish. "Let me take you to that house, we can spend the day there tomorrow!"

"I have to study tomorrow," mumbled Temmin through a mouthful of hothouse grapes; he washed them down with his third glass of wine and gave Fennows a look as dark as a thunderhead.

"Study? Tell your tutor you're busy tomorrow."

Temmin cracked a sweetnut with a significant glare and picked out the brain-like meat. "I can't," he said. "He's not the sort of tutor you can order around."

"So he orders you around? How princely is that? Are you that little a man, then? The Heir of Tremont." Fennows drew his chin down, stretching his face like rubber, and popped his eyes; he fluttered his hands by his ears. "'Oh, my tutor won't let me skip a class!'"

"Who are you to tell the Heir of Tremont whether he's a man or not!" said Temmin.

"I'm a man, that's who, not an unfucked boy!"

Temmin rose slowly, listing from the wine. "Percet Sandopint," he said, deliberately using Percy's name instead of his title, "leave my study."

Fennows seemed to realize the much taller Prince was looking for a good excuse to beat him senseless; he stood up and snatched at the wine decanter. Temmin moved it out of reach, and Fennows left without it, marching out of the room with an affronted but somehow triumphant step.

Temmin played with the cheese-knife, spearing rinds as he drank his last glass of wine. If he were king, he'd have that Pagg-damned dog beaten through the City. He wasn't king, but the mental image of Percet driven behind a cart, shirt in bloody tatters and the crowd showering abuse on him, pleased Temmin anyway.

Nevertheless, the taunts had found their mark; Temmin nursed the wound. Would Allis have paid him any attention if he weren't the Heir? There was no way of knowing. And yet, she seemed so sincere. Her kiss was sincere. So was Issak's. He'd felt wanted. He'd felt like a man in all the best ways.

And then, to have Fennows of all people call him a boy, just because he respected his tutor. Come to think on it, though, when had he paid attention to any of his other tutors? When had he ever let any of them order him around like this? Why should he be so constricted? Wasn't he the Heir? He should be able to do as he pleased—he did at the Estate, and he was a boy, then. Now he was a man, he was the Heir. He would spend his time as he pleased here at the City. Oh, not going to a whorehouse with Fennows, even for a plump girl with a talented tongue. Eddinday looked more like a day to be out in the fields on horseback, away from the Keep, away from Fennows, and away from his exciting but disturbing studies. Temmin thought of Teacher, admonishing him the day before: "You must learn to lead, or at least consciously choose to follow, instead of letting yourself be lulled along."

"Lulled along," Temmin said to no one. "I'll show you 'lulled along.'"

The next day, Temmin wore his riding clothes to breakfast, going straight to the morning room from the stables and returning there straight after, as Jenks discovered too late. "He's gone, Mr Jenks, sir," said the Riding Master when the valet searched for his errant charge. "He wore the chestnut oot this morning an took another horse—Inchari mare, a rare fine un. T'was odd for him to be goin back oot, but it's not fer me to decide what a Prince should do, eh? We'll tell him you want him, sir."

"I'll tell him more than that when I see him, Pagg damn him for a headstrong boy," rumbled Jenks to himself on the way back to Temmin's rooms. "Tempted to chase him down and turn him over my knee."

The "headstrong boy," however, was in fine spirits, and not in the least repentant. Whatever admonition he might receive for skipping his studies was worth getting out of the Keep, and away from Fennows. He couldn't avoid the lordling at breakfast, and Fennows's endless fawning over Ellika enraged him; it was all Temmin could do not to vault across the toast rack and throttle him.

But here in the meadows of the foothills, the fresh air cleared his head. The mare he'd chosen, a black Inchari cross named LeiLei, had a fine comfortable gait and a good temper, far better than a purebred Inchari horse. Too bad Jeb was a gelding; a colt of Jebby's out of this mare would have been a fine horse indeed. Temmin let her wander, cropping the spring grasses. He looked down at the City, spread far below him. He'd climbed high into the foothills over the course of the morning, higher than he'd realized, and the mare hadn't griped at all. No trouble carrying him in the least—a good-sized girl. Wonderful horse, LeiLei. She'd make a good addition to his personal stock.

"C'mon, sweetheart," he said, and guided them back into the forest. He knew a stream ran nearby, and he was sure the mare was thirsty. He found not just a stream, but a lovely pool: a backwater formed behind a rocky outcropping in the stream. The mare dipped her head gratefully, and Temmin dismounted to wash his hot face, and take a drink himself.

When he looked down into the water, he saw his reflection. His mind flitted to Hildin finding his brother in the story, and instantly he realized he'd made a mistake. "Oh, shit," he whispered.

Too late: Teacher's shadowy face appeared, rising through the water towards him. Before he could scramble back away from the bank, Temmin found himself seized by the collar and dragged down into the pool.

He emerged into his wardrobe, a fist clenched in his shirtfront. "I wondered when I would have to cane you," said Teacher. Temmin found himself marched into the study and thrown over the back of the green velvet couch. So many hands pinned him, he knew there were none: magic pinned him. His trousers came down, as did his pants. There was a crack! A burning hot stripe of pain followed across his ass. Before he could catch his breath, five more stripes criss-crossed the first. He struggled against his restraints; his hands jerked in an involuntary attempt to protect himself. As Teacher laid the six stripes down, each worse than the last, Temmin's knees buckled, his eyes streamed, he choked and gasped and howled. For a moment, he wondered if he would vomit.

Instead, he sank to his knees in his puddled trousers as soon as the punishment ended. "Do not ever do that again," said Teacher.

"I—" Temmin gulped, "I should have—more say—in my life! I am a man!"

"Simply disappearing is the action of a boy, not a man. It is ill-mannered, impolite, and inconsiderate of the time of others. If you have a need to be elsewhere, consult me. I am not unreasonable."

"You said yourself I should choose to lead or—choose to follow, not just let myself—be lulled along!"

Teacher burst out laughing, a surprisingly high, rather unnerving chortle. "Do tell! And who lulled you into this course of action? I wonder. It is not your usual behavior at all. You would have tried to bribe me again and then accepted your fate when I refused. Someone has put something into your head. How was your day with Lord Fennows?"

By now, Temmin had risen to his feet and regained his clothing. When he could form words, he said, "Perfectly awful, thank you. He's worse than a prat. He's a little bastard who can't mount a horse without a foot-up, and even then has to be manhandled into the saddle. He thinks Papa's going to give him Elly, and by the Gods, I'll do everything I can to prevent it!" He wiped his still-dripping nose with a savage swipe of his handkerchief.

"And yet you let him goad you into disrespecting me."

"A scrub like Percet Sandopint, goad me? How can you think that?"

"The color in your face tells me everything."

"You just caned me!" Temmin cried, trying for righteous anger, but he dropped his eyes and spoiled it.

"What did Lord Fennows say?"

"…He said I wasn't a man because I haven't had a woman yet."

"Is that all?"

"He said I shouldn't let you order me around, that only boys let their tutors order them around."

"Interesting. I had no idea that is what made a man these days." Temmin glared at Teacher, and took to pacing the room, limping as he went. "I am not at all sure why you dislike me so much," said Teacher. "Please, state your grievances, and I will do my best to make amends."

Temmin stopped in his pacings and gaped. "You just caned me!" he repeated.

"You just wasted my morning," retorted Teacher. "It may surprise you, but I have other duties than your education, sir. And your distaste for me predates today. I ask in all humility, what have I done to earn your hatred?"

"Hatred? I don't hate you, honestly, I don't!" Temmin said. He ran a hand through his hair, threw his long arms open and said, "I dunno! I s'pose I'm just not used to you. You tell me disturbing stories from magic books, you pull me through ponds and I don't get wet—hang on, what about my horse?"

"Shall I pull her through, too?"

"Don't be ridiculous."

The door opened, and in came Jenks. "You're finally here, Your Highness—how did you get home? Temmin, are you all right?" exclaimed Jenks. He stepped toward his still-tear-stained charge, but stopped once he saw Teacher; they exchanged disdainful glances. "Ah—the old crow found you in the mirror?"

"Jenks, would you be able to ride my horse back home to the stables?" said Temmin. "I had to leave her—well…" How to explain why his horse was in one place and he was in another?

"And cover my riding her home how?" said the unfazed Jenks. "The stables are watching out for you, young dolt. First place I looked. Fine bit of work I'd have, coming up with a story about how you got home in under an hour without your horse!"

Temmin peered at his valet. "You don't seem terribly surprised by any of this."

"By what?" said Jenks.

"The magic…thing," Temmin finished lamely.

"I've known Teacher longer than you have," said Jenks. "You'll have to put him back, Teacher, or at least wherever that mare is. Here's hoping she hasn't wandered into the next duchy by now."

They all walked back to the wardrobe. Teacher called up the image of the mare, who had stayed where Temmin left her and was barely visible in the pool. "I'm keeping that horse," he said to himself, just before Teacher pulled him through the reflection to her side. "Come straight back, or I will cane you again," said Teacher before returning to the Keep through the pond.

Caned. He'd forgotten for a moment. He thanked Farr the mare had a smooth gait, gritted his teeth, and swung himself into the saddle.

Temmin took his meals that day standing up in his rooms. He slept on his stomach, and in the morning, skipped his ride. He made it through breakfast with the aid of a fat cushion; Jenks had discreetly tipped off Affton, and between the two of them, they'd gotten the Prince settled in the morning room without anyone in the family noticing. When he returned to his rooms, Teacher already waited, perched just outside the arc of light that crossed the wide library table. "And how was your ride this morning, Your Highness?"

"Do be quiet," said Temmin, easing himself into his chair. The sun toasted his back, and he sighed; it was the only comfortable part on him. "I didn't ride this morning and you know it."

"Oh, I did not mark you that badly. It would not hurt so much if you had not ridden home. I am hoping the time alone may have caused you to reflect on what makes a man."

"I've learned not to listen to a word Percy Sandopint says, if that's what you mean."

"If you cannot face the likes of Lord Fennows, you will have little chance standing up to anyone else."

Temmin rolled his gaze upward to meet Teacher's cold silver eyes, and wished he could find a comfortable position. "I stood up to you," he said.

"For no good reason other than petulance and pride, and it got you caned. Pick your battles more prudently, Your Highness. One day, you will stand up to me for the right reasons. That is one mark of a man." Teacher rose from the edge of desk and fetched the old red-leather-bound book.

Temmin opened it, but paused. "You asked me what I thought of Warin as a man—whether he was a good man or not. I think he was a little cowardly."

Teacher sat back down on the edge of the table, arms folded. "How so?"

"He was hiding from his brother, for one."

"It would not have been a bad reason. Hildin wanted him dead."

"So why didn't he just come through the reflection and kill him?"

"Warin was much, much stronger, both physically and in his magic. Even with Gian's help, Hildin was no match for his brother. Warin would have killed them the instant they stepped through a reflection. A public confrontation was more advantageous for Hildin."

"Then why not just get it over with if Warin was so strong, unless he was a coward? —Ow!" An unfortunately placed button on the seat cushion stabbed him as he shifted to find a less painful position.

"Because he was not hiding from his brother. We are getting ahead of ourselves, Your Highness. Please." Teacher gestured to the book with an elegant hand; Temmin gazed down into it and let the story claim him again.

On the day Warin set off for the village, the snow had nearly melted. The stream nearby roared in a thousand garbled young voices as it rushed toward the river, swollen with the snowmelt. Warin held Emmae at the door of the cottage. A week's worth of wood stood under the eaves nearby, already chopped; Warin's enormous pack sat at his feet, stuffed with pelts and forage.

"Check the fish traps, but don't get too near the banks," he instructed. "If someone comes by on the road, do your best to stay out of sight. Don't worry about me. I can take care of myself, and I'll be home soon. And don't worry about being alone," he added. "You can take care of yourself, too." He kissed her forehead.

"You've taught me how, and I hope I've been a good student," she answered, her determined face wobbling only at her lower lip and the corners of her bright blue eyes.

"The best of students," he said, kissing her again. "You are my brave girl. You came to me brave, and it will serve you better than anything I've taught you." Emmae helped him shoulder his heavy pack; he bent nearly double, even as strong as he was, but straightened, found his balance, and took his leave.

She watched him down the trail. Two days to walk there, two days to trade, two days to walk back. She stood in the doorway, growing cold, until she could no longer see him. She shut the door against the early morning chill, and sat crying near the fire until she stopped shivering.

When her tears ended, she set to work on her chores. By the middle of the day, she had run out of things to do; she picked up the forgotten tray by the cupboard, shining it until she could see herself clearly—a very young woman in a gray wool dress, thick brown hair beneath a plain linen kerchief, round chin smudged with tarnish from the tray. Was that what she looked like? She rubbed at the smudge and wondered if she was pretty. She set the tray beside the hearth. That night, Emmae watched her own reflection in it, to keep her company as she sewed. The banked coals flickered across the surface of the silver just before she closed her eyes and went to sleep, alone in the big new bed.

They came for Emmae the next morning.

She returned to the cottage from the stream with water for the day, to find a blonde, lithe young man in elegant clothes standing near the hearth. He turned away from the fire, and said, "Hello, pretty girl. Don't be afraid, we won't hurt you."

Emmae dropped the bucket; the water beaded on the floor. She heard Warin's voice in her memories: *Run, run and hide.* She backed out the door, but when she turned to run, she found her wrists trapped in the hands of another man—a taller, older, darker man. Warin? No, but so alike: the same angular face and lean body, the same dark hair and eyes, though this man's eyes shone hard, like wet stone.

"I would never hurt a little friend of my brother's, quite the contrary," smiled the man. "Little friend—wife? No, I think not." He held her wrists lightly, but when she tried to pull away from him, his grip tightened and his smile grew. A horrible warmth spread through her, just as it had when she met Warin; her joints loosened, and a flush built in her cheeks. The man walked her backwards into the cottage, into the arms of his companion, who held her firm. A second, confusing fire woke within her, her body responding against her will to these strange, frightening men. Panic and desire spiraled inside her, forcing tears down her face and shortening her breath.

"Don't cry, pretty girl," said the older man. He wiped a tear from her cheek, and tasted it. "Gian, I believe she's enchanted. She tastes of magic. Try her." The younger man's tongue licked her neck; a gasp escaped before she could swallow it.

"I believe you are correct, Your Highness," said the fair one.

"Magic? I have no magic. Please, let me go," she pleaded.

"A Leutish accent! Oh, how charming—irresistible, really," smiled the dark one. "My dear, I have enough magic for the two of us. Not as much as your lover, but then, he is the Heir. I'm only his brother. Poor girl, did he put a spell on you? I'm very disappointed in my brother."

"How could Warin put a spell on me?" cried Emmae. "He wouldn't even if he could!" The blond young man chuckled and nibbled on her shoulder; her eyelids fluttered and she pressed herself into him reflexively.

"So very sure of him. Who are you, sweetheart? How did you come here?" said the dark one, turning her head this way and that.

"I—I don't know…"

The strange man slipped his hands round her waist and pulled her closer.

Had the two men not held Emmae up, she knew her legs would have folded in unwanted, humiliating desire. She sobbed in shame, and the dark one swallowed her cries as he kissed her; the light one's hands closed on her breasts as he sucked at her neck. And then a strange lassitude came over her: shame, desire, resistance, all slipped away into an uncaring, sleepy fog. The last thing she saw before she slept was a silver ring on her finger that hadn't been there before. "Warin said he would bring me a ring," she murmured to herself, and she fell into unconsciousness.

"That's better," said Hildin. "Usually I enjoy it when they struggle, but not when I'm taking them through a mirror. That ring does come in handy."

Gian hoisted the sleeping girl into his arms, and whistled low. "So she's enchanted! How could that be, my Lord?"

"I have an idea," grinned Hildin. "If I'm right, it's a rare thing." He snatched a flame from the fire, fashioned it into a wand, and wrote a message on the table top. The letters smoked, then faded into a soft, golden glow. Hildin returned the wand to the fire, and walked to the tray; he took Gian by the elbow, and the three of them swirled into the reflection.

In a room above the Prince's own chambers stood a small cheval glass. It reflected stone walls covered in tapestries, and no apparent door; the still-weak spring sun struggled through the slats of shutters over a small window, streaking the surface of the mirror with light. The reflection shivered; the interior of a small cottage appeared, and Hildin stepped through, pulling Gian and the girl behind him.

Hildin yanked open the curtains of a capacious bed. Gian set the girl in the middle of it, and hurried to turn the cheval glass to the wall. "Be sure you get rid of that, and make sure anything my brother might use to see into the Keep is covered," said Hildin. "I want him returning on my terms." Hildin sat down on the bed, and smoothed the girl's hair away from her face. She slept on, her pink lips parted. He ran a thumb over them, and she gave a tiny sigh; her head lolled toward him, but she didn't awaken. "Father is failing—I'm likely to be king soon," he said. "I should hate for Warin to show up before the coronation."

"Will Teacher recognize you after His Majesty dies, though?" said Gian, perched on the other side of the bed.

Hildin shrugged, and let his fingers wander across the girl's cheekbones, down her neck, to the laces of her bodice. He pulled a short, jeweled dagger from his belt. "I don't know," he said. He cut the laces and spread the bodice open. He untied the chemise underneath and pushed it down, exposing the girl's breasts. He took one in his hand, and weighed it thoughtfully. "It's why I haven't minded being Regent. As Regent, Teacher must obey me—it was my father's last coherent order. But once the King dies, I'll just have to kill Warin, won't I? I gain the throne, the royal magic, and Teacher's obedience, willing or no." Hildin pinched the girl's nipple. Her back arched, and she moaned in her sleep.

Gian chewed on his lower lip, never taking his eyes off the hand on the breast. "Warin's evaded you all these years," he said. "Why would he let you find him now?"

"This." Hildin smiled, a pleased, savage slash filled with sharp, brilliant teeth, a smile that always frightened Gian into loving him even more. Hildin took up the dagger again and sliced the waistband of the girl's skirt. He put the dagger between his teeth and ripped the skirt to its hem, then used the blade to cut open her chemise. Hildin pushed the ruined clothes aside, and skimmed his hand down her belly to the hair between her legs. "We have her. Would you leave such a woman to a brother you despised?"

Gian wouldn't leave her to a beloved brother, let alone a despised one. Downy, ivory skin blushed rosy across full breasts; rounded hips invited his hand, though he didn't dare touch her until Hildin said he could. "So you think he'll come for her."

"I know he will. All this beauty, and enchanted in some way." Hildin slipped a finger inside her. He chuckled low in his chest. "Oh, perhaps enchanted *this* way, boy, else she's a spectacular slut. She's very needy of attention, let's say." He removed his wet finger and thrust it into Gian's mouth. Gian closed his eyes and sucked it clean, rolling her sweet, musky taste on his tongue; it sparked with the familiar charge of magic. Hildin withdrew it. Gian let out a gasp, and craned his neck toward his master. Hildin laughed, and kissed him, short and biting.

"She still tastes of magic, and not just the sleeping spell, my lord," said Gian when he found his voice again. He looked at her again; on her left hip glowed a familiar sigil, traced in silver. "She bears the Traveler Queen's mark!"

"So she does," smiled Hildin. "How thoughtful of her to make sure my brother didn't get her with child in all his rutting. But soon it will wear off, and we'll present her to him with my child in her belly instead. No," he continued, "there's no doubt who cast the spell. That old bitch is the only one who could have done it, whatever it is." He snatched a flame from the small fire burning in the hearth, lengthened it into a wand, and traced figures in the air over the bed. They glowed gold, until the answer came in silver. Hildin shook his head. "It's certainly hers, but I can't read it all. A kindling spell—sensation, or emotion." He dismissed the wand back into the fire. "Let's ask Warin's little friend." Hildin slipped the ring from the girl's finger, and her eyelids flickered open.

Temmin withdrew his hands from the book, and struggled to free himself from its spell; pain had called him out of the story. "I can't sit any more," he groaned. "I have to stand up!"

"We can discuss things standing up," said Teacher, rising in sympathy.

Temmin's heart still beat hard with Emmae's terror; the knife slicing through her chemise; the taste of magic and sex on Gian's tongue. All of it mixed together in a red confusion of horror, arousal, and the ache in his bottom. Temmin stood slowly, and braced himself on the table until he felt confident of his feet; his breathing slowed, and he took to walking in slow circles around the table. He worked to sort his own emotions from those of Emmae and Gian. "When will it stop hurting?" he murmured.

"In the morning it will be a distant memory. Though after riding tomorrow, the memory may return."

"It's not just the stripes." He changed the pattern of his steps, walking in a slow circuit from Teacher at the one end to the wall of bookcases on the other. Temmin focused his mind on the magic to distract himself both from his excitement and his pain. He'd never seen one of his ancestors perform this much magic, though he wondered if many times great-uncles were ancestors. "Let me see if I understand magic correctly," Temmin said. "At one time, the royal family could control flame—make things out of it; they could use reflections like you do; if they wanted to, they could chop wood without an axe; they could read other people's spells; and they could put people to sleep?"

"And much more," said Teacher. "But the last is women's magic. Men's magic controls the inanimate—wood, fire, stone, metal, water, even the air —anything that is not alive, even if it was once alive. But it cannot control a person."

"Nonsense!" said Temmin, with an accusatory glance. "You held me over the couch yesterday with magic."

"Did you feel a need to be over the couch? An inward compulsion?"

"Certainly not!"

Teacher pushed out a hand, as if commanding Temmin to stop, and said, "Keep walking toward me, Your Highness."

Puzzled, Temmin continued in his track, until he walked straight into an invisible wall. "Fuck!" he yelled through the hands cupping his nose. "Pagg damn it, are you trying to kill me?" He removed his hands, examining them for blood; there was none. He prodded gingerly at his nose, to find it unbroken. He sighed in relief. It would have been horrible to greet Allis with a broken nose. He pinched it in hopes of dulling the pain. "Please excuse my language, but that hurt," he honked. "What did you do?"

"I made the air stand still," said Teacher. "That is all I did yesterday. Air pinned you to the couch. That is the difference between men's magic and women's magic. Women's magic would have compelled you inwardly, coerced your body into doing what the enchantress wished you to do, if she were powerful enough. I simply held you down. Further." Teacher pulled a handkerchief from one pocket, dipped it in a water pitcher on the library table, wrung it out and handed it to Temmin. "Freeze." It stiffened with frost. "Now," said Teacher, "Apply that to your nose to keep it from swelling. It will stay cold as long as needed. I do not think your nose will bruise."

Temmin kept pacing. "What a charming demonstration," he said, holding the frozen handkerchief to his nose.

"You will not forget it. That is the charm," said Teacher.

"Thank you ever so. If that's how it works, how was Hildin able to put Emmae to sleep? That ring? You just said men couldn't do things like that."

"Let us say the ring's manufacture was a collaborative effort."

"Could the royal women do magic as well?" he said. He imagined his sisters with women's magic. Ellika would make everyone throw parties. Sedra would—what would Sedra do? Make everyone talk politics?

"Women have not had magic for nearly a thousand years," said Teacher.

"One did—that Traveler woman," said Temmin. He shifted the icy handkerchief on his nose.

"She is the only one. She has it all now. She—" Teacher gasped, and clutched the table's edge.

Temmin strode across the room, dropping the handkerchief. "Teacher! Are you ill? Let me call for a Sister!" He took Teacher round the waist; his tutor leaned on him for only a moment before standing more firmly. Teacher waved Temmin off.

"No, no, there is nothing a Sister can do for me, now or ever. I am all right." Teacher paused, and straightened the robes set askew in Temmin's attempts to help. "There are things I am prevented from telling you until you are king. I came too close to those forbidden subjects, I fear."

"It hurts you?"

"Oh, yes."

Temmin put one hand on Teacher's shoulder. He put Teacher in the same class as Jenks and his father: invulnerable. What could possibly hurt any of them? "Who does this to you, Teacher? And why?"

"Among the forbidden subjects, Your Highness. Now," said Teacher, moving out of sympathy's reach, "we are done for today. You have an engagement tomorrow to prepare for, and a little more time on your feet will allow you to ride comfortably, I am sure."

"May I ask you one thing? Nothing forbidden, I hope," said Temmin.

"I hope so, too," said Teacher with a small smile. "What is it?"

Temmin put his palms on the table top and leaned forward. "Tell me what Allis likes!" he said. "I'm thinking of a picnic, up in the foothills—well, maybe not so high as all that—"

"Liable to encourage bad memories," agreed Teacher.

"—and I'm wondering what she might like," said Temmin, ignoring the jab. "Little sandwiches with the crust cut off, I expect? Those teeny cakes with the frosting all over them? I don't know what girls like!"

"A healthy young woman like Allis likes food, Your Highness, especially after a ride. I suggest cold chicken, bread, fruit, wine, cheeses—"

"That can't be right, it sounds like what I'd eat."

"Women are not a different species, Your Highness. Perhaps lighter in appetite, but that depends on the woman. Leave it to Mr Jenks and I am sure it will go splendidly. Food is hardly the issue, though, is it?"

"No, I s'pose not," said Temmin.

Fennows drove "the issue" home throughout dinner, making innuendo after smirking innuendo about tomorrow's ride until even

Harsin had enough. Nevertheless, the King took his own chance, closeted with Temmin after dinner. "You're not still thinking about going to the Lovers, are you?" he said, and then proceeded to pepper Temmin with all the reasons why he couldn't. The nobility wouldn't like it. His mother wouldn't like it. His virginity was an embarrassment at his age. He'd be cheek by jowl with commoners. And on, and on.

Temmin's courage ebbed, but he said only, "We're going riding, Papa. I haven't committed to anything. I'm just going riding with a pretty girl."

"Why this one? There are pretty girls a-plenty in the City. You don't have to go looking in the Temple. You saw no one at the balls you've been to? No, I suppose you didn't. I've heard nothing but complaints about your rudeness, staring at the Embodiment like a clodhopper come to town."

Both men stood. Pick your battles, Temmin remembered. May as well start with this one. "I'm going riding with Allis Obby, sir. That's all." He noticed he looked his father in the eye; Harsin was only a hair's breadth taller than he was, now. "Good night, Papa," he said, and turned to go.

"Wait," said Harsin. He took Temmin's face in his hands, and, to Temmin's surprise, kissed each cheek. "Good night, son," he said. "I just want you to think on these things, and make what you know is—what must be—the only right decision."

"I will think on it, Papa," said Temmin. "After I spend a day alone with Allis," he added to himself as he walked back to his rooms.

EIGHT

On Neyaday morning, Temmin skipped his ride. For one, he wanted Jebby to be fresh, and for another, he wanted to give what saddle time his poor bottom would allow to Allis. He would have her all to himself for an afternoon. What would happen once he had her all to himself, he didn't know.

Jenks and Affton made the preparations. A picnic would await them in the Fairy Meadow, not as high in the foothills as Temmin had ridden two days previous, but high enough to afford a lovely view of the City from the comfortable shade of an Inchari-style tent pavillion: opulent carpets, enormous pillows, a low table, and no chairs. Temmin himself found the Inchari style of dining fussy and overly exotic, a decadent, indulgent byproduct of the southern continent's laxity of character and oppressive heat. But with Allis to impress, every luxury the Keep could produce must be brought to bear. All Temmin had to do was show up, and not make a fool of himself.

Given his way, Jenks dressed his charge with a savage fervor, assembling and re-assembling until he found his ultimate combination: a fine dark gray riding suit tailored to a knife's edge, its cutaway coat graced with a black velvet collar; black riding boots so polished Temmin briefly worried Teacher might spy on him through their reflections; a light gray waistcoat patterned with the sigil of the Lovers' Temple—would Allis notice? She seemed to notice everything. Small sapphires winked at his cuffs, a matching stickpin in his simple, dark blue cravat. Gray gloves, a low black riding hat: on the whole, an impression of complete confidence.

"This is why I keep you around, Jenks," said Temmin as he examined himself in the mirror. "I look as if I know what I'm doing!"

"Now you know why the Cavalry is so particular about clothing," said Jenks, beaming. "Looking as if you've already won is half the battle, we say. Now, off with you. Staff will be waiting for you in the Fairy Meadow."

Temmin bounded out of his study, straight into his last obstacle: his mother, or at least his mother's representative in the form of her personal attendant and dresser. Miss Hanston brought Her Majesty's compliments, and would His Highness please accompany her to the Queen's apartments? Temmin blew a breath out in dismay, but trailed dutifully after her. Looking for clues in Hanston's demeanor was pointless; when it came to anyone's dealings with her mistress, she radiated the disapproving protectiveness people showed when a careless child entered a porcelain seller's shop, or when a too-jolly uncle picked up a newborn baby. No one was careful enough with Her Majesty—not even Her Majesty's son—and Hanston wasn't having it.

Hanston ushered Temmin into his mother's private sitting room. The dresser's face broke into soft, doughy benevolence as she announced him to Ansella, and puckered into hard folds again as she gave Temmin a glance that said, "You break her, my boy, and you'll have me to pay."

Ansella put down her teacup, patted the couch cushion beside her, and took his hand as he sat. As soon as the alternately scowling and beaming Hanston left the room, she said, "I know you're hurrying off, Temmy. But I never see you now except at mealtimes, and often not even then. We're both so busy here—I was afraid this would happen." She studied an arrangement of tulips on a nearby console, blood red in the soft cream and blue sitting room, and sighed. "I wanted to speak to you as your mother about your pursuit of Allis Obby," she continued.

"Oh Gods, Mama," he groaned. "I'm just going riding with a pretty girl. I haven't committed to anything at all," he recited.

"She's not a 'pretty girl,' Temmy. It's very wrong of you to call her that," chided Ansella. "You should refer to her as the Holy One, or Miss Obby at worst! I know you haven't committed to anything, sweetheart. But your father is quite adamant that you have nothing to do with the Lovers' Temple until you're…older."

"He can't keep me from doing it."

"No, and he shouldn't."

Temmin raised his brows in surprise. "Are you saying I should chase the Lovers?"

"I can't go that far," said Ansella.

Her face bore a troubled look, and he said, "Would it make you so very unhappy?"

"No!" she said, her face clearing. "No, it wouldn't make me unhappy at all. To have a child of mine called by the Gods? Nothing would make me prouder, even if it is the Lovers and not my own Venna. Your father believes in the Gods, but only because as king he's…he's seen things. I believe because I want to, I believe with all my heart, and always have since I was a small child. Ib—*Sister* Ibbit," she stumbled, "advises me you should not chase Them. You know how much she disapproves of the Lovers, strongly disapproves."

"She disapproves of everything," muttered Temmin.

"I share her disapproval, if not to her degree. But if They want you…I won't tell you to chase Them, but I certainly won't tell you *not* to chase Them."

"Papa didn't ask you to talk me out of it?"

Ansella put her hand over Temmin's. "Oh, of course he did. I told him what I'm telling you…more or less. Your father has his reasons for disliking this, and so do I. But my concern for you is greater than my dislike of the Lovers." She rose, pulling her son with her. "Temmy, you are my youngest," she said, bringing her soft little hands to his face; they smelled of mint-and-chamomile tea. "You are my baby, my only boy. I have to give my girls away. You're the only one I get to keep. I wanted you to stay the same sweet boy you've always been, and so I kept women out of your way."

"What?" he said.

"But if you must go with women," she said in a rush, "this is the best way. Oh, please don't tell your father what I'm saying! But it's true. I would rather see you safely and honorably with the Lovers, than see you dallying with loose women, keeping mistresses, whoring all over the countryside, endangering your children, bringing shame on us, siring bastards on housemaids in my own house—!"

Temmin said nothing. His mother's unintentionally comic tirades against unseen women of dubious virtue were often sources of private amusement for her children. But he'd never connected these tirades with his father. How many mistresses did his father have, he wondered now—how many illegitimate children besides Mattie? Should he worry about sons? "Marriage isn't always a happy ending," Teacher had said.

These thoughts showed in Temmin's face, and Ansella stopped, her face guilty. She recovered herself with difficulty, and resumed, "You know how much I've always hated it that Elly chose the Lovers—"

"Mama, she only goes to Temple but once a year."

"—But you're a man, and you will do what men do, and I'd rather you do it in an honorable way. Your people will be able to look on you with pride, your wife will be able to look on you with pride, I will be able to look on you with pride!" She broke off, choking down a sob.

Temmin took her hands in consternation. "Do I need to call for Hanston?"

"Oh, no, no!" she said. She dropped his hands, fished a handkerchief out of her pocket, and wiped her eyes. "Don't do that or neither one of us will hear the end of it. I'm sorry, sweetheart, your interest in…in women is a milestone I've been dreading. I'm feeling it too greatly," she said. "Go on your ride. Decide for yourself what you will do. And if your father asks if I talked with you, try not to tell him exactly what I said." He left her sitting on the couch again, eyes closed and looking as fragile as the teacup in her hand.

Temmin left his mother's rooms, so deep in thought he barely looked up until he took to the stairs leading down into the family's informal entrance to the Keep, Harsin's sigil in gold inlay upon the huge doors. He wanted to dirty it with soot. How could the King have hurt her so? How could Harsin prefer any other woman to her? She was kind and beautiful, she was cheerful and loving; she was his Mama, and how could any man be cruel to her? The footmen took one look at his scowl and swept the doors open just a little faster than usual, not a ripple of interest on their professionally still faces.

A groom held Jebby's bridle; the big chestnut pawed in good-natured boredom at the fine gravel beneath his hooves. Temmin's anger swerved to apprehensive excitement. He mounted and rode down the switchbacks and the long, long drive to the massive gates at the entrance to the grounds. There he waited, silently rehearsing a little greeting meant to sound nonchalant and sophisticated. "How terribly good of you to come, Miss Obby, or should I say, Holy One, ha ha." No, that didn't sound right...

He stood there only a short while before the heavy stomp of the King's Guard announced someone of importance. The gates shivered as the guardsmen loosed the bolts; they swung inward on silent hinges. The enormous archway framed Allis, astride a delicate black mare with a white blaze on its nose. She turned toward her escort, two Brothers with white swan feathers added to the red horsetails on their helmets, dismissed them with a nod, and walked her mare up the drive. Few women rode so straight-backed and effortless—born to horseback, he thought. A fleeting impression of his mother's skill with horses came to mind and he dismissed it.

Temmin had only seen Allis in formal dress; now she wore a lilac riding suit, much more to his liking than yards and yards of silk. A close-fitting jacket topped a divided skirt; some sort of lace frothed at her throat. She wore her thick black hair coiled beneath a neat gray riding hat—he preferred it down, but what a nuisance on a ride that would be.

She reached him. Dazzled, he forgot to take her hand until she said, "Your Highness," and smiled.

"Miss—Holy One," he stammered as he took her hand at last. He lost the sophisticated little speech and settled for "How are you?"

"No one could be anything but fine on such a splendid day!" said Allis, her smile once again covering him in a foggy euphoria. "Shall we?"

"Oh—yes!" said Temmin, recovering some of his wits. They walked the horses down the drive, taking the road that led up the shallower slope to the stables; the stable hands loitered near the outskirts of the yard with feigned indifference. "Ain't she sumpin!" said a boy in an awed stage whisper, only to have the nearest groom knock his cap off his head.

Temmin responded to Allis's remarks on the weather, his parents' health, and the upcoming Neya's Day ball in happy monosyllables. "Ah— here is the War Road, Holy One. Have you ever ridden it?"

"This is the first unofficial visit I've ever made to the Keep," she said, as they moved from the fine gravel of the drive onto the packed dirt of the War Road into the King's Woods. "Jinny is anxious to stretch her legs, sir, and so—" Off she went at a gallop.

Temmin watched her ride off, wondering if she'd picked the little mare herself. A discerning eye, if so. Such easy communication with the horse, he hadn't seen her tap her heels or anything, and off she'd gone, riding as if someone were chasing her—oh!

He gave Jebby a little swat with the ends of the reins and called out, "Gidyap, Jeb!" The big horse snorted. Letting a snip of a mare outstrip him was unacceptable, and Jebby ran to catch her up. But Allis sensed them coming, and the mare picked up her pace. Soon, they both ran flat-out. But Jebby's stride made nearly two of Jinny's, and soon Jebby ran beside her. Allis reined in, her cheeks flushed and her eyes bright with excitement. They were well down the War Road now, the horses' hooves sending up the sweet, head-clearing scent of crushed cedar.

"How long have you been riding, Miss Obby? You ride extremely well," said Temmin.

"I did ask you to call me Allis," she replied. "Since we came to the Temple, about eight years ago. We didn't live there then—we didn't come to live at the Temple until we turned eighteen, of course. But we were given a very thorough education at the Mother's House where we lived. Lovers and Beloveds came to tutor us, and Teacher, too. That included riding lessons, and they were always my favorite. Teacher gave me Jinny when we took up the Gods last year."

"He told me the three of you are very close."

She slipped into a minute, inward melancholy, but quickly recovered herself to sparkle at him again. He dimly realized her seductive demeanor was in part a facade before she gazed up at him through her dark lashes and the realization left his head. "I do love to ride, and I have few opportunities," she said. "Thank you so very much for this invitation. Issak loves to ride as much as I do. At the risk of presumption, perhaps you might invite him some day? These are such beautiful woods, he would treasure time spent in them."

"I would very much enjoy hosting both of you," faltered Temmin. Issak still confused him. He'd never thought of himself as a lover of men, Alvo notwithstanding, but when Issak looked at him, he felt exposed and unable to resist. He thought of Emmae, and wondered if he too were enchanted. "Do you know anything about magic?" he blurted.

"I'm sorry?" said Allis. "Magic?"

"Never mind, forget I said anything," winced Temmin.

"Nothing beyond fairy tales," she continued. "I suppose one might consider being an Embodiment to be a form of magic. You do realize what being an Embodiment entails, don't you?"

"Well, yes, of course, you take on the Gods at the Spectacles, but surely it's just a mask, you're just—" He stopped himself in time to avoid the word "pretending." Aloud, he said, "I've never been to any Temple's Spectacle in the City—the ones with an Embodiment in attendance," he said cautiously. "I imagine there's more to it than I know."

Her face grew serious, brows together. "There are those who imagine what happens at the Spectacles is play-acting. That all of the Embodiments merely impersonate the Gods when They take us—when They *allegedly* take us. That Issak and I are simply acting out the passion of the Lovers, as if we were performing on a stage at a bawdy house. I imagine you've heard it all. That is far, far from the case. There is no pretending. The Gods possess us. We have no control over our bodies whatsoever when They take us. If puppets had thoughts, they'd be very much like mine at those times, I suppose." She sighed. "It's not an easy thing, but it is also a glorious thing."

"As if we were performing in a bawdy house," Temmin repeated to himself, with the same disgust and arousal as he'd had the first time he'd heard what Allis and Issak did on Neya's Day. His face must have betrayed his thoughts, for Allis drew herself up even further. "I believe you have a question for me, Temmin," she said in a challenging tone.

"A question? I don't think so," said Temmin, dropping his reins. Jebby came to a halt, and turned his massive head to eye his nervous master.

Temmin picked up the reins, and Jebby sauntered away down the Road, until Allis suddenly sped up and wheeled Jinny around to block Temmin's way. "I said, ask your question, Prince Temmin."

Teacher had said Temmin might ask Allis anything, anything at all, but this was far too embarrassing to contemplate so soon into the ride. "I hadn't intended to ask you anything, Holy One," he said, echoing her formal tone, "until perhaps we'd gotten to know one another better—"

"Ask your question!" she repeated, still blocking the Road.

"Very well, then!" he said. "Do you—have you—what is the nature of your relationship with your brother?"

The high, cheerful murmur of birds suspended, waiting expectantly for her answer. Then she smiled, and Temmin heard the birds sing again. "Was it really so hard?"

"Yes, in fact, it was," he said, with an exasperated grunt. "Forgive me, I'm not used to such frank conversation with a young lady like you."

"You are completely forgiven. And there are no young ladies like me." She unblocked the Road, and they resumed their walk. Allis held the reins loosely in her hand. "Such a lovely wood," she murmured, and said no more.

Temmin waited as long as he could, and then said, "Well?"

"Well, what?"

"What is the nature of the relationship between you and your brother?"

"Later," she said, urging her mare into a trot. "The question weighed on you. You needed to let it go!" She gave a whoop, and cantered off down the path. Temmin swore under his breath, and rode after her.

As they climbed into the lower foothills, Temmin showed her all his favorite places: a fine white waterfall misting into a pool so clear they could see every smooth, amber rock on its bottom; maidenhair ferns, frothing in thick, green waves through the underbrush; and a grove of ancient, towering hemlocks, their roots arched and gnarled. "Some say these trees are as old as the Keep—older," said Temmin as they rode past.

The horses moved out of the trees, into the sloping, sunny clearing called the Fairy Meadow. The rivers' confluence lay spread below them, where the Feather let itself be swallowed up by the Shadow before it continued on its way south to the sea.

The tent pavilion stood open to the view, with the Inchari-style picnic within. Allis pronounced it elegant, charming and original, and let him hand her down from Jinny's back as soon as he dismounted himself. Two grooms appeared and led the horses off to crop the grass elsewhere. Temmin took Allis's hand and led her into the pavilion.

A brazier sat by the low table, to keep tea water hot and to dispel any nip that might still be in the air, even on a sunny day. "How pleasant! It's warm enough today to take off one's coat. With your permission?" Allis shed her gloves, coat and hat, and as Temmin removed his own, she arranged herself gracefully into the enormous pile of pillows by the table.

Temmin had never noticed the way a woman's riding costume hinted at the outlines of legs and hips usually hidden beneath layers of skirts and petticoats, perhaps because the only women he'd ridden with were Mama and the girls. He roused himself from his stare, took his place beside her, and poured them each a glass of pale spring wine: "An '88 Bordigalle, pressed on a crown estate, Holy One," said Temmin, dredging up what Jenks had told him in preparation for the lunch.

"Your father was gracious enough to send several dozen cases of the '87 to us at the Temple," said Allis after a sip. "I daresay this is even better. Was last year a kind one for the grapes in Bordigalle? I know our Temples throughout Belleth reported it a most happy summer generally, but I confess I don't know how Bordigalle in particular fared."

Temmin had reached the end of his knowledge of both Bordigallian wine and weather, and so changed the subject. "How long have you and your brother served as Embodiments?" he said, piling her plate with enough to feed every mouth in the Temple.

The corners of Allis's mouth twitched as she took the heaping plate from him. "A year this Neya's Day. Are you very familiar with Temple practices?"

"No," he admitted. "I'm afraid I'm not terribly devout. I make the rounds at the Spectacles every year, say the blessings for my sisters on Nerr's Day, my mother on Amma's Day and father on Pagg's Day and so on —and I must add I haven't been to Neya's Day," he blushed.

"Ah?"

Temmin looked down into his wine. "I can't, yet. I imagine you've heard I qualify to be a Supplicant," he said, and finished off the glass. "But even if I didn't," he resumed, "my mother does not approve of the Neya's Day observances, though I imagine they're different here in the City."

"My brother and I are here. That's the only real difference," she said. "Why doesn't your mother approve? I thought the Queen was among the faithful."

"Oh, she is! She more than makes the rounds. We said our prayers every night: '*Amma as we fall asleep/We give to You our souls to keep/Please keep the Dark One from our door/And we'll be Yours forevermore.*'" Temmin smiled, remembering cozy nights in the nursery, but frowned as he thought of Sister Ibbit's ascendancy in the household. "That stopped after Mama devoted to Venna, and her spiritual advisor became such a fixture. She practically lived with us."

"You didn't care for her?"

"She didn't care for me! She avoided me as much as possible, which was fine with me. I don't think she likes men—she didn't seem to mind the girls, and was always bothering Sedra to become a devotee of Venna. She told Mama that Venna is the enemy of the Lovers—all Her Brothers, actually, and Her Father—and that illness results from 'indulgence in the senses,' which I suppose means enjoying yourself." Temmin filled a plate for himself, swallowed half a ham sandwich whole, and said, "Listen to this: Sister Ibbit told me once that Venna the Sister hates anything to do with men, and that all men were evil boys at heart. But then, she'd just caught me stealing all the sugar cubes from Mama's tea tray. Elly put me up to it," he added defensively.

"Ah, Sister Ibbit. I know of her." Allis shifted on the pillows. "What do you think of what Ibbit says?"

Temmin shrugged. "I'm not very devout, but I know enough. It all sounded like nonsense to me, and Mama told me later I wasn't evil and Ibbit was in a bad mood. She's in a bad mood a lot."

"It's more than a 'bad mood.' Sister Ibbit's mentor was a Sister named Anniki of Litta, who preached that men and women should lead separate lives but for the necessary—rare—getting of children. The Sisters convicted her of heresy some twenty years ago. Poisoned her, of course. Ibbit leads that faction now. She's been very careful to stay within Pagg's Law in public," Allis said, half to herself, "but if she's teaching Her Majesty lies like that..." She stopped with a little laugh, and said, "Enough of Temple politics. I collect your religious education has been neglected?"

He winced. "I didn't know what a Supplicant was."

Allis held out a plate. "This is a wonderfully tender chicken, have you tried it?" Temmin gratefully took both the chicken and the change in subject, and they ate with a minimum of small talk.

"This is a splendid picnic, Temmin, thank you so very much," she said at last. She wiped her lips, Temmin following the napkin's course with his eyes. "Returning to earlier conversation, as we must," she said, "if your religious fervor is tepid, why are you here with me?"

"Truthfully? You're a beautiful girl. But I've seen a lot of beautiful girls since I came here. Every ball I go to, they're everywhere. They throw themselves at me. There's even this girl at the Keep..." Arta twirled through his mind's eye and out of sight. "I met you at my ball," he resumed, "and I haven't stopped thinking of you since. It's more than how beautiful you are, there's something about *you*." He sat up straighter. "I could make up some nonsense about religious devotion, but you'd see through it. And I don't want to make up nonsense. I feel...I feel as if I can trust you."

Her face softened. "You can. And I applaud your candor. Most men try to impress me with their piety. So. You're considering chasing us. Do you understand what happens if we let you catch us?"

"Not really, no. All I've heard is it's some sort of elevated postulancy, which doesn't make sense for me."

"Not all Supplicants join the Temple. The women may marry well—marrying a Lovers' Temple Supplicant is an honor. We get few men, and the ones we get usually become Lovers. But there are many examples of male Supplicants going on to great things, especially in business and politics. A few hundred years ago, one went on to become a Brother—very unusual for a Supplicant to leave one Temple and join another, but it does happen. He rose to be Eldest Brother. They say he read his opponents so well, they surrendered before he ever drew his sword. You might agree these would be handy skills for a king, even though kings seldom take the field now."

Temmin pondered this. It made a good argument for his father. "What would I learn—apart from the obvious, I mean."

"'The obvious?' Here's your first lesson for today," she said, leaning forward. "Call things by their names. What is 'the obvious?'"

"Well…it's the obvious at your Temple, isn't it…sex."

Allis leaned back against the pillows, amused. "You're very sweet when you blush. Do you know how many male potential Supplicants have approached the Temple in the last ten years? None." At Temmin's almost angry grimace, she added, "There's no shame in being a virgin—we're all born one, aren't we? Come, sit next to me and tell me how much experience you do have. I need to hear it all."

"Everything?" he squeaked. She nodded, and patted the cushions beside her. He laid down next to her and stared up at the pavilion ceiling, made of midnight blue silk sprinkled with stars. "Most of 'em were with the other stable boys, when I was younger. Mostly games—seeing whose was biggest, a little kissing, that sort of thing. I just thought of it as something to do until girls came along, whenever that was going to be."

"You didn't know any girls?"

Temmin shook his head. "Not really, apart from my sisters. We had a few dances at the Estate, but it was when I was a boy. They were small and usually just included our cousins. Not many other young people. And then, just as I was getting interested in girls, Ibbit showed up and Mama stopped throwing any dances at all. It drove Elly mad!"

"Maidservants?"

"All of them ancient. It's as if there was a girl-proof barricade around me!" he complained.

Allis shifted slightly on the cushions, thoughtful and amused. "And did any of your stable companions go beyond play? An emotional attachment, perhaps?"

Temmin turned toward her. "If one did, am I still a virgin?"

"For our purposes, virginity is linked with the opposite sex. Go on."

He settled back down on the pillows again, and thought about what to say. An emotional attachment… "My best friend," he finally said. "Alvo.

We've known each other all our lives. He's a groom. I tried to bring him here with me, but Papa wouldn't let me. Told me grooms aren't friends, they're servants." He lapsed into a disturbed silence.

"What happened?" Allis prompted.

"The last night we had together, we were drinking in the stable yard by ourselves. There was this girl." Mattie filled his mind's eye, so pink and white in the dark green hedge. He couldn't tell Allis Mattie was his half-sister; he was too ashamed, and he worried she would interpret his embarrassment as a comment on her relationship with her brother. "There was this girl. We caught her in the hedge with her sweetheart. He ran away, and I thought, here's my chance. Here's this girl, she's half-undressed, she obviously likes that sort of thing, was the kind of girl who did that sort of thing, I thought, why not? She seemed willing enough, at least she didn't say no. Now I think she did, though. Just not out loud. I've learned things since then. I don't think she could say no, even though she wanted to. I think maybe being a servant is like being enchanted."

Allis gave him a bemused smile. "I'm afraid I'm at a loss—enchanted?"

"Never mind. In any event, I kissed her. But I'd had a lot to drink—a lot. Just before I threw up, I thought maybe she didn't like it, but I assumed I wasn't doing it right or something. I don't know," he shrugged. He hadn't said Mattie was his half-sister, and yet he still felt ashamed.

"And this other girl, at the Keep?"

"I'm not done. The girl I kissed had barely left when Alvo went crazy or something. Or always was crazy. He told me he loved me. I mean, loved me as more than a friend. He ended up...I let him kiss me. I s'pose I kissed him back, I don't know, and then he begged me..."

"There's no shame in making love with another man," murmured Allis.

"No," said Temmin, "no, that's not it. I never thought of Alvo that way, not really, and then he got down on his knees...and he begged to take me in his mouth, and before I really understood what was happening, he was doing it, he—it was incredible, his mouth felt so..." He looked up at her, tears pricking his eyes. "It's so damn confusing! He's my best friend!"

"Friends sometimes make the best lovers," she said, taking his hand.

"Yes, but it was the first time he'd even brought it up!"

"He told you over and over, I'd wager, just not out loud. Think back, and you may find dozens of times he told you without saying a word. One thing we can teach you is to see all of the ways people talk to us without saying a word." At his blank look, she continued, "How do you feel about him now?"

"I don't know. I'm as confused as I was then. I still love him, but I don't know if I love him the way he loves me."

He made to sit up, but she pulled his head onto her lap and gently stroked his hair. "That's enough for now. Let's talk about the girl at the Keep."

Temmin waved his hand. "Another maidservant. Very, very pretty—beautiful, even, in her way, certainly not classically beautiful, certainly not like you, but a very appealing kind of girl, you know? We kissed, just last Paggday, but it didn't mean anything. She wanted cheering up after her sweetheart broke up with her, and pretty girls are hard to resist."

Allis's fingers stopped circling his temples. "Then why did you?"

Temmin reached up and touched her cheek. "Because I thought of you." To his surprise, Allis briefly colored and looked away before returning her composed face back to him. A sudden surge of courage prompted him. "You never did answer my question. What is the nature of your relationship with your brother?"

She smiled. "I love him more than anyone in the world. When everyone abandoned us, we had one another, and when everyone abandons us again, we will still have one another."

"That's not what I asked. You know what I'm asking."

"Ask again, and be specific, sir. None of this 'what is your relationship.' Ask me what it is you wish to know."

He sat up, and stared at her; she stared coolly back. "Very well," he said after a long pause, "Do you have sex with your brother all the time, or only during religious observances?"

"Would you blame me if I did?" she said, her poise never wavering. "After all, Issak is very beautiful, wouldn't you agree?"

"Yes, of course," Temmin said without thinking, "but he's your brother!"

"Those brilliant eyes, his silken hair, such strong arms, such soft skin," she said, letting each word roll, fat with meaning, juicy and succulent from her parted lips. At his bilious look, she laughed. "No, we don't! I love my brother more than anything in the world, and fulfilling the Chase is our obligation and our joy as Embodiments, but it's our job, if you like. In public, we are just scandalous enough to make the people happy. In private, we've shared lovers, not often in the same bed—for instance, we share our current Supplicant, an irresistible girl named Anda—you will like her. But that's also work-related. Otherwise, our sex lives are separate." She leaned back; the fabric of her divided skirt draped in graceful folds over the slope of her hip. "Are you disappointed? Were you imagining us wrapped around each other in ecstasy? Or are you in the middle in your fantasy? Oh, look at you blush!" she teased.

Temmin's face grew hot, as the image rose in his mind: Allis before him, Issak behind him, mouths and hands and— He rolled over onto the pillows and pulled her atop him. The smile left her face, but she showed no fear. "What if that is what I want?" he said.

"Then you should chase us," she answered.

He gave her a tentative kiss, a brushing of the lips, shy and unsure after all his bravado. He felt his heartbeat, jumpy and fast, and wondered if she felt it too. Allis took his face in her hands and kissed him again, deeper, and he sighed into her mouth. Everywhere she touched him grew warm and shivery. He cradled her head in one hand, smoothing along her jaw with his thumb, and hoped he did it right. She ran her tongue over the roof of his mouth, and he shook violently. She gave an amused little hum, and did it again to the same whimpering reaction. "Very good," she murmured, breaking the kiss. "Now tell me, what have you learned?"

"Learned?" said Temmin, muzzy-brained. "I was supposed to learn something?"

She laughed. "Did you perhaps notice the ways in which I like to be kissed?"

Temmin raised up further on his elbows, and stared up in confusion. "I…I was distracted."

Allis burst out laughing and pulled him close; the tops of her breasts pressed against his chest. "Perhaps we should try again?" she said, when she let him go. "You lead this time." She slipped off him to one side.

She'd seemed to like it when he touched her lightly. He drew a thumb across her fine cheekbone before following her jaw to the tip of her chin—

a touch that almost wasn't there. Her breath hitched. He kissed her, light, almost teasing, and again, until she let out a soft mew. He licked at her bottom lip, and her mouth opened for him; he tried the same trick she'd done with him, stroking her palate with the tip of his tongue, and she shivered just as he had. He kissed her again, deeper, stopping only when he sensed her pulling away.

"You're a quick study," she said. "What did you learn this time?"

Temmin dragged himself with difficulty from an inventory of all the greens in her eyes. "I think," he said, "I've learned that sometimes when someone does something to you it's something they like themselves. Am I right?"

"One correct conclusion, yes. Shall we continue?"

"Oh, yes, please," he said fervently, and they began again. From time to time, his hand would wander to her breasts, and she would gently redirect it. "See here," he finally said. "Why can't I touch you?"

"In this I teach, Temmin. If you become our Supplicant, you will always be the student. I realize you're used to leading—"

"No, I'm not," said Temmin. "I don't lead at all."

"You do, all the time. You don't think about it, and you only do it to get what you want. Part of what we can teach you is the difference between real leadership and just getting what you want."

"I'm not sure I like that characterization," he frowned.

She kissed him again. "I promise you won't regret coming to us. You may be frustrated from time to time, but you won't regret it."

He wanted to believe her. "If this is all there is, then we had better stop for now," he said, reluctantly untangling himself.

"Are you tired of me already?"

"Very much not," he replied, "but if we keep this up, I'm either going to force myself on you or embarrass myself, and I don't have a change of trousers."

Allis laughed uproariously, a laugh he would never have expected from her that somehow suited her better than her usual demure chuckle. She kissed his nose. "You're already growing wise." She sat up to re-fasten her braid round her head; Temmin filled their glasses again, found a plate of strawberries, and fed one to her as she pinned.

The wine bottle emptied, as did the plates. A pile of bones that had once been a chicken sat next to a single shriveled hothouse grape. Temmin had fallen asleep with his head on Allis's lap as she reclined among the pillows, dozing in the spring sun just slanting below the roof of the pavilion. She roused herself and brushed his hair from his face. "Temmin, I should get back to the Temple soon."

He woke slowly, taking in the starry roof pitched above them, and then Allis's gently smiling face. He pulled her down to kiss her, then sat up and sighed. "I'm glad you came."

"I am, too."

He took her hand and played with her fingers. "What happens next?"

"You need to make a decision by the 40th, a week before Neya's Day. Not right now. Come to us at the Temple in a week for a visit. We may then talk it over with Issak and the Most High Lover and Beloved. After that, you should know."

"If I do decide for Supplicancy, how long will I be committed to it?"

"Two years and two days."

"And when it's over?"

"We'll take a new Supplicant in your place. We only have time for two."

"No…I meant, what happens with us?"

"Temmin, I can't ever be your woman," she said. "Don't be misled. I can't marry or have children or take only one lover. It's against my vows as a Beloved and an Embodiment." She encircled his hands with her own. "I would hope we would always remain friends and occasional bedmates, whether you become a Supplicant or not."

"I s'pose it was silly of me to bring up the future a-tall. We just met," he said, with a weak laugh.

He got up and helped her to her feet. Coats were donned, ascots re-tied, hats returned to heads and gloves to hands. Once they were proper, Temmin stepped out of the pavilion and called for the horses. He helped Allis into the saddle, and then swung up onto Jebby's broad back. "Thank you, gentlemen, for taking such good care of my Jinny," said Allis to the footmen, who nearly swooned with delight.

The horses walked out of the Fairy Meadow into the Woods, Temmin taking them on the more direct route. Once they'd come down the steeper parts of the trail, Allis set the tempo, cantering down the War Road, past the stables, down the slope to the Keep's long drive, and up to the gates. They swung open; her escort of Brothers waited on horseback, as if they'd been standing there the entire time instead of relaxing in the guardhouse.

Temmin took Allis's hand. "Thank you so very much, Holy One, for the honor and pleasure of your company."

"Your Highness," she answered, "the honor and the pleasure were mine entirely."

"So…until next week?" he said, still holding her hand.

"Please remember our discussion, sir, and think things through," she said. "Listen to the counsel of your family, and of Teacher, and we will talk more then." She dropped his hand, and walked Jinny through the gates. The Brothers fell in behind her, and the three rode away toward the City. When she disappeared around a bend in the road, Temmin turned back to the stables, his head full, and his heart fuller.

Only then, in a pensive but happy jog, did he feel the six still-pulsing stripes on his bottom, aching from the saddle. With luck, Jenks hadn't already put the soft cushion away.

Temmin told no one of his plans to visit the Temple—almost no one. He told Jenks that evening, and the happy valet burrowed into the Prince's wardrobe all Paggday to ferret out the proper clothes for a visit to the Temple. Though Jenks was discreet, Temmin himself let it slip to Ellika in the hearing of a footman. It spread through the Keep until it reached the ear of Gram, the King's valet, and thence to the King himself.

"Winmer!" said Harsin as he stomped into his study. "Harla take you, Winmer, I need you now!"

"I'm here, Your Majesty," murmured his secretary from the doorway of his adjoining office. "How can I be of service?"

Harsin flung himself into his favorite chair, and poured a snifter of brandy. "This obsession with Allis Obby has gone too far. He's heading into dangerous territory, spiritually and politically. Find something out about the Obbys to diminish them in Temmin's eyes. Anything."

Winmer paused; his little moustache rose toward his nose. "I'll do my best, sir, but I can hardly imagine anything worse than what they already are. May I speak freely, sir? I have misgivings, political misgivings, about tarnishing the Obbys—certainly not religious misgivings. The Lovers' Temple is nothing but a whorehouse, and the Embodiments are pretenders who perform lewd acts in public once a year for their Temple's financial gain. I am an atheist."

"And let no one other than me hear it, Winmer. I don't care how fashionable it is in certain sets, I'd be obliged to fire you for it, you know, and I rather like you." He contemplated the hearthscreen; it bore a classical scene of Nerr and Neya entwined in one another's arms, blossoming trees above Them, and flowers rising from Their footsteps. "Temmin is a believer, I think. He's his mother's son in many respects. At any rate, he keeps to the forms."

Winmer looked up from his little notebook. "You are a believer, sir," he said.

"Not so devout as to keep this from happening." Harsin put his feet up on a tufted footstool. "I'm slightly surprised at you, Winmer. I would expect, as an atheist, you'd try to discourage my belief in this prophecy."

"I believe in *you,* sir. If this is important to you, I will take the sin on myself—if there were sin to take. I will serve you in every way I can, even against my own misgivings."

Harsin raised a brow. "And what are your misgivings?"

"Letting Prince Temmin become a Supplicant is inconsequential— except in the political sphere," Winmer said, fingering his pencil. "It might portray the royal family as weak for its Heir to associate with the Lovers. Better he should dedicate to Farr, or Pagg, or even Eddin. But it wouldn't be anything a stint in the Cavalry couldn't reverse, and from everything we know about him, Prince Temmin still intends to train with them once he turns twenty. The common people dislike any conflict between the Crown and the Temples. Action against the Embodiments may be perceived as an attack on the Gods Themselves. That's my only concern, sir. The so-called prophecy is not to be feared—murky rhymes, no more."

"Hm," muttered Harsin. "I know better." He blew out a breath. "What do we know about the Embodiments already?"

"We know they're originally from Belleth. They showed up here nearly nine years ago at a Mother's House under the auspices of your counselor."

Winmer put the smallest emphasis on the final word. "Are they possibly his bastards, sir? I've always suspected it."

Harsin gave an uncharacteristically high snicker. "Getting information out of him is harder than simply ordering him to do something—he can always find a way out of doing something or telling me something—but one thing I know for certain: Teacher has no children of any kind and never will. Very well. Send your agents out. Dig, Winmer. Find out who their parents were. The Obbys are young for their positions, and Allis is far, far too good at what she does to have come by it all in less than three years. Now, send word for the Queen. And have them get rid of this," he added, kicking at the hearthscreen. Winmer bowed and retreated to his office.

As Harsin sipped his brandy, the memory of a delightful evening with Allis arose in his mind, complete with an image of her plump breasts bouncing as she sat astride him. Luscious girl, truly remarkable in every way; the visit to the newly installed Embodiment had been a high point of even his extensive erotic life. When his temper cooled, he might pay another visit to her.

He frowned at the Gods making love on his hearthscreen. His son seemed to be of a romantic temperament. Could that knowledge alone turn Temmin away—that his father had Allis first, and could have her again if he wished? Perhaps. Once he'd extricated his son from this mess, he would be sure to send Allis a gift, and present the Gods with a mollifying sum. Where was Ansella? Her rooms were right next door. Damned woman could never be found when he wanted her.

Ansella did not wish to be found. She sat in the pear orchard beneath a tree; her head rested against a knee covered in dark green linen, smooth beneath her cheek. Pear blossoms scented the air, and bees murmured among them. It would be a good year for pears, she thought drowsily. She closed her heavy eyes.

"Annie, don't go to sleep," whispered her lover.

"If you keep playing with my hair, I will." The hand stroking her golden locks stopped, and she sighed in disappointment. It had been so pleasant, dozing in the orchard's dappled sunlight. Lovemaking always made her sleepy afterwards. "Don't stop," she said aloud.

"I won't, if you tell me how goes your foolish son's pursuit of Allis Obby," answered Ibbit.

Ansella hummed as Ibbit resumed her soft touch. "It's proceeding well, actually. Harsin told me to discourage him, but I couldn't do that, darling, you know I couldn't."

Ibbit pursed her lips, and said, "I asked you to discourage him as well —perhaps the first time your husband and I have agreed on anything. Could you not do it for me?"

"I wouldn't go against you for the world," said Ansella. She captured the Sister's hand and kissed her fingers. "But I would go against the Gods even less. I must say I was surprised you thought I should." Ibbit yanked her hand away; Ansella sat up in mild alarm, and searched her lover's face. "Are you angry with me? Please, don't be angry, Ibbit."

"But I am angry," said Ibbit. She fell back against the tree trunk, and petals snowed down. "I'm very angry!" At Ansella's stricken face, she said, "Sweetheart, how can you let your only son fall into error like this? Yes, he is a man, and yes, there's nothing to be done for him—"

"He's a good boy—man—he's the best of all of them!" cried Ansella. "I know Venna doesn't approve of men—"

"She hates them," said Ibbit.

"But how could I hate Temmin!"

"I don't ask you to hate him, darling, I ask you to guide his feet on the better path, and that path leads away from the Lovers' Temple—away from women in general. Much better to send him to Farr. Oh, now there, my girl, don't cry. Don't worry about it now," Ibbit murmured.

Ibbit's strong arms encircled her, healer's hands working at her nape until she loosened again, and opened completely. Before Ibbit came to the Sister's Temple at Reggiston, Ansella had no one to carry her; she was her children's strength, rigid, impervious, closed to everyone but them, and completely alone as a woman. Now, the world moved through Ibbit into her, relaxing every inch of her, disconnecting her joints, turning her thoughts soft and malleable. She still considered herself her children's only strength, but now she had a love—a reliable love—to sustain her.

She let her head fall back on Ibbit's shoulder, and closed her eyes as Ibbit gripped her chin and kissed her, urging her mouth open and capturing her tongue between sharp, sharp teeth. A thrilling fear always split Ansella open from the top of her head to her core when Ibbit bit her; the priestess had broken skin before.

It wasn't always teeth. Sometimes Ibbit would hold her by the neck, as if the bigger woman were assessing the best way to break it. Knowing Ibbit could hurt her, and chose not to, made Ansella weak with desire.

Ibbit let go of her tongue, and pressed her down into the grass. "Don't worry now. Let me take care of you. It's all I've ever wanted, to teach you, to bring you and your daughters to the Sister's true path, and to take care of you, my sweet, beautiful girl, my Ansella. Don't move. Be still, now."

Ansella lay still as Ibbit pinned her to the ground and opened her bodice, still as the sharp teeth left little strawberry marks along the skin at the top of her corset, still as Ibbit's hands and head pushed her skirts up, as the sharp teeth pulled at her lips, and then as they worked at her clit, Ibbit's tongue circling all around everywhere the sharp teeth had been, erasing their traces only to have them mark her again, and again. She stayed still, until she couldn't stay still any longer.

NINE

Temmin set out on his early morning ride the next day with thoughts of Allis. He saw the multitudes of green in her eyes everywhere: pale, tender new leaves; ferns lacy and bright; the deep moss blanketing the tree trunks. Nothing held him back now but his father, who could only disapprove, not stop him. He said the nobility would be angry. Why would that matter? Who could stand against the royal family? And why should he care about what his father feared? The King didn't care about anything other than molding his son into a copy of himself.

He rode through the King's Woods, already knowing it by rote and absorbed in his thoughts, when he noticed a movement up ahead, not far from where he'd found Arta crying. Had she returned, or was it a deer hiding in the underbrush? As he drew nearer, the figure moved toward him, not away from him; it was no deer, but a man.

Temmin pulled up. It might be a Guard—or an assassin. His father had said no one could enter the King's Woods from the far side, and an assassin coming from the direction of the Keep was unlikely. An assassin coming directly at him in plain sight was even less likely. A Traveler, perhaps? The Traveler Prince in the History had red hair, but nowhere near as alarming as this man's.

"Hangin back? Fuckin coward!" the man called, wobbling closer. "Aye, you'd better be careful, you bastard!"

He recognized both the voice and the hair; they belonged to the young footman, Arta's sweetheart, the one who dangled after Ellika. "Wallek?" Temmin called uncertainly. "That's your name, isn't it?"

"Get down from that horse and I'll make you remember my name, you asshole!" cried the footman.

"What's amiss?"

"What's amiss? My girl's amiss! My life's amiss!" Fen waved a small white cloth at Temmin like a little flag. Jebby took a snorting step back, and turned his side toward the intruder. "Get down offa that horse an fight like a man, you beardless shit!" He advanced, weaving as he went. "I'm gonna show you why I'm the bare knuckles champ of Templestone!"

"Bare knuckles—are you serious?" said Temmin, thinking of his training with various fighting masters. Champion or no, Temmin was sure he could beat the footman if he had to.

Jebby was a calm horse by nature, but he sensed his rider's tension, and took great exception to the stranger waving a cloth. The big chestnut pinned his ears back and swished his tail, but the stranger paid no attention, and neither did the confused and preoccupied Temmin. When the stranger came too close, Jebby struck out to the side with his closest hind leg, just grazing the man's thigh. The young footman went down.

Temmin wheeled Jebby around, moved off a short way and dismounted. "Stay put!" he told the unrepentant horse as he wrapped the reins around a branch. He ran back to where Fen lay gasping. "How badly are you hurt?" he said, crouching down. "It's my fault—I should've noticed his mood and moved him away, but don't you know better than to come up on a horse like that?"

"Don' matter," Fen muttered. "Jus stand there an I'll pound you into paste from down 'ere!"

A strong odor of spirits met Temmin's nose. "You're drunker than Farr! Here, let me look at your leg—all right, then, if you won't show me, then let me at least check for a broken bone," he said. "I've seen a horse kick kill a man, you should be more careful—be calm around horses."

"Calm, he says. How can I be calm when you stole my girl!" Fen tried to sit up, and went right back down, sweating and pale.

Temmin ran a gentle hand down the footman's thigh. "Nothing broken. Probably just a bad bruise. Lucky, actually. No, stay down—you must stay down! I'll have to go back to the stables for help, but let's see if we can't get you out of the path first."

Temmin slung Fen over his shoulder and helped the young man onto his good leg as he hissed in pain; they hobbled to an improvised seat in the roots of a tree. "No matter," muttered Fen. "I'll fight you when I can stand up."

A little flask fell out of the footman's jacket; Temmin pocketed it before Fen could catch it. "I'd rather not fight you at all," said Temmin. Fen burst into snotty tears. Temmin took the little white cloth still clutched in Fen's hand—as he'd thought, a handkerchief, but one with a familiar sigil embroidered on it. "Hang on, this is one of mine! How'd you get it?"

"How'd Arta get it, you mean!" cried Fen. "That's what I came to find out! You fuckin bastard! Any girl in the Kingdom—Pagg's balls, you could have Neya's Embodiment! And you want my Arta!"

Temmin sat back on his haunches. "Is that what this is about? Wallek, I don't want your Arta. I didn't lay a hand on her—well—not much of a hand—damn!" he winced. "Besides, she told me you'd broken with her!"

"You admit pawin her, then!"

"I admit nothing of the kind! And, d'you know, I could beat you senseless for having pretensions to my sister!"

"Miss Ellika's the one who got Arta to tell me about you!" cried Fen. He snatched the disputed handkerchief, and noisily blew his nose. "I'd never—I didn't—she made me so mad!"

"Ellika? She makes me mad every other day," said Temmin, sitting down next to the footman. He ran a hand through his hair. This had his sister's pawprints all over it.

"No, no—at Arta! How could anyone ever be mad at Miss Ellika? She's like—bein around her is like bein around a fairy!" Fen stopped crying. "She's so beautiful, so sweet! Otherworldly-like!"

"'Otherworldly-like?'" snorted Temmin. "You wouldn't say that if she were *your* sister."

Fen paid no attention. "The Princess asks me to do somethin, I do it, but Arta, she doesn' understand." He looked so young sitting there wiping his nose, even to Temmin. "S'pose I can't blame 'er. We were goin to get our promise rings, and there I was, movin furniture on my day off."

"For another girl, I might add," chided the suddenly wise Temmin.

"That's what Arta said. Never seen her so mad! And the things she said —I didn't know she knew those words! She said I was an idiot, and who did I think I was, a junior footman danglin after a princess, and I said who did she think she was, a downstairs maid jealous of a princess, like a jenny wren jealous of a swan!"

"I'm sure that went over well."

"If I coulda took it back, I woulda, but she had me so mad! And then she said if she was nothing but a jenny wren, why was I her sweetheart, and I said, we can change that, y'know!" He patted his coat for his flask. "Can I have just a tad? Please?"

"I think not," said Temmin. "What did my otherworldly-like sister do to goad you into this foolishness?"

"She heard gossip—"

"Gossip? She heard it from me! I told her to stop encouraging you, that she was coming between you two."

"She never encouraged me! And you had a hand in the business yourself," glared Fen.

Temmin screwed up his mouth. "People talk... You've probably heard I—I qualify to be a Supplicant to the Lovers' Temple." Fen nodded warily. "All right, then. How could I qualify if I'd done anything...*dishonorable* with Arta?"

Fen stared blankly at the Prince. "That's true! You couldn't go there if... Any road, Her Highness talked to Arta and found out what you done—"

"*I* told her! She already knew!"

"She didn't know about the hankie! Or the kisses!"

"*One* kiss! And I might add I didn't have to talk Arta into it!"

"Are you callin my girl easy?" Fen tried and failed to get up again, and sank back in pain.

"No, no, nothing of the sort. There, now, stay down. Finish the story."

Fen repeated Arta's story, and how she had shown him the handkerchief as proof. "I swore I'd knock you straight into Inchar, prince or no, an she said what did it matter, she wasn' my girl any more, an I said of course you're my girl." He sighed. "Anyway, got myself a bottle for courage, cuz I'm sure to be cashiered or worse for this, and came out here to wait. They lock the Keep at eleven bells, you know. I was so mad I didn' think about bein stuck out here. Oh, Gods, they're gonna hang my head over Marketgate."

"Not if I can help it," said Temmin. "Rely on me. I won't let them touch you. I'll vouch for you."

Fen regarded him warily. "You'd do that?"

"This was a misunderstanding—my sister goaded you into foolishness. And besides, you're the sweetheart of a friend—and Arta is nothing more than a friend. I do my best for my friends."

He gave Temmin a sideways look, filled with grudging respect. "You're all right, Your Highness. Not princely-like a-tall."

"I'll take it as a compliment," he answered. "You're all right, too."

No one bought Temmin's story about Fen meeting him to spar in the woods, though no one contradicted him, least of all Jenks; he only lifted a skeptical eyebrow and said, "Why would you take a junior footman as a sparring partner, sir?"

"We're the same height," Temmin answered. "Fen's a good man. Besides, he's Ar—Dannikson's sweetheart, and I like her."

"Bare knuckle champ of Templestone. Hmf. Do you know how big Templestone is? I hope you haven't made a mistake, sir. You've singled out the girl, and now you've singled out her sweetheart."

"*I'm* not the one meddling with the servants, Elly is!" Temmin said to himself as he stalked off to the morning room and a reckoning with his second sister.

He had to postpone it; Ellika was still asleep. Temmin consoled himself with two smoked fish, a large slice of ham, four eggs, a bowl of porridge, the entire rack of toast and all of the marmalade, washed down with a pot of cocoa. Now and again he looked up from his meal to meet his father's hard stare, until he picked up a newspaper from the stack next to Sedra and pretended to read; his sister cocked a brow at him but said nothing.

Political news, business news, boring boring boring. Ads. Things to buy, a whole pageful. He'd heard of advertisements but never seen them. Look, a mention of his family:

> *ROBIKSON'S PATENT GROATS for more than thirty years have been held in constant and increasing public estimation as the purest farinae of the oat, and as the best and most valuable preparation for making a pure and delicate GRUEL, which forms a light and nutritious supper for the aged, is a popular recipe for colds and influenza, is of general use in the sick-chamber, and is an excellent food for infants and children.*
>
> *Prepared only by the Patentees, ROBIKSON, BELSH, and CO., Purveyors to the Royal Family, 64, Foothill Lodge Street, Newtown, Tremont City.*

They had a Royal Patent Groat Purveyor? He poked at the porridge in curiosity, and wondered what made it patent.

> *The Proprietors of Robikson's Patent Groats, desirous that the public shall at all times purchase these preparations in a perfectly sweet and fresh condition, respectfully inform the public that every packet is now completely enveloped in the purest tinfoil, over which is the usual and well-known hygienic paper wrapper.*
>
> *Sold by all respectable Grocers, Druggists, and others, in town and country, in Packets of 6c. and 10c.; and Family Canisters, at 20c., 50c., and 1s. Each.*

Why would anyone go to a druggist to buy groats? Then again, he'd never had to shop for anything ever in his life, so perhaps that's just what people did. It became dead quiet; he looked up to find everyone at the table waiting expectantly. "I'm sorry?"

"I said," his father repeated, "what are you so engrossed in?"

Temmin thought for a long moment. "Did you know," he said, "that, apparently, we have a Royal Patent Groats Purveyor?"

The King's stare hardened further; he turned with great deliberation to Sedra and struck up a discussion on the recent diplomatic overtures Sairland had made toward Tremont.

Temmin hated newspapers.

Presently, both the King and the Queen took their leave, and Temmin abandoned the pretense, folding up the paper by his plate and addressing a fresh piece of fish.

Sedra rattled *The Morning Capital* and peered at her brother over its top. "Did it work?"

"Did what work?"

"Elly's little scheme. I see you don't have a black eye. How did the footman fare?"

"You knew?" he sputtered. "You should have said something!"

"Couldn't," she said. "It wouldn't have worked if you'd known. You would've changed your usual habits, Wallek would have been cashiered for truancy, and Elly would be very put out with me."

Temmin glared as she folded the *Capital* and took up *The Daily Voice of Tremont*. "As it happens, it did, if leaving me with an injured footman once again engaged to his girl is the definition of 'worked.'"

"Oh good! I knew it would. You've eaten all the toast again, Temmy. Affton, more toast if you please!" chirped Ellika, slipping into the room and taking a place next to her brother. "Oh stop snarling at me. I know you're very cross, and I don't care in the least. Everyone's where they should be, and I'm quite satisfied with myself." She took a long, dainty pull on her coffee.

"What are you doing awake?" said Sedra.

"Avoiding Fennows," she answered, wrinkling her nose.

"Isn't everyone?" muttered Temmin.

"He tried to engage me last night for a private breakfast today, but I got up too early for him. Ha! So there. Now I know you're angry, Temmy," she continued, returning to the original subject, "but it was all for the best."

"Just do me a favor? Stop flirting with footmen," said her brother. "I don't know what I'm going to do with this one if I have to take him into personal service."

"I will on one condition: Come to Mistress Naister's with me on Nerrday."

"The dressmaker's? What on earth for?"

"I'm collecting a new dress for our Neyaday visit to the Temple, silly."

Sedra folded her newspaper and picked up her coffee. "Oh, I'm looking forward to *this* conversation," she said.

"You can screech all you like, Temmy, but I'm this family's current patroness of the Lovers, and so it devolves upon me to introduce you to the Most High Lover and Most High Beloved," said Ellika, removing the marmalade pot from his place. "Oh, you ate it all, you piglet!"

"When did you pick up 'devolve?' Well, done, Elly!" cried Sedra. "Your turn, Tem."

"It's none of your business!" he said, ignoring Sedra. "And I don't have time to spend an afternoon fooling around."

"How does that differ from your usual day?" injected Sedra.

"Be quiet, you," answered her brother.

"Here's a to-do!" came an unwelcome voice from the door—Percet, bleary but vertical. "What are you arguing about? Most unusual in such a close family, I should think!"

"We're not arguing," said Temmin. "What are you doing awake?"

"I want him to come with me to Mistress Naister's on Nerrday, Fennows, and he won't, that's all," pouted Ellika.

"I'd be most charmed to escort you, Elly!" said Fennows with an eager if oily smile.

"Oh, that's all right, Fennows," interrupted Temmin. "I was funning with her. I'm happy to go with you to Naister's, Elly." Ellika gave him a tiny, triumphant smile, and Temmin knew she'd forced his hand. But he couldn't very well let Fennows insinuate himself any further into her life, even if it meant his own trip to a dressmaker. Sometimes, he thought, sacrifices must be made.

Once back in his study, Temmin ran his fingers over the old red book. It had been almost a week since he'd been inside its covers, and though he recalled the story perfectly well, its immediacy had faded somewhat—until the image of Prince Hildin's knife slicing through the girl's clothes, her nakedness among the rags, came to mind. It shot a thrill straight down his center, but whether it belonged to Hildin's henchman Gian, or himself, he couldn't tell. If the latter, what did it say about him? Troubling.

Teacher's cool voice brought him out of his brooding. "A busy time, Your Highness. Both of us engaged in other pursuits, I fear."

Temmin turned to the voice's source, by the door. "I know what I've been up to. What have you possibly been doing?"

"Sir, I am your father's chief counsel," Teacher sighed. "I am always busy."

"Does that mean you've come bearing his stern warnings against becoming a Supplicant, too?"

"Why would you expect me to?"

"Everyone else has!" said Temmin, flinging himself into the library chair.

Teacher sat down on the library table's edge. "I serve the Gods as well as your family. His Majesty would be foolish to ask it of me, and he is not a fool."

"So you approve?"

"I wonder that my opinion would hold much weight with you, sir," Teacher smiled.

"You know more about this Supplicant business than I do. Well? Does serving my family preclude you from having an opinion?"

"In my opinion," said Teacher cautiously, "a call from the Gods should not be left unanswered. Do you feel called? Or something less?"

"Religious devotion hasn't crossed my mind. Not for a moment. But I can't shake her. Or...or him. Issak," he murmured. "Ever since I met her, I've had this strange trust in her, as if she'd never hurt me, as if I just had to be with her no matter what. Issak—I don't know if it's trust as much as just this feeling that…that… Why am I telling you this?"

"Because I am an objective ear, perhaps," said Teacher. "It goes no further, and I do not judge."

Temmin leaned against one arm of the chair, brows knit. "Issak makes me feel as if whatever it is he wants me to do, I should do it. It's the right thing to do. I have to do it. No one makes me feel that way, not even Papa."

"That can be a sort of trust in itself, the instinct to obey another."

Temmin sat up. "Are you saying what I'm feeling toward Issak is like what Gian felt for Hildin? That I have the need to serve like—like that?" Teacher said nothing, and Temmin continued, "Gian trusted Hildin. Is that why he obeyed him?"

"A servant needs to trust his master. To serve is to let someone else make the difficult decisions. You have only to carry them out. Your master is responsible, not you. Gian believed Hildin made the right decisions for them both. In turn, Hildin trusted only Gian, and he took care of Gian just as you care for your horse, though I dare say you treat your horse with more respect."

"Why would you stay with someone who doesn't respect you? Because you love him?"

"Because you need him," answered Teacher. "Are you ready for the next part? Open the book."

Emmae woke slowly. Through the fog of sleep came a beloved, angular face; desire rushed through her, edged in an ominous way. She reached out her hand. "Warin?"

"Not quite," said the face. "Hildin." He seized her hand in a hard grip.

The drowsy fog cleared away; she sat up, and pushed herself to the top of the bed. Stone covered in tapestries replaced the daub walls of the cottage; feathers filled the mattress she sat on, not reeds; and a fire in a generous hearth warmed the room. Her clothes hung in rags from her arms. She pulled them close with her free hand against her chilled skin. "Where am I? Take me home! I want to go home, take me home right now!"

She remembered now, this man Hildin, and the younger one—jarring desire forced into her, just as Warin's had been when they first met. The arousal intensified, insinuating itself further within her. She tried to pry herself loose from his grip, but he pinned both her wrists with one hand to the headboard above her. The remains of her dress fell open. Hildin moved closer and slipped his other hand around her waist. "Oh, please fight me," he purred. "I always win, but breaking the defiant is much more entertaining than taking the docile. What's your name, sweetheart?"

His wandering hand brought hot shivers to her skin, made her light in the head, and she fought to remain in control. "Take me home," she stammered.

"And where is home?" said Hildin. "Leute? The accent truly is adorable, isn't it, Gian—oh, this is my cousin, Gian," he added casually.

"I don't care who he is," she spat. She fought to stay angry. The warmth of his body, and his fingers tracing against her skin, fed her panic and arousal both; she wanted to escape, and she wanted his hand to slip lower. She growled in frustration and despair, struggling against his grip until he took her wrists, one in each hand, and slammed them against the headboard.

"Answer me. What is your name? Where are you from? Where did my brother find you?"

Emmae gathered up the last of her crumbling defiance. "Take me home and ask him yourself, if you're his brother! Or are you afraid of him?"

Hildin gave her a delighted smile. Over his shoulder, she saw Gian shudder, an eager smile on his face. Hildin brought his mouth within a hair's breadth of hers; she turned her head away. He licked a trail down her neck with just the tip of his tongue, until she gasped, and shook in his hands. "There are two ways I could treat you," he said into her ear, each puff of breath maddening and delicious. "I could give you the beating for insolence you very much deserve, or I could just let your enchantment do the work for me."

Emmae's eyes opened wide, and she stiffened. "I told you, I have no magic!" she said to the bedcurtains.

"No, you don't," agreed Hildin. "But it's been practiced upon you, hasn't it? We can taste it on you. You despise me, yes? But look at you. It's all you can do not to spread yourself wide for me right now, even though you don't want to. You desire me. You desire Gian. You want anyone who wants you. Don't you?"

"No, I can't be enchanted!" she cried, but she knew it had to be true. Enchantment alone explained the ropes of arousal coiling around her and crushing the will from her body, her forgotten past, her uncontrollable urge to give in to Warin's passion when she didn't even know him. Did she really love him—and worse, was he the one who had done it? All her strength left along with her certainty in him; she stopped struggling, and Hildin dropped her hands. The sob burst forth, and the fire in the hearth leaped up.

"Never worry, sweetheart, we'll give you what you want. Hush now," said Hildin. He slipped the remains of her clothing from her arms and pulled her unresisting down on the bed. "Now, what's your name?"

She gulped in air between sobs until she could stutter out, "He named me Emmae. I don't know my real name. I don't remember anything before he found me in the woods in the fall!"

"Ah, now we're getting somewhere. No idea who you are—what an interesting, cruel spell! How long did he wait before he had you? Not long, I'd wager." Hildin kneaded her breast until she moaned, pressing up into his hand; the throbbing in her veins prayed he would suckle at it. "He had you the very day he found you, didn't he? But who could blame him—a beautiful woman dropped on his doorstep, defenseless against his lust—I wouldn't even blame him for casting the spell in the first place, to keep such a prize—"

He stopped to take her nipple into his mouth, ending her body's suspense; intense pleasure bloomed inside her. "Yes!" the desire whispered to her. "Now, beg for more, tell him you want him inside you, beg him for it!" Though she had stopped fighting Hildin, she still fought against the enchantment itself; she did not beg, but her hand stole up to his neck, urging him without words. "Warin wouldn't, he wouldn't, he loves me," she whimpered.

Hildin released her nipple, and rolled the other one between his fingers. "And what would he think if he saw you like this, in heat and open to another man—any man? I think he might change his mind about loving you, if he ever did. You're hundreds of miles away from him, at any rate, and you belong to me. This," he said, seizing her mound, "is mine now. Do you understand?" He squeezed until she nodded her head in desperation. Her pain inflamed him further somehow. His excitement drove the spell, and she spread her legs for him, too overwhelmed to resist. He thrust his fingers inside her, and she moved to bury them deeper. "There's my girl," said Hildin, sliding them roughly in and out. "You're mine until I tire of you, mine to do with as I please. Do you want her, Gian? Ah, but you already know he does, don't you, girl?"

Emmae glanced at the flushed page, standing near the bed; he caressed himself through his leggings, staring at her with glassy eyes. Emmae felt invisible hands at her breasts: Gian's desire ghosting against her skin.

"Come here," Hildin ordered. The bed dipped as Gian climbed onto it; Hildin sat up, and kissed the page so hard he groaned. "Behind her," said Hildin. Gian placed himself at the head of the bed and held her against him, his erection pressing into her back.

Though it should have sickened her, Emmae's excitement grew—two men forcing twice the desire on her, far beyond Warin's. Gian's cock twitched against her as he fondled her breasts. She pushed herself faster onto Hildin's fingers, until he took them from her; she cried in disappointment and humiliation.

Hildin laughed, and moved to his knees, unfastening his leggings. He put his hands beneath her hips. "Something better than fingers, pretty thing," he said. His fingers dug into her ass as he pulled her onto him. Emmae let out a guttural scream, arching herself again and again into his hard, fast rhythm. She twined her arms round Gian's neck behind her, to give him better access to her breasts. *Kiss me, kiss me*, she pleaded inwardly—she couldn't find the breath to speak the words aloud, and craned her head back until she saw Gian's face, focused on the Prince. "Let go," rasped Hildin. "I want all of her."

Emmae found herself on her back, her legs as far apart as Hildin could force them; he struck her womb with each thrust. His eyes shone wild and cruel, his mouth pulled into a fierce grimace. He frightened her, and her body had never wanted a man more. "My brother's woman," he growled.

He pinned her to the bed, crushing the breath from her. "But I've taken you from him. You're mine now, Emmae, say it, I want you to say it!"

"I'm not your woman!" she cried, dangerously close to her crisis.

"Did you cry out for more when Warin fucked you? Who's fucking you now? Is it Warin? Is it Warin making you come like this? Who is it, Emmae, who's making you scream, who's making you come?"

"You are, it's you!" she shrieked, and her climax began. She dissolved and reformed around him over and over, shaking in his arms. He pounded into her, refusing to let her orgasm end, until he pulsed deep inside her; he let out a roar and fell atop her, sweaty and swooning.

She lay beneath him, still trembling with desire. Exhausted, frustrated tears ran down the sides of her face; the spell wouldn't release her until the other was satisfied. Hildin's weight shifted off her, and from far away she heard him beckon for Gian. The sounds of begging, wet kisses, the rustling of clothes, and then Gian seized her breasts, licking and sucking in desperation.

His cock matched his body, long and slender, and he shook as hard as she did as he slid into her, never taking his mouth from her breasts, his skin feverish even against her own. His pace grew hectic, nearly bouncing her off the bed, but she'd stopped caring. The enchantment drove her to match him, the inner impulse forcing her hips up and up with no thought left in her, only rhythm and need. He bit the nipple in his mouth, and she screamed and thrashed against him as she fell into the orgasm; Gian followed her in spurts. He lay atop her, whimpering and shuddering.

"As soon as you can stand, Gian, come to me," said Hildin's voice. Emmae opened bleary eyes. The Prince stood in an open door; torchlight flickered behind him in the hallway. "We have arrangements to make." He left, closing the door behind him; it vanished into the wall as the tapestry covering it fell back into place.

Gian rolled away from her and followed her eyes to where the door had been. "The door won't work for you," he said when he regained his breath. "It takes magic."

"Warin could open it," she said.

"But he's not coming."

Emmae wanted sleep; the burning had left her. "He's coming, and when he does, he'll kill you and your master, and I will laugh."

Gian gave a small snort, stood up, and fastened up his clothes. "Warin won't come back. He renounced the throne, and no woman is enough to draw him back. He's afraid of my master."

Emmae gazed up at him: slender and tall; golden hair curling around a tender face; green eyes like a forest spirit. How could one so gentle in appearance be so cruel? "You're afraid of your master," she said. "That's why you did this."

"Afraid?" said Gian. "You'd do well to be afraid of him. I did this because I wanted to, and I'll do it again. Listen," he said, sitting down on the bed, "Don't cry, Emmae. Let him have his way. Give in—to him, to me, to whatever this enchantment is—let go, enjoy yourself. Otherwise, this will be very, very hard for you and not at all hard for my Prince. He prefers a challenge—he'll tire of you faster if you give in. Then, he'll give you to me. I will be kind to you. And I promise you," he added, tracing his fingers down her body, "I won't tire of you for a very long time, no matter what happens."

He lifted the damp strands of hair that had tumbled into her face; she slapped his hand away. "All this magic you claim," she said. "For all I know, I'm a mile from home."

Gian smiled, and turned to the candles burning on the sideboard. He snatched a flame from one and played with it like a ball of clay, drawing it out into a wand. He pushed it back into a ball, balanced it on his fingertip, and threw it back at the candle. Its flame leaped up and ate the tiny fireball. "My magic is nothing. Mere tricks—I'm too far from the throne to have much power. Hildin and Warin are strong, and if the King weren't a drooling wreck, he'd be the strongest of all. And then there's Teacher—no, Emmae, you're far, far from where we found you. This is home now. If Warin returns, he dies. If you love him, pray he abandons you. Look."

He rose from the bed and opened the shutters; she followed him, covering herself with the remains of her chemise. Far below them spread a forest, gray-green in the spring sun. In the other direction, beside an unfamiliar river, lay a small city; smoke rose from its many chimneys. They'd taken her miles from home, perhaps even several days' journey.

"You belong to Hildin," said Gian, placing a soft hand on her shoulder. "This is your life now. If you'll let me, I'll help you accept it, and then we can serve the Prince together."

"I will never serve him, stupid boy. And you can die for all I care," she muttered. Gian shrugged, and left the room as Hildin had. Emmae stumbled back to the bed, exhausted and heartsore, and cried herself to sleep.

When she awoke some hours later, she found herself tucked naked into the sheets, the shreds of her clothing gone; someone had been in the room. She slipped out of bed, wrapped the sheet around herself, and edged along the wall under the tapestries, touching every inch in her search for a hidden latch. Nothing came under her fingers.

The stones began to grind; she pressed herself flat against the wall. A hand emerged from behind a tapestry, followed by an old woman with a bundle under one arm and a pitcher in the other. Emmae sprang forward, but the door ground shut before she could escape.

The old woman jumped with a shriek, but held onto her pitcher. "Goodness, child!" she cried. "You scared me to death!" She was a fat little woman with the look of a grandmother: a broad, pleasant face framed in gray braids. She put the steaming pitcher next to a basin on the side table, and the small bundle she put on the bed. "Now, don't look so fierce, dear, it's just Old Meg. Master Gian says I'm to take care of you." Emmae beat her fist upon the wall, angry tears welling. "Oh, now, don't," said Meg. "You'll hurt yourself. You'll never get out until my lord says you may."

"Please help me," begged Emmae. "I've been brought here against my will—"

"Aye, but not for long, dear, my master always brings them round his thumb in the end," Meg chuckled. "Now, let's clean you up. Don't be shy, we're both women. See?" she said, pouring the steaming water into the basin, "nice and warm. And I have a new chemise for you. Come, you'll feel better!"

Emmae reluctantly took the washcloth from the old woman and put the sheet aside. She did feel dirty, to her bones.

Meg sized her up, and began shaking out the bedclothes. "You are a pretty little thing. Prettiest one yet. No wonder the prince took to you.

You're lucky. Master Gian tells me they rescued you from a shack in the middle of nowhere."

"I was kidnapped!" snapped Emmae. "But Warin will come and take me back." She scrubbed harder, sloshing the water around in the basin as she rinsed the washcloth.

"Warin?" gasped Meg, turning from the bed. "His Highness's brother?"

"So your lord says. I don't believe it."

"Not that you're a girl a prince wouldn't take a fancy to, sweetheart," said Meg, returning to her work. "But if you're Warin's woman—surely you're not married to him?"

"No," Emmae admitted.

"No, I shouldn't think so. Didn't he ever tell you he's the Heir?"

"He's a woodsman," insisted Emmae.

"Don't be stupid, child. Only royals can use the name 'Warin.' He's the Heir, though he gave it up. His birth prophecy, you know."

"No, I don't know."

Meg huffed in disdain and folded her arms. "Heavens, girl, where did you grow up? You have a barbarous eastern accent, so you can be forgiven your ignorance, I suppose. But who doesn't know? Warin is to kill the King before he can take a throne or a wife." At Emmae's blank look, she sing-songed in exasperation:

> *Before this Prince takes wife or throne,*
> *Blood shall be spilled and not his own,*
> *The Lifeblood of the Crownéd King*
> *Must needs be spilled to free his Queen.*

"Warin ran away so he wouldn't kill his father, or so he said. You didn't know?"

Emmae's knees quivered, and she put a steadying hand on the washstand. "I can't marry anyone," he'd said. "You'll always have to wear my ring on your right hand, not your left."

Goosebumps rose on her wet skin. "You said you had clothes for me?"

"The chemise there on the bed, dear, Master Gian said you wouldn't be needing anything else for now," Old Meg chuckled. "No," she added as Emmae pulled the chemise over her head, "I think Warin left out of shame

—shame!—at the way his brother was treated, and at how much more suited to rule Hildin is, even though he's the younger. Since you seem to know nothing about anything, I'd wager you don't know we were sent away when their mother died birthing Hildin."

"'We?'" said Emmae when her head emerged through the garment's neck.

"Oh, I was Hildin's nurse! Last baby I took to breast, and the best. What a love! I couldn't bear to leave him. King Gethin blamed my poor Hildin for the Queen's death. He loved her! Such a rare thing, a royal love match—love match for anyone's rare. I certainly didn't get one! Sit down, let me brush your hair, dear." She chattered in a steady stream as she worked the tangles out. "The King couldn't bear the sight of my poor lamb. They sent us to the King's cousin at Valleysmouth, and there we stayed until Hildin's voice dropped and the King *had* to bring us to court. In a just world, my Hildin would have been raised at court and Warin sent away."

Meg sighed and pulled on a particularly stubborn tangle. "It's only right Hildin hates his brother. Warin had his place at court! At least my Hildin had company in Gian. Hildin was always so patient with him, like a little teacher, and Gian just worshipped his cousin, has done since he was tiny. More a brother to him than his own brother." Emmae thought brothers acted nothing like Hildin and Gian, but kept silent, letting the woman go on. "And then Warin turned tail and ran, like a coward."

Emmae jumped up from the bed. She snatched the heavy silver brush from Old Meg's hand, and brandished it like a club. "Warin is not a coward! Now show me the way out of here!" The door in the wall ground open; the brush grew so hot she dropped it with a yelp.

"I beat my servants myself, girl," came Hildin's cold voice. She twisted toward him, holding her scorched hand to her chest; the Prince stood in the hidden doorway, Gian just behind him. "Never threaten Meg again, or it'll be worse than a burned hand." He advanced on her. "I'll burn you to death, an inch at a time. I'll smother you slowly, give you just enough air to beg me for your life, then start again, over and over!"

Emmae labored to breathe; the air around her grew used, damp and sparse; her vision sparkled black at the edges. She fought for breath, until cool air rushed into her lungs at last. She collapsed, near senseless. Hildin seized her by the hair and shook her until she feared he'd pull it out. "Do not touch her, do you understand? She is as a mother to me, and worth a thousand of you, slut! A thousand of you!"

"There, now," his old nurse said hastily, "she wasn't really going to hit me, my lamb! Put the poor thing down, she's scared enough now she'll never raise a hand to me or anyone else again, I'm sure of it."

"Fetch Warin's bitch something to eat, Meg," Hildin said, still looking into Emmae's face. "We can't have her dying of hunger." He loosened his hold on her, and she fell back on the bed; she heard the stone door open, and knew Meg was gone. "Woman, I will tell you this once: you live as long as you interest me. Your struggle against the spell is intoxicating. And you are my brother's woman—taking you away from him pleases me. But when I've killed him, I will grow tired of playing with you at some point." He swept his gaze down her body. "I admit that may take some time. Your enchantment raises so many possibilities."

He smiled, a wide and unbalanced grin, and walked to the door. "I won't kill you right away. Perhaps after Gian is done with you. Then when he's bored, there's the captain of my guard—he's due for a reward. And he might give you to his men and they to the stable boys when they're done. You might live much longer than you think!"

"You can kill me now for all I care!" she croaked at the closing door.

Despite her brave words, she was terrified, more frightened than she'd been waking up naked without a name in the forest; then, Warin had been there. Would he come for her? Even if he did, Hildin had a point: he might not want her. But did Warin cast the spell? How did she feel about him now? It didn't matter. She could not give in to despair, though it would be so simple to do. She would survive, she would stay true to herself, and in the end, she would avenge herself—against Hildin and Gian, and if he proved to be false, against Warin.

She looked out the window over the deep forests, pulling a strand of hair through her fingers over and over. Warin had said she'd come to him courageous. "I'll need all the courage I have," she said to herself. "I have no one now but me."

Temmin pulled away, shaking with rage and terror, eyes wet. "She wants to kill him. I want to kill him."

"No need. He's long dead," replied Teacher.

"Did she kill him?"

"We'll get to that in time," said Teacher.

Temmin could still feel Hildin's hands all over him—all over Emmae—the Pagg-damned book got him so confused, but then, disgust and desire had overwhelmed and confused poor Emmae. It shocked him how much her plight had stirred him, both to pity, and to deep, uncomfortable arousal.

"Why did Emmae believe Warin might have put the spell on her? Only women could do that—well, one woman…"

Teacher casually flicked a flame from the fire onto a fingertip. "Warin told her nothing about magic of any kind. She knew little of the world outside the cottage."

"Why not?" said Temmin, brushing away the last tears to eye the flame warily. "Why couldn't he tell her who he was?"

"Because he did not want to be who he was."

"I don't want to be me, either, but you don't see me hiding in a forest."

"No, only when you wish to shirk your duties."

The arrow hit the mark, and Temmin bridled. "That's different."

"If you thought you were destined to kill your father, would you feel differently about 'hiding?'"

"Right now I almost wish I were destined to kill my father," he mumbled, then looked up in alarm. "I didn't mean it!"

"It is not an uncommon sentiment among men your age, at least in passing."

"Did you feel that way when you were young?"

Teacher dismissed the little flame. "I do not remember. Why in particular are you so angry?"

"He chooses my friends, chooses my studies, acts as if he can just beat me into doing whatever he wants!"

"He can, about anything other than religious devotion," Teacher answered, face stern. "Cross him too often, and he will have you whipped. He will do it himself."

"What does he want?" Temmin burst out, jumping up from the library chair. "He's brought me here to learn to be king, fine, it has to be done whether I want it or not. But I don't want it, and I don't like it, and you can't make me want it or like it!" He hurled himself onto the green velvet couch, Emmae's anger still jangling inside him. "Why did Sedra have to be a girl? What's the point of all her studying just to marry someone and have children and wave from the dais at Spectacles? Mama shouldn't have allowed it."

"Sedra's fate is her own. Do not be too sure you know what it will be."

Temmin looked up, his fair brows hiding in his unruly forelock. "Does the magic show you what will be?"

"I am not so burdened," said Teacher, following him to the couch. "Do you have an opinion on women ruling?"

"Opinion?" blinked Temmin. "What's there to have an opinion about?"

Teacher sighed. "We will consider the question in future. Meantime, I think your grievances against your father go deeper."

"Are we done for the morning?" growled Temmin.

"We are done for the week," replied Teacher. "I have business to attend to, and you have your Temple visit."

Left alone after lunch, Temmin stretched out on the couch, thinking of Fen; there was bound to be trouble for him. It might be that he'd have to take the footman into his personal service. Maybe he'd send Fen and Arta to Whithorse. It would take some convincing for the rest of the staff to trust them, but if he wrote ahead to Alvo, Alvo'd smooth the way.

Alvo. He'd tumbled it over and over, that admission of love. They'd been like brothers up until that moment, and he still missed Alvo more than anyone. Emmae's observation on Hildin and Gian came to mind: brothers acted nothing like that. Though he always could make Alvy do anything he wanted him to, just like Hildin could with Gian, he pondered, drowsy from one glass too many of the '88 Bordigalle. His thoughts shifted a final time: "I drank this Bordigalle with Allis up in the foothills. Ah, Allis." He closed his eyes, and fell asleep.

On the southeastern coast of Tremont lay Bordigalle's home, the Duchy of Belleth, a land favored with a mild, beneficent climate much inclined to the growing of superb wine grapes, excellent cheeses from the sheep and cattle grazing its lush grasslands, and a tendency towards voluptuousness in its people.

When Tremont drove the Sairish from the continent, Belleth had been the colonizers' last stronghold. It had done nothing to advance its own independence from either Sairland or Tremont, and had never in memory had a king of its own; the Tremontines always said the Bellesians were too lazy to rule themselves. Litta, Corland, Alzeh and Kellen—even Barle, Valmouth and Whithorse, so long a part of Tremont—had strong tribal leaders and kings before their subjugation. But not Belleth. Its people cared too much about great art, great food, and fine living to be bothered with who ruled. Its graceful capital, the port city of Ouve, presided over the great bay at the continent's southernmost tip.

In this ducal capital, the House of Polls once stood to one side of the better districts. Oakwood Street was fashionable at the time the first Mistress Polls founded the House. By the time the building burned down sixty years later, the area had taken a sad turn; fashion had moved elsewhere.

Maleen, the third Mistress Polls, lost everything she owned in the fire, and, temporarily, her eyebrows. But in the end, it was a blessing. A sympathetic patron gave her enough gold to re-establish herself in the best situation a superior whorehouse could hope for: a new building with all modern conveniences, but built on the elegant lines of traditional Bellesian architecture. It stood in the Old Theater district, one never in or out of style, the only building on its discreet lane.

The superstitious Mistress Polls renamed her establishment. Her grandmother founded the House of Polls; in her turn, Maleen founded the House at Greenflower Street. Most mornings she spent in her cozy private parlor, drinking coffee, tallying up the previous night's receipts, and marking down the debts her girls and boys owed against their accounts.

One chemise, she noted in her book, ripped in half by a client: one silver against Shally's account, but 50 coppers compensation for her injury cut the charge in half. Could she charge Shally for the bandage? No, not in good conscience. She only hoped the wound wouldn't leave a scar. A scar would drop Shally's asking price, and then Maleen would be forced to let her go.

She took up the next charge: a chair hopelessly soiled in a scene between Kanae, her current star among the boys, and his best patron. Two gold—a valuable thing, expensive to re-upholster. Besides, a nice, round debt load kept Kanae here at Greenflower Street; he'd nearly balanced his account, after all, and she couldn't have that.

Maleen kept herself well and expensively upholstered, though not to excess. She wore clothes just rich enough without pretension to higher station, their cut befitting the older woman she had accepted herself to be. Before the fire, she had clung to her vanishing youth: gray hairs plucked; asses' milk to bathe her face; softer and softer lighting until she could barely see in her room, though it didn't matter much as she also refused to wear her spectacles.

After the fire, Maleen spent hours before the mirror. She was still a handsome woman. At first, she fretted over her missing eyebrows, but then she reassessed her situation. At 52, a double chin—a *slight* one—could be considered quite appropriate and attractive, while in a 22-year-old it would be repellent. The same with gray hair, the still-faint lines around her eyes, and her more generous figure. Time to capitalize on what she had: experience. Her House catered to all tastes, and a surprising number of clients preferred their women fully ripened...and rather strict.

And so, Maleen cut her soft brown hair to the chin in the traditional Bellesian fashion for older women, stopped plucking out the gray, dressed more conservatively, and wore her spectacles outside the parlor. Flooded with requests for her time, she doubled her rates, and doubled them again; she didn't have time to entertain just anyone, but the few she did appreciated the changes in her body, even though she rarely removed a single item of apparel.

One feature never changed, never aged. Her lovely eyes remained the same expressive, velvety brown, limpid and warm among the patrons in the front rooms, hard, mahogany business in the wood-paneled back room where she counted out the House's fortune. A knock at the door, and she looked up. "Come in! Yes?"

"Gentleman to see you, Mistress," bowed an old man in plain livery.

"A regular, Deck?" said Maleen, rising to her feet.

"No, ma'am, but quality, certainly very high quality. I put him in the best sitting room and gave him tea."

When Maleen entered, she found the gentleman of very high quality on the couch, sipping his tea; he stood at her entrance, and Maleen's quick eye marked him by the cut of his suit and the correctness of his stance and manners not as a lord but a gentleman, and still likely to have plenty of gold in his pockets. "Welcome, sir!" she smiled, taking his hands. "I don't believe I've had the pleasure. I am Maleen Polls. What can my House do for you?"

The gentleman extricated his hands. "Not the House, Mistress Polls, but you yourself." He resumed the couch.

She arranged herself artfully on the chair opposite. "Me?" she said, lips parted in a smile. "Why, sir, I confess I am not often called for at my time of life! Nevertheless, I do have experience to recommend me, especially for *particular* tastes, particular enough that arrangements are more exacting than the norm—"

"You misunderstand me, Mistress Polls. I am here to discuss something more lucrative than whoring."

Maleen abandoned her delicately alluring manner and folded her plump hands in her lap. "Whatever could that be, Mister...?"

The man pursed his lips. "Call me Mr Brown. I am hoping you can provide me with, shall we call them, character references, for two past denizens of your House, when it stood in Oakwood Street."

Maleen allowed herself the tiniest wrinkle of the forehead, and gave him the gaze that made her clientele swoon in anticipation of a tongue lashing. "When you say 'denizen,' Mr Brown, you should know we never speak of our patrons. Ever."

"Oh, no, not patrons. Rather, employees. A nicer term than 'whore,' don't you think? My master is most interested in two former employees, and will pay a great deal to know more about them."

"How much of a great deal?"

"Say, ten thousand gold each—more if the information is useful to him."

Maleen held in her excitement. "My books were destroyed in the fire that took the Oakwood Street House not quite nine years ago."

"A strange fire it was, too, taking only your building," murmured Mr Brown. "Oakwood Street is packed so tightly, one would think the whole district would have gone up. No, your recollections are enough, yours and any other members of your staff who may remember the two we're interested in."

"And those two would be?"

"Allis and Issak Obby."

Maleen laughed to cover the red the names brought to her face. "The Embodiments? Whatever makes you think they were at my House? They would have been children. Not our specialty at all. And children, you know—quite illegal. I am in strict compliance with the law, and pay my fee at Pagg's Temple every spoke."

"They were the children of one of your girls. A Liddy Obby, if my sources are correct."

Maleen calculated the risk in her head. She'd sworn to the one who burned the Oakwood Street house down never to speak of the Obbys. If found out, she would lose more than her business and her eyebrows, but she had a score to settle against those social-climbing twins, and their protector, that Strange Gentleman, though Deck swore up and down it was the Black Man. Twenty thousand gold, with what she had in the safe, was enough to sail across the Anatalian Ocean for a comfortable retirement in Sairland, for she'd have to flee; she'd avoided death once, but in the light of the burning House, the Strange Gentleman had sworn to kill her should she so much as remember the Obbys had been there.

"Ten thousand apiece?"

"Possibly more."

She leaned back in her chair, gave Mr Brown her most conspiratorial smile, and crossed her ankles. "What would you like to know?"

TEN

"You're a Princess—why d'you have to fetch your own dresses?" said Temmin as he handed his sister down from the carriage at Mistress Naister's shop, not far off the Temple Promenade. "I should think the dressmaker would come to the Keep."

"Oh, she does, but I like to come into town, see and be seen and all that," Ellika answered, acknowledging the small crowd through the Guards lining their way to the door.

Mistress Naister's shop looked like the inside of a fragile seashell, pink and cream and gold; Temmin kept his knees and elbows in for fear he'd break something, though what he could break in a dressmaker's shop, he wasn't sure. Mistress Naister curtsied so low, Temmin felt compelled to help her stand again. He impulsively kissed her knobby hand; her fingers smelled of beeswax. Mistress Naister swallowed a girlish giggle, sat Temmin down on a spindly chair made for someone much shorter, and clapped twice. A nervous little shopman came from the back carrying a tiny pink and gilt tea set; he served the Prince while Ellika and Mistress Naister exclaimed over one another like old friends. The cup looked like a thimble in Temmin's hand, and he hastily put it down.

The shopman brought out many heavy bolts of fine muslins and silks; Ellika nattered on to the dressmaker about summer frocks, hats, gloves, shoes, jewels, and whether her current provisioners remained in fashion, until Temmin stopped listening and their conversation turned into a soft, feminine murmur broken by Ellika's familiar, infectious laugh. Temmin conquered his fear of breaking the teacup and drank the entire pot in a quarter of an hour. The shopman kept the pot refilled, but in spite of the tea—and no biscuits, he grumped to himself—he soon grew desperately bored and in need of a bathroom.

Time stretched on, and Ellika hadn't even gotten to the trying-on-the-dress part. A thump brought Temmin out of his stupor, and he looked up to see the shopman had dropped an armful of bolts on the floor; the little man's hands shook as he picked them up, and Temmin wondered if perhaps serving the royal family unnerved him. But he had to have met Ellika before, surely. Temmin tried to keep his observation discreet, but their eyes met more than once before the man looked away. Sweat poured from the shopman's forehead as he shuttled in and out of the stockroom, and he patted himself with a futile handkerchief. Was he ill? He looked as if he might faint.

Ellika and Mistress Naister finally disappeared into the fitting salon; Temmin sighed and rose to stretch, lifting his arms over his head until he brushed against a low-hanging lamp. He heard the shopman's voice, broken and croaking: "I'm sorry, Your Highness, but they have my children!" Temmin turned; the man held a dagger in both hands. The man thrust the dagger at him, like a child attempting to cut his meat for the first time. Temmin jumped back as far from the shopman as he could get, knocking over the gilt chair and its table; the pink tea set shattered on the floor. Cream and tea spilled everywhere; Temmin slipped, but managed to regain his footing as the man sprang forward.

The Prince grabbed the nearest object for a shield, a bolt of sprigged muslin. The shopman slashed at it, shredding the delicate fabric trailing from the bolt end; Temmin parried every thrust, keeping the bolt between them. The shopman tried to thrust underneath it at Temmin's gut, but Temmin darted to one side; the dagger found its mark in the bolt instead, and stuck fast. The shopman struggled but could not free it; he cried in despair, casting about for another weapon, and found an enormous pair of shears, a tool he used every day that fit in his hands. But by then, Temmin had wrested the dagger from the bolt himself; his much longer reach held the man off. Temmin tried talking with him, but kept the table between them. "What is this about? Who has your children?"

"I have to kill you, sir! I don't want to, but if I don't, they'll kill 'em!" said the man. He cried so hard Temmin wondered if he could see.

"Stop!" pleaded Temmin. "I can help you!"

Ellika screamed from the fitting salon door; the shopman turned toward her. Temmin took the opening, came round the display table, and grabbed the shopman's arm. The shears fell to the floor, and Temmin kicked them under the table.

The front door burst open and Guards filled the room, swords drawn. "Don't kill him!" Temmin cried over the noise, but the first Guardsman to reach the shopman stabbed him full in the belly. The man fell to the floor; the spilled cream turned pink, and then red. The Guardsman pulled back what hair the man had to finish him. "I said, *no!*" boomed Temmin, in a voice he didn't recognize.

The Guardsman looked up, startled. "There's no savin' 'im, Your Highness, not with a gut wound like that, and he's going to end up with his head over Marketgate whether he lives or dies!"

"We wish to question him," came Teacher's voice behind Temmin.

"Where'd you come from?" said Temmin.

Teacher raised an eyebrow. "The fitting salon. Guardsman, let him go. He's not going to hurt anyone." The Guardsman shrugged, but released the shopman's hair; his head fell back against the shredded bolt of muslin lying on the floor.

Temmin and Teacher crouched down beside him. The man's face grew gray; he reached out for Temmin's hand, and said, "Your Highness, I've been loyal all my life. I'd as soon kill myself as hurt you. But they took my son and my two little girls last night. Sent me one of the baby's fingers—" He choked. "I told them I was no fighter, but they said you were too well-guarded…they had to take every chance from now on…and that if I didn't kill you when you came today, they'd send all three back in pieces."

"We will find them, and they will pay for this," said Teacher. "Who are they? There's no point in hiding their identity."

The man shook his head, strength almost gone. "Don't know their names, sir," he whispered. "Please don't let them die..."

Temmin looked up at Teacher, who reached out and closed the man's eyes.

"Leave her alone! She's done nothing!" Ellika screamed. Temmin turned toward her; two Guardsmen held Mistress Naister as she begged for her life. A third stood before her with his sword drawn, while three ashen-faced girls, pincushions on their wrists, stood supporting one another in the doorway to the work room. "She's done nothing!" Ellika repeated, tugging at the nearest Guardsman's arm.

"Let the woman go!" called Temmin, straightening. "She's blameless!" The Guardsmen released her, only to catch her again as she fainted. They carried Mistress Naister to a settee in the fitting salon; Ellika waved smelling salts under the dressmaker's nose. When she came round, Mistress Naister told them the dead man's name was Nat Horn. He and his wife Nan kept a tiny house just inside the Old Walls on Tallow Street, and they did indeed have three children. "Nat was a good man, a kind man, worked so hard—he's been with me for fifteen years! Oh, poor Nan! Poor Nan!" wailed Mistress Naister.

Ellika wanted to stay, but the captain of the Guards was adamant: respectfully, the Heir and the Princess Ellika were to be taken back to the Keep directly. The three seamstresses would be able to provide for their mistress better than Her Highness, begging pardon. Teacher assured Temmin they'd find Horn's children, and that Mistress Naister and the seamstresses would be questioned without any harm coming to them.

The two were hurried back into the carriage, past a hushed crowd held far back from their path. They sat side by side on the red velvet cushions, holding hands. Clouds eclipsed Ellika's sunny face, and Temmin couldn't stop thinking about Nat Horn, bleeding to death into the cream. Neither spoke until the carriage passed the great gates; Ellika sat up and cried, "Oh! All that, and I left the dress in the shop!" She gave a high, squeaking laugh that fell into sobs, and Temmin held her the rest of the way, trying not to cry himself.

Temmin demanded his father keep Nat Horn's head off the hooks above Marketgate. Without his head, Nat Horn would spend the afterlife forever separated from everyone he loved; Harla did not permit headless bodies within Her Hill. The Guards found Horn's wife—poor Nan—and their three children murdered, and Harsin relented. The Friends of the Bloody One welcomed the Horns to a niche in the catacombs of Harla's Hill, where their bones would rest together forever.

Temmin, Harsin and Teacher met after dinner that night in the King's sitting room. The fire provided most of the light, and the resulting gloom matched the mood. It glittered in the King's dark eyes as he sat before it.

"How did whoever-it-was know I was going to Mistress Naister's in the first place?" said Temmin. "It's not as if I make a habit of going to dress shops."

Harsin looked up at Teacher, who leaned against the mantel to one side. "We have a spy in our midst," said the counselor. "Brother Mardus, Winmer and Affton are going through recent hirings. So far we have no trace of the men who set Nat Horn on you, Your Highness. Mistress Naister and her women have already been acquitted, but we are shadowing them nonetheless. Now that you've come of age, your uncles are becoming desperate."

"Up until now," said his father, "the attempts have been more subtle. Then the attack at the ball, and now this—much more brazen. You are not to stir from the Keep without a visible guard, Temmin."

"Why? I can take care of myself. I stopped Horn."

"Ellika could have stopped Horn," snorted his father. "This is why you must stay away from the Lovers' Temple. Temmin, it's a weakness to devote to the Lovers, let alone become a Supplicant! You'd be showing my brothers your belly, and protecting you at the Temple—I can't think how we'd do it! Teacher," he appealed, "explain it to him."

"I cannot," Teacher said in a hard, flat voice.

The two stared at one another, until Harsin shook his head and sank back into his wing chair. "Son, I just want you to understand the very real danger you're putting yourself and the kingdom in if you do this—all for the sake of a woman."

Temmin clasped his hands before him. "I promise to think on all that, sir."

"Good night, then," said his father.

Temmin shambled out, lost in thought. The King watched him leave. He turned to his counselor, still leaning against the mantel. "The Embodiment's leading him by the prick, and you're just going to stand there," he said.

"Sir, if there is one thing the Prince can learn at the Lovers' Temple it's how to keep from being led by the prick," said Teacher. "It is a more valuable skill than perhaps you realize."

Harsin glanced sharply at his counselor, but said nothing.

Temmin came to his tour of the Temple on Neyaday. A quiet Jenks helped the Prince dress; Temmin thought it wisest not to ask after his subdued mood, and let him have his way without complaint.

Ellika stayed in her room after the incident at Naister's, and never did send for the new dress. She found an unworn one suited for the occasion in the back of her wardrobe, and insisted on going with Temmin "just to the door if nothing else." Some of her naturally cheerful spirit made its way past the shock of Horn's death, and she came bouncing down the stairs behind her brother to take his arm. She wore a confection of white lace and ribbons against pale pink silk. "You look like a wedding cake," said Temmin, kissing the top of her head.

"Thank you! Put your gloves on, Temmy."

The apprehensive ride to the Temple passed quietly. Even Ellika's chatter limited itself to comments on the scenery as the carriage rolled up the Temple Promenade. First they passed the gray granite expanse of Eddin's Temple, students and priestly Scholars coming and going from the university spreading out behind it; opposite stood Amma's Temple, its Mother's House filled with the orphaned and abandoned children of the City nestled inside its wings; at the Promenade's end loomed the crowded, white marble House of Law bound to Pagg's Temple.

The carriage came to a stop halfway down the graceful boulevard. To his right, through the blossoming dogwoods edging the Promenade's center park, Temmin could just see the busy Healer's House connected to the Sister's Temple. He looked to his left to the graceful, rose marble Temple of the Lovers as the carriage pulled to a halt.

Temmin alighted first, then handed Ellika down. "I'm still not comfortable with your being here," he said.

"Pfft," said Ellika. "I'm the royal patroness of this Temple. And I'm not taking the tour with you, I'm merely introducing you."

"I've met them!"

"Not the Most Highs, you haven't."

Brother Mardus arrayed the security detail around them, and bowed: "Your Highnesses." Temmin followed his gaze to the Temple's roof; sentries in unfamiliar uniforms stood along it, crossbows cocked. Temmin sighed inwardly—would they turn the Temple into an armed camp for his sake? He took Ellika's arm in his, and led the way up the steps. A phalanx of men in the same uniform as the sentries met them midway to the top; they wore helmets like the Brothers, but crowned with swan's feathers instead of red horsetails. He had seen swan's feathers on the helmets of Allis's escorts the day she came to the Keep, but those men were definitely Brothers; these men were definitely not. Then again, swans were one of the Lovers' symbols. "The Temple's Own, sir," murmured Brother Mardus. "They will protect you in public areas, but only in the Temple. They don't leave the grounds, at least in their official capacity. We will be waiting when you leave." Temmin nodded his thanks, and let himself be handed off like a package to the Temple's Own.

At the top of the steps stood two familiar figures and two new ones—old ones, really, he thought. Allis and Issak stood next to a wizened pair he assumed were the High Lover and High Beloved: a surprise. He'd expected them to be younger, though he couldn't say why. All four dressed in the same plain gauze clothing, though the Most Highs' loose clothes were dyed rose, and the undyed clothing of the Embodiments clung. He wondered if they were cold.

Temmin and Ellika stood before the clerics and bowed. "Ellika of Tremont, why are you here?" said the High Lover.

"I am here to present my brother to you," she answered. "High Lover Gan, High Beloved Malla, may I make known to you Temmin of Tremont, Heir to the Throne."

"We welcome you to the Lovers' Temple, Your Highness," said Malla; she took his hands, and kissed him. He expected a kiss like one of his bristly, sour-smelling great-aunts, but her lips were soft, and she smelled warm and sweet, like the clover honey of the Estate. Her hands were warm, too. Before he could recover from his surprise, the High Lover took his hands and kissed him in turn. Both kisses were unexpected, and pleasant; little wonder how the two had come to be Most High, if they could still kiss like that.

He turned to face Issak. This kiss was expected, and when Issak took him by the wrists and pulled him close, he leaned in and closed his eyes. It was less of a kiss and more a sharing of breath, some exchange of vital energy that set his hair crackling, as if a thunderstorm were imminent. Issak broke the kiss first, his expression somewhat surprised.

Temmin turned to Allis. He took her small hands, leaned down and kissed her. It was shorter than Issak's kiss, but it still sent a thrill down his neck to the base of his spine. When she pulled back, she smiled, small and intimate, and the thrill traveled up the way it came.

"Welcome," the twins said at the same time. Temmin walked into the Temple with one on each side, Ellika and the Most Highs following behind and the Temple's Own clustered around them all. The bustle of the Great Hall paused to let them pass, worshippers and clergy bowing and curtseying. They led Temmin up a broad staircase on Nerr's side of the Hall to a private, guarded area, where the Temple's Own left them.

Two servants—an almost ridiculously beautiful man, and a plain, fat girl—bowed them into an opulent sitting room. Two wide, low-backed couches sat close to the floor, more like small beds piled with cushions than couches. Several braziers warmed the room, and Temmin resisted the strong urge to loosen his starched collar. The servants brought tea and cakes on trays and put them on a low table between the couches. Allis poured the tea and Issak passed it round; he let his hand linger on Temmin's when his turn came for a cup, and Temmin swallowed hard.

The talk was formal: Temmin's recent arrival in the City and its differences from life at the Estate in Reggiston; his parents' wellbeing; polite, vague inquiries into the Most Highs' health; the weather. Temmin drank a good deal of tea and ate a huge pile of cakes in his nervousness. To his surprise, Ellika didn't filch a single sugar cube from the bowl.

At last, his sister said her goodbyes, accepting kisses all round. "Be good," she whispered to him as she kissed his cheek, then let the beautiful young man lead her away.

"And with that, we shall take our leave and return to our duties," said High Lover Gan. The plain, fat girl helped each Most High to stand. Temmin bowed. They inclined their heads, their eyes filled with mirth more than gravity; the beautiful servant opened the doors, and they left the room with the fat girl trailing behind. Odd they'd employ an ordinary-looking girl as a servant, and then pair the poor thing with that man, thought Temmin. Almost cruel.

Allis took his arm on one side, Issak on the other, and they began their tour, four of the Temple's Own trailing before and behind. Temmin observed politely as they looked into the neat dormitories, the vast library, and the erotic art collection. He wanted to spend more time in the last, but the twins propelled him out the door into the gardens.

The gardens contained many little nooks and niches; tucked away in more than one were passionate couples—or more than couples. Deeply embarrassed, Temmin didn't know whether to stare or look away, but neither Allis nor Issak seemed to care, sometimes ignoring the lovemakers, sometimes stopping to observe and even comment, and then moving on. "Were those Lovers and Beloveds, or...?" asked Temmin.

"Most of them," said Issak absently.

They entered the sculpture garden. The statues portrayed Neya and Nerr: alone; together; with Their Sisters or Brothers; or with any number of the human lovers They took in Their Sagas. Temmin found staring at statues less embarrassing, and he studied them with real curiosity. At times he wondered if the statues' positions were even possible.

"Ah—I knew we'd find someone using 'Nerr in Repose,'" Issak said, stopping before what resembled a bench, but turned out to be a life-sized statue of Nerr, lying on His back. His erection rose into the air, or so Temmin assumed; a young postulant Beloved straddled the statue, hiding it completely. The girl blushed and stammered, lifting one long leg as if to dismount, but Issak stopped her. "Your teacher sent you out here, didn't he? Then finish your assignment."

The girl sank back down on the phallus, her brown hair half-covering her face. But as it filled her, she let her head fall back; her mouth opened. She let out a tiny grunt and closed her eyes. She rose up, and Temmin could see the phallus now, thick and curving. She lowered herself onto it again. A flush bloomed across her skin, and her breasts bounced as she rocked in earnest, one hand between her legs. Temmin forgot his embarrassment. Though he'd seen Emmae's body in the Intimate History, he'd never seen a woman's body with his own eyes. He remembered the way Emmae's crisis would build inside her, and just as he wondered if the girl experienced the same pressure, pushing against some invisible wall until it burst through, she cried out, one hand working between her legs, the fingers of the other pinching a nipple. Her movements on the phallus slowed, and she braced herself on the statue's chest as she caught her breath. Temmin realized he'd been holding his own, and let it out in a small whoosh.

Issak helped the still-shaking postulant off the statue; she laughed, thanked him, and then kissed him, a long, full kiss Temmin could feel from ten feet away. He wanted to kiss the girl himself, kiss Issak, kiss Allis, kiss *someone*, or at least get a few minutes to himself to recover his equilibrium. Instead, he shifted on his feet and hoped his erection wasn't too visible. The postulant cleaned the phallus, and Issak shooed her back toward her classroom, arms full of clothes. "That was an assignment?" said Temmin.

"I would imagine lessons here are quite different from your lessons with Teacher," said Allis as they resumed walking.

Not as different as one might think, reflected Temmin.

They strolled back inside the Temple. "Now we'll show you the petitioning rooms," said Allis. "Few visitors get to see them from the gallery—the only reason we're showing you is that you're considering Supplicancy."

"What's a petitioning room?" said Temmin.

"It's where we meet with petitioners to the Temple," said Allis. "People asking for a blessing."

"I know what a petitioner is. I've made a few petitions myself, mostly to Amma to help my foaling mares—to Venna, when someone's been sick, but that was always done in private, at home." That was how Ibbit wormed her way in, he thought. "Why do you need rooms for it? I thought that's what all the people in the Great Hall of the Temple were doing—petitioning the Gods."

"These are rather more personal requests," answered Issak. "Blessings, the laying on of hands."

"I thought healing was more in Venna's line," said Temmin.

Allis squeezed his arm. "It's not that kind of healing." They came to a vast warren of little rooms, a steady stream of people moving among them. "The ones wearing Temple garb—what we've got on—are clergy and lay devotees. The rest are petitioners," she continued. She opened a door set between two ranks of rooms. "This is an observation gallery—there's one between each row. When we're by a window, keep silent. If you have a question, write it down." She handed Temmin a little pad of foolscap and a pencil from a pocket on the wall.

Walking inside, Temmin saw little, screened windows set into the walls. Each let into a room, staggered so the rooms could not see into one another. The odor of sex, quite fresh, filled the small, warm corridor; the pierced screens cast stars onto its walls, the only light.

Temmin peered into the first room. It held a low, wide Temple couch piled with pillows, a dressing screen, and no other furnishings. A middle-aged woman reclined into the pillows, feet on the floor, Temple skirt rucked up around her waist; all her attention focused on the man in street clothes kneeling before her. The man gave a muffled groan, his face buried so deep in the woman's sex he seemed to be pushing his way inside her. "Can they see us?" he whispered.

Issak took the pad and pencil. He wrote in big block letters, "NO BUT THEY CAN HEAR BE QUIET!!!" Temmin made an apologetic face and turned back to the room, fascinated. Neither the man nor the woman was beautiful, but watching such an intimate moment drew him in; the man seemed so desperate, and the woman watched him with such intense serenity, stroking his hair. The man held his cock in one hand, and she murmured encouragement as he pumped it: she could see how much he needed her, how hard he was for her, how good he made her feel, how close she was— The woman curved her back, hips rising off the couch; the man's smothered cries became louder and more pleading in response until his seed spurted from him in a stuttering arc. He laid his balding head on her thigh, gasping, face glistening, and sobbed like a child as she soothed him with comforting nonsense. Just before Allis tugged him away from the window, Temmin thought he saw movement behind the dressing screen, as if someone watched.

"What was that all about?" whispered Temmin in her ear. "Should we have been watching?"

"They know staff may watch them," she whispered. "I don't know the story, and I'd wager he doesn't either, poor soul."

They came to the next inhabited room. Inside, the fat young woman who'd served them tea lay on the couch, large breasts exposed. She cradled a dark-haired woman in her arms. Temmin thought they might be asleep until he realized the dark-haired woman was suckling like a baby, softly playing with the other nipple as she nursed; the fat girl gently rocked her, a somnolent ecstasy playing over her face, her mouth just open. She opened her eyes, looked straight through the screen at Temmin, and gave him a smile that went directly between his legs.

Before he could think much more about it, Allis pulled him down the hall again to a window where a burly young man already stood, watching through the screen. He ran a quick, appreciative eye over Temmin, nodded a greeting, and returned to his watch. "NECESSARY OBSERVER," Issak wrote on the pad.

A smack and a cry: Temmin's eyes followed the sound. A naked man lay sprawled across a heavyset older man's lap. His knees trapped the younger man's legs, arms pinned down with one beefy hand. An angry red handprint already branded the young man's flank; his captor ran light fingers over the mark, and the young man writhed. "Be still!" hissed the older man. The young man fought to stay motionless, wailing as the spanking continued.

To his shock, Temmin noticed the young man's hard length forced down against the other's thigh. He liked it? Why would he like it? Why would anyone like it? But the more the young man begged, the more Temmin himself stiffened.

The big man settled the smaller one's legs so that his cock dangled freely; the man reached down between them to take it, slowly stroking as the other hand circled the already-red ass. "Not till I say," he growled, and rained down slaps.

"Please!" the young man begged again. "Please, sir, please!"

"Shoot for me." He squeezed his partner's crimson ass with one huge hand as the prick in his other visibly throbbed. The young man let out an agonized scream, half pain, half pleasure, and came.

As soon as the throes ended, the older man swept him up in a crushing embrace. "Oh, you were so, so good, such a good boy, you took it so well," he crooned, tears in his own eyes as the other man sobbed in his arms. "Now here—" He unbuttoned his trousers, revealing a purple enormity. "That's what you want, eh? Take it." The crying man dropped to his knees and swallowed the giant prick down to its root.

Allis tugged Temmin away again, nodding to the observer as they moved away. "We set a watcher in those kinds of cases," she whispered. "We can't let the petitioners hurt the staff."

Down the row they went, looking in on men and women, men and men, women and women, threesomes and more—dizzying and confusing.

They came upon another stocky observer; inside the room, a woman lay tied to the couch, her head dangling from one end. One man drove in and out between her legs, another thrust into her mouth as he squeezed her breasts. Thoughts of Hildin and Gian raping Emmae, flashed through him, his body reacting just as before. He glanced at the dispassionate twins. The woman thrashing against her bonds aroused him, a horrible, inescapable arousal; what kind of man was he, to feel his blood surge like this? When the men finished, they untied her. To Temmin's confusion, she fell into their arms and covered them with kisses.

It wasn't all sex. Some sat side by side, or reclined in one another's arms, talking, sleeping, or just touching one another. One blissful woman slept, dangling naked from the ceiling in an elaborate rope harness; a second woman watched over her. In another room, a man scribbled in a notebook while another man made love to a woman. In time, Temmin realized the woman was the note-taker's wife.

As they left the gallery, none of what Temmin had seen stayed so clearly in his mind's eye as the fat girl's smile, the woman tied to the couch, and the older man and the younger man. The images left him flushed, flustered and somehow angry.

They walked into the Great Hall, an enclosed courtyard where entwined statues of Neya and Nerr rose three stories high. In niches along the wall stood individual statues of the Twins in all Their various aspects; hundreds of flickering candles stood before each one. Elaborate offerings lay before the giant statues spilling onto their feet: towers of sweets, a profusion of flowers.

Allis and Issak led Temmin through a door peeping out from the great statues' legs. Inside, the room held several of the low, wide couches, and two large beds recessed into rose silk-covered walls. Braziers warmed the already-overheated room, and Temmin once again longed to remove at least his cravat. The fat young woman he'd last seen suckling a petitioner had regained her clothing and now glided around the room with the tea things.

"This is the Supplicants Chamber," said Issak. "It's where you'd be spending a good part of your time. Supplicants live with us, but I can't imagine His Majesty letting you live outside the Keep."

"My father has nothing to do with it," said Temmin, pulling away from their hands and pacing off. "I live where I please."

"Do you, now?" said Issak, folding his arms. "So will you be living here?"

"Yes! No! What?" said Temmin. "I need to use the—the facilities!"

"The facilities," said Issak. "Yes. Anda? Please show His Highness the lavatory." The fat girl led Temmin through a hidden door past a modesty wall to a room with a urinal, sink and toilet, and left him standing before the urinal, but he found himself too hard to piss. None of his usual methods to ease his erection seemed to work. Did he have time? It shouldn't take long in this state, and who'd bother him in here? He put one hand against the wall, and stroked his almost-painful cock.

"No," said Issak from the doorway. "Not here. If you need to come, you'll do it in the other room." Before Temmin could tuck himself in, Issak seized him and shoved him back into the Supplicants Chamber, where

Allis waited. Issak stood behind him; he pinned Temmin's arms to his sides, his cock twitching in the air.

Temmin turned crimson. "I would advise you to let me go. I am the Heir."

"And here that means nothing," Issak murmured in his ear.

"Why are you so angry?" said Allis. She slipped his already-unfastened trousers and pants from his hips. "Tell us." Her hand slid down the band of muscle from his hip to his groin.

He flinched under her fingers. "I'm not angry!"

"You are," said Issak. "Why? I think I know. You watched the rooms, and we watched you."

Temmin flexed his arms, but Issak kept him pinned. "And so?" Temmin began; Allis lifted his balls with gentle fingers, and speech left him.

"It was easy to see which rooms fascinated you the most," she said. "Were you the powerful or the powerless, Temmin? You like Issak holding you like this."

She rolled his balls deftly, and he choked out, "I—I can't think with you doing that—"

"Don't think," she said; her fingers squeezed, and for a moment the world vanished. "Just tell us, without thinking."

When the world returned, he whimpered, "I don't know, I just don't know!"

"I think you do," said Issak.

"Why would anyone want to hurt someone else, why would anyone want to be hurt?" Temmin managed to get out.

"You wanted it," said Issak. "Your cock jumped every time that big hand landed on that red ass."

"It wasn't the pain," said Allis. "Any time one had power over another, you were interested."

"I don't understand."

"Who was in control in those scenes that captivated you so much?"

"That's obvious! Those petitioners raping that woman, the man spanking that boy!"

"He isn't a boy. He's a Lover," said Allis. "And why did you think the woman was a Beloved?"

"What woman could want that?"

"She was a woman who wanted that," said Issak.

It hadn't even crossed Temmin's mind that the woman was the petitioner; he'd just assumed the men were. "She was the one with the power," said Issak. "She gave it to them. She trusted them not to hurt her, and to give her power back in time. If she had signaled she wanted to stop, it would have ended immediately."

"You didn't stop when I told you to let me go," said Temmin.

"You said you would advise me to let you go, not that you wanted me to let you go. Do you want me to let you go?" said Issak.

Temmin didn't answer him. Allis poured something slippery over her hand, and he groaned as she stroked him. "No one wants to be raped," he managed to say.

"It wasn't rape," said Issak. "It was about power, and trust. Rape is also about power, but trust is absent. Sex is absent, for that matter." Issak took Temmin's earlobe into his mouth and sucked on it; a burst of feathery shivers spread from his mouth down Temmin's side.

"Power is a king's stock-in-trade," said Allis. "And so is trust. Who will take your power? Whose power will you take? Who will you trust? And can you be trusted with power?"

Temmin felt Allis's breasts against him; Issak's arousal pushed against him from behind. Too much, and not enough. He thrust helplessly into Allis's hand as a jumble of images came to him: Hildin and Gian; the young man begging to be spanked as he came; Issak's commanding eyes; tears running down Alvo's face as he knelt between Temmin's legs; the woman tied to the couch; Mattie in the hedge; Arta in the forest; Emmae enchanted— Issak bit his neck.

A long, strangled cry, and Temmin came. He sagged in Issak's arms, near swooning.

When he'd recovered himself somewhat, he found he'd been deposited on the couch. The anger left him, replaced with fear and shame. Tears filled his eyes. The twins held him, soothing him like a child. Was he the powerful or the powerless? Powerful, he supposed—he was the Heir to an empire, but he hadn't thought much about it until recently. Did his soul really crave power? If not, why did it attract him so? Ibbit was right; men were inherently depraved, or at least he was. What had Fennows said about patronizing whores—"the Lovers' Temple makes you think about it."

"I don't want to think about it, I don't want to be like that," he sniffled as his tears subsided.

"Tem, you already are 'like that,'" soothed Allis. "You know so little about yourself, but you told me everything on our ride."

"Did I? Then tell me how evil a man I am."

Issak raised up on one elbow and handed him a damp towel from a bowl on the table. "Why do you think you're evil? What does 'like that' mean to you?"

Temmin wiped his face, his swollen eyes grateful for the towel's coolness. "I have this ancestor—a sort of ancestor—" He started again. "I assume you've told Issak everything? Well, then. You remember the girl at the Estate—the maid I kissed? It never even dawned on me that she didn't want to kiss me, not until I was well into it. If I hadn't gotten sick, I think I might have kept on going. I might have raped her."

"But you didn't," said Allis. "You stopped."

"That's not the point, I had to stop—I didn't want to! And it took…it took me some time to understand I was wrong to have kissed her at all."

"Temmin, it hasn't even been a spoke since you came to the Keep," said Issak.

Temmin's stomach lurched. "I changed my mind about it because I found something out. I found out…I found out she's my sister. Half-sister —I didn't know. My father told me when I got here. It changed everything about the way I saw it. She was my sister!"

Allis pushed an errant lock of hair behind his ear. "She became a person to you when you found out who she was. The next girl—the one in the forest?" she added at his confused look.

"Arta?"

"You were in a fine position to take her whether she wanted you or not. What could she have done?" said Allis. "Nothing. She even invited a kiss, to hear you tell it. But you knew her. She was a person to you already. And so, when she made it clear she wanted you to stop, you did."

"So it means I'm only a danger to girls I don't know," said Temmin.

"In the simplest of terms, it means you need time in an atmosphere where you can't be indulged," answered Issak.

Indulged. The word sat heavy in his ear. Inside, he knew he was indulged and even petted, but his conscious mind preferred to think of himself as rather put-upon. "I am not 'indulged,'" he said.

"Temmin, you're Heir to one of the greatest nations on earth. Of course you're indulged. You can have or do anything you want," said Issak.

Temmin awkwardly jerked himself upright, out of their reach. "No, in fact, I can't," he said, as haughtily as he could with his fly open; he tucked himself back in. "I didn't have a choice in leaving home, I don't have a choice in my studies, I don't have a choice in my friends"—and here the spotty face of Fennows rose again, sneering. "And I can't choose my path in life. I'll be King, and that's all I can be," he finished.

"You have a choice here," said Allis.

Temmin sat with his elbows on his knees, head down. "I have to think about it."

"We understand, but you need to tell us soon," said Allis. "We need time to prepare. *You* need time to prepare."

"I should go now," said Temmin.

"Anda," called Issak, "please tell the majordomo to bring the Heir's carriage around."

Temmin looked up at the rustle of fabric; the fat servant girl rose from a nearby couch. "Hang on, how long has she been here?"

The girl paused at the door. "The whole time. You're very pretty when you come."

Temmin rose to his feet, turning an appalled purple. "I don't like it when servants turn their faces to the wall—though in this case it would've been the least you could have done!" he sputtered. "I don't believe servants are to be treated impolitely, and I count many servants among my—my dearest friends. But a servant I don't know, sneaking in and observing a... *private moment* that has nothing to do with her in a place where she shouldn't have been—!"

"Where am I supposed to be?" said the girl. "This is my room."

"Your room? This is where the Supplicants live... Are you trying to tell me you're a Supplicant?"

"Prince Temmin of Tremont, may I present to you Miss Anda Barrows, Supplicant of the Lovers' Temple," said Issak.

Anda crossed the room; Temmin hadn't noticed her grace before, and his eyes followed the sway of her hips and breasts. She gave a fluid curtsey, then to his surprise drew him into a kiss so expert it penetrated to his toes. The scent of tea time came from her skin—vanilla cakes, red currant jelly, cream, black tea—and when she pulled away from him, disappointment replaced his astonishment. "You'll like me once you get to know me," she said, patting his cheek.

"Take your impudence off to the majordomo, Anda Supplicant," said Issak affectionately.

The twins' goodbye kisses lingered on Temmin's lips as he rolled back up the broad Promenade to the Keep; he acknowledged the strolling gentry with an occasional distracted wave or nod, but looked straight through even the prettiest young woman on the Promenade.

"My choice. It's my choice whether I do this or not. It's not up to Papa, or Teacher, or anyone—it's up to me alone." He savored the idea, rolling it around and around long after the gates of the Keep closed behind the carriage.

ELEVEN

Dinner that night was a thoroughly uncomfortable meal, but no matter how fast Temmin ate, it never seemed to end. His father kept a stony silence; his mother watched them both with apprehension. Ellika bounced with impatience; Sedra merely crooked an eyebrow at him. Fennows smirked and grimaced and nudged his way through all five courses.

When the ladies left and Affton brought in the port and cheese tray, Temmin swallowed a polite glass and rose to excuse himself. To his surprise, Harsin rose as well. "Fennows, we're leaving the ladies to you," the King said. "I'm sure you won't mind."

"Oh, I should think not!" said Fennows, brightening. "P'rhaps I can finally convince Elly to listen to my poetry!" The lordling knocked back his port, scattering nutshells and cheese rinds, and hurried toward the Small Sitting Room.

Once father and son sat before the fire in Harsin's study, the butler re-appeared with another decanter. "I had Affton set aside the best port for us. No point wasting it on that ass Fennows," snorted Harsin.

As his father filled their glasses, Temmin said, "If you think Fennows is an ass, why is he here?"

"I'm placating Lord Corland. He wants King's laws against slavery repealed. Perfectly legal in Inchar, you know, and he wants to bring his best slaves there up to his northern estates. Seems unlikely to succeed if he does. I'm hesitant to bring masses of them into the country. Corland says it's just a few, but that's how it always starts, and I have enough trouble with revolts in Inchar itself without watching for it inside the country. The Fathers are against importation if only because it will cut into the fees they receive for indentures—why pay for an indentured servant when you can just buy a slave. Besides, Incharis are creatures of the tropics, they mightn't stand the cold. I may still have to let him do it—it's unclear whether King's law actually covers Incharis."

"Don't you decide what King's law is?"

"It's not so simple." They sat in silence, Temmin wishing to be back in his own rooms. "So," said Harsin, "how was the tour?"

Temmin braced himself for the dreaded conversation. "The tour? Oh…it was—it was interesting."

"What did they tempt you with? Platters of sweets laid out on the bare breasts of Beloveds?"

Temmin shot his father a sullen look. "It wasn't like that," he said.

"Really? That's what they offer me whenever I tour it. My last visit with her was about a year ago. I'm due for another."

Temmin's belly clenched. "'Her?'"

"Allis Obby, son, who d'you think I mean?" At Temmin's ashen face, he added, "It's the King's duty, but she and her brother have sex with every influential man the Temple has to tea. Some of the women, too, if more discreetly."

"You've…been with Allis?"

"Just the once. So far."

Temmin's mouth framed silent words. The world became as focused and clear as when he'd defended himself against Nat Horn, and the assassin in the garden.

"I understand your captivation, completely," Harsin continued. "She's beautiful in evening clothes, but she's incomparable out of them, let me tell you. Her breasts are so firm for their size, and she's remarkably flexible. Perhaps the most beautiful woman I've ever bedded."

The blood returned to Temmin's face in a rush, draining his heart dry. This was his, this was his decision, Allis and Issak were his, and now— "And you've bedded a few, haven't you," he said aloud.

"You say that as if I should be ashamed of myself."

"Perhaps you should be, sir. I think of my mother, even if you don't."

"My marriage is no concern of yours," said his father. "It has no bearing on my other activities. Fucking the Embodiment is a royal responsibility, not just an enjoyable afternoon."

"Don't say 'fuck' when you talk about her!"

"Temmin, what do you think she does all day? Who do you think they are, these Obbys?"

"They're the Embodiments of the Gods!"

"They're prostitutes!" shouted Harsin. "They're prostitutes from Belleth! That's where Teacher found them—in a whorehouse in Ouve!"

Temmin shook, half in rage, half in shock. "Who told you this?"

"I didn't really care who they were before now, but with my son and Heir falling under their sway, it was incumbent upon me to find out. They were born at a brothel called the House of Polls. When they reached a certain age, they became prostitutes themselves."

"That can't be true," Temmin insisted, though he remembered something Allis had said at their picnic: "*We've been training for our positions since birth.*"

"Do you see what they are? Will you stop now?" said his father.

A sick green mist crept into Temmin's vision, and the port he'd downed threatened to come back up. "Merciful Amma," he said, and fled the room.

Harsin watched him go. He leaned back against his tufted leather chair and closed his eyes, opening them when Winmer entered from the King's office. "It's done," said Harsin.

Winmer nodded. "His Highness is a romantic young man, sir. These revelations can do nothing but tarnish her in his eyes, possibly beyond cleansing. I must say I wasn't surprised when I got the report."

"Nor I. Poor things," Harsin murmured. Louder, he said, "Well done, Winmer. I'm impressed by the speed of your agents." Harsin closed his eyes again, the firelight casting shadows along the lines of his face.

"Your Majesty, are you well?" said the secretary.

"I blasphemed, Winmer. I called the Embodiments prostitutes."

"I don't believe in blasphemy, sir. Let me refresh your port."

Harsin took the refilled glass. "I don't believe, Winmer—I *know*. I blasphemed, and They'll demand Their price for it. But if it keeps Temmin from the Temple, I'll pay it. Have you sent for Lord Litta?"

"He'll be here in the morning, sir," nodded Winmer.

"Good." Harsin filled his glass again and quickly tossed back half. "I want reinforcements, just in case."

Once in his rooms Temmin spent a restless evening, pacing about his study and running his hands through his hair, to the point that Jenks enquired after his trouble. Temmin refused to answer and tried to dismiss the valet early, but Jenks insisted on preparing him for bed. "If I don't, sir, I'll come back in the morning to your clothes all over the bedchamber and the bathroom turned inside out."

"I'm not a child! I don't need a keeper, or a nurse, or a valet, or anyone. I order you to leave!"

The older man unfolded his arms, and braced himself on the green velvet couch. "Temmin, what's wrong?"

"Everything!" he roared. "Just go away!"

Jenks thinned his mouth into a concerned line, said, "If you need me, I'm near, sir," and left.

Temmin choked on tears as soon as the door closed. He collapsed onto the couch, but returned to his pacing in moments, uneasy in his skin. He hated himself, he hated his father, he hated Jenks for making him lash out, he hated Teacher for encouraging all these erotic notions, he hated Allis and Issak...

Did he hate them? He didn't know. If the Embodiments were simply prostitutes, Fennows was right; they played pretend for the worshippers' titillation and the filling of the Temple's coffers. Allis and her brother wanted political advantage for the Temple, and nothing more. What should he do?

Hours of this, and Temmin tried sleep. As Jenks predicted, he flung his clothes about the room and left his wet washcloth on the bathroom floor, despite an earlier resolution to prove his man wrong.

Lying awake, he obsessed over everything Allis and Issak ever said and did, digging for reasons to believe in them. On that splendid day in the foothills, Allis had said, "When everyone abandoned us, we had one another." What did she mean? It had to be important—perhaps it held his solution. He fell asleep to her pensive voice whispering "abandoned," over and over.

Nightmares assailed him in his sleep; in most, Allis compared him to his father and found him lacking. He woke heartsore.

A silent Jenks attended to him. Temmin couldn't muster the energy to apologize, and Jenks left the study with few words between them, adding to Temmin's heartache. He took Jebby out for a short run, avoided his father's tense, triumphant eye at breakfast, and stomped upstairs in perhaps the worst mood of his short life. Teacher awaited.

Temmin launched into the night's revelations without a greeting. "Is it true, Teacher, what my father said? They whored themselves out? How can I believe anything they ever tell me? How can I believe anything *you* ever tell me?"

Temmin didn't think Teacher could be any paler, but his tutor's face went a silent, deadly white. "Forgive me, I have sudden business to attend to," whispered Teacher.

"What business? What are you going to do?"

"If you want to know the truth, I suggest you not delay. Ride to the Temple and ease your mind. Allis and Issak will answer any questions you put to them, even these."

"But I asked *you* a question!" he said to Teacher's retreating back. "Pagg damn it, answer me! How can I trust you! Augh!" He ran his fingers through his hair, setting it on end. "Jenks! Where are you?" He stuck his head out the door. "Find Jenks now," he said to the nearest footman.

Temmin strode into his wardrobe. Jenks hurried in not long after, still pulling on his coat. "I was taking my morning tea. What's amiss, Your Highness?"

Temmin shoved a coat at him. "I need to ride to the Temple. Will this do?"

"No, try this one, sir," said Jenks, professionalism overtaking concern. "Your linen is fine. Buff waistcoat and breeches, your best riding boots, the low topper. And this cravat. The amber studs and cufflinks, a plain pin. You need to brush your hair, and I should have shaved you this morning."

"Doesn't matter." He pulled off his morning trousers and waistcoat.

"Temmin, will you please tell me what's wrong?" pleaded the big man.

Temmin stopped, one leg in the breeches and the new waistcoat unbuttoned. He slumped onto a bench. "If you found out that...that people close to you, people you cared about, might not be what you thought they were..."

"Oh?" said Jenks, his face still and apprehensive. "Who?" He waited as Temmin slipped his other leg into the breeches and pulled them up.

"The Embodiments," said Temmin.

Jenks relaxed a fraction, then tensed in shock.

"What if you found out they weren't holy," Temmin continued, "that they were...what if you found something like that out?"

"Where are you hearing such things?"

"My father told me last night they were born in a whorehouse in Ouve. That they...damn it, Jenks, he said they were prostitutes. And that she's his leavings," he bit out. "He had her a year ago."

Jenks paused, Temmin's gloves in one hand. "I understand why you're upset. It would upset me, too, were I in your shoes. But it's the King's duty to lie with Neya's Embodiment, just as it is for him to hold council with Pagg's Embodiment, and fight with Farr's. As for the Holy Ones, they were chosen by the Gods, sir. Why would their past have any bearing on their suitability?"

"They were chosen by Teacher. He may think he's a god, but I don't see his temple on the Promenade. How can you be holy and have sex for money?" He snatched the gloves from Jenks and marched from the wardrobe to the study. "Of course, everyone says that's what they do now."

"That's blasphemy!" said Jenks, trailing behind.

"If it's blasphemy, my father said enough last night for the Gods to strike him down where he stood, and I saw him at breakfast, quite well. And then there's Fennows."

"So we're taking Lord Fennows' word, now, sir? You said he was a 'fathead.'"

Temmin wheeled on him. "You forget yourself, Jenks! You are speaking of a peer. And you're addressing the Heir, not a little boy!" He slammed his hat on his head and ran from the Keep to the stables, boot heels scattering the pathway gravel. Once there, he brushed off every groom, saddled and mounted the barely-dry Jebby himself, and dashed down the long drive to the gates.

The Guards saw him coming. They shouted for him to please wait, Your Highness, you must have a detail with you, sir, please, sir, slow down! But he showed no signs of doing so. The Guards managed to open the gates enough for a single rider, and he thundered past. If he saw a gateminder gallop off toward the Guards' compound, he paid him no mind.

Snow melt swelled the Feather River; its roar swallowed the sound of Jeb's hooves as they pounded across Kingsbridge into Old Town. Traffic brought his pace to a trot, giving the crowds a chance to recognize him. He heard the now-familiar cheers, and a path cleared enough for him to reach the Promenade without slowing to a walk.

At the Lovers' Temple, he gave the chestnut to a groom standing at the foot of the steps, and charged into the Great Hall. There he stopped, unsure what to do next, until the beautiful young man from the day before appeared, bowing before him. "Your Highness, you're unexpected," he said. "My name is Senik. Please, let me offer you refreshment while I find a senior—"

"I don't want a senior anything. You will find the Embodiments, preferably both of them," interrupted Temmin. "I don't care where I wait. I want to speak with them and only them immediately."

"Of course," said the startled young man. "Please, follow me, sir."

Senik led him to the same reception room where he'd had tea with the Most Highs and left him on the low couch, until the unlikely Anda Supplicant broke his solitude. She sailed in with the tea things, her Temple clothes flowing around her over-abundant curves. "I don't want tea, I want Allis," he snapped at her.

"Don't we all, and hello to you, too," she replied, sitting opposite. Her brown eyes sparkled with good humor; Temmin wanted to pull her hair out. "Never worry, Senik is on their trail. Don't let looks fool you, he's very efficient. Milk? Sugar?" Temmin scowled, but took the proferred cup. "Merciful Amma, I haven't seen such a look since I told my mother the Temple accepted my Supplicancy. Speaking of which, are you joining us?"

"It's none of your concern, and you're being awfully familiar with me."

Anda rose to sit beside him. She fixed his eye, despite her plainness; her curves reminded him of the rolling grasslands and grain fields of Whithorse. Her light brown hair fell to her hips in a shiny river, and she still smelled so good, of tea and jelly cakes. She struck him less as fat, and more as delicious. "Titles don't mean much in a temple," she said. "If you take Supplicancy, I'll outrank you. I'll be helping teach you. Which involves a great deal of intimacy, if you haven't guessed, and intimacy breeds concern, or should."

"I don't want you as my teacher," he said. He moved away but the couch's arm blocked his escape.

Anda leaned in. "Oh, yes, you do. I make you uncomfortable. You tell yourself you don't like my body, but your eyes linger a little too long on it." Temmin reddened, remembering her kiss. "You want to see my breasts again. You want to kiss me again." She brought her face nose to nose. "You want to make love with me," she whispered. She settled back against the cushions again, a smile rounding her cheeks. "Some day soon, maybe you will! Oh, don't be angry, Your Highness," she added at Temmin's deep frown, "I'm not mocking you. I'm reading you. It's not my place to take your virginity. I don't want to be responsible for you. I like you, and you're very pretty and all, but someone like you needs the Embodiments, not me."

"Someone like me?"

"Someone with so much potential power and skill, more than my own —ah! Holy Ones." Anda stood and bowed as Issak and Allis entered; Temmin remained fixed to the couch.

Issak put his fingers under Anda's chin. "Have you been teasing him, Anda?"

"Oh, yes, Holy One!" she answered.

Issak pronounced her a baggage and kissed her, then gave Temmin a questioning look. "Your Highness?"

"What's wrong, Temmin?" said Allis. "Anda, you may leave us."

"I've tried to jolly him up," said Anda as she departed, "but he won't be jollied."

The door closed. Temmin said, "I know about you."

Allis took Issak's hand. "Know what about us?"

"…That you come from Ouve. That… My father said some things about you, told me things about you I'm having a hard time believing or understanding."

"Coming from Ouve isn't so bad, Temmin, despite its reputation. We're not so lazy as all *that*," said Issak, pulling his sister to sit next to him on the opposite couch.

"No, no," said Temmin, studying his shoes. "He told me about…about your mother."

"Our mother is dead," said Allis. Her voice pulled his eyes from the floor; she looked back at him, wide-eyed and tensed as if expecting a blow.

"What about her?" said Issak in an even voice.

"That she was a prostitute," Temmin forced out, dropping his eyes again. "That you were prostitutes."

Neither twin spoke. It must be true, then. Temmin didn't trust himself to look up again, and had almost resolved to take his leave, when Issak said, "Yes, she was, and yes, we were. She died just before we turned ten. We were ten, Temmin. Do you understand what I'm saying? We were ten."

"Maman worked for Mistress Polls, and owed her a great deal of money when she died. Mistress Polls made us work it off," murmured Allis.

"Couldn't you have done something else there?" Temmin said to the floor. "Cleaned? Run errands? Washed dishes?"

"Don't you think we would have if we could have?" said Issak. "We were worth too much." Temmin looked up from beneath his golden brows to meet Issak's intense stare. "Do you know how much our virginities brought, Your Highness?"

"Virginities?" he faltered. "But you were only ten, who would—"

"A thousand gold apiece is what she sold them for," said Issak. "After that, clients had us both, or separately, or watched us together. You look a little ill, Your Highness. Didn't you know some men enjoy the company of children? How old do you think we were when this happened? We turn twenty-one this year."

"I hadn't thought it through," he said miserably. "I just…it seemed so wrong, prostitutes as Embodiments, especially after everything some people have said about you… Why didn't you go to a Mother's House?"

"Mistress Polls said a Mother's House wouldn't take us because we were the children of a whore—we were dirt, we couldn't even pray at a temple let alone live at one," said Allis.

"She was lying, of course," continued Issak, "but we didn't know it. The House of Polls was all we'd ever known. We were born there. We'd still be there if Teacher hadn't rescued us."

"How big was your mother's debt?"

Issak glowered. "We paid it ten times over, in just three spokes. Polls always works the accounts in her favor. No one who's worked for her has ever balanced an account. Her people are no better than slaves, but that's how it is in some houses. Maybe most."

"The House isn't there any more, though," said Allis in a far-away voice. "Teacher says it burned to the ground. I wish I'd set the fire myself."

"But it's illegal, using children like that, isn't it?" said Temmin.

Issak gave an uncharacteristic, barking laugh. "Why do you think she charged so much? You can buy anything if you have money, Temmin. Anything."

"Teacher bought us, I suppose you could say," said Allis, returning her attention to the room. "He settled our debt with Polls, and brought us here."

"I'm glad he did, it must've been awful," said Temmin, his blue eyes filling with tears. "Awful. Merciful Amma, I can't think about how awful! I'm so sorry. My father made me so angry, I just—I didn't think it through. He kept saying you were prostitutes, and he kept talking about how beautiful you were naked, Allis. That's also true, isn't it? You've had sex with my father."

"He's the King," she answered. "It's our duty, both his and mine. Once a year. If he enjoyed himself, I'm glad, but it has nothing to do with anything other than duty. I've tried to tell you, Temmin, it's what Issak and I do."

A sob escaped before Temmin collected himself. "I'm sorry. I'm sorry. I thought of you—of both of you—as mine. Not mine like you belonged to me, or anything," he amended, waving his hand. "But like this was special. It wasn't something my parents were giving me, or anything—it was mine. My choice. It's my choice, not his!"

Issak rose, Allis close behind him, and they sat next to Temmin, one on each side. "It's still your choice," said Issak. "You can choose to come here or not, it's no one else's decision but yours."

"Don't make it now," said Allis, taking his hand. "Go home. Think a little longer. Pray—I wish you'd pray. You've been called, but it's up to you whether you answer. Now, don't cry, Tem, our past is past for us."

"Why are you comforting me?" he asked through his tears.

Issak put his arms around Temmin, and Allis crawled into his lap. "In this Temple, we comfort people," said Issak, touching his forehead to Temmin's, "and in the end, it comforts us."

In Greenflower Street, Maleen Polls stood before an already-overloaded hackney. Workers loaded trunk after trunk on the carriage under her man Deck's eye, until the springs wheezed in protest and the coachman advised her to hire a second carriage. "I'm in a hurry," snapped Maleen. "I must be aboard the *Crescent Moon* as fast as I can, and if you take much longer I'll walk!"

"Will you ever explain to me why you're leaving so hastily? You never showed the slightest inclination to sell, though I've asked you a thousand times," said the tall blonde woman standing beside her.

"I am tired, and I've always wanted to see Sairland. I know I've left the House in good hands, Diria." Maleen caught curious eyes peeping from behind the windows' heavy curtains. Shouldn't she be sadder about leaving? No, not with the Strange Gentleman on her trail.

"You haven't 'left' the House with me," huffed Diria. "I paid good money for it!"

"You got a bargain, and you know it. Finally!" The workmen tightened the last strap, old Deck clambered painfully onto the driver's box beside the coachman, and she pulled herself into the carriage, too hurried to accept a hand up.

"Goodbye, Maleen!" called Diria as the carriage rolled away.

Maleen neither answered nor looked back, her mind focused on her getaway. She might have some time before the Strange Gentleman caught up with her, or even heard what she'd done, but she wasn't taking any chances. She wouldn't feel safe until she boarded the *Crescent Moon*. If the Strange Gentleman were the King's agent, as she could only suppose, once she left dry land he could not touch her.

She cast her mind back to the trunks weighing down the carriage. One held clothes adequate for the journey and the sparest of wardrobes; she would bespeak new dresses and linen in Apecto. The other ten contained nothing but gold in small chests wrapped in clothes enough to muffle any sound—in all, fifty-thousand pieces. To be on the safe side, she'd sewed another thousand into the hems of all her traveling clothes; it made her dresses drape oddly, but she didn't care. If she landed at Apecto with nothing but the thousand, she could establish herself in a small house with two or three young ladies, perhaps a youth as well, and train them up to her standards. It wouldn't be as grand as the ten trunks full, but she'd be alive.

At the docks, hired men hoisted the trunks down from the carriage, its springs groaning in relief; the men continued onto the *Crescent Moon* and piled all but the one holding her clothes in a heap before the gangway. Deck went aboard to see to their stowing. Until then, the trunks blocked her way; she couldn't come aboard.

Maleen stood on the harbor's high rock wall, watching the loading and fidgeting. She sat atop the trunk, amusing herself with her reflection in its shiny new brass fittings.

A mist rose up through its bright lock.

Maleen bounced off the chest in alarm. How could it be on fire?

The mist formed into something like water; she put her hand over her heart in sudden dread, and turned to run for the ship. Unseen hands clamped around her. "Hello, Mistress Polls," said the cool voice she still heard in nightmares. The Strange Gentleman walked into her sight. "I thought you'd hold your tongue rather than see me again. I did promise to kill you, and promises are to be kept." The icy silver eyes scanned her as she stood gasping, the air around her head damp and heavy with her own breath. "The shorter hair suits you. Shall I light it on fire? Or shall I smother you?" The Strange Gentleman cast an appraising glance at her dress. "No. I shall be merciful. This will be faster."

A gesture, and the invisible hands swept her over the harbor wall. The black, oily water closed over her head; she stared upward as she sank, arms stretched over her head reaching for the surface, the gold coins in her hem pulling her after them to the harbor's bottom. Her screams sent fat bubbles up through the foulness until her lungs contained nothing but water.

Teacher watched until the last bubble popped, interrupted at the end when Deck ran down the gangplank to the harbor wall. He seemed to consider diving in after her, but in the end only wrung his bony hands. "Ai! Mistress!" Deck wailed, his thin chest heaving. He saw the figure dressed in black, and flinched away, making the Sign of Amma. "The Black Man! Ai, Mistress, what have you done!"

"She has left you an independent man," said Teacher. "My friends say you were kind to them, and for their sake, I will not kill you. Keep her trunks, continue your voyage to Sairland, and never come back. When you land, give two of those trunks to Amma and two each to Nerr and Neya in return for your life. You never knew Maleen Polls, nor anyone else who lived in her house. Am I understood?"

Deck stared. He nodded, turned and ran aboard the *Crescent Moon*, leaving Maleen's last trunk behind. Teacher kicked at it absently, then shined a brass corner with a handkerchief. If anyone saw the black figure swirl into a fluid mass and disappear, he never told a soul.

Temmin stayed with Allis and Issak until late in the afternoon: long talks about their mother, and coming to the City under Teacher's protection; lunch with the irrepressible Anda; and kisses—only a few. Pressing past a kiss reminded him of the twins' past, and though they didn't speak of it, Temmin saw flickers of memory pass through their eyes.

When they gave him their final kisses and saw him to the Temple's entrance, Temmin found Brother Mardus waiting, a Guard contingent ranged around him. Nervous petitioners picked their way up the steps under their stern eyes. "Your Highness," said Mardus.

"Brother Mardus, I'm surprised to see you!"

"You shouldn't be." The two men walked down the stairs; at the bottom stood Jebby, with Mardus's own horse. "Now, sir, you are going to get on that horse, and you're going to follow our lead. You will not break away, and you will do what I tell you when I tell you. Are we clear?"

"Yes, of course, Brother Mardus. I just don't see what—"

"When we are not in public, I will explain the obvious to you, sir," rumbled Mardus. "When His Majesty and I say you will not leave the grounds without an escort, we mean you will not leave the grounds without an escort. Bad enough you had to come here," he added.

Mardus and Temmin mounted their horses. Guards blocked the Promenade in both directions, and the Temple's Own crossbowmen once again lined the rooftop. "All this?"

"All this, sir, because you rode out undefended. Don't do it again," said Mardus.

"I was on urgent business!"

"As a priest of Farr I support your candidacy, sir, but nothing involving that Temple is urgent." Mardus tapped his heels into his horse's sides, sending them all into a trot; the ride passed in silence.

Temmin found tea laid out on the little table by his study window, but no Jenks. He demolished the cakes and sandwiches, and pondered how best to apologize. Jenks must be deeply offended this time, and who could blame him? What possessed him to put Percy's dignity above Jenks? Jenks was worth a hundred thousand Fennowses.

The man himself entered with the late post, and Temmin jumped up, rattling the teapot lid. "Jenks, I'm so sorry..." He trailed off at his man's grim face. "Oh, I've really done it this time, haven't I?"

"Your Highness, you must learn to school your temper," said Jenks, depositing the post beside the now-askew teapot and picking up Temmin's discarded riding coat.

"I know, I know," he moaned. "What is the matter with me! Was my temper ever this bad at home?"

"No, sir."

Jenks kept walking. After a moment's hesitation, Temmin followed him into the wardrobe, and found him brushing out the riding coat. "Will you forgive me?" Temmin persisted.

"I would find it much easier if you would tell me why you're so upset. If I am going to be chewed on for something that has nothing to do with me, I deserve to know what it is."

"Oh. It's...complicated."

"Then best start now."

Temmin laid it all out in an impassioned rush—an edited version of the Temple tour, his father's accusations and boasts, the twins' revelations, and Brother Mardus's anger and paradoxical support. "But it was what my father said—do you understand why this has been hard for me to talk to anyone about? And you especially!"

Jenks had stopped tending to the coat and sat on the wardrobe bench, listening intently. "What do you intend to do, Temmin?" he said.

"I'm taking Supplicancy. I think."

"Is it because you're angry at your father? That's a terrible reason to take orders, even temporary orders."

Temmin stopped. "...Maybe. I don't know. Allis says I should pray. I'm not used to praying—I mean, not proper prayer—and I don't want to go back into town to pray at the Temple. Not with a Guard detail, and Mardus pursing his lips on the front steps, and the Temple's Own following me around, and everyone staring at me."

"The servants tell me the family has a chapel. It's at the foot of the Tower. I don't think it's used much now. It would be quite private. Perhaps you might pray there."

Temmin took dinner in his room that night. Another meal under his father's withering eye curdled even his stomach, and the true story of the Obbys' past angered him enough to loosen his tongue past wisdom.

After dinner, Jenks inquired discreetly as to the chapel's exact location. Despite serious doubts, Temmin took a bowl of ritual sweets and a bouquet of flowers, and wound his way through endless hallways and galleries until he found himself in the Keep's oldest part, called the Fortress. He'd walked this way when Teacher dragged him through a reflection into the Tower, though in the opposite direction. He recognized the stairway leading up and up to Teacher's library. To one side stood a set of wooden doors, covered with archaic carvings. He recognized the sigils of Temmin the Great on one door and Gethin the First on the other as he pushed through them into the chapel.

Someone kept the windowless, ancient room within well-tended. Its style pointed to the Keep's founding a thousand years before; vaulted stone rose above tapestried walls to meet in graceful apexes. Eight altars had been carved from the bedrock, each with its God. Purple and gold seasonal draperies wreathed Pagg's niche, in honor of His spoke, Spring's Beginning. Candles flickered before all the altars, reflecting off the smooth, polished wood of the padded kneeling benches set in rows.

Empty glass vases waited before Nerr's statue, a silver pitcher of fresh water beside them. He settled the flowers, and carefully stacked the pink and white candies at Neya's feet. He knelt on the bench nearest the Twins, and prayed. "Lord, Lady, I don't know what to do. Are You calling me, or is this just about wanting the Embodiments? Or being mad at my father? I want to do the right thing. I know I haven't been the most faithful person —no, actually, I've always believed, I just haven't gone through the forms perhaps as much as I should. Just send me a sign. Let me know what I should do."

Minutes ticked by. His knees hurt, and his eyes watered from staring at the candles. He sighed, and sank back on his heels. "I just want a sign, from either of You!"

"Do you expect the statues to speak?" came a voice near the doors.

"Gah!" Temmin leaped to his feet. "Why do you always have to sneak up on people!"

"I do not 'sneak up on people,'" said Teacher. "Some people do not pay attention. What brings you here? I did not think prayer in your line."

"It was Allis's idea," said Temmin, spreading his arms wide and dropping them to his sides. "I don't know what I expected. I hoped something would happen."

"Are you giving up? How long have you been here?"

"Oh, Gods, forever. Well—ten minutes." Temmin consulted his pocket watch. "Oh. Five. Five minutes."

"Hm." Teacher walked up the aisle toward the altars. "Every Temple has its ecstatic practices. One tends to connect more directly with the Gods that way. Lovers dance themselves into a trance. Sisters deny themselves food and sleep. The Scholars of Eddin hang upside down, sometimes for days."

"All of them?"

"That kind of communion does not appeal to everyone."

"I just don't know what I'm listening for."

"You will not know until you hear it. Do you truly want an answer?"

Temmin paused. "Yes. I want to make sure I do the right thing."

"Then give it more time, Your Highness. If you cannot kneel, stand. If you cannot stand, pace. When you find your mind wandering, direct it back to listening. Do not force it. Just…listen. You may not get an answer, and you may not do the right thing anyway. But prayer will take you further than thought sometimes. I will leave you now."

When Teacher left, Temmin resumed kneeling, but abandoned it for pacing. He always thought best when pacing; perhaps he prayed best when pacing. He took up a circuit around the chapel, doing his best to focus without straining. His mind flitted to Jebby; he returned it to listening. His father, Allis and Issak, Ibbit's polemics against men ever attaining any sort of spiritual life, Fennows, Sedra, Jenks, Ellika, his mother, the scenes in the petitioning rooms, Mattie, Anda, Fen—Alvo—all thoughts threatening to distract him. But he let them float away, sometimes, as with thoughts of Allis, with difficulty.

He emptied his mind, and kept pacing. He emptied it again, and kept pacing. Two hours of emptying, and a tiny voice in his mind, a voice not his own, whispered, "Temmin."

He halted. The emptiness filled, and the voice vanished. But he had heard it.

He left the chapel, and took the long walk through the castle to the Residence at a trot; he banged on his father's door. Temmin brushed past the King's valet into the receiving room. "Is he awake, Gram?"

"His Majesty is closeted with Mr Winmer, Your Highness," said Gram stiffly.

"Uncloset him. Winmer should be done with him at this hour."

Gram's eyebrows shot into his hairline. "Indeed, sir?"

"Indeed. Tell him I'm here." Gram bowed just enough, and disappeared into the King's private rooms.

Harsin entered in shirtsleeves, to find Temmin helping himself to brandy from the sideboard. "To what do I owe the pleasure, son?"

"I doubt you'll get much pleasure out of it. I've been to the Temple and talked with Allis and Issak," said Temmin. "They were ten, sir. Did you know? I'll take your silence as 'yes.'"

"I'm surprised you had the courage to confront them."

"Confront them?" shouted Temmin. "I can ask them anything! And they told me everything. I trust them! They tell me the truth! I'm going, Father. The Gods have called me, and I'm going."

"You don't understand! This is a mistake! You are costing me—"

"I don't understand your political situation and I don't care. You are King. You rule absolutely. Everyone's always going on about what an astute ruler you are—figure out how to turn it to your advantage. Ask Sedra to help you," he snarled. "It's only for two years, and I will come out of it the stronger, with skills I can use when I am king in my turn."

Harsin purpled. "You will make me a laughingstock."

"Because I'm a virgin? That's hardly the main measure of a man."

"What would you know about the measure of a man?"

Temmin downed the brandy's dregs and smacked the snifter on the sideboard. "More than you think." He stomped from the room, slamming the door behind him.

"There's the Gods' revenge for my blasphemy," said Harsin to the empty room.

TWELVE

Temmin sent a message to the twins that night, by way of a sleepy footman. The next morning, a postulant Lover delivered the response; it sat on the library table when Temmin returned from a solitary breakfast.

"Disregard me," said Teacher, lounging by the window. "By all means, read your letter."

Temmin sat down and ran a finger over the Lovers' Temple sigil stamped into the wax. Breaking it felt like sealing his fate, though he'd sealed it the night before in his father's study. "Your Highness," it began. "Your presence is required at the Lovers' Temple from Farrday, the 34th day of Spring's Beginning, through Ammaday, the 35th day of Spring's Beginning to prepare for your admittance as our Supplicant." The elegant writing included no signature.

"That is from the Embodiments, I assume. Did you find your answer last night, then?" said Teacher.

"I would've thought my father told you this morning."

"I have not seen him yet, though I wager when I do we will have quite the spirited discussion." Teacher moved to sit atop the table. "What did you decide?"

"I'm taking Supplicancy."

A flicker crossed Teacher's dispassionate face. "You are sure? You may change your mind, right up until the moment you take orders."

"I'm as sure as I can be," said Temmin. "I heard…it sounds ridiculous, but I'm talking to a man who walks through mirrors, so…I heard a little voice calling my name. That's all." He looked up into the pale silver eyes. "I think I've been called. It feels like the right thing to do. Allis and Issak have been more trustworthy than my own father. So…I told them I'm doing it. Paggday—it's not my initiation, is it?"

"No," said Teacher. "That will be at the Neya's Day Spectacle."

"In front of everyone?"

"You must be sure of yourself. Public proclamation confirms that surety. You will be learning all about it when you are there on Paggday."

Temmin fingered the old red book, still lying on the table since his last lesson. "What if I'm wrong?"

"We pick a path, we walk it as best we can, and we change course if we find we have taken the wrong way. How gracefully a man adapts is one of his greatest measures. Shall we continue?"

Temmin opened the book.

Warin arrived home leading a laden pack horse. The door swung open at his touch, unlatched; he tripped on an empty water bucket just inside. Ashes filled the stone-cold hearth.

He called for Emmae, but no answer came. He ran outside and called again, ran to all the places he thought she might be, but he didn't find her. His heart gave a great thud, and he ran back to the cottage. There, beside the hearth, he found the newly-shined silver tray. A message glowed on the table top, burned into the wood:

> *I found a girl left all alone and took her home for safekeeping*
> *—H*

Warin seized the tray. "Show me Hildin of Tremont!" he shouted, but it reflected only his own stricken face. He threw the tray against the chimney to clatter against the hearthstones.

Hildin had Emmae. Warin had worried about Travelers and wanderers of all sorts, but never thought his brother would take her. How had she found the tray? What had possessed her to polish it? How could he have been sentimental enough to bring it with him in the first place? He should have told her about the danger, about reflections, about Hildin. How could he have told her without telling her who he was—or about her enchantment? He should have told her everything. No, he should have kept going ten years ago, across the river into Leute, where Hildin couldn't find him. But leaving the kingdom meant losing his magic; leaving his father and the throne behind had left him cursing the Gods for his prophesied fate, and now he cursed himself for his weakness and pride.

He shuddered, thinking of her enchantment. Hildin had to have discovered it by now.

Warin unloaded the horse. It had no saddle, but he didn't need one. He sorted through the new supplies, pulling out what he wanted and storing the rest in the cottage. Perhaps he and Emmae might return; perhaps the leavings might serve some other poor man. He came upon Emmae's ring and promised ribbons, and tucked them in his pouch. He would give them to her yet.

When he had what he needed for his journey strapped to the horse's back, he went to the cupboard a final time. He lifted up its false bottom and took out a sword, still kept sharp in its scabbard, and a little box. He shouldered the sword's harness, added the box to Emmae's presents in his pouch, and picked up the silver tray.

Warin propped the tray against a tree. "Show me the Traveler Queen," he shouted. His image faded, and the old crone appeared, grinning and beckoning. Warin led the horse into the reflection.

He emerged into a clearing; the Travelers' bright caravans surrounded him.

"And a horse, too!" chuckled the old woman. "What took you so long to find me, Warin?"

"I couldn't leave Emmae to search for you on foot, and I couldn't risk Hildin finding me if I searched for you by reflection."

"Emmae?"

"That unfortunate girl you enchanted!"

"Ah, you found her, then! I knew you would. How is she?"

"How do you think she is, you cruel old bitch?" said Warin.

The woman laughed. "An old bitch? Perhaps. But you have no idea what real cruelty is, Prince."

Warin scooped a ball of flames from the cookfire and bounced it. "Hildin has her, and you owe me an explanation. You owe her one—you owe her your help!"

"Or what?" she said. "Do you honestly think I'm frightened of a little fire ball, Your Highness?"

"Perhaps not for yourself, but I'm willing to wager your wagons would burn nicely."

A rusty-haired young man approached and put an arm around the old woman. "You are among friends, Prince Warin, truly."

Warin frowned, studying the young man. "You look familiar. I'm sure I've traded with you—you're her son. And yet the man I knew—"

"Had a wall-eye," grinned the Traveler Prince. "I've been cured. Now is not the time to threaten. Calm yourself."

"Give me a reason to be calm!" said Warin. He pulled a second ball from the fire and stood, one in each hand.

"Stop playing, you'll burn someone," said the Traveler Queen. "Connin, return those to the fire."

The Traveler Prince flicked his fingers; the fireballs shot into his hands and from there back to the campfire, leaving Warin breathless and even angrier than before. He drew his sword, and Connin stepped back, arms spread. "Friends, Your Highness. We've always known who you are. If we meant you harm, we could have killed you in your sleep any time in the last ten years. Please, eat with us."

Warin sheathed his sword, uneasy but pragmatic, and sat down by the fire. The old woman handed him a bowl of rabbit stew and a hunk of brown bread to sop in it. "Prince Warin, I gave you your prophecy at your naming, as I do for every royal son. You didn't like yours, and so you ran away."

Warin stared into the fire until his eyes dried out. "I swore I would never take the throne, or marry, if it meant my father's murder."

"Your Highness, our fortunes find us wherever we are," murmured the Queen.

"I never understood Hildin's prophecy: 'As a rabbit, so a man.'"

"You will," she said in a changed voice.

He looked up; a beautiful, dark woman with a round face and bright eyes had taken the crone's place. He blinked. She became grizzled and withered again, but her dark eyes still twinkled and danced. He shivered. "I want to find Emmae and take her home with me. She's mine whether we marry or no. You know who she is, don't you?"

She nodded. "Her real name is Edmerka. She's the only child of King Fredrik of Leute."

"A princess?" he gasped. That changed everything. He couldn't take her back to the cottage; her father would never allow it, and in good conscience he knew it would be wrong to keep her from her duty. Besides, he couldn't marry her. When he guessed she was the daughter of a merchant, not standing before Pagg sat easier in his mind, but it wouldn't do for a princess.

The Traveler Queen told him everything: the unpaid debt revenged; the gift of amnesia paid for in maiden's blood. "It cured my son's eyes. Powerful stuff. You noted the mark on her hip? No babies will come before it fades, but the kindling spell will not fade, nor can I remove it."

"Tell me why I shouldn't kill you for this," said Warin.

"That you'd be dead before you raised a finger is beside the point," answered Connin. "We'll help you get her back."

"I have always aided your family," said the Queen. "I bear you no ill will personally, Warin, but the Tremonts are no friends of mine. And yet, I have had no choice but to aid you. All of it done for love, Your Highness." She paused. "The Leutish princess was meant to be enchanted. The Tremontine Heir was meant to find her. The two were meant to fall in love." She leaned forward and patted his knee. "You tried to escape your fate, but fate brought you Emmae. Will you return to the Keep for her? Even with your prophecy?"

"Yes," rasped Warin. "I can't leave her with Hildin, even…even if she'll never be mine."

"Then we will go with you. It's faster and safer with us than on your own."

"Is there any way to remove her curse? Any way at all?"

"She must bathe in the blood of a king," replied the crone.

Warin shuddered; if it meant killing his father, or Fredrik of Leute, she was doomed for life. He murmured his thanks, and rose to fetch his bedroll.

"One last thing, Your Highness?" faltered the Queen. "Have you seen Teacher?"

"Teacher? Not since I left the Keep," said the startled Warin. "You'd have more recent word than I do. Why not just summon his image in a reflection?"

The Queen gave him a faint, sad smile. "Good night, Your Highness. It's many days to the Keep, and we start early tomorrow."

Warin lay on his bedroll, eyes following cinders into the night sky. If he went back for Emmae, he would be forced to stay and take the throne some day himself. In his youth, he'd dreamed of ruling his people well, until the full import of his prophecy weighed down on him. He had schooled himself then to renounce the throne in spirit as well as fact, and lead a quiet life far from the Keep. That was all over now. His father faced a violent death at Warin's hand.

He reached into his pouch for the little box; it tangled in Emmae's ribbons, but he fished it out at last. It contained nothing but a mirror inside the lid. "Show me Emmae...Edmerka of Leute," he whispered. When no image came, he tried Hildin, and then Teacher. But the mirror showed him nothing but himself. Warin closed the box, sad but relieved; he hadn't seen her, but he also hadn't seen what his brother might be doing to her.

He closed his eyes. If he had to return to the Keep, he would become king in time. Perhaps, he thought as he drifted off, he could then atone for his father's death and remove Emmae's enchantment with his own life's blood.

As the days passed, Hildin and Gian came to Emmae every night, and sometimes during the day as well; she had no choice but to enter into everything they did to her. "I will break you soon," Hildin said once. "Every time I take you, you are a little less hesitant, a little more eager.

Fight harder, darling, I'm not tired of it yet!" She cried aloud, in ecstasy and despair, and Gian licked the tears from her cheeks.

Emmae grew despondent. Meg told the Prince the girl never slept; Hildin took to using the enchanted ring to force sleep upon her.

Meanwhile, King Gethin fell from madness to near-unconsciousness; his time drew short. Hildin sat with him, watching him sleep, until his father roused and took his hand. "Warin? I knew you'd return," said the King, his voice weak and crackling, as if he breathed through water.

"I am Hildin, sir," grated the son. "Warin is dead."

"Warin dead?" wept Gethin. "Oh, my son, my only son!" Hildin snatched his hand away. Gethin cried himself into stertorous insensibility.

The Prince scowled into the fire; he planned to use Warin's girl harshly tonight. Teacher entered, a man in Leutish livery following. "A messenger from King Fredrik of Leute, sir."

The messenger bowed himself in half, and presented a parchment to Hildin; Hildin unrolled it to find a drawing of a handsome older man with an aquiline nose and a grave face, a jeweled circlet above his brow. "My master, King Fredrik," said the messenger. "The scroll is keyed to the King of Tremont, Your Highness," he added.

"The King is indisposed," said Hildin. "He named me Regent, and as such I stand in his stead." He shot a gloating look at Teacher. "If a magical object…say, a scroll, or even a person…is tied to the King, I may command it." The messenger bowed again.

"Speak! I listen," Hildin said to the parchment.

The drawing blinked as if awakening from a nap. "King Gethin?" it said. "Oh—Prince Hildin! Where's your father?"

"He is on his deathbed," said Hildin. "I am Prince Regent and act for the kingdom."

"Your brother?"

"Is dead. I am the Heir."

Fredrik's drawing nodded in thought. "I see. Very sad. I grieve for your father already. He was ever a good neighbor, and a pious man, and your brother was a brave warrior whose counsel I have missed." Hildin ground his teeth, but nodded. "I have need of a good neighbor and counselor now," continued the drawing. "I seek news of my only child and heir, the

Princess Edmerka. She disappeared near our mutual border three spokes ago, and though I fear bandits, I've received no request for ransom. We've searched everywhere to no avail, though I have respected our treaties and have not crossed the Western Branch of the Leute. I beg for your assistance, since my magic stops at our border."

Hildin's ears pricked up; Warin's hut lay near the border. "We share your deep concern," he said. "Why did you not contact us sooner?"

"For the first two spokes, we thought she lived safe at Allerach, the seat of my wife's family, until the captain of her guards was found raving in a village many miles from there. He had no memory, not of my daughter nor even of himself. When I arrived at Allerach, Baron Aller was completely unconcerned—said he assumed we'd changed our minds. He is also no longer a Baron, as he is missing his head." The drawing drew its brows together. "We have searched for my daughter ever since. We've found most of her retinue, all witless and raving. I am frantic. If you find her, Your Highness, I shall give her to you in gratitude. Your father and I have often spoken of alliance. There is no one to rule after me, though I have tried and tried to get a son. I have no nephews, nor cousins however distant—not even bastards. Our blood has grown thin over the centuries. Through marriage to my daughter, perhaps my grandson—your son—will rule here in Leute. After the way King Gethin and Prince Warin led us against the Northern Incursions—"

"Your Majesty," interrupted Hildin, "We will undertake the search this very night. I shall find her for you and happily take her to wife. I will speak to you in this way again as soon as I have word." Hildin rolled the parchment up, the drawing's mouth still open to respond.

Hildin dismissed the messenger and strode from the King's chambers, Gian and Teacher close behind. "Gian, quickly. Two mirrors to our guest's room." Gian ran off.

"Guest?" said Teacher as they climbed the stairs. "Your Highness, is there something you have not told me?"

Hildin laughed. "Nothing that would concern you until now." He arrived before the chamber above his own, and pressed his ring against a small stone in the wall. A hidden door opened. "After you," said Hildin.

On the bed lay Emmae, the sleeping ring upon her finger. "Who is this girl? Why have you put her to sleep? Those rings were not meant for this," said Teacher, crossing to her side.

"I forbid you to touch that ring," said Hildin. Teacher's hands pulled back as if burned. "Such a glare, but so obedient," chuckled the Prince. "Who is this girl? We shall see."

Gian arrived, carrying two small mirrors. Hildin set one on the bedside table, Emmae's slumbering form reflected in it. The other he set before him. "Show me the Princess Edmerka."

Hildin's reflection rippled and faded. In its place appeared Emmae.

"I have her!" cried Hildin. "I have the Princess, and soon, two thrones!"

"Where did you find her?" said Teacher, the usually impassive face thunderstruck.

"With my brother Warin—oh yes, I found the coward living in the woods near the Leutan border, almost two weeks ago. I'm not entirely sure he won't follow her here. If he does, I shall kill him. Yes, your favorite, everyone's favorite," mocked Hildin.

"Has she been asleep this whole time?" said Teacher.

Hildin snickered. "Oh, no," he said. "There's a very entertaining spell on her."

Teacher snatched a flame from a nearby candle and formed a wand. It danced in the air, drawing golden sigils, until the now-familiar silver answer formed beneath them. Teacher gasped. "How cruel! How could she do this?"

"Ah, you can read it! I discovered its meaning through trial and error, you might say," said Hildin. "The girl has no idea who she is, and I doubt Warin does, either. He found her near his shack and named her Emmae. She thinks he's in love with her."

"And you think he will come for her," said Teacher.

Hildin shrugged. "It doesn't matter either way. If he comes, I kill him. If he doesn't, I take the throne."

"If your father dies and Warin is still alive, I recognize Warin as king. No one can do anything to change that, even were I willing to recognize you."

"Warin dies the minute he appears. I will kill him, and since I am of the blood, you can't stop me, nor can you hurt me yourself. Once I've married the Princess here, I will be king of Tremont and Leute both."

"Not until her father dies," said Teacher.

Hildin smiled, sharp and frightening. "Very true! Now, Teacher, you will not aid my brother in any way. As Regent, my commands over you are as binding as the King's. Go to your library and stay there. Gian, set a guard on the room. Let no one enter or leave. Search the library and Teacher's person for mirrors—anything reflective. When you return, we'll take the ring off, and have a little celebration with Her Highness."

"Will you tell her?" asked Gian.

"Not yet. Give her forgetfulness a little longer."

Hildin waited a day before unfurling Fredrik's parchment again. "King Fredrik, hear me!" he cried.

The drawing came to life, as if Fredrik had been waiting for him. "Speak, I listen—Oh, Your Highness, news so soon?"

"I have found your daughter and have her safe at Tremont Keep."

The drawing became quite animated. "Where? Is she all right?"

"She is happy and safe. We found her held captive in a squalid hut. The scoundrel is dealt with, and he did her no harm—well, the Sister's Temple can be bribed, and I have nothing but compassion for the poor girl. I'll marry her even in her condition," Hildin smiled.

"She's not with child?" gasped the drawing.

"Oh, no, no, nothing of the kind. At least we don't think so at present. Are you near the boundary river?"

"Within a day's ride."

"Bring a mirror across the border into Tremont. I will bring you to the Keep by reflection as soon as you send word through this enchantment."

"Thank you! That saves me countless days of travel! I shall leave you now to prepare," said the drawing; it stilled, and became a parchment portrait again.

*   *   *

Emmae awoke the next morning to find Old Meg bustling about the room. "Child, get up! See here, the Prince has given you new dresses!" She spread out a fine blue gown.

"What?" yawned Emmae. Her sleepiness fled on seeing the clothes, and she sat up in bed. "He's giving me clothes? Why?"

"I'm sure I don't know, dear, but I'm to get you ready as fast as ever I can."

Emmae ate and then let Meg dress her, as impassive as a doll. Meg brushed Emmae's lustrous chestnut hair and set a soft blue veil and a golden circlet over it. "Ah, to be young and have such skin again!" said Meg. "My Hildin will be so pleased! You look like a princess, dear!"

"I'm not a princess. I'm a woodsman's wife. Or was meant to be." Tears pricked at her eyes, but after days of crying, she had few left.

Meg shooed her out the door, where Gian waited to escort her. "Welcome to Tremont Keep, my lady," he smiled. "You look more beautiful than ever. That dress is the very color of your eyes."

"Why are you letting me out?" she said.

"It's time."

She said nothing more as they walked down flights of stairs and through long passageways, focusing her attention instead on her opulent new surroundings. Tapestries covered even the hallways; real wax candles lit every space. Nothing that might serve as a weapon appeared to her.

Hildin stood before the huge doors to the Great Hall. "You may leave," he said to Gian, "and take the servants with you." Hildin waited until Gian cleared the hall, then said, "My Emmae, you're as regal as a queen. Fitting, since you'll be one soon."

"Queen of what? I don't want to be a queen," she growled.

"My father is dying. In fact, he may not last the night."

"My condolences."

"My brother has renounced the throne and has abandoned you. And while I'm not one for Warin's discards, I can make exceptions. I will take his throne, and you as my queen."

"You're assuming I'll marry you, and you also suppose your nobles will accept a commoner as your wife."

"But you're not a commoner," he said. "You, my dear, are the only child of King Fredrik of Leute. Your real name is Edmerka—horrid name, isn't it? I shall continue to call you Emmae. The man you marry will inherit Fredrik's throne, and that man will be me."

"I am not this Edmerka!" she cried, stamping her foot. "You are wrong! And I will never marry you!"

"Yes, you will." He pressed her into the tapestried wall. "Under this fine gown, you're wet for me, Emmae," he whispered in her ear. His fingers found a hard nipple through her bodice and pinched it; she gasped, and closed her eyes in pain and arousal. "I know you burn for me because I burn for you. If you refuse me, I will take you before the entire court, make you straddle me on my throne, everyone knowing you are the Princess Edmerka. And you will not only let me, you will scream out your pleasure before them like the slut you are!" He ground his hardness into her; she whimpered, but spread her legs. "I will fuck you, Emmae, in front of the whole court, in front of your father, and then after? I will let anyone who wants you have you, right there. I will watch you scream and beg under my lords. Your father will disown you—he's uneasy enough you've spent the last three spokes with your 'abductor.' And after I have thoroughly shamed you, I will give you to the stablemen. No one will lift a finger to help you. That," he finished, "is how I know you'll marry me."

Hildin released her, but she stayed pressed against the wall, choking on her breakfast. "Now," he said, "We are going before your father, his retinue, and my nobles. Oh, yes, he's here. I brought him through a reflection just to see you. Your feelings of shame at your captivity and its implications will explain away your obvious emotional turmoil. Nevertheless, you will do your best to be grateful to your rescuer. Won't you?" he said, shaking her just enough.

Emmae nodded wordlessly, and followed him into the Great Hall.

Temmin broke from the book, filled with Emmae's despair and Hildin's resentment. He thought of something his father once said about finding coercion arousing, and wondered if it ran in the family. "Poor girl! Did she live out her life like that, under the spell? How did the King keep her safe? What a sentence, all for refusing to pay a Traveler!"

"Never cross a Traveler, Your Highness. Never. They have nothing to lose, and so fear nothing. By contrast, you have a great deal to lose, for the King is always the hope and possession of his people. Always keep that in mind. The King is not his own man."

"Then why does everyone want to be king?" said Temmin. "If it's such a burden, why take it up?"

"Because not all kings fulfill this hope, nor recognize their servitude. Many of your ancestors ignored their real responsibility and ruled for themselves alone. Even Warin tried to escape it, to live for himself rather than his people."

"You're always going on about being my own man. How am I to be my own man if I serve the kingdom?"

"Servants are their own men and women, even slaves. Even in straitened circumstance—" Here Teacher paused and the long white fingers flexed minutely on the edges of the tabletop. "Even in straitened circumstances, there are choices in one's own conduct, and many decisions to make independently. If a servant cannot make the right decisions for himself, he cannot make them for the ones he serves." Teacher paused, and the silver eyes searched Temmin's face. "By taking Supplicancy, you shoulder a great responsibility that will serve your people as well as yourself. Obeying the Gods and walking among your subjects will bring you closer to both."

"Father says it will hurt the kingdom."

"Do not confuse the kingdom with the nobility, Your Highness." Teacher shifted on the tabletop. "I note you have stopped calling the King 'Papa,' as your mother prefers."

"He doesn't deserve it," said Temmin sullenly.

Temmin returned to the dinner table that night, tensed for a confrontation. Instead, his father ignored him, giving him no more than a cursory "Good evening" and a withering look the one time he spoke. Sedra and his mother watched them both, while Ellika chattered on. Temmin supposed Fennows took his dinner in town; he didn't bother to ask.

After dinner, when the women had retired, Harsin left for his own rooms after one silent glass of port, bolted back and the empty glass deposited on the table. Temmin told himself he didn't care, drank his own glass and joined his mother and sisters in the Small Sitting Room.

"Small" at the Keep meant smaller than the Grand Salon where hundreds of dignitaries and large receptions might be entertained, but larger than the average cottage; it was considered a private room, for the family's use alone. Books and portraits of Temmin's ancestors lined the walls. Despite its high frescoed ceiling covered in gilt and Gods, it had a cozy feel to it, especially in the circle of warmth around the fireplace where the women sat with their handwork; Ellika picked fretfully at her embroidery and Ansella knitted a little silk reticule, while Sedra drew in her sketchbook. At his entrance, Sedra stuck her pencil at a non-regal angle behind her ear.

He could see from their faces that news had traveled fast. He wasn't surprised his mother knew—his father probably spent half the morning berating her for not changing his mind. His sisters hearing of it surprised him. "I saw the envelope that came for you this morning, you see," explained Ellika, so excited her hair seemed curlier.

"I thought it best not to bring it up around Papa," murmured Sedra.

"Can we not talk about it?" he said, folding himself up on a footstool by Ansella's chair. He leaned his head against her knees.

"No, sweetheart, we don't have to," she said, brushing his hair back from his forehead. Ellika deflated in disappointment, but returned to her haphazard stitching; Sedra plucked the pencil from behind her ear and resumed sketching. Mama's familiar perfume of chamomile and roses mingled with the scent of the lavender sachet she used in her wardrobe, wafting faint from the violet silk of her dress. It reminded him of quiet nights in the nursery when he and his sisters were still small: Mama and Nurse knitting and mending, Sedra reading aloud, Ellika playing at paper dolls or stitching, and Jenks cracking nuts by the fire, all at peace with the world and each other. He should be ashamed of himself for this longing, but Temmin longed not for his boyhood as much as the peace with the world he'd had at the Estate. He closed his eyes, listening to the gentle voices, the soft but determined scratch of Sedra's pencil, and the tiny, comforting click of Mama's steel knitting needles, and knew this rare, restful moment would have to carry him through his increasingly complicated life for a long time to come.

Upstairs, the King paced his study; Winmer stood to one side, notepad at the ready as always, and to the other stood Teacher, white hands folded before the long sweep of black robes and the severe black suit beneath them.

"He spent two hours in the chapel last night? Gods," said Harsin. "I don't suppose he was meeting a girl there? That little housemaid? No? Luck is failing me."

"He told me he was praying, Your Majesty, on the advice of Neya's Embodiment," said Teacher.

Harsin groaned. "He said the Gods called him, but I didn't know he believed it!"

"The Gods?" said Winmer; he cast an accusing eye on Teacher, who returned it so coldly that Winmer looked away and shuddered. "Regardless whether he feels divine inspiration," the secretary continued, "there is still hope he might be turned away from his present course."

"Let him go," said Teacher, brows lowered.

"So you've advised," retorted Harsin. "We disagree, and we order you to stay out of it from now on. I would send you to your library for good, but I need you, and you know it. Now, Winmer, give me hope."

"Hope dusts the downstairs rooms, and wears a white cap on its curly little head," smiled Winmer.

"That maid?" snorted Harsin. "He's too timid to do anything on his own."

"Perhaps we might give him a little push, then, sir," said the secretary.

"He's furious," said Temmin to Jenks on Ammaday morning as he tugged on his riding boots. Paggday had been difficult; a usually pleasant day off had turned into a constant reminder of his father's anger, every glance falling like a blow to his forehead.

"You knew he would be, Your Highness," Jenks answered, laying out the prince's morning clothes on the dressing rack. He stepped back to survey the effect.

"You're not still mad, are you?"

"No, no, Temmin. I never can stay mad at you for long," said the valet.

On his ride, Temmin pondered how nice it would have been to have Jenks as his father instead of Harsin. Harsin was forbidding; Jenks was not. Jenks approved of him; Harsin did not. Harsin had been absent most of his life, coming to the Estate twice a year. (He overlooked the times when his father came, with no fanfare or preparations, whenever the children or the Queen took ill.) Jenks, on the other hand, had always been there, a presence as constant and reassuring as his mother's.

Jenks loved him; his father did not, he told himself.

He ate breakfast in his room, avoiding the tension of the night before. When Teacher entered the study, Temmin already sat on the green velvet couch, the old red-bound book on his lap. "I want to sit here today. It's more comfortable."

"To be sure," said Teacher in mild surprise. "There is no real reason to do otherwise."

"So, how bad was it with my father?"

"I have been ordered to 'stay out of it' from now on," replied Teacher. "I can no longer advise you on the subject in any capacity. Just remember what I have told you in the past. That is all I may say."

"I don't need any more advice anyway," Temmin said confidently. "He couldn't have been too mad—he didn't lock you in your room!"

A small smile wavered on Teacher's lips. "He threatened it. But he knows I have endured long periods locked in my room over the centuries. By now it makes little difference to me, and my counsel and support are more valuable than satisfying his pique."

"Did Hildin really lock you in your room?" asked Temmin. He was done thinking about his father.

"Only for a little while. Are you ready to continue?"

Temmin slid a hand over the book's cover and opened it. The blank pages blossomed into words, then pictures, and finally swallowed him up.

King Fredrik found his daughter changed. She'd been so willful, so disdainful, so...*loud*. But now, she rarely met anyone's eyes, and seldom spoke. She kept herself apart, staying in her rooms at dinner. She trembled whenever Hildin came near her, and once almost dropped the wine goblet his page Gian gave her. Even her name had changed. Hildin called her Emmae; he told Fredrik he'd fallen in love with the Princess as soon as he'd set eyes on her, and since "Emmae" meant "worth loving" in the Tremontine, Fredrik chose to believe him.

The changes in her troubled the King at first, but when he dwelled on the three spokes she'd spent with some lout in a shack—Hildin overlooked the possibility that she might carry a commoner's brat, and so Fredrik overlooked his daughter's unhappiness. It would fade in time, along with the doubtless horrible memory of her captivity. From what the old serving woman Meg said, it had been quite the ordeal, though Meg was an odd thing, possibly addle-pated; for instance, she said something about the dead Prince Warin that made no sense at all.

The night before the wedding, Teacher stood in the library at the top of the Tower, surveying the chaos the Guards left behind in their daily search for reflections. Against one curved wall, a large, empty frame that had once held a mirror stood; scrolls and books, once carefully stored on shelves, in drawers and cubbyholes of all kinds, covered the floor in haphazard piles.

Teacher sighed and waved a long-fingered hand. The scrolls slithered to their cubbyholes and drawers. Books floated one by one onto a table, their pages riffled through by an invisible hand. Those whose pages had torn were set aside for mending, and the rest found their way back to their shelves.

The last book, an old one bound in dark red leather, made its way back to the lectern standing by a shuttered window. Teacher listened for Guards. Silence. Teacher waved the book open to a blank middle page and said, "Reveal." The page turned transparent, and resolved into a mirror.

Teacher smirked at the reflection. "Show me Hildin." The mirror shimmered; a blurry scene before the Prince Regent's fire appeared. Hildin was drinking hot wine with his future father-in-law. "Mirrors have returned," murmured Teacher. "An open invitation to Warin."

Teacher scanned the room, and frowned. "Show me Gian of Valleysmouth." The scene changed again; Gian stood behind a fat, cheerful old woman holding a candle in an otherwise dark room. A waxy, almost green, pallor covered the young man's face, but his expression was determined. The old woman rattled on about something, peering quizzically about. Just before she turned back toward him, Gian slipped a cord around her neck, and began to pull; the woman's eyes bulged, her hands flew to her neck, the candle fell, and the image went dark.

"Worse, much worse than I thought," muttered Teacher; a wave of the hand, the mirror returned to parchment, and the book closed with a grim thud.

"I must thank you again for finding her, Hildin," Fredrik slurred, emptying the wine pitcher into his goblet.

"You've thanked me at least a thousand times already, brother King, and tomorrow you thank me with the gift of your daughter," said the bored Hildin.

"I'll thank you a thousand times more for marrying her. She's all I have, especially now. I've set my wife aside, I think I said? I let her live, but the men in her family have all seen the executioner's axe. Missing for two spokes, and no one thinks it worth mentioning!"

"Most trying," said Hildin.

"I tried to get a son, mind. Sacrificed every flawless white bullock born in the kingdom to Pagg and gave the meat to Amma, for twenty years. Nothing. Only the one girl, even among my mistresses. I finally consulted the Traveler Queen," he confessed. "She took my money and told me nothing could be done. Can you imagine it!"

"A treacherous female, I've always said it," remarked Hildin, rolling his eyes when Fredrik turned away. Eventually, Fredrik stumbled off to bed, crossing paths at the door with Hildin's golden-haired page, who bowed him out of the room and shut the door.

Gian gave his master an appraising glance. "At least your father-in-law will be in Leute," he said. He upended the wine pitcher only to find it empty, and sat at Hildin's feet.

"I don't think he'll be anywhere," said his master.

"Where will he be, then?"

"Harla's Hill. Warin is coming, don't you think?"

"Yes, but—"

"He hasn't come through any of the mirrors I've returned to the Keep. They're traps, of course, but Warin never was stupid. That's what I expected, and that's what I want. I want him to confront me at the wedding, or at my coronation when our father has finally died. Somewhere in public."

"What will that accomplish, my lord? Everyone thinks he's dead already. Wouldn't it be better to kill him in private?"

"In public, everyone will see a pretender attack me without provocation. The people will side with their king—me—and even if they don't, I imagine there will be a great deal of confusion. People might get killed."

"Warin, certainly."

"Oh, not just Warin." Hildin took a long drink. "I want Leute. I want it sooner than later. I'd have taken it by conquest if it weren't for our lucky discovery of Her Highness. Once we're married, I'll have no use for her father. If he were to die in a fight between Warin and my Guards, Leute would be mine, as well as my son's. And at that point, it won't matter whether I'm a husband or a grieving widower."

Gian looked up, stricken. "You would kill Emmae?"

"Would you have that slut to wife? With the enchantment on her, I'd never know if my children were mine or the wine steward's."

"Teacher would know! We could lock her away—it's been done before. Remember Temmin the Great and Elees of Whitehorse! Please, master, please don't!" said Gian.

Hildin paused, his cup in midair. "You care so very much, boy? You surprise me. We shall see. Have you taken care of the...other matter?"

Gian steadied his quivering voice, and answered, "Yes," before he gave up and buried his head in the folds of his master's robes.

"Don't cry, Gian," said Hildin, his hand on the young man's head. "We had to do it. I didn't want it any more than you did. She was like a mother to me. But she was old, old and stupid. Already she'd said things that might have given away the girl's presence at the Keep before her 'rescue.' If we'd let her live—Oh, Meg, why were you so foolish!" wept Hildin.

*   *   *

The brief betrothal gave Emmae some consolation; Hildin and Gian stayed away from her, for appearance's sake. She might move through the Keep, but stayed in her rooms instead, avoiding the casual desire that eddied whenever a man passed his eye over her.

But now, the hated day had arrived. Fredrik presented his daughter before Pagg at the temporary altar in the Keep's great hall, and tried to ascribe her violent trembling to excitement. They repeated their vows, Emmae sullen and dull, Hildin ringing and proud, almost insolent. The Little Father knotted the marriage cord three times around Emmae's left wrist: "Obedience, humility, fidelity." He gave the free end to Hildin, who pulled her to their marriage bed through hallways deserted by custom as the two kingdoms' nobles cheered in the great hall.

Gian met them in the wedding chamber. "What are you doing here?" snapped Emmae.

"Gian is always with me," said Hildin. "Even now. Perhaps especially now. I need…assistance." His excitement coursed through her, familiar and horrifying, but she stayed still before the fire. "You've stopped fighting? How disappointing, little wife, I've enjoyed your struggles against the spell. Don't stop for my sake." He undid the laces of her cloth-of-gold overdress and let it fall in stiff folds around her feet.

"I will never do anything for your sake," she said, closing her eyes.

"It doesn't matter," he whispered in her ear. "Fear or need? No, it doesn't matter." The purple silk underdress followed the cloth-of-gold, as did her chemise, until she stood in nothing but her purple-gartered stockings and gold slippers.

Hildin drew her by the cord to the bed, fastening it tightly to a ring in the center of its headboard; he left a good deal of slack. "I do love tradition, don't you?" he drawled. He sat beside her, ran a hand down her side, and gestured to Gian; the page sat at the foot of the bed and stripped off her shoes and stockings. He kept her foot in his hand, running his fingertips up and down her sole until she wriggled in spite of herself. He took her toes one by one into his mouth, nibbling gently; the spell crushed her down into the bed and up again, stronger than ever.

Hildin slipped a hand between her legs, forcing a sob from her. "Oh, she's very wet for us, Gian, aren't you, poor wife? Wet and pulling at my fingers." The moisture trickled from her; she wanted their hands on her, she wanted them sliding into her, and silently swore she would see them both dead.

The two men rose from the bed. Gian reverently removed the Prince's own purple and gold wedding garb, dropping to his knees to undo the leggings and free the hard length within. He took it into his mouth. Hildin watched intently, shifting his gaze to Emmae. His lust clawed at her insides, tearing at her and softening her at the same time. "I've been saving your mouth for when I'm bored with the rest of you. Besides, Gian is so much better at this than any woman—" his hand fisted in Gian's blonde hair, and the young man groaned. Hildin pulled out. "But you'll teach her, won't you, boy?"

"Yes," gasped Gian. "Yes, please!"

The idea disgusted her, and yet her lips felt swollen and eager; the men wanted it, and their will bore down on her. "I'll bite it off, I swear!" she cried.

"No, you won't," laughed Hildin as Gian stripped off his clothes. "You'll love it. But tonight I have something else in mind. You first, boy, I'm in a mood to watch you and my lady." Gian slithered up the bed, and wrapped her free hand around his cock.

"That's not for me," she said. "It's for him."

"Not for you? And here you're in such a state. If it's not my desire, it must be your own." He ran tracing fingers over her breasts, teasing the nipples and then returning to soft circles. "If the spell isn't raising my desire in you, then you must want me yourself. Is that it, Emmae? Have we won you?"

"You will never win me!" she said, though her words ended in a breathy moan.

Gian molded her breasts and rolled the nipples roughly between his fingers. "Yes?" he smiled.

She stumbled out, "It will always be the spell!" A chilling, reminding wave broke over her, and she undulated in his arms. Gian suckled at her, kneading her soft breast until she let out another groan.

"Your dilemma, my dear, is that we just don't care," came Hildin's amused voice. Gian released the nipple with a wet pop and moved to the other side. Hildin stretched out beside her tethered arm and stroked Gian's hair. "We have your body, and that's enough for our pleasure, and my ambition. You're already having trouble telling the difference between your own desires and ours. In time the spell will simply wear you out."

Gian slipped two fingers inside her; she heard her own wetness with each thrust. He took the nipple between his teeth, and bit harder as the pleasure spiraled up and up, until her free hand beat at his back all on its own, and she let out a long, agonized cry that left her hoarse and shuddering, clenching so tightly inside that Gian laughed. "She nearly broke my fingers, my lord." He moved over her, sliding against her sweat-covered skin.

Gian circled her in his arms; she spread her legs, shamefully eager. But then, the sooner she satisfied Gian and Hildin, the sooner her anguish would end, at least for the night. He pushed hard against her belly, but to her surprise, he flipped them over. He pulled her down and kissed her, running his tongue across the roof of her mouth until she straddled him, ready.

A hand came to rest on her flank. "Hold her tight," said Hildin behind her. Gian pinned her to his chest, though she struggled and tried to push away from him. Hildin's hands painted circles on her bottom, and she relaxed—he'd taken her from behind before, it would be over soon—until something cool and slippery dripped onto her, slicking her crevice. A thumb slowly pushed inside her ass. Emmae took in a ragged breath, realizing what he meant to do. "I beg you, I beg you, don't do this to me!"

"Beg all you want, wife, but a virginity is called for on a wedding night, and this is the one I will take." The thumb retreated. Relief and disappointment vanished as two fingers replaced the one, stretching and twisting inside her. She tensed every muscle in her body against pain.

"Hush, sweetheart," whispered Gian as she struggled and wept in his arms. "The more you fight it, the worse it will be. You must relax—the spell will work to give you pleasure whether you want it or not, but it won't guard against pain!"

"More to the point, you will hurt yourself," growled Hildin. "Give me entrance, Emmae, or I will take it."

Emmae sank into Gian's mouth, despairing. She lost herself in kisses as she willed her body to loosen. Hildin's desire unfurled and grew within her, building at the base of her belly to join Gian's. Beneath her, Gian's hardness slid just outside her opening; behind her, Hildin seized her hips. He placed his cock against her ass and slowly pushed inside. Gian sucked her scream into his mouth.

It hurt, a burning ring until the head was well inside her. Hildin advanced and retreated, advanced a little further and retreated, again and again, and she found herself pushing back, opening herself; the pain receded, and a horrifying ecstasy crawled over her. He worked his way inside her to the root until his belly pressed against her buttocks. Every hair on her body stood on end, every inch of skin achingly aware. "Oh, Emmae, I possess you completely," he rasped. "He never had you this way, only I have, you're mine now." His hands gripped her, flexing and squeezing as if to gain control over himself, his breathing deep and guttural; Emmae ground helplessly against Gian, the spell urging her to find release. "You like Gian beneath you, eh?" said Hildin. "Shall we both take you, then?"

Gian slid closer to her opening, his tip pushing against her. "Please, no!" she cried and struggled, until both men laughed.

"Not tonight," said Hildin. "Perhaps some day, when you've grown used to this, oh yes, you will have us both at once. You will beg us for it."

Gian slithered a hand between his body and hers, finding its way to her clitoris. "Give way, let it happen," he said. Bright lights gathered at the edges of her vision, her eyes bulging; her throat tightened. She breathed in harsh wails, keeping time with Hildin's thrusts and Gian's circling fingers.

Confusing, overwhelming pleasure rolled up her spine, fighting against her revulsion, one long orgasm that went on and on; she rocked back against the penetration, wanting more, her rough breathing turning to screams until Hildin went rigid against her and came, pulsing inside her. He dug his long fingers into her hips, steadying himself as she shuddered and twitched; he withdrew and rolled to one side. "Take her, take your pleasure, Gian."

Gian put her unresisting on her back and plunged into her dripping folds. Boneless beneath him, spread wide, no strength remaining to fight, she shook, lightly at first, and then harder. "It's all right," soothed Gian, kissing her flushed face, "I shake afterwards when he takes me. It passes. Emmae, you are so very beautiful, never more so! Oh, I could love you!" He looked almost drowsy, lips parted, but the eyes under their casual, drooped lids glittered, sharp, broken shards of green glass. Gian clutched at her breast, twisting the nipple, and his release came tumbling inside her, working its way up her body. She curved into him, crying as she came.

Emmae floated, every nerve suspended in bliss, until the spell played out; the men were sated. She sank back into despair. Gian already slept, his smooth young face slack and innocent. A wipe between her legs, and a pricking of her finger; she jerked her eyes open. Hildin squeezed blood from her finger onto a square of silk, wet from her sex. "That's enough," he said. "Some virgins don't bleed at all, you know. I wonder if you did." He pulled his shirt down over his head, then took up the silk. "This will satisfy them. Oh, didn't you know? The Little Father, King Fredrik and my highest lords are waiting for proof of our consummation. It is our custom."

She feigned sleep on Hildin's return; she felt his gaze as he settled down next to her. "Mine," she heard him whisper. "Mine, Warin, she's mine, until she's Harla's." He gave a faint chuckle, closed his eyes, and was asleep in moments.

Hildin's dagger lay somewhere in the room. If Emmae could reach it, she could kill at least one of them and then herself. But the marriage cord still tethered her wrist to the bed, and the men draped themselves over her; every time she moved, they stirred. She wept silently, cursing the knife for its tantalizing nearness. Harla would come to this house—if not tonight, soon—and somehow, she would be the one to bring Her.

Temmin withdrew from the book. He brimmed with desire, outrage, disgust and a deep need to see Emmae revenged, every hand on her, every one of Hildin's infuriating strokes imprinted on his body. That such a personal violation could bring on such ecstasy—it had to be the spell.

"You're shaking, Your Highness," said Teacher. "Take a moment."

Temmin closed his eyes, marshalling his emotions. "I want him dead, I so want to see him die," he muttered.

"You will."

Temmin concentrated on the velvet upholstery under his fingers, and the soft dry heat from the low fire. He closed his eyes; the insides of his eyelids shone coral in the sunlight falling across his face, until a shadow crossed him; Teacher blocked the light from the window. "Every time the book tells her part of the story, it takes me a bit to feel myself again— especially to feel fully male again. You think that's funny?" Temmin added in irritation.

"Oh, not exactly," said Teacher, lips twitching. "Go on."

"I just thank Farr I'm not a woman. I haven't even had sex yet, not really, and here my head's filled with her experiences. I'm just glad I was made for—ehm—*doing*...not...being done to?" he trailed off, wincing.

The twitch turned into a smile. "What do you think goes on between Mentors and Students, between lovers of men?"

"Isn't it like what Hildin and Gian...or what Gian does to Hildin...isn't it just mouths? And hands?" said Temmin, thinking of the men in the petitioning rooms, and of Alvo.

"It depends on the lovers involved," said Teacher. "Remember what Gian said to Emmae. Hildin took him in that way, too. More shall be revealed at the Temple, I am sure."

"I should hope not."

"I should bet on it, were I you, sir."

"Let's not talk about it," he said, waving his hand to dispel the thought. "Why didn't Emmae's father stop the marriage? He knew something was wrong, he had to have known."

"Think about it as her father would have. Whoever held her, probably had her—at least, everyone assumed so, including Fredrik. Royal women especially must come to the marriage bed virgins. Emmae's captivity damaged her, destroyed her reputation. The only way Fredrik could get her decently married was to swear his kingdom would pass to her husband. If she had had a brother, even another sister, Emmae would have been sent to a Temple and forgotten." Temmin couldn't read Teacher's face, shadowed from the sunlight, but the cool voice retained a pragmatic tone.

"Hildin seemed genuinely pleased to have her, even though she was broken."

"But she *wasn't* broken," said Temmin.

"She was not a virgin."

"No…" Marriage required a girl's virginity; if the groom's family wouldn't look the other way at an unfortunate Sister's Temple evaluation, the wedding would be canceled, but Temmin had never heard of it happening. Though how would he know, he admitted.

He thought of the sentimental songs Nurse liked to sing sometimes in the evenings, especially if she'd had a bit too much barisha. Ellika would play the nursery spinet, Sedra would roll her eyes and retire to read in the furthest corner; his mother would tut-tut as Nurse crooned about naughty boys who didn't obey their mothers and fell down wells, sad young men dying on a battlefield, a lost love's name on their lips, and ruined girls, ravished and abandoned by noblemen, throwing themselves over bridges, their drowned bodies floating past the battlements of their evil seducers. For such a cheerful, busy woman, Nurse loved her maudlin tragicals, reflected Temmin.

"Imagine were one of your sisters somehow compromised like this," said Teacher. "What would happen to her? What do you think your father would do?"

"You'd have a far better notion than I would."

"Even so, cast your mind on it. You are king. You have two daughters. One of them has been shamed, everyone knowing she is likely no longer a virgin, though no one would dare say anything."

Temmin thought of Ellika's bright, golden smile and Sedra's dark, amused eyes as they sat before the fire the night before. "I'd think anyone would marry either of 'em," he answered. "Sure, they're annoying, but they're both pretty, especially Elly, and Seddy is very good company when she cares to be. And they're the King's daughters. I can't see where virginity would make a difference."

"But it does. No man wants another man's leavings."

Temmin blanched. He'd called Allis his father's leavings, just two days ago. That was different, wasn't it? Going after one's own father had to be different than going after some random man. Allis was no virgin, far from it, and it didn't bother him, did it? Or was this an example of Percy's *species in the species*? "I don't think that's necessarily true."

"You are thinking of Allis. She is a Beloved. Beloveds are by definition experienced, as are mistresses, courtesans and prostitutes. One takes them to bed, not to wed."

"So tell me what Father would do."

"He would marry her off as quickly as possible," said Teacher. "She would be given to the first consenting noble."

Temmin put his feet up. "I don't see how that's all that different than what he has in mind for them now."

"Your father is trying to make good matches for your sisters both for the kingdom and for their own sakes. If he can possibly combine the two, he will."

"But the kingdom comes first," said Temmin.

"Yes, it does," admitted Teacher.

"Then kings should never be fathers," grumbled Temmin.

That night, Temmin decided to brave the dining room. If his father wanted enmity, he'd return it, Pagg be damned.

He got no chance to show his father unpious incivility; the King dined elsewhere, and so Temmin found himself staring at Fennows over the after-dinner port. "Well!" said the spotty young lord. "Bit of a time you're having with the old man! Damned unhappy about the whole Temple thing. Still doing it, eh? Well, I suppose you'll live it down at some point."

"Serving the Gods is not something to live down, Percy."

Fennows snorted. "Among the common people, no. You'll be celebrated in story and song as the Virgin Prince, I should think. It's not the peasants and merchants I'm thinking of, but our sort of people."

"Here's what I want to know," said Temmin, cracking a walnut between his fingers and tossing the shell in Percy's general direction. "Why is it so important that a man should be sexually experienced as soon as possible, when women must be virgins until they marry?"

"What?" said Fennows. "You can't be serious. Let me hand round the bottle, old thing, your gears are stuck and in need of lubrication."

"I'm quite serious!" said Temmin, automatically pouring himself another glass. "For instance, if you loved a girl, would you care if she wasn't a virgin? You'd marry her, wouldn't you? I mean, she's not supposed to even know about all the women you've had."

"That's because I'm a man," explained Fennows in a slow, singsong voice. He sat up straighter. "You're not implying anything about Elly, are you?"

"Elly? What? No! Of course not. Why d'you always talk about Elly as if she's practically— I'm speaking in general," he ended impatiently.

"I wouldn't pay for a dinner where someone else had eaten the main course, would I? No man wants a slut for a wife."

"I'm not talking about a slut! I just mean—what if something had happened—she was tricked, or she was forced, or something?"

"Women are weak-willed, true. But damage is damage. She'd be lucky if anyone took her. End up at a Temple, I should think." Fennows cocked his head; his small eyes studied Temmin's face. "You can't marry Allis Obby, you know, Temmy."

Temmin gaped. "I'm not talking about Allis," he said.

"Then what are you talking about?"

"I'm not sure I know," Temmin murmured.

THIRTEEN

Temmin vacillated several times before Farrday's overnight visit to the Lovers' Temple. He talked himself back into it each time with a combination of wrath against his father, desire, pride, and the memory of the tiny voice in the stillness of the chapel.

On the dreaded and anticipated day, he took out his nerves on Jebby's legs, riding hard over the countryside through the King's Woods into the unknown fields beyond—another thumbing of his nose. He'd been ordered to stay within the safe confines of the Woods, but today he was invincible. Jebby was less so; the hectic ride had left the big horse flecked with foam, and Temmin decided to leave him at home to rest rather than ride him into town.

Once breakfasted and dressed, Temmin's nerves overwhelmed his coordination; his hands shook too hard to saddle LeiLei, and he gave the task up to the grooms before he'd begun it. By the time he gave LeiLei's reins to one of the servants at the Temple's steps, he wished he were back home in bed with the curtains drawn. He trudged up the steps, Brother Mardus and a Guardsman flanking him; four Temple's Own crossbowmen and a supervising Brother crouched on the roof. He took off his hat and went inside.

Allis and Issak waited for him in the Great Hall, in a respectful circle of space left where the stream of worshippers parted around them. The soft waterfall of voices echoing against the rosy marble trickled away. Every face turned toward Temmin. A young man said, "It's him, Tess—is he…?" into the quiet.

"A word, Your Highness," said a rasping, cultivated voice. Temmin turned; the Duke of Litta stood to one side, rigid and disdainful.

Temmin stopped, uncertain. He'd been introduced to Litta—he'd danced at his ball—but he knew the Duke only casually. Even so, he crossed the floor, holding out his hand and projecting as much dignity and confidence as he could muster. "Good morning, Lord Litta," he said in his best imitation of his father.

Litta took his hand, and pulled him closer. "What I have to say is for your ears alone—for now."

Temmin let himself be led to an altar dedicated to the Wingèd Neya; he noted Mardus and four Temple's Own hovering nearby, out of earshot. "What may I do for you?" he said.

"You may stop this," Litta replied brusquely.

Temmin gaped briefly, but recovered and said, "I hardly see how this is your business, sir."

"It is the business of every noble in this land. You are making a grave mistake, and we are willing to go to some lengths to stop you."

Litta was the more powerfully built, but Temmin was taller; he took refuge in his height against the other man's intimidating manner, and pulled himself upright. "Exactly how far would that be—hang on," he said, his temper rising, "are you threatening me? In the *Temple*?"

"Threatening you? No. I am a loyal subject of His Majesty, and bear scars endured in the King's service," bowed Litta. "But you are aware of the prophecy, 'When Nerr gets the Heir,' as the vulgar people summarize it?"

"What of it? I'm amazed you believe in it. And even if it is true, why would the country's prosperity be bad for the nobility?"

"Not the country's prosperity—the common people's prosperity. *We* are the country. *They* are our subjects. Should they prosper too much, they will begin to consider themselves our equals. Your Highness, if you take Supplicancy, you may bring down a thousand years of Tremontine rule."

"Prophecy is often misinterpreted," said Temmin, thinking of Warin's prophecy.

"I am not willing to gamble on that."

Temmin crossed his arms, his confidence less and less feigned as his temper rose. "And how do you propose to stop me?"

Litta flicked a glance over Temmin's shoulder. "From your behavior, I assume it's more than just a physical urge that leads you into the arms of the Embodiments." Temmin said nothing, his eyes narrowing. "Mm," murmured Litta. He gazed dispassionately at the twins, letting his words take their time. "I would imagine, then, that if they were harmed in any way—"

"If you or anyone acting on your behalf lay a finger on either of them, I will see the Brothers hang your head over Marketgate. Pagg damn me if I don't do it myself!" said Temmin.

"Keep your voice down, young sir."

"I remind you I am an adult, *sir*, and the Heir."

"If you are an adult, then you will understand that I don't have to lay a finger on them, *sir*."

Temmin stared into Litta's triumphant eyes, his confidence fading. "What do you mean?" he said.

"Word of the Obbys' past has reached me." Litta stepped closer. "If it got out, it would ruin them. They'd be cast out of the Temple. I dare say they'd have to return to their former profession."

"I'm sure the Temple knows what happened to them when they were children."

"Oh, of course. I can't imagine their sponsor kept it from the Most Highs, nor do I think it would have mattered. It doesn't matter to me— what happened to them is sad, really. Deplorable. But I wonder what the common people would think. The Obbys explained it all away to you, but they can't...*charm*...everyone in the kingdom, can they? It would ruin them," he repeated.

Temmin blanched. "This is blasphemy—are you a believer?"

"I care more about my children's inheritance than my soul." Litta smiled. "Do you think I wouldn't do it? If you take Supplicancy, I promise you, everyone in the City will know the day after Neya's Day. If you turn from the Temple, I promise you, no one will know other than the King and myself—and you. And you'll still be able to see the Obbys. Just not…right away. Do think on it, *sir*." Litta patted Temmin's shoulder, and strode out of the Temple with as close to a saunter as his military bearing would allow.

"Temmin?" said Allis's voice at his elbow. She put a hand on his back; he mechanically took her on his arm, and walked toward the Supplicant's Chamber. Issak joined them, kissed Temmin without a word, and took his other arm. They left the Temple's Own at the door to the Supplicant's Chamber. Once inside, Temmin paced away from the twins into the room; Issak glanced at Allis as they followed behind.

"You're upset," said Allis. "What did Litta say?"

"Nothing of consequence."

"Ah, that explains your shift in mood from apprehensive and excited, to apprehensive and frightened," said Issak. "What did he say, Temmin?"

Temmin sighed and folded himself onto a couch, setting his hat beside him. "He knows about your life in Belleth. Pagg damn my father, he told Litta about your past."

"And?" said Issak.

"And Litta says if I take Supplicancy, he'll tell everyone!" said Temmin, spreading his arms. "It'll ruin you! I can't let that happen to you, and I can't swallow letting him win like that, especially when it's really my father's doing. Gods, I hate him!"

"It's not hard to see it from the King's perspective," said Allis, sitting next to him. "He's worried about you."

"Worried about politics," said Temmin.

"In his mind, the two are linked. You will inherit the throne. He worries he won't have one to give you," she said.

Temmin pushed his hair out of his eyes. "You think Eddin's priests are right, that if I come here it's the end of the monarchy?"

"No," she said, "I think your father loves you."

"I wish he'd leave me alone."

"And I wish I had a father," she murmured.

Issak fixed his sister with a warning look, and said, "Temmin, you knew the nobility would not approve of this."

"No, but I thought they'd just try to talk me out of it!" Temmin answered. He grimaced and threw up his hands. "Who'd think they'd dare threaten the Heir, or Embodiments—who does something like that? It's blasphemy!"

"Not everyone puts faith above personal advantage," said Allis.

Temmin put his head in his hands, pushed his hair back again, and stood up. "So that's it, then? I just go home?"

"Do you want to go home?" said Issak.

"Pagg's balls, will you stop that!" he shouted. "Aren't you worried? At all? My father's won! I can't let him ruin you! There's nothing to say he won't do it anyway!"

Issak took him by the shoulders and shook him once. "You are going to calm down, and we are going to take care of it. All right? We decide what happens here, not you. We will take this to the Most Highs, and among us, we will sort it out. You are to focus on becoming a Supplicant."

"How can I focus, when my father's threatening you? He's the King. He's a believer who fears for his soul, but apparently he has others who don't, who'll do his bad business for him. If he wants to hurt you, there's nothing I can do—I can't protect you except by leaving!"

"Tem, you don't have to protect us," soothed Allis. "It's all right."

"No, it's not! This is a bad idea anyway, just let me go!" He wrenched himself from Issak's grip and ran from the room.

Allis rose from the couch as if to follow, but took her brother's hand instead. "I think it's best if we let Teacher deal with him at this point."

"I agree," nodded Issak. He sighed, and took Allis in his arms, kissing the top of her head. "One thing I love about people," he said, "is that however much I know about them, however well I think I can read them, they still manage to surprise me now and again. I knew his sexual frustration is mounting, and then he wants his father's approval so badly, but—"

"No, it's more than that." She looked up, eyes troubled. "I think he's in love with us."

Issak paused. "You may be right." He rocked her in his arms a moment longer, and kissed her nose. "We have time to take care of that. What concerns me is that you react to him more than you ought."

"It concerns me too," murmured Allis.

"Come on," said her brother. "Let's go bother the Most Highs and decide how best to deal with His Grace the Duke of Litta."

"There's a cheery thought, at least," she smiled.

Temmin's charge down the Temple steps caught Mardus off-guard. "Your Highness," he called as he ran after the Prince, "I was in conference with the captain of the Temple's Own—I thought we were here for the day —"

"There's been a permanent change of plans. You won't need to talk with the Temple's Own for some time yet, if ever," said Temmin in a thick voice. "Where's my horse? I want to get out of here."

Mardus gestured to one of his cohort, who took off running toward the Temple stables. He pulled on his helmet, his unsettled gaze on Temmin. "Sir, is there anything we as your guard should know? Do you not feel safe here?"

"The only danger here is me," snapped the Prince. "Where's my Pagg-damned horse—finally!" Temmin thrust his hat onto his head and leaped into the saddle. LeiLei danced impatiently until the Guards mounted their own horses. Mardus did his best to keep Temmin from cantering on ahead of them, but once inside the gates, the Brother gave up, and Temmin pelted down the drive; his hat blew off. Mardus stopped, picked it up, and carried it to the mudroom entrance.

From there, the somewhat dusty hat made its way up to the Prince's rooms atop a silver salver held by a footman, finally ending up in the hands of Jenks, who accepted it without comment. The last sound before the door closed was His Highness's voice, raised in anguish and anger: "What do you mean, you're leaving?"

The footman put the salver under his arm and walked silently down the Residence Wing hall, until the King's secretary stopped him before the open door of his office. "The Prince has returned?"

"Yes, Mr Winmer," said the footman. "And may I say, not in the best of moods."

"You may not say, Caid," he answered. "The Prince's business is not a subject for the gossip of servants." At the young man's abashed face,

Winmer added, "Very good, it's all right, carry on." He spared the footman a final glance, then shut the door and walked through his green, book-lined office to the King's private sitting room, smiling. "He's home, sir, and 'not in the best of moods,' says Caid."

"Gods bless Litta," sighed Harsin. "Sulky, is he?"

"I would spend the day engaged elsewhere, sir, until tonight's events have unfolded."

"You've arranged things?"

"Oh, yes. The girl is dependable. By this time tomorrow, he will no longer be eligible for Supplicancy. And I should think he'll be considerably more cheerful as a result."

Harsin laughed slightly. "Perhaps, but I think it will be some time before he forgives me. I love my son—I'm his father. But we are King first." He paused, considering. "I'm concerned that someone may try to convince him to stay the course and not accept his gift tonight."

"Colonel Jenks has been called away. His train leaves in two hours. Gram has called in his nephew, Harbis, a gentleman's gentleman of great repute, while the Colonel is away."

"Vetted?"

"By Brother Mardus and Teacher. He is completely reliable. Speaking of which, I must ask, sir, about Teacher himself."

"I've given him further instruction not to advise Temmin in any matter involving the Lovers' Temple."

Winmer frowned. "I do not question your judgment, sir, but is it wise to let Teacher out of the library until this is settled? He always looks for loopholes."

"Not this time. He knows my mind."

When Teacher found him, Temmin lay on the green velvet sofa in his study; his eyes hurt, and his hair tangled around his head. "Jenks left," he said.

"I know, Your Highness," Teacher murmured, taking up the habitual post by the hearth. "What did he tell you?"

"That his sister Justice needed him in Reggiston, something about her oldest son getting drummed out of the cavalry. I said, why can't you

handle it by post? And what could a former corporal—Uncle Pat's servant!
—do about it anyway? He insisted he had to go. And I need him. This is
my father's doing. Why won't he leave me alone!"

"I have heard that Mr Gram's nephew, a Mr Harbis, will be here
shortly to take care of your attire, sir."

"What do I care about my attire?" cried Temmin, flinging himself
backward with one arm over his face. "Harbis can go to the Hill, along
with my clothes. I'll send him away. I need Jenks!"

"Why do you need him so badly?"

A sob escaped from under Temmin's elbow. "I'm not going through
with Supplicancy."

"Ah?"

"Lord Litta threatened to spread the story about Allis and Issak and
everything that happened to them in Belleth."

"Ah."

Temmin lifted his elbow, his sleeve now damp with tears. "'Ah?' That's
all? You have nothing else to say, no advice on what I might do?"

"There is nothing I can say," shrugged Teacher. "Your father has
ordered me not to advise you on matters involving the Lovers' Temple, sir."

"Pagg damn him! I order you to talk to me about it! I have to talk to
someone!"

"Your orders do not supersede his, Your Highness," said Teacher gently.

"You obeyed Hildin!"

"King Gethin had named him Regent, an order that bound me to
Hildin as long as Gethin lived, or until he ended Hildin's regency." Teacher
gave a small but sympathetic smile. "I can listen, but no more."

Temmin sat up. "Can you advise me on politics?"

Teacher's smile widened. "Certainly, sir."

"All right, then. How might I counter the Duke of Litta?"

"You do not need to, Your Highness. Others will take care of His Grace."

"Others? Who?" he asked, puzzled.

"Alas, I cannot advise you on that," answered Teacher, with a smile
both pensive and mischievous.

"The Temple? But what can they do?"

"Alas, I cannot advise you on that," repeated Teacher, "though I may advise you on anything else."

Temmin frowned in thought for a moment, then said, "Let me try it this way: were someone wishing to counter Litta, what could one do?"

"Be more specific in your questioning, sir. What is Litta doing that one would wish to counter?"

"He's blackmailing me! He's a blackmailer!" shouted Temmin, waving his arms.

A triumphant smile, and Teacher said, "Few of us have clean hands. That is why the wise man, especially a man whose public credit is important, never resorts to blackmail. To counter a highly placed blackmailer, one goes digging."

"But how can I?"

"I am telling you, sir," said Teacher intently, "you do not have to. Others have it in hand. Trust that anyone attempting to blackmail an Embodiment of the Lovers would find himself in deep water before long, and in this life as well as the next."

Temmin's heart lightened. "You're taking care of it for me!"

"Not at all, sir," said Teacher through thinned lips. "Others have it in hand. More than that I cannot say."

Temmin sighed. He knew full well Teacher's meaning; the Temple would take care of Litta. "I just don't see what those others can do."

"Have patience, sir. In the meantime, I suggest perhaps studies might take your mind off His Grace."

"Oh, Gods," he groaned. "I'm still upset from the last part of the story." Even so, he fetched the old blank book from its shelf, and settled back onto the sofa. In truth, he was glad to leave his own problems behind; at least, he thought before the book swallowed him up, he didn't face a murderous, insane brother.

Warin and the Travelers reached the City the night of the wedding, making camp well outside its walls. Travel by mirror had been considered and discarded; the chances of Hildin finding them were too high. The

Traveler Queen had insisted on riding with them, and to Warin's surprise, she kept up with the men, never tiring.

They sat before the camp fire, Warin thoughtlessly poking at it with a stick and watching the sparks rise. A sudden vitality burst inside him, a brilliant light overwhelming unknown inner barriers, a million doors to a million rooms filled with the light of the sun, the moon, every star, opening in his soul all at once.

"Are you all right?" said Connin.

"I don't know—yes, I think so. Something's changed inside me…" Warin trailed off, gasping. A dark foreboding fought with the great sun bursting inside him. The exhilarating incandescence felt so very wrong and so very right, all at the same time. What was its source, what did it mean?

Suddenly, deep bells, mourning bells, sounded over the dark walls of the City.

The Traveler Queen groaned and clutched herself in pain as the bells reverberated; her son rushed to her side, and Warin jumped up, but she waved them away. "No, Connin, take Warin into the woods—you know where, and why. I must move—I'm too close…" Two Travelers helped her away from the fire, solicitous and soothing.

"Is she all right?" asked Warin. "What's wrong?"

"Come," said Connin, walking into the woods. The moon struggled to shine through clouds. Even in the dark Connin knew the way, as if it were an old, familiar trail. They entered a small clearing, and Connin called, "We're here."

"Is Warin with you?" said a cool voice. A black figure moved from the shadows into the clearing.

"Teacher? Gods, it's you!" cried Warin, running forward. "Oh, my old friend, how I've missed you!" He kissed the offered cheek and hugged Teacher close.

"You need not have, Your Majesty. You should have stayed."

"I know that now." Warin paused. "You say, 'Your Majesty.'"

"Gethin is dead," said Teacher. "The bells are for him." Warin dropped his hands from Teacher's shoulders and allowed himself to acknowledge what he already knew: the source of this over-bright new light bathing his spirit meant his father was dead. "Your power has come to you, and so have I. There is a mirror hidden in these woods, and one hidden in my library. Hildin's power over me as Regent broke the minute the King died, and I escaped. *You* have Tremont's magic now."

The glorious, consuming light inside Warin turned harsh, and he blinked back tears.

"Do not grieve, Warin, your father has been dead a long time," said Teacher. "His body merely lingered. You are here now, and you are needed. We must try to reach the Father's Temple before Hildin's coronation tomorrow. If we do not, the Guard will have no choice but to follow him."

"Why not use a reflection?" said Warin. "True, I've had little luck finding one into the Keep, but at the Temple there must be something."

"No," replied Teacher. "If we find one, it is sure to be a trap."

"The one in your library?"

"I must be there for it to exist. It is a one-way journey, even for me. We must go by foot."

"There are always the Brothers," said Warin. "They will follow only the rightful king, no matter who's wearing the crown, and between the two of us, we can make it plain I am king."

"More importantly, we must hope that the people believe you. Otherwise, we might face a long and painful war." Teacher took Warin's hands. "One last piece of unwelcome news. Hildin has married the Princess."

Warin dropped his head; bitterness joined grief. "She's made her choice, then. I'm too late."

"Choice?" said Teacher. "How could you consider this a choice? Consider what she faced, with such an enchantment upon her and the disgrace of nearly three spokes with her 'captor.' Fredrik has no illusions—he knows Tremont wants Leute and will take it one way or another. Uniting through marriage is always better than uniting through conquest, and her honor is damaged at best. She had no choice." Teacher considered what to say next. "Your Majesty, I strongly believe he intends to kill King Fredrik as soon as he himself is crowned. He may kill the Princess as well."

"Take me to her now, then! Let me go to her!" cried Warin, crushing Teacher's hands. "Merciful Amma, take me to her!"

"Calm yourself, sir! Hildin has ensured a certain death were you to enter the Keep through any reflection we might find, and as for entering the city, the gates are locked, and the moon is too new for a reliable reflection. My mirror in these woods is kept magically lit— Oh!" Teacher leaned on Warin's arms, staggering. "Lead me further away from the camp! Please, now!"

Connin took one arm, Warin the other, and they guided Teacher away from the clearing. "Mother must have gone back to the fire," said Connin.

Teacher straightened, waving away Warin's arm. "We cannot be near one another, not even in earshot. I am all right—this is far enough. When you see her, tell her I would not wish pain on her for the world, Connin, but I had to come."

"She knows," he answered.

"Go back to the camp, then, both of you," said Teacher. "Rest now. You will need all your strength tomorrow."

Warin hugged Teacher one last time. He said nothing to Connin on their way back, his hand on the pommel of his sword.

At the camp, bedrolls circled the banked fire. Once inside his own, Warin seethed with rage. His prophecy had been wrong. His father died alone, in bed, and not at Warin's hand. For that, he rejoiced, but as for the rest...

All his anger at the Gods came roaring back. For years, he'd wondered what he'd done to deserve his prophecy. Now the punishment was compounded; he'd given up his throne and his beloved father for nothing. In his grief and anger, he yearned for Emmae, and feared for her more. He stared up into the dark sky, thinking of his brother in the marriage bed that belonged to him, and willed Emmae to be safe.

"King Warin," murmured Connin from a few feet away, "master yourself. You've relit the fire."

Warin glanced to his left; flames licked up from the coals, burning angry and bright. "Bank," he sighed; the fire subsided. "Apologies. I have yet to reconcile myself to my father's power." He pulled his magic inward and focused on his breath, forcing himself to sleep.

The next day dawned clear and fresh. The air in the field where the company camped smelled of trampled grass, wood smoke, and horses. In soft half-sleep, Warin dreamed he was a child again, waking up in his father's pavilion during maneuvers. He waited, dreaming and dozing in the dawn light, for his father's booming voice to call him to breakfast with the Cavalry.

He woke fully. The dolorous toll of the bells had ended. His father was dead. Today he would kill his brother, and take his father's place.

He pulled on his clothes and sword, found the little mirror box at the bottom of his pouch, and flicked it open. "If she still lives, show me Emmae," he said. The reflection flickered, and Emmae appeared. She wore an overdress of stiff brocade, its deep Tremontine red contrasting sharply with her pale skin. Her hair hung loose and limp to her waist; she smoothed a strand through her fingers over and over, a gesture he knew well. He jumped to his feet to throw himself into the mirror, but the reflection resolved again to his own pinched, hollow face; she must have moved away.

At the Keep, Emmae glanced back at the cheval glass in the corner, willing Warin not to look for her. "Cover the mirror," she said to a serving woman; confused and dutiful, the woman threw a sheet over the glass.

A flood of flowers, food, gifts from dignitaries, silk dresses embroidered in gold thread, furs, satin slippers flowed into Emmae's apartments, borne in by countless maidservants; a dozen more had dressed her and now hovered about, twitching the folds of her ermine-lined mantle into place, offering perfumes, and otherwise annoying her.

To her surprise, Old Meg was not among them. Of all the servants, she expected Meg to be the one to ready her for the coronation; Hildin relied on her as spy and watchdog. Even so, Meg was familiar, the closest thing she had to a friend. She would never cross her Hildin, but she had been kind in her way, and gentle. Emmae asked several of the women, but none of them knew her whereabouts.

Against the tide of riches and women came Gian. He wore the yellow and blue of Valleysmouth, the yellow giving his skin an unnatural pallor, and he carried a jewel casket in his hands. "Leave us," he said to the servants. One last reluctant twitch to the mantle, and the primary dresser left, shooing the rest of the maids before her.

Gian pulled strand after strand of pearls from the casket, so many that Emmae wondered if there were oysters inside the box. "These belonged to the King's mother. He wished to see them on you," he murmured tonelessly.

"You don't seem to take much joy in your master's coronation," she said.

Gian looked up from the casket, a pair of long pearl earrings in one hand. "We have waited for this day since we were children." He fastened the pearls in her ears and stepped back. "You make a magnificent Queen, Emmae. Your dressers did well."

"The dressers—Gian, where is Old Meg? Is she unwell?"

The young man went paler still. "She is dead."

"Dead? What happened? Was she ill?"

"I killed her."

"Why would you do that?" she said after a long, astonished pause. "Stupid boy, why would you do such a thing?"

"He required it of me. I've never killed for him before. I am sick at heart." Gian took her face in his hands. "Emmae, listen. I care what happens to you, more than you will ever believe. Tread carefully. Do as you're told. Tell no one about Warin, nor that you were brought here long before you were officially found—your confidante would be dead in a day. Give my lord no excuse to do you harm. Do you understand me?" Gian choked, then continued, "She was as his mother, and yet he had me kill her for fear she'd give us away. He'd waste no tears on you." He dropped his hands and took up the casket again. "I won't see you again until the ceremony at Pagg's Temple," he said.

Emmae's breath returned, uncontrollable. "Why are you warning me?"

Gian stopped halfway out of the room, his face twisting with emotion and his green eyes bright and full, but he said only, "I will see you at your crowning." He let the door stand open, leaving the Guards outside watching for Warin.

Emmae mastered her breathing and focused her mind. She pulled the cover off the cheval glass in hopes Warin would see her, but she saw nothing, no indication he was watching. She sighed, and took the habitual lock of hair between her fingers.

Hildin meant to kill her; if he'd kill Meg, her own life meant nothing. As soon as he possessed Leute, she was expendable. She might tell her father, but what good would that do? He didn't listen, even when he was sober, and he was unlikely to believe her—if he did, he'd probably kill her himself. Then again, if Hildin wanted Leute badly enough, why let Fredrik live? She had no love for him; they said he was her father, but she didn't remember him at all, and she could only think that a real father wouldn't throw her away on such as Hildin. As an unmarried woman, she lived under her father's thumb, now as a married woman, under her husband's. But what if she were neither a daughter nor a wife?

As a widow, she might live on her own terms. Perhaps she might then set a search for Warin, if only to discover why he hadn't come to her. She could separate herself from men, attended only by women—safe from the spell. Though occasionally she'd caught eddies of interest from certain women, it would be easy enough to weed them out.

Though she had thought often of suicide in her captivity, now the will to live filled her, fierce and eager. She searched her room, rifling through the gifts of jewels in hopes of a ceremonial dagger, but not even a stickpin came to hand.

She refused to sink back into despair. Whether today or a spoke from now, she would find a way to kill Hildin before he killed her, and live.

Warin and his men entered the city at Marketgate without remark, the Guards assuming they were Travelers come to entertain the crowds for coppers, or perhaps to sneak into one of the public feasts setting up in the city squares. Times were pinched, but there would be at least a little for everyone, if not a feast for all. Turning away the poor and unwashed from such a banquet would earn Amma's wrath, though the harvests had been small enough in the last few years that some thought She was angry already.

The Market was empty of sellers, all business suspended for the coronation celebrations, but even taking that into consideration, the City seemed threadbare and patched, its people moving slowly, and far too many beggars in the streets. Its shabbiness appalled the returning Prince. Had times been so very hard?

The band paused at a fountain among a small knot of men refreshing themselves in the midst of assembling long boards into feasting tables. "I tell you what, old son," Warin heard one huge, scarred man say to his neighbor, "I can't help but think what that Prince Warin wouldn't have let things come to such a pass. He was always good to his men, never put himself above us. Ate same as we, slept same as we. Never his like, even braver than his father, Harla carry him home."

The Prince cast an eye over the man, and then out onto the milling crowds. He hadn't commanded in ten years; time to see if he'd forgotten how. "Did you serve with Warin?" he said.

"Where d'ye think I got this?" said the scarface, tapping the mark on his cheek, an ugly thing that ran from his left ear to his chin. "That I did, against the Northern Tribes up at Montesurbis—in Leute, too, at Dordemon, when we was nigh-on boys. Pagg-forsaken heathens, we drove 'em back into the Wastes, didn't we! Prince Warin, rest his bones, was a great man, and would have been a great king. Not like the Regent, who already taxes us past the fat into the lean. Takes the milk *and* the cow, he does."

"And the farm, and the farmer's wife," added another man.

"What is your name?" Warin asked the scarred man.

"What's yours, there, Jemmy Rustic?" snorted the man.

"My name is Warin."

"Ha! And I'm Prince Hildin!" he said to the chortles of the other townsmen.

"You served with Warin, you say, and you do not know him when he stands before you?" said Connin.

"Clear off, Traveler!" said a ruddy man. "Ain't you got a bear to lead, or your mama to whore out or sumfing?" The townsmen drew together, anticipating a fight. Connin held his men back with a sharp word; they formed a sullen wall, with Warin before them.

Word spread; the Travelers were putting on a play, something about the dead Prince Warin: cheek enough on the coronation day of the Regent to draw attention. The curious and the bored gathered around the fountain, and Warin leaped up onto its lip. "Men of Tremont!" he cried. "I am Warin, son of Gethin, come back to take his throne!"

A squadron of Guards pushed their way through the growing crowd, led by a ferocious-looking Brother. "Clear off!" he roared. "You up there! Get down!"

"It's Prince Warin, come back to us! Don't you reckonize your King, Brother?" jeered the ruddy man.

"The King's in his Keep and all's right with the world," said the Brother, but he peered up at Warin anyway. Trouble creased his brow, just visible under his helm. "I knew the Prince in his youth. You are very like, I admit it, and your speech is fine, for a Traveler. But it's been ten years since he disappeared, and His Highness says the Good Prince is dead."

Warin jumped down from the fountain's lip. "Even if you don't know me, I know you, Brother Cor." The Brother started at his name. Warin glanced over to the feast preparations; a cooking fire burned beneath a spitted lamb. He snatched a flame from it and formed it into a wand of light.

The crowd murmured uneasily. "I seen nobles do that," said the scarred man, shifting from foot to foot.

Warin spread his hands; the wand lengthened and thickened into a staff. He spun it, and struck the ground with one end. A wall of flames sprung up around the panicked townsmen, flames licking at their feet and rising high into the sky, filling the air with the scent of fire and smoke.

All but the Brother screamed for mercy; instead, the cleric stood still and silent, and the flames shone bright on his steel chestplate and helm. Warin waved his hand. The fire leaped back into his staff, leaving only the smell of scorched air.

The Brother dropped to his knees. "Your Majesty," he said, presenting his sword. "Kill me for my offense."

"Never would I do such a thing, Brother," answered Warin, raising him up. "Keep your sword, and use it for Tremont."

The townfolk had dropped to their knees along with the Brother. The scarred man spoke up: "Only seen Old King Gethin and his sons do sumfing like that, or the Black Man"—he and the other men made Amma's sign—"and that's the truth. Please forgive us, Your Majesty. I am your loyal man, and always was!"

"Rise, please, rise, all of you!" Warin took the scarred man's hand, lifted him up, and said, "What is your name?"

"Willum, sire."

"Willum, you were with me in the north?"

"Aye, I was a chief pikesman, my lord, under Brother Gerral of the King's Own. After Montesurbis and Dordemon, I'd follow you anywheres!" His face contorted with emotion, puckering the slash down his face. "Sire, we thought you was dead. We thought as how your brother would rule and we'd be under a rougher thumb than we was already. Now you've come back from the dead—it's a miracle, sire, the hand of Amma come down and give us a miracle!"

"No miracle—I was never dead, nor will be until I see my brother in the Hill," said Warin. He leaped nimbly onto the fountain's rim again to stand above the crowd. "My father is dead of old age, not by my hand. The prophecy is broken, and I have come home to find my brother has lied to you, stolen from you, and taken the throne. Will you stand by me and take it back?" A full-throated howl of assent went up from the crowd. He nodded. "These men around me—Brother Cor, these Travelers and their Prince, and Willum here who was with me at Montesurbis and Dordemon"—Willum swelled with pride, and his fellows elbowed him—"are to be accorded respect as my companions. Listen to their counsel. Cor, send the Brothers at Farr's Temple the news, I'll need them by my side."

"I'll send a Guardsman to the Armory as well, sire," said Cor, but Warin stopped him.

"No. There's a chance we may not get there in time to stop the coronation. If they see the offering fire smoke rise from the Temple, the Guards will turn against us." Warin turned back to the gathering. "All you women, spread the word throughout the city—I am home! I go to the Father's Temple to oust the usurper and take my rightful place. Let my people come with me!"

Clumps of men joined the crowd as they passed through the City until there were at least a thousand, with twenty Brothers beside and more on the way. Warin led them on towards the steps leading to the Temple of Pagg, on the highest and sheerest of the six Temple-crowned hills within the city's walls—a bluff, its long, steep switchback roads wide enough for four to walk abreast. It would be a long climb; he walked faster.

Warin let the people's love, relief and trust wash over him. Any doubts he'd had about becoming King vanished.

Atop its steep, oak-covered hill, Pagg's Temple flew the flags of the King, dark red with three triangles in gold; in the shade of the trees surrounding the sanctuary, the bearers who'd carried the nobility up the long climb rested beside silken and gilt litters. At the entrance to the Temple, hidden in shadow, Hildin, Gian and the Little Father watched the mass of people already climbing the sharp switchbacks. "Is it him?" said Gian.

"I'd wager it is," answered his master.

"Him who?" said the elderly Little Father, looking from one to the other.

"How many do you think will side with him?" said Gian.

"Not enough. I have purchased the Brothers over years with donations to Farr's Temple—the Guards, too, and the Fathers. He won't find much support after all this time."

"Who are we talking about!" said the old high priest, peevishness wrinkling his face further.

"A man pretending to be my brother, Little Father. He says he is Warin, but Warin is dead."

"A pity he besmirches your dear brother's name, Your Majesty," said the Little Father, his head shaking more than usual. "But you have your father's power now. Surely there will be little difficulty? What is that bright flashing I see down below?"

It was the sun glinting off polished steel, the kind that made up the Brothers' armor. Hildin said, "Little Father, go. Make your preparations. We shall start the ceremony momentarily. I wish to take a moment here and watch this pretender." Once they were alone, Hildin hissed, "Pagg damn him, he has Brothers! They're standing in front of him! I see Teacher, too. How did that old bastard get out of the library?"

Gian considered for a moment, then answered carefully. "You are no longer Regent, sire, and not yet the oldest brother, despite what we say. He obeys Warin because he must."

"You're challenging me, Gian. Don't," said Hildin, not bothering to give his cousin a glance. Gian dropped to one knee, and kissed the deep red brocade of his master's tunic.

Hildin ignored him, scanning the crowd far below. At the head of the rabble, Teacher stood beside Warin, who looked more like a Traveler than a prince; that could hardly endear him to the people, but then how had he gathered such a crowd? Peasants with sticks, but so many of them—at least a thousand, maybe twice that. Directly behind Warin and Teacher were about twenty Brothers; more were joining the back of the crowd. Troubling.

Hildin waited until both Teacher and Warin turned to speak with a Brother. He took a deep lungful of air, let it out between his hands, and threw it before him.

A fierce wind rushed down from the Temple toward Warin and his men, still some 300 feet down the nearly-vertical slope. At the sound, Teacher and Warin turned and threw up their hands just in time; the wave of air broke around their magical shield, but still sent the several dozen Brothers leading the pack crashing into those behind them in an avalanche of men and armor; one, bowling sideways, knocked Warin off his feet.

An appreciative mutter broke out among the Guards looking down from the Temple. "*That's* for traitors," said one to his neighbor. "Though the Black Man is with them," he added, troubled.

"Knowing Warin, he'll stop to care for his wounded," puffed Hildin, his hands on his knees. "Then he'll come charging up the hill straight into the teeth of the Guards. They'll mistake any magic of his for Teacher's. Bar the door behind us—I've already warded it with most of my power, but that blow took the last of my strength for a while. By the time Warin breaks through the Guards, the ward on the door, and the bars, it won't matter. I'll be crowned, and everyone across the City will see the smoke from Pagg's altar and know that it is so. Let him watch Fredrik and Emmae die, and then I'll be recovered enough to kill him. Help me inside, I'm tired now." With a final order to his Guards to defend the Temple to the man, Hildin leaned on his cousin and entered the Temple.

*　　*　　*

Scores of men lay still or groaning on the steps at the forefront of Warin's impromptu army: among them, Warin himself. Calls for Sisters filled the air.

"I failed you," said Teacher. "I did not see him."

"I didn't see him, either, and I hardly thought he'd waste such a goodly amount of power this far down the hill," said Warin. "You and I took the brunt of it, but I couldn't get my defense up fast enough to protect all of the Brothers."

"Nor I."

Brother Cor gently prodded Warin's shoulder; Warin paled and choked down a heave. "Broken collarbone," said the Brother. "Your Majesty, you cannot stay. We must find you a Sister."

"Would you let a broken bone stop you?" said Warin, dragging himself to his feet. "No, not as long as you could walk. Sling it. How many hurt?"

"That I saw? One Traveler, two Brothers, a good handful of townsmen, all dead outright. Maybe more. Perhaps a hundred wounded, some badly enough they might yet die. Broken bones, split heads, many bruises." Cor sighed. "Our armor made us better weapons than anything else the Usurper could command."

Warin shuddered as Cor helped his left arm into a sling. "Call the Sisters for the wounded. The dead Traveler—find Connin and tell him—there you are, Connin. Are you all right?"

"Unhurt. I don't know how I'm going to tell Tom's mother, is all." Connin eyed the Temple, its windows shuttered tight. "The Usurper has about a hundred Guards around the Temple, fifty bowmen on the roof, who knows how many inside, and the entrance magically sealed. We'll get through the ward among us."

"The King's injury weakens his ability to wield magic, and I cannot break a seal that Hildin has set," warned Teacher. "It will be up to you, Connin."

"We will rely less on magic, then," said Warin, "and more on persuasiveness." He ran up a few steps, shaky at first, then more confident as he pushed pain aside; he faced his few hundred remaining men—armored Brothers and unprotected townfolk intermingled, armed with swords, spears, daggers, axes, kitchen knives, staves, and nothing at all.

Without thinking, he tried to raise his unslinged right arm; he nearly swooned with pain and kept himself upright with an effort, though he hid it as best he could. "Men of Tremont!" he shouted. "We have suffered at my brother's hand. But now, his magic is weakened. He will not be able to strike such a blow again before we reach him, and I hold my father's magic now." Warin stopped for breath; his shoulder ached, reminding him that though he held the magic, he might not be able to use much of it.

"Hildin has barricaded himself inside Pagg's Temple," he continued, "but we will breach his enchantments, and his Guard will join us when they see their true King has returned. Many in the Leutish nobility, their King Fredrik, and his daughter the Princess—the Princess Edmerka are also inside," he continued, his voice catching on Emmae's title. "They are not to be harmed. Is it understood? Respect King Fredrik as you would me!"

"The Leutish woman is the Usurper's wife," called a townsman. "Don't spare her, Your Majesty, she may carry his child!"

"She is innocent in this," said Teacher in a surprisingly loud voice above the murmurs. "Protect her." Teacher drew sullen, frightened looks from the crowd, but the cries for Edmerka's blood died down.

"We outnumber the Guards, but I will not have them die if I can help it," called Warin. "Stay well behind until I call for you, and then be ready. Be sure your fellows understand what I've said!"

As Brothers and townsmen shouted his orders, bawling in relays to the back of the crowd, Warin walked up the road, with Teacher a step or two behind and the men following at a distance. Strange how quickly he'd put the Woodsman aside and taken up the King, he thought, as he and Teacher raised a shield of solid air before them. Just as he feared, arrows from the Temple's roof rained down on them as soon as they came within range.

This time, they were not caught off-guard; the arrows cracked against a barrier of air, but a few lucky shots passed over their shields to land with resounding thunks far behind them. A strangled cry told Warin at least one of the arrows had hit its mark; he looked back to see a dozen men, arrows protruding from arms, legs, throats, eye sockets. "Stay out of range!" he roared, and climbed faster up the switchbacks, Teacher and Cor keeping pace.

When he was sure the Guards could hear him, he shouted, "Cease fire! I am Warin, returned to take up the throne!"

"Warin is dead, pretender!" returned the Guard commander, a burly man with a many-times-broken nose.

"Would the Black Man stand with a pretender?" countered Brother Cor. "Would the Brothers stand with a pretender? Look to the bottom of the hill. Even now, more Brothers join the rightful King."

The commander shifted uneasily as he eyed the growing assemblage of shining steel on the long ascent, and then the massive door to the Temple. "We're locked out, sir," muttered a Guard behind him. "The Regent has locked us out."

The commander scowled and straightened his great shoulders. "Prove to me you're the Prince come back."

Warin climbed the broad, white Temple stairs, stopping within arm's reach of the commander. "What would prove it to you?"

The commander considered, hand flexing nervously on the hilt of his sword. "I—well…" He cast about. He straightened, more confident, and pointed to a white boulder, its top flat as a table; rusty stains flowed down its sides, as if blood had run down it over and over again. "The Father's Rock. Lift it."

A gasp went up from the crowd. The Father's Rock predated the Temple itself—in fact, it could be said it was the original Temple. Sacrifices to the Father had bled down the sides of the Rock until Temmin the Great built the white marble Temple sanctuary nearly two hundred years ago. Warin strode up to it and placed his good hand on the dull white stone, surprisingly warm against his skin. How much magic could he muster, with his broken bone, and still have enough left to see the day through? He closed his eyes and focused his newly-inherited, still-unfamiliar power around the rock. He gathered it up, and pushed with his mind.

The Rock shifted under his hand. He opened his eyes and stood back as it rose from the stones around it. Up, and up, until it hovered in the air at the height of a man. His control wavered, new power and his injury combined against him. "Enough," he said brusquely, and let the Rock drop as if he'd meant to do that all along. The Rock struck the stones beneath it with such force that it split in two. Stillness, then murmurings of astonishment, until a roar broke out from every Guard, Brother and townsman.

"Only a Prince—or a King—could do such a thing," said the Commander, head bowed. "You *must* be Warin. Forgive me." One by one, the Guards joined him on their knees.

Warin felt the long climb and the broken bone; he swayed on his feet, and Teacher steadied him. "I'll be all right," said Warin. "I have to be. Teacher, once we're inside, protect Emmae. I order you to protect her at all costs."

"Unless it endangers you, I will," replied Teacher. "But I must defend any man close to the throne first, even your brother, much as it pains me. I must allow only you to kill Hildin. I cannot lift a hand against him."

Behind the barred and warded door, a hundred members of the Tremontine and Leutish nobility sat on padded benches in the Temple, the Tremontines on the right, the Leutans on the left. All wore subdued colors for the old King's passing, but not Hildin. He wore a cloth-of-gold mantle encrusted with jewels over his Tremontine red silk tunic, and fairly danced up the aisle to stand before the Little Father, Emmae following behind.

The great door shook with a force that scraped the wood against the stone lintels, though the door would not give way. Nervous murmurs began in the crowd; more than one lord snuck his dagger from its sheath, and the hundred Guards within took defensive positions.

Three Fathers ran up to their high priest and whispered in his ear; the Little Father whispered loudly to Hildin, "I don't understand. They say Prince Warin is outside, with a great crowd of Brothers and commoners who say he is the rightful king. Teacher is with him, too. A good hundred are dead, but ten times more are coming up the stairs!" His words reverberated off the Temple's stone archways; the murmurs turned to astonished and alarmed babble, punctuated by the shaking of the doors.

Hildin hissed, "Shut up, you old fool! Prepare to light the altar fire." He turned to the nobles in their rows. "Warin is dead," he said over the noise. "Anyone who claims to be Warin is a pretender! Now, Little Father, get this over with!" He kneeled, dragging Emmae down next to him.

The cleric abandoned his planned chant after a glance into the Prince's face, and switched instead to a quick blessing. He took the crown from Gian's hands, held it up before the assembly, and settled it on Hildin's head. Hildin stood, took the queen's crown from an attendant, and placed it none too gently on Emmae's chestnut hair, the weight of it bearing down on her brow. Hildin raised her up beside him. Whatever was trying to open the doors slammed against them again, sending a tremor into the stone that Emmae felt through her slippers.

"I don't care for this, at all," said Fredrik. "Who is this man who claims to be your brother? You told me he was dead!"

"This man is a gross pretender!" shouted Hildin over the increasingly anxious crowd. "A pretender has come with Travelers to kill us all!" he continued. "Guardsmen, defend your King!"

The Guards tensed. The lords herded their ladies toward the altar, as far away from the doors as they could get them, and drew their own swords; the hilts and scabbards were covered in gems, but the blades were sharp and deadly all the same.

The door complained against competing enchantments, until the ward broke, then the bars, and it finally it gave way. Connin stood in its ruins; Warin strode past him into the Temple. The assembly drew a surprised breath all at once, and even the Guards stood still, uncertain.

Warin looked nothing like the smiling, happy man Emmae had seen last; his skin was waxen, dark hair plastered to his forehead. A sling held his left arm, and pain flashed over his already spent face with each breath. His eyes met Emmae's, and shone with hope and purpose. He stepped toward her, but at the sight of the crown on her head, his spirit seemed to droop. His gaze both implored and doubted her.

Emmae flung the crown to the floor.

Warin smiled then and strode further into the hall, the Brothers and Travelers fanning out behind him. "I am Warin, and I have come back with the Brothers beside me for my crown and my wife," he shouted.

The hall erupted into arguments and exclamations. Many of the benches were overturned as some Tremontines dropped to one knee and declared Warin king; others cuffed them to the floor and cursed them as idiots, while the Leutans stood uncertain.

Hildin grabbed Emmae by the arm and threw her at Gian. "Guardsmen, you are sworn to obey the crowned king," cried Hildin. "I wear the crown—kill this pretender and his rabble!" The Guards took a step forward.

Suddenly, Brothers swarmed past Warin, their armor shining in the sunlight now streaming in; beside him, an absence of light but for pale skin, appeared a figure in black. The Guardsmen hesitated, taken aback at the Brothers' strange allegiance, the presence of the Black Man, and the sheer number of their opponents, until Hildin gave a flicker of a signal to the high gallery of the Temple. A hidden archer sent an arrow into King Fredrik's throat; he crumpled at Emmae's feet, his blood spattering Hildin's mantle. "They've killed King Fredrik!" yelled Hildin.

Emmae's eyes flew to the gallery. An archer in the red and gold uniform of the Guard stood hidden in the shadows; he looked not at her face but at her heart, and she knew the next arrow was meant for her. She closed her eyes.

A thud against her chest, a sharp stab, a weight that fell into her arms and dropped her to the floor. She opened her eyes.

She held Gian. He had taken the arrow meant for her, through his heart, through his back, through her dresses, the tip just piercing her skin. "No more death, not even…for him," he whispered. "I loved you." Gian groaned once; blood bubbled from his lips; and he died.

"Gian! Damn you, I have need of you…" said Hildin in a rough, low voice, though his eyes filled with tears. "No matter. No matter. I'll kill you myself when this is over, bitch." He returned his attention to the melee. Flames licked weakly at his fingers as he tried again and again to summon his spent magic, but the great wind and the destroyed ward on the door had taken too much.

Emmae held Gian's body, shock, triumph and a confusing grief mixing with the blood running over her hands and dress, some of it her own. Dimly, she realized the men around her had no thoughts of her body, perhaps for the first time. She collected herself and slipped Gian's long ceremonial dagger from its sheath. "Thank you," she whispered, and closed his eyes.

A howl rose up from the Leutish lords; they launched themselves at Warin and his men, including the much better-armed Brothers, who did their best to defend themselves without killing their attackers. "Emmae!" cried Warin above the din. "Emmae! Teacher, can you see? Is she dead?"

"I see her moving, but your cousin is dead," Teacher replied. Warin and Teacher set their shields before as many of the men as they could reach, and pushed forward against the fighting, but the air before Warin quickly began to tremble. "Your Majesty," said Teacher, "you are exhausting yourself—behind me! You must stop using your magic!"

Warin gave up his shield and fell in, gasping in pain but still calling out to as many as could hear him: "Leutans!" he cried, "Hildin betrays you! He killed Fredrik and means to kill your Princess—see where he hid the archer!" He took a flame from the branches of candles lining the Temple, and threw the resulting fireball into the galleries. Every head turned to see a Guardsman illuminated in the shadows, arrow nocked. He let fly at Warin, but Teacher gestured; the arrow quivered in the air, stopped, and turned. Flying faster than it had left the bow, the arrow sank itself into the archer's heart up to the fletching.

A new, stronger howl arose from the Leutans, who turned from the Brothers and attacked the Tremontines, Guardsman and noble alike. A Leutish lord took up a Guardsman's dropped spear, brought it to his massive shoulder, and sent it straight and true toward Hildin. Teacher cried out, and ran toward the altar; the spear stopped as the arrow had, but did not return; instead, it fell at Hildin's feet.

"Why stop you me?" shouted the Leutan. "Kills he our King, kill us he will! Kill him you must! *Damn this Tremontine tongue!*" he added in Leutan.

"Because he is of the blood," answered Warin in Old Sairish. "Do you recognize me, sir? You are Hendas Baron Holset. You fought with me at Dordemon."

Lord Holset squinted. "You are much changed...but yes, you are Warin of Tremont."

"I swear to you, Tremont is not your enemy, only Hildin," said Warin. "Help me. I would take your hand, but I cannot."

Holset pondered a moment, then hoisted Warin up on one of the richly padded benches that hadn't been knocked over in the fighting;

Warin nearly fainted from pain. Holset set himself at Warin's back and shouted in his own tongue, "*Leutans, to me! We stand with King Warin! Leave off those nobles who support him!*"

"Lords of Tremont!" Warin called, strengthening the sound of his voice with the last shreds of his magic, "leave off our guests! Guardsmen, if you cannot bring yourself to act against the crowned king and follow me, then drop your weapons! I swear to you, you will be protected!"

The first to drop his sword at Warin's feet was the broken-nosed commander, with a "Gladly, sire"; the remaining Guardsmen quickly followed suit, the only sound now in the Temple the clatter of swords and spears falling into the growing pile. "You have no one left, Hildin," said Warin into the new quiet.

Hildin pulled his jeweled knife. "I have my Queen, which means I have you. Oh, yes, I think with her at my side, I might do anything." He glanced briefly down at the bleeding Emmae, still crouching by Gian's body with the dagger hidden in the great folds of her brocade overdress. Emmae felt nothing from Hildin, though a desperate, searching desire flowed into her that she recognized as Warin's.

She gathered her strength, and sprang, clutching at Hildin's leg. A quick, calculated slash down his inner thigh, as she'd once bled a rabbit with Warin. She heard Teacher's shout, and the dagger grew too hot for her to hold, but by then she knew she'd aimed true. Hildin's blood covered her, pouring from the severed artery. She scrambled backwards; Hildin stumbled after her with an ineffectual stab of his dagger, then fell to his knees. "Warin's whore has killed me…Gian, Warin's whore…"

"As a rabbit, so a man," spat Emmae. She crawled further away, but Hildin already lay in his gore, eyes rolled back in his head.

Teacher was at Hildin's side then, ineffectually trying to stanch the bleeding, pale white fingers dyed red and shaking. "I cannot stop it. I was not fast enough to stop her. Your Majesty, I cannot stop it!"

"Let him finish dying, Teacher," said Warin, running up the altar stairs. "You can't save him, and I don't want you to."

"I do not want to either, but I must!" A moment longer, and Teacher's trembling increased as the river of blood subsided. "He's dead. Your

Majesty, you must forgive me now, or—" A spasm, and Teacher folded inward, crooning with pain.

"You're forgiven, Teacher, with all my heart!" said Warin. Teacher uttered a deep, relieved sigh, and the pale face relaxed.

"He's dead?" murmured Emmae into the shocked silence. "He's dead." She stood up. Hildin's blood covered her head to foot, soaking through her heavy clothes, thick and clotting in her hair, coating her hands, trickling into her face, warm blood that seemed to grow hotter.

Warin didn't care about the blood. He took her as best he could in his uninjured arm, but the blood grew hotter still and forced him back. "Emmae! Teacher, what's happening to her?"

"The spell is ending."

It seemed so long since the silver smoke had entered her—silver smoke? When had there been silver smoke, she wondered. It seeped out of her bones, trickling up through her flesh, to seep from her skin in long tendrils rising toward the high stone arches above the altar. As the smoke left her, air rushed in; she gulped great breaths. With each one came a rush of memory: her mother's beautiful, loving face; oh, her mother's death, and the tears she wept, tears that never completely ended; her distracted father; the long, lonely days with stupid Olka and the rest of the simpering servants; her horrible stepmother; the carriage—the Travelers. Their Queen. The cards. The spell. Connin.

"I remember," she said. "I remember everything." She looked past Hildin to Fredrik's body, and ran to kneel at its side. "My father—*oh, no, oh, Father!*" she sobbed in Leutish. "*And I didn't know you! Why did you send me away? How could you marry me to that horrible man? How can you be dead!*" She cradled his cooling hand against her cheek.

Warin moved toward her, but Teacher stayed him. "Let her grieve."

Wincing, Warin shook the pale hand off his shoulder, and crouched beside Emmae. "Emmae, my love, are you all right?" he said, his voice breaking. "Oh, how I've worried! When I discovered you'd been taken… You—you remember who you are now?" She nodded and cried into her father's hand. "I'm so sorry for your father's death, truly. We will wait as long as you wish to be married, even the year and a day for full mourning."

The spokes of fear, loneliness and horror spun before her eyes, spokes not knowing who she was, or why her body answered anyone's call. Her throat constricted with anger, and she snarled it open. "Married?" she cried in Tremontine. "And who am I marrying?"

"Why…Emmae, we're promised to one another!"

She sprang to her feet. "I was promised to a woodsman, not a king, and as it turns out, both are false men!"

"How have I been false to you?" he said, staring up at her. He rose to his feet, face an appalled red until he jostled his broken collarbone and paled again. "Emmae, I have given up everything to come for you."

"Giving up a tiny cottage and a hard life for a throne—what misery!" she jeered.

"We were happy there," he said, his voice dark with yearning and anger. "*You* were happy there!"

"Who was I then?" she shouted. "I didn't know, but you did!"

"No, I didn't!" he shouted back. "I knew you were Leutish, and likely from a wealthy family but I never guessed you were the princess!"

"Harla take you, you knew about my enchantment!" she said, breaking into sobs again. "You knew, and you didn't tell me, and you—you *used* it!" His face crumpled; a bitter triumph rose in her throat.

"I should have told you, but I didn't know how. I didn't want to frighten you, and I couldn't lift it—"

"Only the blood of a king, the Traveler Queen said."

"—And I would have been that king for you!" he shouted. "If the only way to save you from that spell was to bathe you in my own blood, I swear by Pagg right here in His Temple that I would have come back, taken the throne and died for you! Emmae, I love you!"

The bitterness clawed at her heart. "My name is Edmerka, Princess Royal of Leute, Dowager Queen of Tremont, and I will not marry you or anyone else, ever! I hate men!" She ripped at her dress. "I want that bastard's blood off my body, now!"

Warin's hooded, dark eyes glittered with a rage so like his dead brother's that she instinctively stepped back. "My lady, as my brother's widow, you will always have an honored place in my court unless you decide to make your home elsewhere," he said. "Little Father, may we beg the use of your baths? The Dowager Queen wishes to use them." The astonished cleric agreed, and Edmerka, Dowager Queen of Tremont, let the servants lead her off.

Her temper had gotten the better of her. She was angry with him, yes, and she had every right to be, she told herself as the serving women poured bucket after bucket of hot water over her until the red stream eddying down the drain ran clear. She had every right to cry, she told herself as a Sister bound up the wound above her heart: her father had died, right in front of her; she'd discovered the depth of her enchantment; she'd faced Warin's outright treachery. Then why did his hurt and anger stay so fresh in her mind, why did his suddenly hard eyes make her wilt with remorse, why were her tears more for her lost love than her lost father?

Temmin came out of the book sobbing. Her years of loneliness, her yearning for love: her father broke her heart, and when she finally thought she'd mended it, Warin broke it again. He felt every ache of it, but unlike Emmae, he knew what Warin had gone through, and why. "Warin loved her! Why didn't she know? She was so lonely and unhappy, how could she turn him away?"

"A handkerchief, Your Highness," Teacher said, handing it over. "You have seen this story through her eyes. Is it not possible he did betray her? Is it not possible he expected too much, too soon?"

Temmin wiped his eyes, his tears as much for himself and his present troubles as for Emmae's long-ago heartache. "Because...because it's what she knew?"

"Which was...?"

"That men would always betray her—that's what she felt. She had no experience of anything else, and so she saw Warin in the same light. But that's unfair. He wasn't like them. He didn't mean to do what he did."

"He knew exactly what he did."

"Then he's evil!" said Temmin. "Except...except he's not evil."

"Sometimes, good people do evil things," Teacher replied. "They use duty, profit, expediency, desire of all kinds, to justify their actions, and however strong the justification, somewhere inside they know they have done wrong and must make amends somehow. That is the difference between real evil and transitory error. The irredeemable are those who commit evil with no self-justification whatsoever. They commit it because they can. The question is, should good people in error be forgiven? Are some offenses so great that no amends can be made?"

Temmin's head ached. "I don't know. I don't want to talk about it."

"Then think about it until our next lesson."

"I don't want to think about it!" shouted Temmin. "It's all I've done, is think about things, and morality, and gods, and—and what to do for the good of the people!" He jumped up from the couch, and advanced on his tutor. "This was supposed to take my mind off of things, not torture me with them!"

"What tortures you?"

"*You're* torturing me!" he said, clutching his throbbing temples. "This is a horrible day! Just go away!" He stalked into his bedchamber and threw himself on the bed. Teacher did not follow him.

No matter how he tried to sleep, he kept coming back to "things." Hildin and the woman who'd whored out the Obbys as children—they were certainly irredeemable. Gian made amends with his life, but that was the least he could do. And when he was king, Temmin intended to track down that brothelkeeper and kill her himself, the Obbys and their cavalier attitude be damned. Maybe he'd kill Lord Litta while he was at it. Maybe he wouldn't wait until he was king. He had two years to fill now, after all.

Harbis entered and inquired after His Highness's preferences for dinner dress. His Highness said his preference was for the substitute valet to piss off because he wasn't coming out of his bedchamber until Jenks came back. "Very good, sir," murmured Harbis, wasting a masterfully outraged twitch of the chin on a young man with his head in the pillows. The valet tiptoed out again.

And then, Temmin thought, there were the people who might still make up for their sins and restore their honor. Warin might still make it up to Emmae in the story. Yes, he knew they married in the end, but were they happy? His parents weren't. Maybe married people didn't get to be happy. And Emmae was so frustrating! What else could Warin have done?

Here was this girl, half-naked in the hedge…no, she'd been naked in the woods…

"Why does everything lead back to Mattie!" he shouted, and burst into tears again. "Where is Jenks?"

Harbis the valet, chin still twitching, walked down the short flight of stairs from the Residence Wing to the mezzanine where the senior staff and personal servants lived. There in the hall by his door stood Mr Winmer, the King's personal secretary. "How is the Heir?" said the dapper little man.

"Indisposed, Mr Winmer," said Harbis after a discreet pause. "I believe His Highness will be dining in his room."

"It's a perfect evening for an intimate dinner," said Winmer, his smile widening. "Take the evening off after dinner service, Mr Harbis. I've made other arrangements for Prince Temmin's comfort at bedtime."

"Thank you, sir," said Harbis, his professional facade breaking into genuine pleasure. He opened the door to his temporary rooms. "I am much obliged to you."

"Not at all," said Winmer. "We are obliged to you for stepping in on such short notice." He watched the door close behind the valet, then turned to his own rooms, set apart from the rest of the floor closer to the King's apartments. By the fire stood a young woman in maid's livery, wringing her hands. "Ah, Miss Dannikson!" said Winmer. "Promptness is a rare quality in the young female. It is one of your many charms."

"Mr Winmer, sir," said Arta, bobbing a nervous curtsey.

"Are you frightened? Don't worry, my dear, it's merely time to collect on your little debt."

"My debt…?" she quavered.

Winmer circled behind her and unpinned the little starched cap from her hair. "I didn't tell Mr Affton about your very shocking behavior at the Heir's birthday ball, and you promised to do anything I asked. Didn't you?"

"Yes, sir," she whispered, squeezing her eyes closed.

FOURTEEN

Yellow and blue banners flying from Lord Valmouth's city residence proclaimed His Grace was in town. The crest of the City's social season began next week at Neya's Day, and lasted until the season ended on Nerr's Day, the first day of Summer's Beginning; everyone of note in the Kingdom would be in the City for that last spoke of gaiety.

Tonight, Lady Valmouth held a ball. Partygoers' carriages clogged the street before the hulking, old-fashioned townhouse on Park Square, waiting with varying degrees of patience as the King entered with his entourage of attendants and Guardsmen.

Harsin climbed the stairs, acknowledging onlookers. Once inside the tall, narrow entryway, he gave over his cloak to the waiting servant and shot his cuffs; he absently admired the three gold triangles inlaid in his dark ruby cufflinks, a symbol of both his family and its empire for a thousand years. An evening's entertainment while his son got over the sulks and cemented his path away from the Lovers' Temple was the perfect thing. Two of his mistresses would be here tonight; which one he favored with his presence afterward would depend on which charmed him more. His favorite was beginning to fade; the second seemed more likely. Perhaps some enchanting new thing might even catch his eye. It was so hard to tell how the evening would go.

And then he hoped to see Litta. Obviously the conversation with Temmin had gone as expected, but he'd like to know more. The boy so far was completely predictable; his mother's upbringing had left him with an over-abundant idealism and little to no subtlety of conduct. Right now, Harsin found that useful, but Temmin needed training in the ways of statecraft to be an effective king, or even an effective Heir. Harsin resolved to talk with Teacher, and entered the throng to the usual fanfare.

He entertained himself by taking the youngest daughter of the house onto the dance floor first. The lady was far too inexperienced to interest him, barely out of the schoolroom, but something about a flustered, pretty young girl, blushing and stammering, amused him no end; to boot, the King's attention would fill her dance card faster than her still-unformed looks would, which amused him even more.

The second dance he gave to his waning favorite, a slender, long-legged woman who realized her sun was setting; an understated desperation lingered in her clasp, the color high in her cheeks as his ear missed every third word. He left her at the sidelines with a dismissive bow. She bored him. He'd set her aside before Neya's Day with a nice present of a costly necklace, perhaps a country house—something that would please both her and her cuckolded husband. His eye roamed over the dancers to land on his rising favorite, the dark-eyed, olive-skinned daughter of an Alzehni merchant, a Miss Selvaci; their eyes met, and his satisfaction with himself grew.

He turned toward a commotion at the top of the stairs. Applause and obeisances rippled through the crowd: the Obbys had entered. A surprise: Harsin expected they'd absent themselves from any social situation where they might encounter him, at least for a few days.

A tug in Harsin's groin brought sympathy for his poor foolish son. Though Harsin's tastes didn't run to men, Issak might change anyone's mind, and Allis was in astonishing looks even for her, long black hair brilliant against luminous skin. He regretted keeping Temmin from them, but only momentarily; after tonight, Temmin might make any number of appointments with them with no more thought than Harsin ever gave it. A fluttery young man buttonholed Issak, and they disappeared into a side room.

Unexpectedly, Allis met Harsin's eye. Always be gracious to the defeated, especially the beautiful defeated, he said to himself. He strode through the parting crowd to her side.

"Your Majesty," Allis smiled, curtseying low.

"Holy One," replied Harsin with a bow. The musicians began the introduction to the next dance; he took her on his arm and they twirled onto the floor. Harsin's hand fit so delightfully at her waist—such a delicate woman for such curves. "I will be calling on you in our official capacities, soon, I think," he said.

Allis lifted a brow. "You surprise me, sir. I should have thought we would suffer from your disfavor for at least, oh, two years."

"My disfavor? How could anyone be angry with you, Miss Obby?"

"I have heard that your son's plans to join us as Supplicant have displeased you. Nevertheless, you are welcome at the Temple any time you wish. If you don't care to run into him, we're happy to offer you the Door of Discretion."

"Oh, Miss Obby, I thought it quite clear that Nerr will not be getting the Heir, at least this Heir." Harsin whipped her through a turn, but she stumbled nary a bit.

"The conversation with Lord Litta?" she said, returning his smile. "You may note His Grace's absence this evening."

"I hadn't noticed. You have my entire attention."

Her smile revealed the tips of her teeth, shining white against her rosy lips, intimate and promising, but she said nothing.

Curiosity overcame him. "What explains Litta's absence?"

She danced on tiptoe, and leaned in toward his ear. "Two things stop blackmailers," she said. "Prompt disclosure of the horrible secret they threaten to reveal, and horrible secrets of their own."

They danced in silence, Allis keeping her eyes on his face, and Harsin staring absently over her head at the yellow and blue draperies, the yellow and blue livery of the servants lining the walls, the yellow and blue flowers —Lady Valmouth's over-use of her husband's colors was giving him a headache. "I must say, Miss Obby, that I do admire your nerve," he said.

"I cannot return the compliment, I fear."

"Have a care, my dear," he said, tightening his grip around her waist. "I am an embodiment myself, the embodiment of this empire."

"Your Majesty, I am the Embodiment of a Goddess. I'm not the one who must have a care. However powerful you think you are, you are nothing compared to my Mistress."

"Your Mistress has strict rules about confidentiality. And yet you risk displeasing Her."

"You and your proxies risk your souls, sir, with far fewer qualms," she replied. "As to confidentiality, of course we would never betray any confidence given in worship, but we have many, many sources of unprivileged information. Devotees of the Lovers are in all walks of life, you know, especially one particularly intimate profession. It is not at all difficult for us to learn useful things about anyone, however high or low."

The dance ended. Allis curtsied again and sailed into the crowd, a trail of men following her.

Harsin's dinner curdled, and his restless eye skipped from face to face. Lady Litta stood in a knot of older women, jowls a-wobble, but no sign of her husband. Never mind. Winmer's plan unfolded tonight, and after that it wouldn't matter.

Temmin woke to a gentle clatter of dishes, and a savory smell of roast beef, potatoes, warm bread, and a bit of a cabbage-y smell that might be broccoli. He must have slept through tea. Did he have lunch? His stomach seemed to think he hadn't. "Jenks?" he said. He sat up and pushed the hair out of his puffy eyes.

"Harbis, Your Highness," said the valet in his irritating, melodious tenor, nothing at all like Jenks's gravel-filled baritone.

"Oh, it's you," grumbled Temmin.

"It is me, to be sure, sir," said Harbis. "If you please, sir, your dinner has been sent up. You seemed ill-disposed to dine with your family." He had perfectly appointed the little table; its damask cloth shone clean and white, and the valet's elegant, slender hands fluttered among the dishes, removing silver covers with unfamiliar gestures Temmin found annoyingly graceful.

Despite his mood, Temmin wolfed down two bowls of broccoli bisque, a plate full of oysters, most of a roast of beef, potatoes, asparagus, the whole basket of rolls, and a good-sized pudding with custard. Even after all that, he had no objection to the decanter of port, a bowl of sweetnuts and a small, aged cheese. "Thank you, Harbis," he said, remembering his manners even with this overly suave substitute for Jenks. "Now, push off. I don't want you. I'll put myself to bed," he added. Harbis bowed, eager to be gone, and nearly scampered out of the room with the service cart.

Temmin cracked nuts, setting the meats aside. He wasn't hungry any more, but the brittle crunch as he crushed each shell satisfied. He did not hold back on the port; he hadn't intended to get drunk, but drunk suited the gloom of the single lamp, and his mood. He hadn't realized how much Supplicancy had come to mean. Here the twins had just shown him part of what he might learn, what he might do, what he might see... How he suffered for their kisses.

Maybe he could still learn from them. His father might not see the utility in reading people, but he certainly did. Reading people made it so easy to lead them. Look at Issak, bending people so effortlessly, and so gently, to his will.

Warin seemed to read people. He brought them to his side, and he hadn't had Lovers' Temple training: charisma, that's what it was. His own father had it. Maybe it was genetic, and Temmin didn't need training. Harsin had only to look at you, just like Issak—but not like Issak. People feared his father, but they loved Issak; they wanted to do what he wanted them to do, whether it was pour him wine or kiss him. That was part of the twins' skill, perhaps, making you want to be led.

They'd be disappointed, but better disappointed than shamed. The tiny voice in the chapel, it would be disappointed too. Maybe angry. But what could he do? It would be worse to let Allis and Issak be hurt, wouldn't it?

He wondered what he might face when Harla took him home to the Hill, when She would weigh his crimes against his soul. How long would She torment him before he was allowed to rest forever? Centuries? Millennia?

Litta didn't seem concerned, nor did his father, even though Temmin knew he believed. Litta must be an atheist, in spite of what he'd said. To

Temmin, atheists were semi-mythical creatures; no one would admit to unbelief, not if they valued their livelihoods. Or lives in some parts of the kingdom.

Worshipping a God, worshipping Allis and Issak—it was the same to him. And if it brought luck to the common people, that was for the best. Why would Litta think otherwise? Warin wouldn't have gotten his throne back without the commoners. There wouldn't be a throne without the commoners. The people were the kingdom, not just the king. But now it didn't matter, and to be honest, it figured only tangentially into his desire to take Supplicancy. It would be easier now, he told himself. He'd find some girl. There were plenty, according to that prat Fennows. Then he'd get it over with, and go to the twins. But it wouldn't be enough. He glanced at the decanter. Nearly empty, though he couldn't remember drinking it, and he didn't feel that drunk.

A whisper of fabric against carpet, and he looked up, expecting that useless Harbis. Instead, a girl stood just inside, with the door closed behind her. She quailed when she saw him, and reached for the doorknob, but steadied herself instead. She walked further into the room until he could see her more clearly.

He rose in surprise. It was Arta. She wore a gown of soft green like the fine ladies she'd admired at the ball. He'd been wrong that night; she was even more beautiful dressed as a lady than she was as a maid. Pale gold freckles dusted the fine skin of her shoulders, just as he'd imagined, and her hazel eyes were brilliant even in the low light. She dropped a curtsey all the way to the floor, stumbling on the way down, and he helped her up; she quickly pulled her loose, dark curls over her shoulders in an unsuccessful attempt to cover her cleavage.

"Arta, what are you doing here? Why are you dressed like that? Not that you don't look nice—you look wonderful, actually, quite beautiful… Gods, really, really, quite, quite beautiful." She stood now, very straight and rigid, her small, shaking hand still in his. She was blushing, and she wouldn't meet his eyes. "Arta," he said more forcefully, "what are you doing here?"

"I…I am bid to say—that is, no, not bid to say…" She blinked rapidly, and began again, her voice stronger, working hard if not successfully to overcome her northern Valmouth accent. "I am here to comfort you in your disappointment, Your Highness. They—I mean, I thought you mightn' want to be alone tonight, an as you an I are friends…we might be better friends," she finished, daring a guilty glance up at his face before fixing her eyes on his shoes again.

Suddenly, she wobbled on her feet, her eyes rolled, and Temmin caught her with a "Whoa!" just as she toppled over; a whiff of perfume hit his nose, heavy roses and lilacs, not at all her usual clean smell of hay and tea. He half-carried her to the green velvet couch and sat her down, reclining against the cushions at one end with her feet still on the floor. He found the brandy decanter on a table by the wingback chair he never sat in, poured her a glass, and ordered her to drink it as soon as she could hold the glass herself.

The brandy brought color creeping back to her face. "Oh dear," she whispered. "Oh, dear, dear, I got all rickety-tick. I'm so sorry, Your Highness, I don' know what happened."

"You locked your knees. Happens every inspection back at the Estate, especially on Farr's Day. Some new man in the Guard, or a postulant Brother, always goes down from trying to stand up straight. One Farr's Day when I was eight, a whole platoon went down one after another, boom boom boom, like ninepins. *That* was funny," he smiled. "Feeling better? Good. Now, tell me what you're doing here, all dressed up like this."

"I told you," she mumbled into her glass. "I'm here to keep you comp'ny." A tear found its way out of her eye, and she scrubbed at it in alarm.

"And so happy to do it, I see."

"No, no, sir!" she said, sitting up all the way. "No, I like bein with you!"

"Then why are you crying? Arta, tell me. You're under my protection. No one can do anything to you, I won't let them."

"Yes, they can," she said, stumbling over words and tears. "They can! They can turn me away without a ref'rence, an Fen, too, an if I lose my position without a ref'rence, I can' get a new one, you know, and my family needs the money, sir!"

"Stop, stop, stop! Who's 'they!'"

Arta's nervous babbling stopped. "Did I say 'they,' sir?"

"You certainly did." He gave her the handkerchief from his pocket. "Now, don't give this one to Fen," he said.

She laughed and wiped her eyes, but the tears kept falling. "I shouldn' cry, I really shouldn'. T'isn that I don' like you, sir, I do! I do, very much! You're kind, an handsome, an you make me laugh. I know we should get on very well together."

He took her in again: the perfume; the carefully loosened hair; the dress that left just enough to the imagination that removing it seemed best. "Someone sent you to seduce me."

"Why did you think I was here?" she said into the handkerchief.

"Merciful Amma, d'you think girls just show up at my door at all hours? Who sent you, Arta? No tears! Just answer!"

"Mr Winmer, sir," she said, wrenching herself into such a knot that he took to rubbing her back, soothing her loose again.

"And what did he say you were to do?"

"I was to lie with you, sir. That's why I'm all dressed up." She glanced up, guilty. "He knows you like me. You do like me, don' you, sir?"

"I don't know any man who wouldn't. You could charm Farr Himself."

"Oh, I don' think so, sir, especially with my eyes all puffy an red." She wiped her nose. "Mr Winmer knew you liked me because he saw us dancin in the hall that night. I am so sorry, Your Highness! It was my fault for peekin. He caught me just after, an said he could either tell Mr Affton an have me turned away, or I could owe him a favor. So I owed him a favor. An here I am."

A clear image of Winmer came to mind, the little man's eyes bulging as Temmin throttled him. "Why tonight?"

She bit her lip, and took his hand. "Mr Winmer said you'd gotten some bad news and couldn' go to the Temple after all, an that you were sad an lonely, an that I should make you feel better because you think I'm pretty an you'd like it if I did. An that wouldn' be so bad, would it, because we do like each other, and then he'd make sure I was taken care of an that Mam an Dad would be, too, an if you liked me well enough, you'd take care of me even better, so here I am, to make you feel better."

"He threatened you."

"Oh, no, sir! He just…he *explained* things to me. It's all right." Arta gave him an unsteady smile, and cradled his cheek. "You're so kind to me. If this is what you want, if this will make you feel better, then…" She rose up on one knee, her breasts nearly spilling from the neckline of the dress, and kissed him.

The kiss edged away the misery of the day, mixing with the port that suddenly made itself evident in the languor of his limbs, a drowsiness that shifted to arousal as she opened her mouth to him. He remembered kissing her before; he'd brought himself, more than once, remembering that kiss and her slim waist in his arms. He slipped his arms around her now, and kissed her down against the cushions. She was here for him, his consolation. She was the girl who would open the road to Allis and Issak in the most delightful way possible.

One hand slipped from her shoulder to the tops of her breasts, mounded above her corset, and the pulse between his legs nearly burst the buttons of his trousers. He kissed her jaw and her soft, soft neck, where the perfume she wore mingled with her own natural scent. She wriggled beneath him as he worked his hand further into her bodice and freed one breast, the nipple hard between his fingers. He pulled away, wanting to see all of her.

Arta lay back, panting, hazel eyes full, face pink and turned toward the couch's cushioned back, her breast white and rose against the dark green velvet. White, rose, green.

Temmin started away, sick. "This is not what you want. You're afraid. Someone's making you do this."

"Oh!" said Arta, blinking back tears. "Oh, no, sir! I mean, yes! Yes it is what I want!" She wiggled the other breast free. "D'you not like me any more? Please say you still like me! Please!"

"Of course I like you, good Gods, look at you! Augh, no, not looking at you, *not* looking at you!" He got up from the couch with an effort and turned away. "Dress yourself, Miss Dannikson!"

"Please, Your Highness, please!" she begged. He heard the rustling of fabric. "Please…Temmin…" He turned at the unfamiliar sound of his name on a servant's lips, to discover she hadn't covered her breasts, she'd taken off her dress; she trembled above the green puddle of fabric, in only stockings, little boots, a short chemise and her awkwardly skewed corset.

Temmin did his best to think of Jenks in his underwear, but the charm had no chance against a nearly-naked Arta; his only defense was distance. He groaned and backed away. "If you don't put your clothes on, something's going to happen here, something neither of us want."

"You don' understand," she pleaded. "We have to do this. It's bad trouble for me, worse than you know. They can bring Fen in after what he did that time in the King's Woods—everyone knows what really happened. If Fen's taken for treason—oh, sir, they'll hang his head over Marketgate! Please! If Mr Winmer finds out you wouldn', he'll blame *me*! It's as good as killin Fen myself!" She broke into sobs.

Winmer would die, there was no way around it. He'd pluck out that little mustache a hair at a time, and then he'd stomp what genitalia the man possessed into a pulp, and then he'd hang him by the heels and let him bleed to death from his groin. "It's going to be all right," he finally said. "Come here, you goose. No, with your dress. I'm not going along with this little trap my father's set. Tuck yourself in—I refuse to do it for you. How d'you fasten this thing up?" Arta wept so hard she couldn't speak, but she let him maneuver her arms into their sleeves, resigned and limp. He figured out the fastenings himself, and when he finished, said, "No one's going to kill Fen. D'you hear me? No one's going to kill him. I won't let them." Arta fell against his chest, and he let her cry. "Dannikson, this is a very bad habit of yours."

"Yes, sir."

"Do you believe you are safe with me, and that Fen is safe with me?"

"Sir, he said—"

"I am the Heir. Winmer is a secretary."

"Secretary to His Majesty!" She went to wipe her eyes with the handkerchief, found it sodden, and shook it out as if to flick the tears and snot from it.

"Give me that," he said, replacing it with the last one in his pocket. He led her back to the couch and sat her down again. "Now listen, I will get us all out of this."

"It's no use, sir," she said mournfully. "Even if we don', you'd have to make them think we did. The staff prob'ly already think it. Fen'll leave me for bein untrue. But he'll be alive." She propped an elbow on the arm of the couch and rested her chin on her hand. "I wish I'd never left home, but when Auntie said there was a place for me here…"

Temmin only half-listened, but at that said, "I can't send you home. It's the first place they'll look. I have to send you both someplace else, at least temporarily." He got up and paced the room.

Home. Home was the answer.

He was the Duke of Whithorse; his word there was law now that he'd come of age. He would send them to the Estate. He would send them to Alvo. "Don't go away. Here—finish your brandy."

He sprinted to the door, and called for a footman. When the young man ran up, a discreet smirk on his face, Temmin realized that Arta was right: her reputation was already ruined. "Does something amuse you, Caid?" barked Temmin. A more sober expression quickly took up residence on Caid's face. "Find that footman Wallek, and bring him here. Then go fetch Teacher. I need him."

Caid goggled, but did as he was told, hurrying down the hallway past the other footman posted in the hall. "What's amiss?" whispered the duty man as Caid passed.

"Prince has finally gotten round to it," said Caid, pausing once Temmin was back inside, "but looks like 'e wants the pair of 'em!"

The other shook his head. "No accountin for royals."

In short order, Caid brought a rumpled, confused Fen Wallek to the door, still limping slightly. "Why does he want me?" said Fen.

"Damned if I know why anyone'd want a freckled rustic like you," muttered Caid. "Maybe he just wants to complete the pair, like."

"What's that supposed to mean, you cock's egg?" But Caid had knocked on the door and was now trotting down the hall toward the oldest part of the Keep.

The Prince himself appeared in the open door in his shirtsleeves, his hair pointing every which way. "Wallek, very good, stop gaping and get in here."

"Yes, sir," said Fen, bobbing from the waist before entering. "I'm sorry for my dress, sir, I was just about to turn in—" He stopped short at the sight of Arta, her eyes red and a fancy, inexpertly fastened dress barely draped over her shoulders. "Pagg damn you, you lyin bastard!" he shouted. "You said—you said— Pagg damn you for a liar! Pagg damn me for believin either of you! Marketgate it is, but I'll fuckin pound you into the ground first!" Arta launched herself at Fen, begging him to listen, but he thrust her away. "Don' touch me! Slut! Bitch!"

"Keep it down, or you'll ruin everything!" hissed Temmin, circling away as Fen put up his fists. "She's neither of those things, idiot. You can think what you want of me, but Arta's innocent in this. My father sent her here against her will. She's trying to save your life, and I have to get you both out of here without anyone noticing."

"Fen, truly!" she cried.

"Noticin? Oh, god, that's what that fathead meant—half the Keep must know about *her*, and now they'll think I'm part of it, too! I'll fuckin kill you both!" said Fen.

He lunged at Temmin, but the Prince danced out of reach. "Would you rather be humiliated or dead?"

"Oh, I already know I'll be dead, as soon as you call the Guards!" He lunged again; this time, Temmin caught him. They grappled, until Temmin brought a hard kick down on Fen's already-injured thigh; the redhead dropped to the floor, cursing.

"Think! Why haven't I called the Guards yet, if I'm so anxious to see you dead?" said Temmin. "And why would I invite a hothead like you into my rooms if I were busy seducing his betrothed?" He stepped back out of reach again. "Just listen, will you? Arta, tell him."

The story poured out of the girl, rushed and frantic: the guilty dance in the hallway; Winmer; the threats against them both. "Fen, I didn' know what else to do! I knew I'd lose you, but better me alone and ashamed than you dead!" she said. She crouched down beside him, and cried what tears she had left.

"You could have told me!" said Fen.

"And have you do something even more stupid than this? We're telling you now, and I can help you both if you'll let me," said Temmin.

Fen glared at him briefly, then took Arta in his arms there on the floor. "There, now, sweetheart, you shouldn'a, but here we are, and I love you still."

"Just trust him, Fen, please," she said, and clung to him in relief.

"What can he do?" said Fen, tears now slipping from his eyes. "If I'm taken up for treason—I don' care for myself, but Bern'd lose his place at university—that's my brother, sir."

"You won't be taken up. You would never have been taken up, but I'm going to hide you anyway just in case," said Temmin. "I'm sending you to a friend—" A knock at the door, and Temmin ushered Teacher into the room; Fen and Arta made Amma's sign. "Oh, stop that. He won't hurt you," Temmin said in exasperation.

"How can I serve you, Your Highness?" said Teacher, surveying the crying couple on the floor.

"You can do things for me, yes?" said Temmin. "You're not forbidden to help me?"

"I may do whatever is in my power for you, save in that one matter."

Temmin laid out the situation, with interruptions from both Arta and Fen until he ordered them to be quiet. "I want to send them to Whithorse. Take them through the mirror."

"No," said Teacher.

"No? What d'you mean, no? You said you'd help!"

"Taking them through the mirror will not help. The King will suspect something if they suddenly disappear, and then I will just have to bring them back. You must send them in plain sight. Let everyone believe what they already believe, and that you are sending your new lovers to take up residence near your home."

"But how can I send Fen with her?"

"Sir," said Teacher, "let them believe what they already believe."

"Oh. Oh!" said Temmin.

"Give them new clothes, gifts. Put them day after tomorrow on the train to Whithorse, first class. In fact, have Winmer make the arrangements. No one will question it, not even your father."

"Does anyone aim to ask us whether we want to go to Whithorse, with everyone thinkin we're—we're—" Fen grimaced, coloring.

"Better no honor than no head," whispered Arta, leaning into him.

"What's to prevent 'em from killin us later?" said Fen.

"The King is not vengeful," said Teacher. "By the time he discovers the full story, the matter of His Highness's Supplicancy will be resolved. Hurting you would mean nothing." Temmin walked Teacher to the door, leaving Arta and Fen holding each other on the hearth rug. "I must say, Your Highness, you have impressed me this evening. Well done."

"You're sure my father won't hurt them once he finds out Arta's not my mistress?"

"Once you have either lost your innocence or become a Supplicant, it will not matter."

"I'd better find a real mistress, then."

Teacher put a long-fingered hand on his shoulder. "Time will tell, sir, who is your Mistress. Or Master."

Fen and Arta slept in Temmin's bed that night, while Temmin turned fitfully on the green velvet sofa. In the morning, Harbis blandly served breakfast for three on the little table, pulled up before the morning's fire. If he noted Temmin's haggard face, he said nothing. No one spoke as they picked at their food, and not even Temmin could empty the toast rack.

He could take care of Fen's things, but he knew nothing about outfitting or buying gifts for girls. Oh, certainly, for his mother and sisters, but—perhaps one of his sisters might help? The three of them scorned tattling on one another as children, but this was more important than who put salt in his tutor's sugar bowl.

In the end, he chose Ellika. She already took an interest in Fen and Arta, and she'd know exactly what sorts of things to pick out. Still in his dressing gown, he sent Fen into the wardrobe with Harbis to find whatever might fit him, and called for Winmer.

Temmin managed bare civility to the little man, and his resulting rather haughty demeanor added credence to his orders: that Affton should ready temporary rooms for Arta and Fen in the guest quarters nearest his own; that Harbis, with Winmer's assistance, should arrange gentleman's clothing and accoutrements appropriate for Fen; and that two first-class tickets be obtained for the Neyaday train to Whithorse. Winmer gave

Temmin a satisfied bow, and went so far as to kiss the cringing Arta's hand. "Oh, how I hate him!" she said as soon as he was gone.

The outraged but professionally resigned Affton arrived next to escort his former employees to their suite; Harbis followed, arms full of princely attire he deemed low enough for a former footman. Temmin, dressed by now, sent for Ellika, who bustled into his study in a disapproving burst of rose and gold silk. "If what Iddie's telling me is true, you are a horrid young man, and I am loathe to speak to you," she sniffed, dropping gracefully onto the sofa.

"If she's telling you I've taken Arta Dannikson as my mistress, she's mistaken—no, not her sweetheart, either—but listen, Elly. You can't tell anyone, not Sedra, not Mama—not anyone, d'you hear? You must let them believe I've taken them both."

"But Temmin, whatever for? Everyone thinks you've dropped your plans for Supplicancy!"

Temmin's heart sank; he'd been so worried for Arta and Fen that he'd let the Temple slip to the back of his mind. "I have, but not because of this," he said. "Later, I'll tell you later. For now, just know that if you tell a soul, you'll get them both in serious trouble, the killing kind. You can't even tell Iddie how things really stand." He put the matter before her.

"But of course I'll help!" cried Ellika, jumping to her feet. "I'll send Iddie with a tape measure this instant, and set Naister on a full wardrobe for Arta right away. She'll put aside her other work, I'm sure, she always does when I ask, and why shouldn't she. We'll have to send the things to Arta by messenger later, but I'm sure I have a few old things that'll fit her for now, or that we can alter quickly. Our coloring's so different—well, Iddie and I will figure it out. Oh! Your secret's safe. I love intrigues! And that Winmer—I always thought he was too smug by half." She paused at the door. "Poor Arta. Poor *Fen*—somehow it's always worse for the boys. Well, we'll get them safely off, Temmy, never worry. And you will tell me why you decided against Supplicancy, soon. In the meantime, I shall play outraged and put-upon sister! Hooray!"

When the room finally contained no one but himself, Temmin slumped onto the stool at his writing desk and pulled out a sheet of paper; he would write a letter to Alvo for Fen to deliver. He dipped his pen.

36th SpB, 990 KY, at Tremont Keep

Dear Mr Nollson,

I have the pleasure of introducing to you—

He started again.

Nollson—

Please make these two friends of mine welcome.

No.

My Dear Alvo,

I am sorry I have not written before now. I did not know what to say. I do not like that between us, who have been so close, but you shocked me greatly. I am still unsure what to say or even think about it. I wish you had told me your feelings a long time ago. We might have discussed it before I left instead of leaving it as we did. It makes me unhappy to think of you as unhappy, because I do love you, Alvy, you know that, yes? I just do not know about the other.

There will be a less honest letter from Winmer to Crokker as well sent by special messenger, but I wanted to write to you specially about these two friends I have sent home. You will hear all kinds of nonsense about how they are my lovers. They are not, but you cannot let anyone know—no one, Alvy, not even your mother, no one. Do not say anything. Let people think what they will. My friends are in danger here, and I have to send them somewhere safe. Please treat them kindly for my sake. I don't think they are likely to see kindness otherwise, but try to encourage it among the staff anyway. They are blameless. Teach them to ride if they do not know already, especially Fen. I do not think he knows much about horses, even though he says his father is a blacksmith. If I am to take him into my own service, and it appears I will have to, he will need to know how to ride. You will like him, even if he does have red hair. You may have heard that I stood to become a Supplicant. That is all off.

One more thing I must tell you, and it is about that girl, Mattie. She is my half-sister. My father had a dalliance with a maidservant when Mama was confined with me. He did not know about her, though Jenks suspected. Do not tell anyone that, either, but I thought you should know. I feel terrible about what happened that night, and not just because she is my sister, though that is bad enough. Speaking of Jenks, if you see him at the Estate, or if you get in to Reggiston and see him there, tell him to come home immediately. I need him.

I do not like the Keep. I have only been here a short while, but it feels like forever. I thought when I turned eighteen that I would be grown at the turn of the clock. I would know what to do and how to do it. I would be a man. But I am more confused than ever, even though I have learned a great deal. I must grow up very quickly indeed, and I am not sure how to go about it.

They have given me Percet Lord Fennows as a companion. He was Percy Sandopint before his grandfather died. Do you remember him? He visited us briefly. He is even worse now. I wish you were here, and so does Jebby.

Your true friend,
~~Whithorse~~ Temmin

What a noodlehead, signing Whithorse, but then, he didn't sign his given name with anyone outside the family, and he'd never written Alvo a letter before. And he was tired. He hadn't gotten much sleep last night. He left the letter on his desk, shambled into the bedchamber, took off his clothes, and crawled into the still-unmade bed, not bothering with a nightshirt. The sheets smelled of Arta and Fen: disconcerting, but he was too tired to care. He fell asleep.

A knock came at the study's door, then again, more insistent. "Halloo?" called a voice. "I've been knocking and knocking, and no one's answered!" The door opened, and Lord Fennows let himself in. "I know you're in here, Temmy, and I want to hear about last night! The two of 'em! That's the spirit! Don't fancy the boys meself, but to each his own, I should think!"

Fennows walked to the open bedchamber door and peered in. Sound asleep. Not surprising after the night before, he thought. Was that perfume he detected? Not an inexpensive one, either. He bounced on his toes for a moment, wondering whether to wake Temmin up, finally deciding to let him be; after all, Fennows himself had had many a long night cavorting among the ladies. The poor thing probably had a hangover to boot.

He slipped away from the door and ambled around the study at his ease, fingering Temmin's belongings: a globe; a music box with a Farr's Day inscription from Ellika—he made a note, she liked music boxes—books. Books, whatever for. He was sure Temmin wasn't much of a reader; that was his old man's line, and that horrid oldest sister of his. Must be the loathsome tutor, the one called Teacher, though some called him the Black Man. Servants and their superstitions. He ran his fingers over an old, red leather-bound book and flipped through its pages. Blank. "What a stupid thing to have in one's library," he said.

Fennows spotted the desk, and the paper atop it. He listened; Temmin had begun to snore, loudly. Safe to see what the Heir was writing. Fennows crept up to the desk.

What an interesting letter. Who was Alvo Nollson? He consulted his memory, since apparently he'd met the man—hang on, Nollson was Temmin's groom! Strange letter to send to an undoubted illiterate. Who would teach a groom to read? "A dangerous innovation, I should think," Fennows murmured to himself. He took a small notebook from his breast pocket, and wrote down the salient points. He neglected to write down the passage about himself, preferring to add it instead to the long list of injuries he would one day repay.

When Temmin woke up, Fennows was gone, no sign of his presence left behind.

FIFTEEN

The letter was folded and sealed, and pressed into Fen's hands early the next day at the train station. "Give this to my groom, Alvo Nollson—only him, d'you understand? You can trust him. He will help you," said Temmin. "He's my best friend."

"Must be some groom if he's your best friend, sir," said Fen.

"Friend and groom, the best of both. Crokker should be expecting you. He's fierce, but don't let him frighten you."

"Never worry, sir, we worked for Mr Affton," said Arta; she smiled, though her pale face and trembling hands betrayed her.

For appearance's sake, Temmin kissed Arta on the forehead and Fen on one cheek. Though the kisses were innocent, he'd grown increasingly fond of both of them, he thought absently as they waved from their compartment window through the steam of the train's departure. He was responsible for them now, the first time he'd felt responsible for someone else's well-being, and it frightened him somewhat.

Perhaps it was another small taste of kingship, something like the rush of power that came over him when crowds shouted his name, waving and calling as they were now, as his carriage rolled through the streets towards the Keep, though there was a surly undertone this time he didn't like. He waved back, but wondered all the way home. Would that he could turn people to his cause the way Warin could, but what cause was that? What did he stand for, now that the Temple had been taken from him?

Teacher waited in Temmin's rooms, looking out over the lawn. "Are they on the train?"

"Yes," answered Temmin, "and it was a strange thing. Well, no, *they* weren't strange, neither was the train. The people round the station were. They don't seem to like me very well right now."

"You disappointed them," said Teacher.

"Disappointed? What right do they have to be disappointed in me?" said Temmin, flinging himself onto the couch. He changed his mind as soon as he hit the cushions; he still hadn't unkinked himself from the night he'd spent on it, and he rose and resettled himself into the wooden chair by the library table. "Why d'you always have to stand with your back to the sun? I can't ever see you properly, you're just this thin black stick," he said, shading his eyes.

Teacher didn't move, remaining a dark shadow haloed in the sunlight. "The common people have every right to expect greatness from their rulers, though they are usually disappointed. They very much wanted you to go to the Temple and fulfill the prophecy. Now they think you have taken a mistress, and a young man as well. They are disappointed in you."

Temmin slumped in his chair, ashamed. "I'm just like the rest of the nobility, or will be. They'll have to get used to it."

"Are you like the rest? You do not seem so to me, at least, not yet."

"It's what I am," he mumbled. "I should get it over with now, just go with Fennows to his stupid brothel and get it over with. Then I can go see Allis and Issak and do whatever it is I can do there, and then go home and be a good princeling and turn into my father."

"Is that what you want?"

"No, it fucking well isn't what I want!" Temmin said, banging his fist on the table top.

"I will excuse your improper outburst, this time," said Teacher, unperturbed. "What, then, do you want?"

"I want to go home. I want my best friend back. I want Jenks! I want Allis and Issak, and in the right way, not some state visit. I want to hit someone! And I want Fennows to go fu—to go back to Corland!"

"You cannot go home. Alvo in time will be allowed to come to you. Jenks returns in a few days. Allis and Issak would welcome you as a Supplicant, especially now that they have dealt with Lord Litta. You may arrange with Brother Mardus to hit someone, but someone will undoubtedly hit you back. And Fennows returns to Corland on tomorrow's train."

"What? Wait, slow down," said Temmin in astonishment: a great deal of news to absorb at once. "Fennows is leaving?"

"He told His Majesty that pressing business takes him to Corland."

"Merciful Amma, there's a sweet bit of news!" he said. "As to the rest, I don't care if someone hits me back, a few days are too many, and what about Litta?"

"Do you not read the papers?"

"I hate newspapers," said Temmin.

Teacher pulled a slim tabloid from an inner pocket of the black robe, and tossed it on the table. *The Afternoon Spectator*, said the ornate nameplate at the top of the front page. Beneath it, a headline in large type, stretching over two columns: *A Terrible Trade—Lovers' Embodiments Call for Ministerial Action—Dreadful Suffering of Children.*

Temmin clutched at the newsprint, wrinkling it almost beyond legibility. "Oh, gods, Litta did it. Why did he do it? I did what he said!"

"Read it."

"I already know what it says!" But Temmin did as he was told, scanning the columns. "*They* told a newspaper—they told everyone! Why would they do that?"

"To remove the only weapon anyone had against them. It went quite well, actually. Almost every newspaper in the kingdom is calling for a crackdown on certain brothels. Litta and your father are powerless against the Obbys now. In fact, they are stronger than ever."

Temmin sat back in his chair and squinted. "I thought you weren't supposed to advise me on this."

"I am not. I am merely stating where affairs stand." A pause; Teacher moved away from the light to sit on the edge of the table, and resolved from a black figure to a pale one again. "Is your brain a-whirl, or may we return to study?"

The story. Just today, he'd wished he were more like Warin, that he had Warin's charisma and decisiveness. "Yes," he said slowly, "I think I'd like to study. Ugh, the book's sticky!" He rubbed at the old red leather with a handkerchief. "I don't know, though. Warin and Emmae were so angry with one another. I almost don't want to know how bad their marriage was."

Temmin opened the book, and fell in.

In the aftermath of his ascension, Warin weeded out the faithful from the traitorous. To everyone's shock, he spared the Duke of Valleysmouth and his family, who had raised Hildin and Gian, and gave Old Meg an honorable entry to the Hill, but he tracked down the family of the archer who'd killed Fredrik of Leute and slew all its men. Even so, the hooks above Marketgate went largely empty; few had stood with the Usurper.

The rest of the Travelers caught up with their Queen, making camp at the edge of the King's Woods; their caravans flickered bright among the cool green leaves of late spring. "Will you not let me entertain you at the Keep?" said Warin.

"No Traveler may spend the night beneath a solid roof, Your Majesty," said the Traveler Queen, "but thank you."

"Well then, take the freedom of these Woods as a reward for your service, now and always."

"Thank you, cousin," said Connin with a bow, his leg extended just into mockery.

"In return," said the Traveler Queen, "and to protect ourselves, I will set an enchantment on the far side of the Woods. Anyone may leave them, but only your direct descendents, and my own people, may enter from that side. With your consent, of course." Warin gave it, the usefulness of such a thing undeniable; with such an enchantment, the Keep became unassailable, bounded by the Feather and Shadow Rivers, by the steep cliff overlooking the City, and now by the impenetrable Woods.

Warin kept his distance from the grieving Edmerka, Dowager Queen of Tremont and Princess Royal of Leute. There were those in his court who whispered that perhaps Edmerka's tears and black dress were tears of regret for killing her husband, not tears of grief for her father; they also whispered that perhaps the black veils hid a belly swelling with the Usurper's child. The new King made it clear there was to be no such talk, but after a spoke of rumors, Edmerka herself bowed to the advice of the Eldest Sister and submitted to an examination; the Sister's Temple subsequently announced that the Usurper had left no offspring. The whispers ended.

For her part, Edmerka's first act was to take the marriage cord that had bound her to Hildin and burn it. She kept to her bower and refused to dine in company, and would admit no man for some weeks. She finally bent enough to allow her own nobles to visit her, though she pulled a mourning veil over her face. She surreptitiously watched through her window for sightings of Warin on the grounds, or in the courtyard—her spacious rooms had views of both—but let no one know that she yearned for him, her pride at odds with her heart.

An uneasy triad of nobles, all sworn to relinquish the reins of the kingdom to Edmerka's eventual husband, returned to Leute to rule it in her absence; Hendas of Holset remained behind as Her Majesty's advisor. "I don't see why I mightn't rule by myself," Edmerka said to Holset one day in late summer. They sat in the breeze of an uncovered window on the garden side of her receiving room, and he noted the restless eyes watching for any movement among the flowers and hedges.

"Lady, the nobility will stand with tradition," answered Holset. "Two spokes have passed. Fall's Beginning approaches, and Leute remains without a king. You must remarry soon and give us one."

"I wish never to marry again," she answered, savagely stabbing her embroidery in its tambour frame.

"You will not even consider the hand of King Warin?"

She pushed away the tambour. "Warin is a false man. And he has no partiality for me now." She drew the ends of her braids through her fingers under her long black veil.

Holset smiled; so Warin still might hope. "No, madame, Warin is true to you, in spite of your over-proud conduct. Yes, I say it, and you may storm and rage all you like: you are well-matched, the two of you. Your lords will give you until Fall's Beginning to make up your mind. After that, I cannot guarantee their patience."

So he repeated to Warin that night. "She loves you still, Your Majesty, I would stake my life on it. All that is needed is some wooing. Yield to your own inclination, sire. You cannot tell me you do not love her."

The next day, Warin waited at a hidden intersection in the garden among the late season flowers; Edmerka had taken to walking there alone, and when she passed, he fell in step beside her. She stiffened, but did not run. "How long do you intend to stay in mourning, sister queen?" he said.

"Until I am done, brother king," she answered. "It is tradition."

"Did you love your husband so very much?"

Her startling blue eyes pinned him through the veil. "I despised him even as I loved my father."

"Your father was a lighthearted man. I am sure he would have you put aside mourning. I myself look forward to seeing you in colors again."

"Do you," she said. She pulled a little curved knife from the tasseled belt at her hips, and began to cut the asters, white and violet, that spilled onto the graveled pathway.

Warin struggled for words. He couldn't see her face through the veil, though he recognized the way she stood, the slight tremble of frustration and temper that used to run through her at the cottage. "Emmae—"

"Don't call me that!"

"Very well, then, Your Majesty." He watched her hack at the flowers. "I…I am sorry."

"Indeed? For what?" she said, seemingly intent on her task.

"For not telling you who I am, or what had happened to you."

"You should be," she said, pointing the knife at him. "You should be very sorry!" She returned to butchering the flowers. The little knife was none too sharp, and crushed more than cut the stems; the air filled with their astringent, green and somewhat bitter smell.

Her trembling increased, though whether from fury or misery he couldn't tell; it wrung his heart, and broke his pride. "And how might I express that sorrow to you?" he said. "I will do anything you want, anything to earn your forgiveness and love. What must I do?"

"I don't know if there is anything you can do," she choked. She dropped the flowers and ran back to the Keep's courtyard, her long mourning veil tangling so badly in the rose bushes that she left it behind.

After a moment, Warin bent down and picked up the discarded flowers. He tried to untangle the veil, but in the end, he ripped it from the thorns and trod it underfoot as he stomped back to the Keep, through the courtyard to the tower stairs leading to the upper hall, and finally to pace and brood in his own quarters.

"Let her come to you again in her own time, Your Majesty," came a voice at his elbow.

"I don't think she will, Teacher," said Warin heavily.

"She is wounded, and you have let the wound fester. Show her your love, but be steadfast and patient."

Warin fingered the flowers in his hand. "I waited for her to heal from a wound I gave her once. I can do it again, but I wonder if she will heal a second time."

"It is the same wound, sire," murmured Teacher.

That night as she sat down to eat in her bower, the Dowager Queen found the flowers she had dropped, in a little nosegay tied up in simple ribbons and placed atop her tray. A note beside it read:

> These are the ribbons I bought with our furs. They belong to you.

At first, the maidservant thought Edmerka would throw the flowers across the room. Instead, the Queen took one long breath in, let it out, and gave the nosegay to the maid to put in water. When the flowers died, Edmerka slipped the ribbons unseen into the silk purse she wore at her waist.

Warin let a day go by before he sent another gift: a tiny, delicate wooden rabbit, the twin of the one carved into her broomhandle, and clearly from the King's own hands. It, too, went into the purse with the ribbons. She gave no thanks, and when the King inquired of her women whether Edmerka had accepted the gifts, they told him truthfully they had no idea what she'd done with them.

Undaunted, Warin sent a gift every day. He sent her a rabbit fur pillow, stuffed with lavender from the bushes outside their old cottage, and her unfinished embroidery fetched on the same trip back through the silver tray. He sent her a length of silk for a new dress, the same color as the flowers she favored in the garden, with a note: "Asters are for patience." Many small gifts he sent, none returned, until finally he sent her the ring he'd bought with their furs in the village: a simple, golden band.

That night, the Dowager Queen joined the company at dinner for the first time. She sat at the King's left hand, as was proper, but said only, "Tolerably well, Your Majesty, thank you," when asked how she did. There was some small progress: she had exchanged black for gray and set aside her veil, though she kept her hair covered in a widow's coif. Her right-hand ring finger remained bare, where his promise to her should have shone in gold.

From that day, Edmerka rejoined the daily life of the Keep. She walked more often in the garden, ate in the Great Hall, and dressed in colors, if drab ones, but she rebuffed every attempt Warin made to engage her in conversation. "I am not inclined to speak privately with you, Your Majesty," was all she would say, until finally Hendas of Holset came to her in frustration.

"Lady, I am here to tell you that you will either marry King Warin, or you will marry the Leutan lord of your choosing," he said, settling his thick frame into an equally thick chair in her bower.

"And if I choose none?" she said.

"Then you bring civil war to your kingdom, or worse. The lords ruling in your name will only do it for so long before their ambition overtakes them. And if you reject him, the King may decide to take Leute by force in his anger. Either way, you will destroy your people. Thousands will die, either by the sword or from the starvation and sickness that always follow war."

"I will not be threatened into marrying Warin of Tremont!" she said, stomping her foot. The ring clinked faintly against the little wooden rabbit inside her silk purse.

"No threat, Lady, merely a statement of fact. I will tell you this: Whoever wins the war will either force you into marriage, a Temple, or Harla's Hill. I would not see the daughter of an old friend meet such an end," said Holset. "Several Leutan lords and envoys remain in hopes of winning you. Make up your mind, and soon."

"And you?" she said, lip curled. "Will you bid for my hand, Lord Hendas?"

"No, Lady," he answered promptly, "for I have a wife, and I love her." He stood, and he cast such a stern, cold gaze over her that she froze inwardly. "Be assured that if war comes to Leute, I will be in its thick, either fighting to win the throne for the worthiest man, or fighting to save our people from Tremontine swords."

She pondered this conversation until dinner. Once, Edmerka would have screamed and thrown things faced with choices that were no choices at all, but she had changed, fundamentally.

Seated beside Warin at dinner, she waited for a pause in the general conversation. "Your Majesty," she said.

Warin turned, instantly attentive. "Yes, my Lady?"

"I recognize there is wide interest in my future. Before I decide what my future might be, I must speak with you before this company." Her voice was heard so infrequently that the diners fell silent, some studying their plates, some the Dowager and the King, Hendas of Holset among them. "You have said you would do me any service I might require, brother king," said Edmerka.

Into the quiet, Warin said, "You know I would do anything in my power to accommodate you, sister queen."

"Then make me a promise." She stressed each word, first in Tremontine, and then in Leutish. "Swear that no matter what I decide for my future, you will not march against Leute as a result."

Several Tremontine lords rumbled deep in their throats; one put his hand on his dagger, but the Leutans sat straighter. "My friend," one whispered gleefully to another, "she must have decided against him in favor of one of us."

Warin put down his wine goblet and frowned. "I do not speak Leutish well," he answered slowly. "So you will have to translate for those who can't understand me, Lady." He stood. "On my honor, and that of my kingdom, I swear I will not march against Leute if you decide against me. For that's what you mean, isn't it?" he added more quietly to her. She coolly translated all but the last for the few Leutans who didn't speak Tremontine.

The Tremontines broke out in angry exclamations; the Leutans called for wine and noisily toasted the King in both languages. Edmerka smiled to herself and slipped out of the Great Hall.

"I have enraged my lords, Teacher, and am not entirely sure they are wrong," sighed Warin late that night.

"Your Majesty, you have cleared the way for the lady to make a true choice. You have proven yourself an honorable man."

Warin shook his head. "I wasn't sure what my final gift to her should be until tonight. If she doesn't accept my wooing then, I am done."

"A bird?" said Edmerka to her maidservant the next morning. "He sent me a bird?" She peered into the cage in the maid's hands.

"A nightingale, Your Majesty," beamed the maid. She hung the cage near a window. "They sing, oh, it's so beautiful! It'll break your heart, it will. They say they sing for their lost loves."

"We have nightingales in Leute," Edmerka snapped. She stomped out of her bower, down the stairs to the upper hall where the King met with his counselors, and demanded entrance.

Inside, Warin and several Tremontine lords bent low over a map. "Should civil war come to Leute," the King was saying, "we must be on guard against attempts to take these castles along our borders—" He straightened as Edmerka burst through the door, a protesting servant at her heels. Her eyes were bright with anger; he might have expected this.

"Explain yourself, sir!" she said, stuttering on the words.

"Explain myself, how, my Lady?" he said. "Perhaps you may excuse us, my lords?"

"Let them hear how cruel you are! What do you mean, to give me— me!—something in a cage! Something that sings because it cannot help itself—crude, cruel, unthinking man, explain yourself!"

"My lords, please excuse us," said Warin firmly. He took Edmerka by the elbow and steered her under protest into his private chambers, where she did her best to straighten the coif that had gone askew in her rush to confront him. He longed to take it off entirely, to remove the last reminder of his brother. Perhaps that was why she wore it—to remind him.

"Well?" she said. "What do you mean by this?"

"I bought it from a bird trader in the City. He had hundreds of songbirds, all kinds."

"And you thought I'd like to keep one locked up in a cage for my amusement?"

"No," he said quietly, "I thought you might like to set it free."

Her mouth dropped open in astonishment, and she stared for a good while. The angry splotchiness of her face resolved into a full blush before retreating altogether. "Yes," she said finally, "I think I might." She extended a shy hand. "Would…would you care to open his cage with me?"

They met in the pleasure gardens his mother had planted, Edmerka bearing the cage, Warin keeping a careful but approachable distance. "Should you not still be in conference, sire?" she said.

"This is more important," he answered. He took the cage from her hands. "Whenever you are ready, my Lady."

Edmerka looked in at the little dun-colored bird. He peered back at her with one black eye, then the other, ruffled up the feathers at his neck, and let out a trill, modulating to a sob. "Such a lovely song," she whispered. "Go sing it to your ladylove." She fumbled with the latch. The nightingale stopped singing and hopped back in alarm. "Now, it's all right, just give me a moment—there!"

The cage sprang open, and she stepped away. The bird paused, then hopped onto the threshold and took flight before his captors could change their minds. He flew low over the flowers, gathering speed quickly, until he flitted over the meadow beyond and into the King's Woods. They gazed after him long after he'd disappeared, as if they might actually see the flash of brown wings in among the leaves.

"Thank you," she said, her voice soft and tinged with the loving sound it had once held for him.

Warin bowed. "I am gratified." He offered his arm. "May I—would you care to walk the gardens before we go in? This is such a cool breeze for the warmth of the day."

The next day, Edmerka put off her widow's coif. For two weeks, as the sun began to slant lower and Fall's Beginning drew closer, they walked together in the gardens every day, Warin offering his arm and nothing more. She came to dinner in a gown made of the violet silk he'd given her. Another day, she appeared in the gardens with her braids tied in the ribbons she'd hidden in her purse. One night, he came to his bedchamber to discover she'd sent an elaborately embroidered favor for him to wear at the Farr's Day tourney: her initials, a pair of rabbits arched above the letters, the work begun when her name was Emmae and she didn't know her initials. His heart swelled with hope.

Every night, each lay in their separate beds, remembering their lovemaking in the cottage. He felt her soft hair slipping through his fingers, the curve of her hip, her moans; she, his beard brushing her neck, his weight holding her down on the bed as he entered her. But in the daylight, she kept her reserve, and he remained patient.

Two days before Farr's Day. Hendas of Holset was making pointed remarks to the Dowager now, and several Leutan lords gave up their wooing and were preparing to return to Leute: time to raise their armies. The day was warm and pleasant, and Warin took Edmerka out into the gardens for what he feared might be the last time. He'd made it clear that he waited only for word from her, but she had done nothing more than walk with him. Though they usually spoke in general pleasantries, today they spoke of past times, even the time in the cottage. There was a wistfulness in Edmerka's voice that struck both dread and hope into the King's heart; on the one hand, she might finally be reconciling past love with present, but on the other, she might be taking her leave, though with a certain sadness.

As for Edmerka, she had made up her mind.

An arbor hitherto unseen on their walks appeared, covered in honeysuckle still bearing its fragrant trumpets of red and pink even so late in summer. Beneath it stood a secluded bench. She drew him down to sit with her.

"I decide what to do today," she said. "My lords have made it clear they are done with waiting. In fact, I may have waited too long." Warin kept his silence, tense and afraid to look at her. "Don't you want to know my decision?" she said impatiently.

"Lady, you will tell me in your time." He sighed. "Let me speak plainly, though I've tried to let my actions speak for me. I love you. I will always love you. And I ask nothing of you, not even your decision, though I want nothing more than for you to stay beside me the rest of our lives. If you have something to tell me, tell me. If not, then…"

She reached up to touch his cheek, freed from some internal bond, and said, "I choose you, Warin." She closed her eyes and raised her lips for a kiss that never came, and she opened her eyes in hurt confusion.

Warin gazed down into her face, desire and amusement on his own. "You're a grown woman who makes her own decisions," he said. "If you want a kiss, take one."

Emmae smiled, fierce and happy, and slipped her arms around his neck, though he kept his at his sides, passive; she crushed his mouth against hers. The kiss ended as quickly as it began, sudden and passionate, leaving them both panting. "If you want me, you must ask me, no matter how much I might want you. Ask me. Show me. What do you want?" said Warin desperately.

"I want you." She half-crouched on the bench, pressing herself against him.

"Then take me," he murmured, his low voice shivering its way from her ear to her center. His lips were soft and unresisting when she kissed him this time. She opened his mouth with her tongue, to a groan deep in his throat. Emmae crawled into his lap; she whimpered at the tightening of his arms around her, a trap she could escape whenever she chose. His head fell back so that she might kiss his neck, his desire plain against her thigh.

She slid a hand beneath his tunic, brushing his hard, furred belly, and freed him into her grasp. He whispered something that might have been a prayer, or perhaps her name—her true name—against her skin. "Warin, my name is Emmae, I am Emmae, I am your Emmae." She kissed him again. The taste and smell of his skin mingled with the honeysuckle, and she bit at his neck as she stroked him. "Help me with my skirts," she said.

He bunched them around her waist, and she slipped her legs around him, straddling his lap. Warin put his hands under her naked bottom; she guided him inside her; she sank down his entire length. His dark eyes widened, showing their clear whites before he closed them briefly. "I dreamed of this," he said. "Every night I dreamed I was inside you—I cannot stay still..."

"Then move."

He pushed up into her. She met him each time, impaling herself over and over, wetter than ever the enchantment made her. Warin gripped her bottom tight, helping her rise and fall, and she felt her climax begin. It was nothing as it had been under the spell. She filled with some strange power entirely her own—as if she were swallowing his every thrust and cry and turning it into something golden inside her that built and built until she locked her legs around him. The melting gold overwhelmed her, and she threw her head back and screamed for joy. She pulsed around him; he pulled her down hard onto him, shaking as he came. His head fell against her breasts as he gasped and moaned, and she clasped him closer, crooning in Leutish as they shuddered together.

When she regained enough breath to move, Emmae untangled herself enough to gaze down into his face. It was open, unguarded, no longer cautious and reserved. She smiled, and kissed him again. "Marry me," she said.

"As soon as my legs can hold me up," he answered promptly. She laughed, but he continued, "I'm serious. As soon as we return to the Keep, I will call for the Little Father and we will tie the marriage cord today."

"You were so sure that you had one braided?" she teased.

"I've had it braided in some hope this last spoke, though I thought perhaps I'd burn it tonight. But I'd rather see it knotted round your wrist. Do you agree, my lady?"

"Very much, my lord," she said. She kissed him again, then slipped from his lap and stood up. She brushed ineffectually at her rumpled skirts. "We look and smell of sex. Everyone will know what we've been about."

"Do you care?" he said, fastening up his hose.

She considered. "No."

"Then let's be married!" cried Warin. He caught up her hand, and they ran through the gardens, into the courtyard, scattering ducks and chickens before them as they hurried into the Keep and a new life.

Temmin came from the book laughing for the first time: a delirious happiness, a yearning sated. The lovemaking's intensity left him out of breath, aroused but somehow satisfied. "They were happy," said Temmin. "They married happily! Were they always happy? Please tell me they were."

"Emmae gave King Warin twelve children, the last of whom became a Supplicant of the Lovers' Temple and eventually Most High Beloved— Finnia. The King and Queen were devoted to one another all their lives. Warin never took a mistress, rather to the astonishment of his subjects and his own sons."

"Is it that uncommon in a king?"

"He is the only Tremontine king inclined toward women who did not take mistresses."

Temmin's mood deflated, brought abruptly down to the present. "I suppose I should get on with it, then," he grumbled.

"Far be it from me to discourage you from a natural inclination—if that is yours," said Teacher, "but the past does not predict the future. You do not have to walk directly in the footprints of your ancestors."

"I find that advice astonishing coming from someone who's always going on about prophecy."

"Prophecy is unrelated to the past."

Temmin frowned. "Is prophecy always right, though? What about mine?"

"In my experience, prophecy is always right. What is wrong is how prophecies are interpreted. I hesitate to interpret yours, and wonder whether interpretations to date are correct."

"I wonder if an Heir will ever fulfill the prophecy and become a Supplicant," said Temmin, tracing the worn gilt lettering on the book's cover. "I mean, I wanted to be one, but…maybe it's not even a prophecy. Warin's prophecy didn't come true."

"It most certainly did."

"He didn't kill his father."

"Hildin was the crowned king," Teacher said patiently. "The prophecy was not at fault. Rather, it was the interpretation. Warin's fate found him however much he tried to escape it, and it was not the fate he had always expected. Then, too, remember Hildin's own prophecy: 'As a rabbit, so a man.' Nerr will get the Heir, some day." Teacher paused. "Do you still wish to fulfill that prophecy yourself—to become a Supplicant?"

"You're not supposed to talk to me about it."

"I am not supposed to advise you on it. This is not advice. Do you?"

"I don't see how I can. Everyone thinks I've lost my virginity to Arta."

"The Gods know differently."

"I can't just walk into the Temple and say, 'Whatever you've heard, it's not true.'"

"The Gods always know the truth. One does not have to convince anyone of anything."

Temmin sat up straighter. His father thought he was no longer eligible. The nobles thought so, too. The only ones who knew different were himself, and Teacher. Arta and Fen, and Ellika, they might assume it, but they didn't know for certain. "I can do it now, can't I? No one can stop me, because they think they already have." He turned a shining face to Teacher. "No one can stop me!"

Jenks came home from Reggiston the next day, grumbling about some stupid captain taking a severe dislike to his nephew, "but I gave him a severe disliking. He was dished, oh yes, sir, he was dished within an inch of his life." Temmin wondered how a former corporal could "dish" a captain with no repercussions, but said nothing. Nor did he say anything about the resolution of his difficulties. The less said, the better; if he followed through on the plans rapidly forming in his head, he wanted Jenks to have nothing to do with it. As for Arta and Fen, all the gruff valet would say was, "I saw them when I visited my sister on the Estate. I told you to leave the maids alone, but left out the footmen. Ah well, at least he's spirited. And she has a sweet way about her. Just…try not to hurt them, sir."

"Nothing is further from my mind," said Temmin.

That Ammaday, the 40th of Spring's Beginning, was the day the twins had originally set for Temmin to make up his mind; instead, he was to visit the Temple for the day, perhaps the night. Harsin knew, but paid no heed; the night before, he smiled indulgently at his son across the breakfast and dinner tables, and the son smiled indulgently back. "I do wonder why you sent your…friends to Whithorse, Tem," said the King over after-dinner port one night. "Rather hard to see them, that far away. You can only go up to Reggiston once every other spoke, at most."

Temmin made a show of bashful thoughtfulness. "It was a kindness. It bothered them to be here in the Keep, or even in the City. And I want my privacy. I'm sure you understand, sir."

"Oh, very much so," grinned Harsin. "I know the last few weeks have been difficult for you, son. I wish to make it up to you. I will tell Teacher to take you to your lovers. You can go to them whenever you wish, as often as you wish."

"Take me to my lovers. Why, thank you…Papa," said Temmin, hiding a smile of his own.

The war of the wardrobe began. In the end, Temmin and Jenks reached a compromise: correct but comfortable clothes, not too formal, in exchange for the finest new small clothes the favored royal tailor could make on short notice. "If you're going to sit around in your underthings…" mumbled Jenks, letting the thought go unfinished.

On the day, Brother Mardus and his men escorted the Heir through the city and down the Promenade, handing him off to the Temple's Own at the top of the pink marble stairs. In their midst stood the ridiculously handsome Senik. To his surprise, the postulant kissed Temmin full on the lips. "That's how we say 'hello' here. It's also how we say 'goodbye,' 'thank you,' 'you're welcome'…" Senik waved an encompassing hand. "This way."

Up the broad, grand stairs on Nerr's side of the Great Hall, and into the reception room, where the Most Highs and the Embodiments waited for him. "I must say that we were pleased to receive your letter, young Temmin," said High Lover Gan once greetings and tea had been passed around.

"What did you do to Litta?" he said without preamble.

"The young, so blunt," sighed the High Lover, drowsily patting Issak's thigh.

"We are here to speak of you, dear heart," said High Beloved Malla. "The Holy Ones tell us that you left before your last visit even began, in some distress."

"I should say so," answered Temmin. "Litta cornered me and threatened to blackmail the twins if I didn't call off my candidacy."

"Litta is no longer a concern. We will leave him behind," said Issak firmly. "What concerns us now is why you're back. Are you reconsidering Supplicancy, or is this a state visit?"

"I am reconsidering. In fact, I'd like to formally submit my name, and ask if we might keep it among us. I don't want anyone else to know."

"Indeed?" said the High Lover, the sleepy look leaving his face.

"But do you still qualify?" said Allis. "We have heard things."

Temmin wanted very much to see if perhaps his shoes were untied, but kept his head up. "Gossip. I qualify. Those whose names have been linked to mine will be in some danger until after I take my vows if it becomes known that we didn't—we didn't…"

"Be very sure, Temmin," Aliis said. "If you've already lost your innocence, when the Gods come down that day—"

"They'll kill you," finished Issak. "Nothing and no one could help you. Not even Teacher."

"I swear," he said. "I swear on whatever God you want—I swear on my own soul, on my mother's soul."

The two elderly high priests and the young Embodiments considered silently among themselves for a long moment. "Very well," said Allis. "We accept your chase. You will take your first vows on Neya's Day Eve. You have a week to prepare. Will you stay today?"

"And tonight?" added Issak quietly.

This time, Temmin dipped his head. "Yes."

"Then go down to the Supplicants Chamber and change your clothes for Temple garb," said Issak. "We four have business to discuss."

Temmin walked down the broad staircase to the Great Hall alone, and stood uncertain in the light crowd of Ammaday worshippers, many radiating what Teacher had called disappointment, though Temmin would have called it outright anger. He fidgeted at the feet of the entwined statues of the Lovers, and finally walked between their legs and through the door of the Supplicants Chamber.

"Close the door, please," called a rich, lazy voice. "It lets in a draft." He did as he was told, and came further into the dim, rose-silk-covered room.

Anda was shedding her last stocking, her simple Temple clothing draped on the couch. She let down her mouse-colored hair, each lock falling thick and wavy to her full hips before she unpinned the next. She smiled. "I'll be with you in a moment."

"I'm not here for you," he thought. All this time, and he'd now seen Anda naked twice and neither Allis nor Issak once. Nevertheless...

"The way you stare," she tsked, ambling toward him. Her large breasts bounced and jostled with every strangely graceful step, and to Temmin's irritation, the low twitch began again. She was plain, she was fat, she was not Allis, she was everything he didn't want, she was kissing him senseless, her hands loosening his cravat. "Hello," she said when she ended the kiss. "Get undressed. I'll get your Temple garb, shall I." She walked, hips lolling, toward a set of shelves lined with neat piles of folded clothes and a great many towels.

As she sorted through the piles humming to herself, Temmin absently tugged at his cravat. Naked, Anda had a look of abundance, he grudgingly thought. Swelling breasts, rounded arms, a soft belly, full hips, lush thighs. "Fertile" came to mind; her body reminded him of the rolling hills of oats near home, of wheels of cheese, of bowls of ripe fruit, of jugs of cream, of honey, and nuts, wine, and good, thick bread. Not plain, or fat. Edible.

"You're still dressed, for shame," she said. "Didn't they tell you to change?" She was much closer to him than he'd realized. He'd managed to shed his coat and untie his cravat as he'd stared at her, but nothing more. "Oh, all right, if you're that eager for my attention." She slid the Tremontine red cravat from his collar, and removed his waistcoat.

"I'm not eager for your attention," he quavered as she undid his shirt studs and slipped them into his trouser pocket; her fingers grazed his erection, and he jumped.

"Really," she chuckled, slipping his braces down his shoulders, followed by his shirt. "Off goes the vest," she ordered, and he stripped it off without thinking twice. She unbuttoned his trousers, delicately avoiding touching him this time, and let them puddle at his feet. "Off with the pants and shoes and stockings," she said, moving to recline on one of the low, wide couches that seemed to be the only seating the Temple possessed. "Everything over on the pegs."

He hung his clothes slowly, contemplating a dash toward the pile of linen garb beside the Supplicant and a second dash toward the bathroom. He was not in the habit of displaying his erection; doing so now was to let Anda win, though what the contest was, he couldn't say.

"Turn around, Temmin," ordered Anda. "I've seen it before, and by the time you're through, you'll have seen a few, too. In fact, come to think on it, I've already seen you come."

He spun around, stung. "You are a very impudent girl."

"I'm a very truthful girl. You'd best get used to it, as you'll be getting a great deal of truth here." She smiled, and nodded her head toward him. "I told you, you'd like me."

The imprint of her kiss still tingled on his lips—this fat girl with nothing to distinguish her, so arrogant in her confidence, so transparently artful in her arrangement of her curves. He remembered seeing her half-naked in the petitioner's room, the peaceful, absorbed face of the woman suckling at her breast, and how the wish to take the woman's place had flashed through him before he'd turned away, humiliated: he grew harder.

"The way you stared at my breasts through the window of the petitioner's room," she said as if reading his mind, "I thought you were going to burst through the screen. Come satisfy your curiosity. I won't lay a hand on you."

"I'm not worried about you laying a hand on me," he said, not moving. "I'm worried about my laying a hand on you."

"Go ahead. Touch me, touch my breasts. I won't stop you. You can't touch them enough, in fact," she whispered.

Temmin crossed to the couch and sat down, covering himself with his hands. If he touched her, what would stop him from flinging himself atop her, spreading her legs, holding her down and taking her? "I have to stay— to qualify until Neya's Day. If I touch you, I can't—I don't know if I can stop myself…"

He hadn't realized he'd closed his eyes until a strong hand took his and placed it on Anda's breast. "You're safe," murmured Issak in his ear. "Never worry, you're safe here."

"From what?" said Temmin, his voice cracking.

"From yourself."

"You don't understand, do you know what I want to do to her?" Temmin's hand gripped Anda's breast so hard the flesh flowed between his fingers.

"I have a pretty clear idea of what you want to do to me," said Anda in amusement, "though I do wish you wouldn't squeeze quite so hard quite so soon."

"Gently, start gently, Tem. There will be time enough for pain," said Issak, stroking his arm. He relaxed his grip without thinking, Issak's touch comforting and solid as he guided Temmin down on the couch beside Anda, then settled himself behind Temmin. Whatever happened, Issak was here.

Temmin slid his arms around Anda from behind until his hands closed on her breasts, so soft and heavy, heavier than Arta's, kneading until she tilted her head back against his shoulder with a low growl. Under his fingers, her nipples grew hard, the wide circles of brown skin around them puckering and pebbling. "Are they supposed to do that?" he asked shyly. "It's not because I'm hurting you?"

"No, you're not hurting me, it means I like it—or that it's cold out," she laughed. "It's normal. Don't yours do that?"

He rolled her nipples between his fingers; he remembered Emmae liked it. "I hadn't really thought on it. So…it means you like my doing this?"

"Very much." Anda turned over in his arms.

"Show me what to do, what do you like, may I kiss—would it be good, would you like it if…?"

She gathered up her breasts and offered them to his mouth.

Hesitantly, he licked at a nipple; her scent was different here, a musky apricot. He pushed his nose between her breasts before his mouth found the nipple and took it in, running his tongue over its soft, crinkled skin. He ground himself against her, his worries that he might hurt her or push things too far gone, Issak's breath against his neck reassuring and warm, the hardness that had to be Issak pressing against him arousing and somehow comforting. He was safe. He took the nipple fully into his mouth and sucked.

"Just like that," she whispered, rolling onto her back. "Pinch the other. No, both at the same—" Her words dissolved. Temmin growled and clutched at her breast, biting the nipple harder before releasing it and attacking the other one; Anda undulated beneath him in a fleshy wave, her thighs opening.

A hand took his and guided it between her legs, slipping his fingers just inside. "This is a woman, this is what a woman feels like," murmured Issak.

So wet, hot, and wet, and slippery, so different from anything Temmin had ever felt, though Emmae and Warin's lovemaking ghosted against his fingers and mouth. He rumbled deep in his chest, sucking harder at the nipple in his mouth, and tangled his fingers with Issak's in his eagerness. "Slowly, slowly," said Issak; he moved their joined fingers in maddening, gentle circles that left Anda squirming. He guided Temmin's fingers to the top of Anda's opening, grazing a hard nub there; Anda gasped and whimpered, jerking her hips. "That little bump? That's her clitoris," Issak said in his ear. "We call it the pearl. It's like a little prick, but you can't treat it like one." He set their fingers in a tight, soft spiral around the nub; a sort of hood of skin covered it, and more and more, Issak guided their fingers to slide it up and down. Anda's fingers tightened in Temmin's hair; her breathing became disordered, and he clung to the breast in his hand as she twisted beneath him. He took the nipple between his teeth again, just as Issak sped up the rhythm of their fingers inside her. She bucked and begged them not to stop, begged, and swore, and sobbed, until her climax rippled through her body, sending every inch of her shivering like an aspic. Issak slowed their fingers down and withdrew his own hand, but Temmin kept up lazy, amazed strokes on the inner lips, memorizing the silky, soaking fleshiness.

"Owtch. That's enough," she giggled, pulling his hair. He stopped his fingers, and let go the nipple with a pop. "He needs his nails trimmed, Holy One."

"He needs many things," said Issak. He plucked a cushion from the piles around them, tossed it to the floor, and knelt beside the couch, stroking Temmin's back.

A rushing ache spread from his testicles; he rolled to one side and wrapped his hand around his shaft, but Anda stopped him. "On your back." He did as she said, and Issak kissed him, kissed him and didn't stop:

insistent, firm, controlling, safe, maddening, absorbing until Anda's breath blew hot between his legs. A groan forced its way from him into Issak's mouth, and he fought against the restraining hands against his shoulders. A tongue licked at his balls, tasting him thoroughly, and he blurted a muffled "Holy Mother!"

Tiny licks up the underside of his shaft, a ghost of a touch and somehow penetrating, ending at its slit. Anda took the head into her mouth, softly working at it, playing with the foreskin and running her tongue along the groove running down its underside. She swallowed all of him now, doing something intricate—teeth, tongue, he had no idea. It differed from his experience with Alvo: urgency without desperation, deliberate and directed, a pleasure that swelled and retreated in tides, instead of bursting from him in surprise.

Issak forced his tongue inside Temmin's mouth just as Anda pressed firmly behind his balls, still sucking. His body curled up in response, but Issak kept him pinned and struggling. "Let her finish you," he whispered in Temmin's ear. Two long, harsh breaths, and Temmin came with a roaring sob.

Issak put his head on the pillow beside Temmin, who lay there red, sweating, and barely awake; Anda crawled up beside him and kissed him, an unknown yet familiar taste on her lips. "Different," Temmin mumbled. "Was different."

Issak ran his fingers gently up and down Temmin's golden-furred belly. "Men are better at it than women," he agreed.

"Not this time," said Temmin.

He fell into a doze as they petted him, and when he awoke, they were gone. He was starving, his stomach threatening to digest itself unless he ate, quickly. Something smelled good. A luncheon sat on the table: cold meat, cheese, fruit, pickles, cider, the good-smelling something being a loaf of still-warm bread. He ripped the top knot off, a habit that back home resulted in Cook chasing him out of the kitchen with a wooden spoon. He slathered a large knife-full of butter on the bread and devoured it, licking the melting butter from his fingers.

He tore into the rest of the meal just as avidly, until Allis's voice said, "Do you always eat like that?"

"'M growin'," Temmin answered through a mouthful of beef and cheese. He swallowed. "I'm always hungry. Please, sit. There's plenty," he added, gesturing at the still-laden table.

Allis sat down next to him; the soft rasp of her linen Temple skirt against his thigh reminded him that he wore nothing at all, and he grabbed a pillow to cover himself, staining it with his greasy fingers. "You must accustom yourself to nudity, your own and others," she admonished him, tweaking the pillow away.

"Why are you in clothes, then?"

Her face broke into the closest thing he'd seen to a grin from her. "There will be time for that, never worry. Did you have a good nap?"

"About that," he said, putting down the tumbler of cider. "Why did I fall asleep?"

"You weren't tired from your exertions?"

"I was wide awake during them, I assure you. I mean, at night I—that is—if I have trouble sleeping, it can help..." he trailed off.

"Issak told me you said it was different. I take it you meant, different from your one experience of that kind with Alvo. Anda was practicing a certain technique. It works best on men. If one does it correctly, the receiver is so sated he falls asleep almost instantly."

"Tell her from me she doesn't need to practice. She's mastered it."

"We use it in many situations, often at the Healer's House—oh yes," she said at his dubious expression, "we work with the Sisters—with all of the Temples. We serve at the Healer's House, caring for the emotional needs of their petitioners, and Sisters serve here, caring for the physical needs of ours."

"There are Sisters? *Here?*"

"The Sisters help us with contraception training, recognizing illnesses, that sort of thing. Sometimes, the sick come to us first. They're too ashamed to see a Sister, and go to one of these modern doctors..." She shook her head. "Frauds. By the time people finally come to us, and from us to someone who can really help them, it's often too late. Once a year or so, a man's heart will give out in the throes of passion. First the Sisters try to help, and if they can't, the Friends are called to take him to the Hill."

Temmin shivered. "I can't imagine a Friend here. All hooded in black robes." The robes brought Teacher to mind, which led to the voice in the chapel, and from there to thoughts of the upcoming Supplicancy vows on Neya's Day. "Allis," he began, "what's going to happen? I mean, on Neya's Day. Do I just swear a vow before the Most Highs and that's the end of it, or...?"

"You will take two sets of vows. The first will be before the Most Highs the night before. The second will be in communion with the Goddess on the night itself."

"What kind of communion?"

"She'll take your virginity, Temmin, what do you think?" Allis said, amused.

He went pink. "Then you'll be responsible for me, yes?"

"No," she said. She flicked her slender fingers over the remains of his lunch. "Are you going to eat these grapes?" She popped one in her mouth, seeds, thick skin, and all. "Mmm. In a way, I will be. But really, Neya will be responsible for you. She will be bound to you, and you to Her. My body, but Her Spirit."

"I remember what you said about puppets. But tell me, what's actually going to happen? Where will we be, what words must I say?"

Allis nodded to herself, absently peeling and seeding a second grape. "You don't need to memorize anything. You'll be told the words to repeat. The night before, you will take your first vow. The next night, you will help bring down the God into Issak—Anda will help bring down the Goddess into me. It's not a comfortable sight, I warn you now. The Gods will then enact the Chase, the people will watch until They are through, and then you will present yourself. If They accept you, They will take you back to the ceremonial bedchamber."

"*If?*"

"They may judge you unacceptable. In that case, the blame falls on the Most Highs, Issak, and me, and we will pay for it, not you. But if you've lied about your status, They'll kill you—at the least, you. Maybe us, too."

"I swear, Allis, I swear—"

"Neya will initiate you and accept your final vow to belong to this Temple for two years and two days. And then your Supplicancy will begin."

Temmin spent the rest of the day trotting after Allis and Issak, with Anda and Senik trailing behind all three. They met with higher clergy, sat in on a nervous postulant class identifying anatomy on one another before a stern but surprisingly unpuckered Sister, and then a quiet tea with Anda and Senik.

Perhaps, thought Temmin, he should begin his studies on his own if he were to be serious about this business. For instance, Senik fascinated him. As the handsome postulant moved first among the hallway crowds and then the small group in the Supplicants Chamber, he changed from moment to moment, instantly shifting to reflect whoever he spoke with. Was he really as beautiful as Temmin had first thought? Yes, and that affected how others treated him, certainly—it was clear Senik was a great favorite, much called on by the Most Highs for various tasks, and the Embodiments' servant of choice. Even so, Temmin detected a deep desire to please behind the sly, insinuating smile. Or was that just the face he turned toward Temmin? Either way, Temmin was pleased with himself for his growing discernment, until Senik caught him looking and to his surprise rebuked him. "Don't think you know me, Your Highness. You haven't learned a thing yet."

Dinner ended the evening, a dinner served communally at low tables in a dining hall. Temmin, the Most Highs and the Holy Ones sat a little above the ranks of Lovers and Beloveds in their linens of varying shades of rose; the postulant Lovers wore red and sat each with a Beloved, the postulant Beloveds in white and paired with a Lover. Issak and Allis alone wore undyed linen. As visiting royalty, Temmin wore the dark red of his family.

The lightweight linen clothes made life in the warm rooms much more bearable—pleasant, in fact—and Temmin grew more used to feeling underdressed and overexposed. By the time the evening ended back on the wide couches of the Supplicants Chamber, he was comfortable and acclimated, in mind as well as body, and anticipating the night. "So," he began, "what happens now?"

"Oh, lots of things," said Allis. She stood and raised her arms over her head, stretching back and away in a smooth, shallow curve; her breasts strained against the linen of her shirt, and her belly peeked from under its hem. "I'll leave you to it."

"Where are you going? When will you be back?"

"In the morning," she said. "I'll see you before you leave, never worry."

"Tonight is for us," said Issak, sliding his hand up Temmin's neck to play with the hair at his nape.

"I thought it was for all of us," said Temmin, disappointed.

"Don't be greedy," she laughed, and kissed him. "One thing at a time. Good night, now." She kissed her brother, and glided out of the room.

"Is it so very bad to be left with me?" said Issak.

"No, no," stammered Temmin. "I just—generally speaking, I prefer women, and Allis in particular, and—"

"To serve here, you must enjoy male company as well as female, regardless of your natural inclinations. It's not difficult, with training. Few people are focused exclusively on one sex or another, though it's true the Temple attracts those with the most fluid ideas about sex."

"Is sex with men like Mentoring?"

"Nothing like. That's a temporary arrangement—it's more about the submission of the young to the old. This is more a matter of service, though power often plays into it. Politics as well. All of society is about dominance and submission, really."

"I don't understand. What does sex have to do with politics?"

"Sex is about everything, and everything is about sex, at least as you contemplate the Mysteries this Temple is trying to teach you," said Issak. "I don't know what they teach in the other Temples. For all I know, Farr's priests teach that everything is about battle and battle is about everything, in fact, I'd bet on it. But I am not the Embodiment of Farr, or Eddin, or Pagg. I am the Embodiment of Nerr. I'm here to teach you what I know, and to guide you closer to the Gods on Nerr's path." The stroking fingers against Temmin's nape turned into a fist tangled tightly in his hair, pulling his head back. "Don't be disappointed. What you learn tonight will bring you closer to understanding women."

Temmin thought he already understood women, or at least Emmae, but how could he explain that without sounding ridiculous? He leaned his head into Issak's hand to relieve the painful grip on his hair, but Issak redoubled it, pulling Temmin close against his chest. "You're hurting me."

"Nerr's path is sometimes painful. But this only hurts if you fight it," murmured Issak.

A faraway voice came to Temmin: Gian telling Emmae, "The more you fight it, the worse it will be."

"Oh," said Temmin. "Oh, you can't possibly—what are you going to do, Issak?"

Issak slipped his free arm around Temmin, pinning him. Temmin had a height advantage, and had always assumed that with it came physical superiority, but he soon found out Issak was stronger. "I'm going to fuck you, and you're going to let me," Issak laughed, a low rumble that sent a shiver through Temmin.

"And why would I do that?"

Issak gave his hair a sharp shake. "Because I am your teacher, and you are my student. Because you have been spoiled all your life, and you need to give in to someone else's desires for once. Because you want me to."

"I *don't* want that," groaned Temmin, though his head swam; all of his blood had rushed between his legs, and his cock pressed insistently against the thin linen trousers.

Issak yanked him not unkindly to his feet; Temmin gave no resistance to the untying of the drawstring round his waist. Issak let go Temmin's hair, pulled his shirt over his head and pushed him back down on the couch, then undressed and joined him. "On your side away from me," murmured Issak. "You obey me so easily. Why is that?"

"I don't know," whimpered Temmin. Issak smiled against his shoulder. Cool, slippery liquid poured down the crevice of his ass; Issak spread it with teasing fingers. Temmin gasped, and Issak sank a slippery finger inside him.

"Relax," purred Issak against his neck.

"It—it's very—I'm not—"

"It's just the tip of one finger. Don't fight me. Let go. It will hurt otherwise. There—there, just relax. Push out. That's right, good boy." Issak pushed the finger in, pulled out, and pushed back in, always slow, always advancing. Odd, shivery pleasure overtook the initial pain, so like what Emmae had experienced until Issak hooked his finger and pushed at one spot. Stars went off behind Temmin's eyelids; Emmae had never felt anything like that. It forced a low shout from deep inside him, and Issak chuckled. "That's your walnut. You like that, eh?"

Temmin's voice refused to work. He pushed back against the finger and it worked in deeper, stretching him gently. It moved in and out, always coming back to brush against the spot that made him lightheaded, near dissolving into white nothingness. A second finger joined the first. He was ready for it, wanting it; his moans grew more guttural, deeper. The fingers stayed on that spot, massaging until the fingers were all there were in the world.

"You're all stretched out for me," said Issak in his ear. "D'you know what I'm going to do now? I'm going to fuck you." The fingers withdrew; the world returned, and Temmin exhaled in a soft wail. Issak rolled him over on his back; his eyes glowed green and dangerous, even in the low light, and his hair hung wild and black around him. And yet to Temmin, giving himself to Issak seemed like the safest, most natural thing in the world. Issak slicked himself with the slippery liquid; Temmin's cock was longer, just as he was taller, but like his body, Issak's had more weight, potent and heavy in his hand. "This is for you, and you will take it all. Won't you?"

"Will it hurt?" whispered Temmin.

"Do you care?"

"No."

"Do you trust me?"

"Yes."

"Then hold your legs back." Issak smiled, slipping a hand up and down Temmin's length. He slid his fingers back inside, gently stretching, then removed them and centered himself, the head pushing against Temmin's opening. "Push out," whispered Issak. "Let me in." Temmin pushed out, and Issak pushed in.

The ring of muscle burned, just as Emmae's had, but once the head pushed all the way in, the burning receded and left nothing but the strange thrill. Issak advanced by small, gentle degrees until he was entirely inside, and he stayed there, his dark-shadowed jaw flexing until he began to move.

Temmin had always thought it was Emmae's enchantment that had brought her such unwanted pleasure on her wedding night. But with each stroke the shivering ache pulsed through him, his skin a-quiver. Issak touched that spot again, sliding past it over and over, and Temmin's eyes rolled back in his head in unending, shuddering bliss. Even so, when he reached down between them and discovered his erection was gone, he let out an involuntary gasp of frustration. "It's normal," soothed Issak. "In time you will learn to stay hard, but going soft is normal."

"I still feel hard," said Temmin, forcing the words out between ragged breaths. "I think—I think I have to piss!"

"No, you don't, I promise. Let it be. Am I hurting you?"

"No!" blurted Temmin. "Don't—don't stop!" Sweat beaded on Issak's forehead; his white teeth closed on his bottom lip. His eyes shone with a gentle cruelty, and Temmin swore he was even more beautiful than Allis.

Issak let out a long growl and pushed deep inside, to the point of pain. A great twitch, a pulse, and Issak leaned in temporary exhaustion against Temmin's legs, stretching them back even further. "Push out again," Issak said when he'd regained his breath. His softening cock slithered out, and he collapsed onto the couch. He gathered Temmin into his arms and kissed him, licking at his lips. "You are very, very tight," he mumured dreamily. "I could've held on longer—all night, actually—but I couldn't ride you hard your first time. Some day, I will."

Temmin lay dizzy in the safe circle of Issak's arms as his mind began to work again. It should have hurt. He should have been frightened. He should be angry with himself for letting Issak lead him into it. He shook, and gasped in dismay as he tried and failed to stop, just as Emmae had. "It's normal, the shaking," muttered Issak. "Never worry. It will pass."

"What did you do?" he said through chattering teeth.

"What do you mean?"

"I didn't want that...and you made me want it."

"I did nothing of the kind. You wanted it and you didn't know it yet. That's all."

"I didn't even know men did this! I thought it was all hands and mouths." He shook harder; Issak responded with a reassuring tightening of his arms, and Temmin burrowed into him, relieved and humiliated.

"Sometimes it's like this," said Issak. "Not all the time. It depends on the men involved. You've had sex with a man before."

"Alvo?" frowned Temmin. "I don't really think of that as sex."

"And yet you're getting excited again." Issak slapped at Temmin's cock; it swayed in the air. He slid down the couch and put his head between Temmin's legs, licking him in one long, wet swallop from his balls to the tip. Temmin's cock vanished into Issak's mouth, disappearing and reappearing, glistening. His hips moved in time with Issak's sucking, until a finger pushed inside him and right to the spot, that spot, oh Gods, it was that spot. Issak's mouth picked up speed, until the world vanished. He arched up into the tight wetness that was all that was left of reality, shouting as his seed shot out of him. He twitched in the void, suspended and sparking, until the world filled in the space around him once again, and he fell back onto the couch panting Issak's name.

"I don't know if I'll ever walk again," Temmin said after a time. "I don't know if I want to walk again."

"We're not falling asleep here," said Issak. "Up with you." He half-dragged, half-led Temmin to one of the alcove beds in the wall, large and soft; Temmin tumbled into it. Issak washed himself at the sink and tumbled in after him. They fell asleep in minutes, Temmin's blond head on Issak's chest, his fingers tangled in Issak's black hair.

All through breakfast, Temmin wondered about his behavior. It was a silent, musing meal in which the twins respected his mood; indeed, it didn't even seem to surprise them. He wondered all through his leave-taking with the Most Highs and the Holy Ones, his enjoyment of the goodbye kisses muted and absent-minded. He wondered as he climbed gingerly onto Jebby's back, trying to form the questions as well as the answers.

Why had he submitted to Issak—how had Issak persuaded him, when after Emmae's experience had consumed him, he'd sworn it would never happen to him, ever, assuming it would ever come up, which it wouldn't. She'd been humiliated, shamed, used, and didn't that come with it? But with Issak, he'd felt nothing but trust. Had he told Issak to stop, Issak would have stopped. He'd told Issak *not* to stop. He'd gone to the Temple simply for Allis. The spiritual trappings were confusing, and possibly useful; he wanted to gain the kind of control over himself and his world that Issak seemed to have. Now, he wondered if there were more to it than even that.

Questions usually angered him. He preferred answers, absolutes, not ambiguities. He liked his world in black and white, and these questions were a stubborn gray. He wanted the answers, even though they promised to lead to more questions. He wanted to stay at the Temple, and learn.

On the remaining ride to the Keep, he endured the sullen streets with greater equanimity, staying his heels from Jebby's ribs, and holding his head high. The barriers to Supplicancy both within and without him were gone.

Let his father choke.

At the Dunley Arms, in the High Street of Reggiston, lived a Corrishman. He hadn't lived there very long—only two days. He didn't look Corrish, nor did he sound Corrish, at least now; his voice lacked the melodious, doleful, singing tone largely all that was left of the Corrish language, but if need be, he could sound as posh as any Maryakuspan gentleman, as coarse as any borderlands deerherder, or as sophisticated as any fashionable gentleman on the Capital's Promenade.

His eyes turned down at the outside corners, and when his handsome face was in repose they gave him such a naturally melancholy appearance that old women passing by in the street were likely to stop, take his hand and ask him how he did. In the course of his work, the Corrishman had schooled the melancholic, meditative gaze so characteristic of the far north from his sad eyes, the Corrish gaze that could turn on a moment's notice harsh and cold as an icy wind whipping around a corner; the long northern winters taught the inhabitants too much about the fickleness of the world.

He'd pelted down the highway from Corland to Whithorse on his master's business, stopping only to change horses and snatch a scanty few hours of sleep before settling at the Dunley Arms. His handsome face, his demeanor of quality, and his generous purse quickly made him friends in the tap room, especially the innkeeper.

The innkeeper was not the first Dunley at the Arms; his older brother had owned it first, he told his wealthy guest over the pint of ale the Corrishman had bought him. The brother died, leaving no son. And so in course the present Mr Dunley turned the widow and her daughter out and took the Arms for himself. "It's Pagg's Law," said the man somewhat defensively.

"Oh, to be sure," murmured the Corrishman. "You did what was right and proper, to be sure. I do wonder, though, if the mother and daughter ended up in a Mother's House?"

"Oh, no, no, sir!" cried Mr Dunley. "For shame, no, for who could see his own people living in a Mother's House? No, sir. Tellis—that's my sister-in-law—took in washing, and our Mattie—that's my niece—she's a grown girl. Mattie went into service at the Estate, and sent her wages to her mama like a good girl. Her mother'd served at the Estate when she was young, you see, born on the Estate. They 'most never hire from out of the Estate, oh no. No need. Plenty of help to be had, born and raised there. But the Old Duchess, she made an exception for Mattie. Even took her into the Estate school, taught her reading and writing—waste on a servant if you ask me, especially a girl, but the Old Duchess has advanced idears on such things. Much good it did Tellis," Mr Dunley snorted. He took a deep draft of his ale, and nearly wiped his mouth on his sleeve before remembering he wasn't in the back by himself. "Pretty little thing, Mattie. Very taking. Just like her mother. Would've had Tellis to wed myself, but Darwas got there first, didn't he. Ah, well."

"I wonder if your niece is as pretty as my sister. I'd lay wages she isn't," smiled the Corrishman, producing a miniature from his pocket. "I'd lay a five silver piece on it."

"Aye," said the innkeeper, squinting, "a lovely girl you have, but not as pretty as our Mattie." He stretched out his hand for the silver.

"But I should like to see her myself before I pay my fiver," laughed the Corrishman.

"Well, sir, I'll tell you," said his host. "I don't know where she is. Tellis come to us not a spoke ago, and said they was leaving Reggiston! And her, born on the Estate!"

"How odd," said his listener.

"Aye, sir, passing odd! Said she had money come to her from a distant uncle. Distant uncle. Her people are all Estatesmen! None of 'em have that kind of scratch, sir, and that's a fact. But she and Mattie, they're gone. Last I saw of 'em, they was off to the Owl. Hired a post and four, if you can believe it! I'm supposing they went north after this *uncle*. Poor Darwas, I'm glad he's dead rather than see it." He took back his hand glumly.

"Oh, good host, never be sad. Here—I will take you at your word. Here is your fiver. And another pint for the both of us, eh?"

"Thank you, sir, thank you very kindly!" cried Mr Dunley, happily bustling back to the taps.

"Oh, no," murmured the Corrishman, "thank *you*."

SIXTEEN

The Keep's servants slept little the week before Neya's Day. All the rooms, even the bedrooms in the Old Residence Wing, were turned out and prepared for guests who might or might not be staying. As they did at the turning of every spoke, the maids received new pinafores, and the footmen new shirtfronts. The maids beat every carpet, brushed every curtain and tapestry; the footmen, under Affton's hypercritical eye, polished every piece of silver, every candlestick, every brass doorknob, grand entrance and mudroom alike, even though their sheen already blinded the onlooker.

On Neya's Day Eve, the King traditionally hosted one of the last great balls, a high point of the waning social season that would end a spoke later, along with the spring, on Nerr's Day. This year was no exception, and the day found the Keep in an ever mounting frenzy of decorating; garlands draped every bannister, huge sprays of hothouse flowers filled every alcove, topped every table, and more flowers hung in swags from the ballroom ceiling, gigantic ropes of pink, white and red. Even the servants' quarters boasted little bouquets of more common flowers, and those rarer blooms whose stems had decided not to cooperate and snapped short instead.

Temmin let the family know he would only be attending briefly, wishing, he said, to spend Neya's Day elsewhere. His mother pursed her lips in silence; his father clapped him gently on the shoulder and said, "Why wouldn't you, indeed?"

For her part, Sedra sighed and wished the ball already over and done. She was twenty-one, and tired of her siblings' teenaged drama. Temmin could take the whole staff to his bed for all she cared, though she wished he'd be more discreet; at least Papa stopped his whoring at the door to the servants' quarters. Ah, well, it was time. Mama couldn't keep him a child forever.

She marched down the ballroom stairs on her father's arm, a good daughter of Tremont, if one in pinching shoes. To her relief, Temmin led Ellika out on the floor first for the opening dobla, the two near as well-matched as the Obbys, as she overheard one of the footmen whisper in exchange for an elbow in the gut from his fellow.

At the end of the dobla, Temmin relinquished his second sister to her throng of admirers, and offered his hand to Sedra. "Just the one, Seddy," he wheedled, "and then I'm off." The orchestra struck up a modern dance, one their mother frowned on and thus irresistible even to the straitlaced Princess Royal; she fastened up the train of her dark gold gown and let him whirl her onto the dance floor.

Temmin beamed down at her. "You're in wonderful looks tonight." He himself looked older; his beard had filled in since his arrival at the Keep, and he held his head more confidently. Perhaps he was growing up more quickly than she'd thought.

"And you are looking suspiciously cheerful, baby brother," she replied.

"Baby, am I?" he cried. He seized her firmly round the waist and romped her down the room double time, scattering the other dancers. Temmin's hair flew all around his face, a gangly, exuberant, golden puppy in spite of his newfound poise. He danced her around in such a hectic way that she hung on for dear life, a task made harder by her own helpless laughter.

"Temmy, do slow down!" she gasped.

"Say I'm not a baby!"

"You're not a baby! You're not a baby!"

He smirked, and resumed the usual pace of the dance. "You're entirely too serious, Seddy. You should laugh more."

"You're entirely too ridiculous," she said, smiling up at him as she caught her breath against her corset. If she were queen, tight-lacing would be the first thing she outlawed. "I take it your giddy demeanor can be traced to your trip to see your little friends."

"Ah," he said, his face closing in a way she'd never seen before, irritatingly secret and a tad superior. "You might say that." The dance ended. Temmin kissed both of her cheeks before he released her. "Wish me well, Seddy."

"Wish you well? It's Neya's Day Eve. You should be wishing your sisters well."

"Even so. Please."

She studied his face, open once again and earnest, a seriousness her little brother rarely wore. "Yes, of course, Temmin. I pray for you every day, just as I've sworn to on all the Nerr's Days of your life, you zany."

"'Zany,'" he repeated. "Yes. That's me." He kissed her cheek again. "Goodbye." She watched him out of the ballroom, ignoring several attempts to lead her into the next dance. Troubling and unlike him. His infatuation with that maid and her man had changed him.

Two hours later, Ansella retired for the night, leaving her daughters with the King; unlike the Queen, neither princess could leave until he did. To Sedra's frustration, Harsin, his white smile sharp within his salt and pepper beard as he worked the room, showed no signs of boredom.

And then: "Where is Prince Temmin?" She was tiring of the question.

Usually by now her father had made his excuses and slipped off with one of his mistresses. Sedra saw his new favorite, the odd little thing with a pointed chin and dark, feral eyes that already sparkled with too much wine, and wondered again why he would not leave. Her shoes hurt, and she wanted to go upstairs and curl up with a book by her fire.

Lord Corland appeared in the corner of her eye, in urgent conversation with her father—when had Corland come back to town? She prayed he'd left his odious son Fennows in Maryakuspa, for Ellika's sake if no one else's.

*   *   *

The urgent conversation appeared to be one-sided from a distance, but on closer inspection, both parties were fully involved, a small pulse in the King's jaw the only sign of increasing tension. "Master yourself, Corland. What do you mean, Temmin's lovers are a sham?" said Harsin, keeping the smile on his face.

"I mean, he's pulled the wool over your eyes!" hissed Corland. "He still qualifies! Your son means to take Supplicancy!"

"How do you know this?"

"Fennows found it out—His Highness must have confided in him," Corland said evasively.

"He would never have thought up such a plan. He doesn't have it in him—doesn't have the courage. He's as guileless as a child…"

"He's not a child any more. He's fooled you. You must stop him. Where is he?"

"He went to Whithorse to spend Neya's Day with his—with his lovers…" Harsin thought back over his conversations with Temmin. In none of them had the Prince said outright that he'd taken those servants into his bed. "Pagg damn him. Pagg damn him!"

He left the purple-faced Corland and exited the ballroom as naturally as he could. Winmer fell into his wake as he climbed the Residence Wing stairs. "Call Miss Selvaci out of the dance, as if I'd sent for her. I don't want my absence to raise suspicions. Take her to one of the suites connected to mine—you know which one. Send Teacher to my study. See if Temmin is in his rooms, then send the Colonel to me as well, damn them both. Then go back and keep the girl busy—get her drunk. She loves sparkling wine and it won't be long until she passes out. Put her to bed, then come to me yourself." Winmer nodded, and peeled off as Harsin tried not to slam the door to his study.

Colonel Jenks and Teacher came in not long after, the former in a hastily-donned and rumpled coat, the latter as smooth as ever. "Where is my son?" said the King.

"Where is he? He's off to Whithorse! The old crow took him," said Jenks with a jerk of the thumb at Teacher. "Outright refused to take me with him, said he wouldn't need me. It's time we told him what I am, sir. I can no longer insist on my presence in—in some situations."

"We both know Whithorse security is up to the task," said Harsin, "but we both know that's not where he is." He measured the Colonel's unfeigned look of surprise, and turned toward Teacher. "Tell me where he is and how he got there. I order you."

"I took him to the Lovers' Temple, as he requested."

"Show me."

Teacher paused, then murmured at the mirror over the mantel. A foggy image formed of a great bath: men and women milling about in various degrees of nakedness; towel-wrapped heads just visible above the surface of a steaming pool. The image moved closer to a naked, golden-haired young man covered in soap and sitting on a stool. The most beautiful young man Harsin had ever seen was dumping buckets of water over the other's head. Temmin—for once the suds were gone, it was clearly him—spluttered under the stream, though Harsin couldn't hear him. A last bucket poured over him, and once he'd shaken off the water, a buxom young woman Harsin recognized as the current Supplicant of the Lovers pulled Temmin off the stool, threw a towel over his head, and vigorously dried his hair, kissing his laughing face at the end.

"I gather you didn't know, Colonel Jenks?" said Harsin.

"No," said Jenks slowly.

"I believe you. It would appear that our boy has become a man capable of lying to almost anyone." The King sank into his chair, the leather creaking. "Teacher, when I said take him to his lovers—you know very well what I meant!"

"But that is not what you said," replied Teacher. "I regret that my lessons in precision of speech—"

"I would call down Pagg's curse on your head, but it's too late for that, isn't it?" snapped the King. "You're dismissed, Colonel. No, no, not for good," he added at the tightening of the man's broad jaw. "For the evening. Go on."

In the doorway, Winmer stepped aside to let the Colonel pass, then closed the door behind him. "Miss Selvaci is asleep, sir," he said to the pacing King. "She'd entertained herself quite well at the ball already. I've instructed one of the upstairs maids to nurse her through tomorrow's expected hangover."

"He's gone, Winmer. Slipped through our fingers," said Harsin, watching his feet as he paced slowly back and forth.

Winmer bounced on his toes, thinking. "You could still force him out. Send Teacher to Whithorse, bring those two servants back—"

"You said that girl was reliable."

"Indeed, sir, but we underestimated his determination. They can still be of use, though. Have Teacher bring them back. We can use them as leverage against the Prince. If he thought them in immediate peril…?"

"He cares about them enough to shield them. True." Harsin stopped pacing and ran through the possible scenarios in his head.

Two deaths to possibly save the kingdom. Harsin had killed more men than that in battle with his own hands, and caused the deaths of thousands more in Inchar. But those were Inchari, stubbornly refusing what was good for them. These were Tremontines, and innocents. The prophecy might be wrong, or the Scholars of Eddin might be interpreting it incorrectly.

"If he balks, the death of the young man and a sword at the throat of the young woman would bring him to heel quickly," said Winmer. "Do it in the Great Hall of the Temple. Teacher can take us there without anyone knowing."

Teacher's silver eyes radiated contempt. "I am the servant of the King, except when I am the servant of the Gods. No outsider may enter a closed Temple without an invitation, and the Lovers' Temple is closed until the Spectacle tomorrow." Teacher pointedly turned away from Winmer to the King. "You have come perilously close to outright disrespect, Your Majesty, astonishing from a man who does not believe but *knows* what the Gods can do. Have I taught you so poorly? Have you paid no attention all these years to the Gods made manifest over and over in your life?" At Harsin's shaken expression, Teacher added, "It comes down to this, Your Majesty. You fear for the Kingdom's fate. Will you murder two innocents on the steps of a Temple, and perhaps bring down an even worse one?"

"No," whispered Harsin, dropping his head. Winmer rocked on his heels in disapproval. Harsin raised his eyes to his secretary. "But if Temmin knows I'm aware of his deception, the threat of murder might be my only recourse. You," he said, glaring at Teacher. "Find my son's spurious lovers—no, let's be exact, shall we, Winmer?"

"Arta Dannikson and Fen Wallek, sir," said the secretary.

"Find Dannikson and Wallek. Bring them here to the Keep. Do it now. Is that specific enough?"

"Yes, Your Majesty," said Teacher, with only a hint of reluctance in departing through the mirror.

Freshly bathed, Temmin pulled on his new Temple garb—red, the color of the postulant Lovers, a happier, somehow less serious shade than the official Tremontine red garb he wore the last time he was at the Temple. "Will I see the Holy Ones again before tomorrow?" he asked over a late supper with Anda in the Supplicants Chamber.

She put her wine glass down and replied, "No. You won't be seeing them until it's time to draw down the Gods tomorrow night. It's not at all an easy thing, you know, Tem."

"Allis says it's something like being a puppet."

"I am happy to say I don't know," said Anda. "I only know what it looks like, and frankly, that's enough. It's exhausting. The twins'll only be able to serve ten years or so. Most of the Embodiments serve at least twenty, but they only take on their Gods once a year. Ours do it twice a year, in quick succession. By the time the Gods were through with Idia and Hendas, the last Embodiments, they were spent. They're still at the Temple in Kellen, I think, just taking the sea air and resting the last two years. They chose me, you know. I miss them," she said, looking off into memory. She came back to the room. "It's so tiring we treat the serving Holy Ones like glass for a whole spoke afterwards, even Allis and Issak, young and fresh. No one sees them."

"Even me?" said Temmin, who to his surprise hadn't seen them since Teacher had unceremoniously dumped him in Issak's sitting room three hours ago.

"Oh, no. You'll see them. Just don't expect much. You'll be training with the Postulants anyway."

"I've been wondering—who will be watching tomorrow? In the crowds, I mean. It's—it's not all nobility, is it?" he winced, thinking of Litta;

he wasn't sure if the sight of that white scar among the onlookers would frighten him or anger him.

"Social standing doesn't matter, here or in any Temple, you know. We hold lotteries. All are equal before the Gods, at least on Spectacle days— except virgins. No virgins at Neya's Day. And royalty. Royalty's expected. And then this year, there's extra precautions because of you. When royalty stays up on the dais where it belongs—"

A loud to-do in the Great Hall erupted outside their door. A Temple's Own knocked briefly and thrust his head inside. "Your Highness," he said, "you'd better come. The King is on the steps, calling for you."

Temmin shook the crumbs from his clothes, still indifferent when it came to tidiness at mealtime, and strode from the room behind the warrior Lover, a small cadre of Temple's Own forming around him as he walked. In every corner, servants and clergy filled the Great Hall, cleaning and polishing in a frenzy. No worshippers were in sight for the first time in Temmin's brief experience; everyone was barred from the Temple but staff until the doors opened for the celebrations the next evening.

Temmin and his guard emerged onto the rosy marble steps. The air was cold; he could see his breath. Halfway up stood his father, flanked himself by Royal Guardsmen in a respectful standoff with a line of Temple's Own. A few steps behind him stood that dratted Winmer with a small knot of others including, to his surprise, Teacher. Behind them gathered a small crowd made up mostly of late visitors to the Healer's House across the Promenade, drawn by the unexpected martial sounds at the Lovers' Temple.

Temmin drew a deep breath, hoping to quell his shaking. "Well?" he called down, with a creditable attempt at bravado.

"Well, indeed," said Harsin. "I've come to take you back."

"I don't think so. This is my choice, and I've made it. You can't come in and cart me off bodily. No one's allowed in tonight."

"He's right. Pagg's Law, sir," murmured Brother Mardus at his side.

"Do not think to lecture your King on Pagg's Law," snapped Harsin. "Even were it an ordinary night, I would not dream of defiling this Temple —any Temple—by bringing Guards into it to cart you or anyone else off bodily. You will walk out on your own."

"Will I," said Temmin, his temper rising.

"Don' you do it, sir!" a young woman called in a sweet, familiar voice. "Don' you do it! If we come to harm, that's as it should be!"

Torches had finally been brought, and a young man's flaming red hair blazed plain in their light. Fen flexed against the Guards pinning his arms back, but made no move; they held Arta far too tightly for him to risk it.

Who had betrayed them? Jenks didn't know where he was going, and fully believed Arta and Fen were his lovers; Ellika knew they weren't, but had no idea he'd decided to join the Temple and wouldn't have stopped him if she had. That left Teacher; he glared into the strange silvery eyes. Teacher didn't look away, and gave a barely visible shake of the head, as if knowing Temmin's mind.

"I'm not for the idea of us dyin in general," said Fen, "but I don' beg anyone for anything, and I'd rather die than be damned. This whole thing is blasphemy, and I want no part in it. Go ahead, sir, and let the Guards be damned, not us!" At this, the men holding him shifted uncomfortably, looking at one another and then at the Temples surrounding them.

"You'd kill them to stop me?" said Temmin to his father. "You'd place their deaths on your soul?"

"We are King, Temmin. We do what we must, and we must stop you. Their deaths will be on you if you don't come down from there."

"You speak to me as if I'm a child up in a tree!"

"When you act like a child, I'll speak to you like one!" roared Harsin.

By now, the Most Highs had joined the flock of Lovers and Beloveds at the top of the stairs, Gan leaning on Senik in his sleepiness. "What do you wish to do, Your Highness?" said Gan.

Steel glinted against Arta's throat, and in Temmin's imagination red bloomed against the white of her skin. But here and now, the steel wavered ever so slightly. He cast about for anything he could draw upon for guidance. He thought of Jenks: "Who are you more afraid of? The Gods, or your father?" Now that he feared for two innocents, not for himself, he wasn't sure.

What would Warin do? He would try to rally the Guard to his side, but as his ancestor had discovered, their bond to the crowned king was stronger than their bond to justice.

Senik said he knew nothing about reading people, that inborn talent notwithstanding, inexperience doomed Temmin's attempts to do it. Even so, it was all he had, and he studied the King, calling on everything he knew about his father. Harsin was angry, that much was clear. But he'd seen his father angry before. This time, a desperation tinted his voice. The question was, would his desperation lead him to do something horrible, something unforgivable, something that would both damn him and destroy the nascent ties between him and his son; he had to know that if he killed Temmin's friends, it would be the end of any intimacy between them. It might already be too late, he thought, tasting bile.

Silence filled the Promenade. Temmin finally said, "Fen, Arta, are you sure?"

"Yes," said Fen, speaking for them both in a voice choked with emotion. "I would go to the Hill for you, sir." Arta nodded vigorously, unable to form words, the curls at her forehead bobbing and tears coursing down her face. The dagger at her throat openly trembled.

Temmin turned to the Most Highs. "I'm staying." Each word appeared in a white puff before him, expanded and dissolved.

"Very well, then. Take your first vow," said High Beloved Malla, her voice filled with a power he hadn't suspected the gentle priestess possessed. "Crouch down before us. Now, put one hand beneath your feet, and the other atop your head." Temmin kept his balance until he looked up at the priests and began to wobble. "Say: All between my hands I give to the Lovers for a span of two years and two days."

Temmin took a deep breath, looked straight at his father, and said, "All...all between my hands I give to the Lovers for a span of two years and two days." Everyone—the Guards, the Temple's Own, the Most Highs, his father, the crowd below—exhaled, a long, surprised sigh, and he rose to his feet.

"No more 'Your Highness' will you hear in this Temple," said the High Lover. "You are now as a Postulant, no more, for the first year. You will address us always as Most High, and the Embodiments always as Holy One. You will obey your superiors immediately, and that includes all sworn Lovers and Beloveds. Do you understand?"

"Yes, Most High," said Temmin. His ears rang, and unexpected tears pricked the corners of his eyes. He had never broken Harsin's gaze, and said now, "Do what you must, Father."

"Sir," said Winmer in an urgent undertone, "a crowd has formed. Do what you must."

Harsin trembled with rage and glared up at the assembly on the landing. "You have brought doom on this kingdom, Temmin," he said in a low voice. He mastered himself, stood straighter and turned to face Arta and Fen, and by extension the crowd below, already agitated in uncertain joy. "Neya's Day is a time for love and celebration," he said, an artificial smile in his voice. "We rejoice with you at Prince Temmin's instatement as Supplicant of the Lovers' Temple!" He turned back, and once out of the cheering crowd's sight, his face contorted. "There will be many unprecedented changes in store for this Temple, I'm sure!" With that, he descended with his escort and rode up the Promenade toward the city's center, leaving Fen, Arta and Teacher alone on the steps.

Arta swayed as if ready to drop; Fen caught her in his arms, even though he himself looked faint. "It's all right, we're alive, sweetheart," he murmured into her hair. "We're alive."

Temmin ran down and embraced Fen and Arta, then turned to Teacher. "Is there any reason you can't take them back to Whithorse?" he said.

"None in the world."

"Perhaps they might like a cup of something hot first?" called the High Beloved.

"Something stronger, I think," replied Temmin. He stayed Teacher as the other two climbed the steps into the Temple, and said, "Did you betray me?"

"I have helped you in this matter time and again," said Teacher. "Why would I try to thwart your ambition now?" The pale, smooth face, usually so empty of anything but intelligence, beamed.

"Then who did?" said Temmin earnestly, one hand on Teacher's shoulder. "Who was it?"

"I do not know, but I am extremely invested in finding out, Your Highness. Now, go on. They are waiting for you."

*   *   *

Despite Anda's light, musical snoring in the alcove bed across the room from him, Temmin slept late on Neya's Day. Or at least, he assumed he had; the Supplicants Chamber had no windows. Anda's bed was now empty and made, and his only gauge of time was his roaring appetite. With his breakfast, he learned that he had in fact slept until lunch, "A good thing on the whole, as it'll be a long night, with little sleep for anyone and much exercise for everyone," smirked Senik.

All Temmin knew about the upcoming ritual was this:

There was to be some sort of trial for Allis and Issak to bring down the Lovers, something that might be painful for them, or perhaps it was the presence of the Gods Themselves that was painful. He and Senik and one of the senior Lovers, a man called Barik, would help Issak prepare for it, though the preparations were obscure to him.

There would be a Chase. Neya and Nerr would run until the Brother caught the Sister. It would end as it did in the Sagas, with lovemaking. The people would pass by one at a time to watch Them and receive the blessing, then find a corner of the gardens to imitate their Gods; everywhere, all over the kingdom, over much of the world, people with no chance of seeing the Gods in this life would do the same, going out into the fields and gardens to ensure their fertility. Temmin was to help hold the people back until the Gods were satisfied.

There would be some kind of acknowledgment of his dedication as Supplicant, and he was to follow the Gods back into Their bedchamber, a room used only when They were in residence, as it were. Neya would take his virginity and that would be an end to the ceremony as far as he knew.

With this scanty knowledge in mind, Temmin made his way to the gardens, already filled with worshippers waiting for the Chase. The Most Highs sat in state on a dais above the crowds. Beside them, rigid and fidgeting, sat his mother.

He climbed the stairs quickly, and sank down on his knees before her. "What are you doing here?" he cried, taking her hands. "I'm happy to see you, truly, Mama, but I'm very surprised."

Ansella gave him a shaky, rather liquid smile. "The pious parent attends the investiture of a child into a Temple, sweetheart, no matter how

I myself feel about…" She stole a glance at the Most Highs, who graciously pretended deafness.

"You heard what happened last night," said Temmin. "He's not making it hard on you, or Jenks, or Teacher?"

"Your father is putting a brave face on it. He has decided it is more politic to downplay the significance of 'Nerr getting the Heir.' The commoners, however, are jubilant." She nodded at the milling crowds, most gazing happily up at him, some bowing reverently. "As for consequences at the Keep, as soon as Teacher returned from Whithorse, he was confined to his Tower. That's the only good thing that came of it. Col —Jenks is under suspicion of helping you, as am I now that I've come here —I couldn't let you do this alone, with none of your family here to witness! Sister Ibbit didn't want me here, and neither did your father, but they couldn't stop me from attending Temple." She sighed. "You were wise to send your friends to the Estate. I've never seen Harsin so angry, or so frightened. I wouldn't come home for a good while, my dear."

"The Keep is not my home," he answered. "I'm happy to see you, Mama. This is all…I'm sure this is the right thing to do, but I confess… Everything's upside down, except for here."

"Temmin," called Senik from the foot of the dais, "it's time to get ready." Temmin kissed his mother's little hands, made his obeisances to the Most Highs, and turned to go, his step unsteady. Malla stayed him, her warm, thin-skinned hand on his. "It's all right to be afraid, Temmin Supplicant. But don't withhold yourself, any part of yourself, from Them. They will take all of you, and if you resist Them, so much the worse for you."

"Respectfully, Most High, I didn't go through all this to resist."

She smiled pensively. "Ah, but there is so, so very much more still to come."

Senik led Temmin down a long corridor that ran parallel to the gardens. Temmin carried a basket full of little muslin bags, Senik two small but heavy caskets. "Barik Lover will lead, we will assist," said Senik. "Have you met Barik?"

He had; he'd met all the senior clergy. The biggest thing about Barik Lover that he'd seen were his eyes: soft, sympathetic brown pools often lit with some unheard, inner joke. Otherwise, Barik's balding, close-cropped head came only to Temmin's shoulder. He was middle-aged, and beyond good looks in Temmin's estimation—a long nose, square-set mouth, and rather well-furred forearms. They entered the anteroom of the Gods' Chamber, a long oblong with two doors. One was red and led to Nerr's side of the Chamber; the other was white and led to Neya's.

Barik sat before a long, low table. "Senik Postulant," he muttered, "why do you go all the way to Inchar to fetch me something?" He took the basket from Temmin and laid out the bags on the table. "They're already on the frames, and I don't like them hanging up there any longer than necessary."

Barik began taking practised pinches from the muslin bags, depositing them in the center of two large pieces of thin paper: dried herbs and flowers, spices, barks, and a bitter powder that made Temmin sneeze. Some substances were common to both; some, Barik added only to one of the papers. "There's an exact sequence of sensations—hunger, scents, tastes, caresses, even blows—that bring the Gods down into their Embodiments," he said, "and these mixtures provide the incense. We'll burn these in a brazier. Stay away from it." He folded the papers into packets and directed Temmin to reseal and stow the muslin bags back in their basket.

Barik handed one of the packets to Senik, who still held one of the caskets. "Take these to Glaes." Senik disappeared through the white door; when he returned, the three men opened the red door, and entered Nerr's side together.

Temmin thought of the last time he'd seen Issak naked: thick-muscled, almost cruel, bending Temmin's will to his own. And now here he was in near-reverse, bound naked to a frame, sweaty, already half-erect and bending himself to Nerr's will, whatever it might be. There was a sadness to the set of his mouth, and Temmin wished he could see Issak's eyes, but the Embodiment wore a blindfold. "Why is he tied up like that?" said Temmin.

"It's part of the sequence, and it's for everyone's safety including Issak's. When the Gods come down, They're on the exuberant side at first," said Barik, depositing the remaining paper packet on a brazier at Issak's feet.

Smoke curled up from the brazier, smelling of rich woods and amber, and that bitter powder; it made Temmin a little dizzy in the head. Issak took it in, long steady breaths ending in sighs, and hardened further, Temmin's own arousal responding.

Another scent wafted into the room: white hothouse flowers, tuberose, gardenia, and the little trumpet-shaped ones Ellika loved—freesia—but underneath floated that same bitterness. "Neya's scent," murmured Senik. "They've begun the greater preparation with Allis."

Allis tied and blindfolded, helpless and open to his touch: a deeper breath, and the image became clearer, almost physical. He had yet to even see her naked, but he could imagine the rise and fall of her breasts, sweat trickling between them, her soft mouth open and panting; it shot between his legs in a burst. He reached out to touch her.

Barik's suddenly booming voice in his ear brought him back to the room. "Don't stand near that brazier, I said! It's for the Holy One, not you. I need you here, not hallucinating in a heap. Back away." Temmin dutifully stepped back, and though his head cleared somewhat, his arousal stayed with him, tight against the red linen trousers.

Issak's sighs turned to groans, his thick cock fully erect and straining. Temmin's eyes slipped down his body and came to rest on a mark he hadn't noticed before, on Issak's left hip: a birthmark? Who had a glowing silver birthmark? He stepped further away from the brazier, and took in a few lungfuls of clean air.

Senik offered the box to Barik with a hitherto unknown solemnity; Barik opened it with a quiet click of its clasp, and pulled out three heavy clusters of rubies, earrings Temmin supposed, though far heavier than an ear could support. The clusters altogether must have weighed half a pound. Barik stripped the earrings and handed their gems back to Senik.

Senik smothered the smoking brazier with sand. Whatever the effect of the incense, Issak was firmly in its grasp; he strained against the binding straps, the tendons and veins in his arms standing out in sharp relief. Barik ran a gentle hand up the Embodiment's broad chest and stopped at the first nipple he came to, stroking it gently. Issak flinched and whimpered, and then Barik took what Temmin had thought was an earring and fastened it to the nipple.

The Embodiment let out a long, roaring groan. "Gently, gently, now, Holy One," murmured Barik as he fastened the second clamp. He stepped behind the frame and pulled Issak's head back by his thick, black hair, kissing him; the Embodiment returned it, hungrily. "Come take my place, Temmin Supplicant," said Barik. Temmin hesitated. "Supplicant, here. Now. Hold his head. Give him what he asks for."

Temmin took Barik's position behind the frame, and wrapped Issak's hair timidly around his hand. "Temmin, please," crooned Issak, lips searching. His voice held the same frantic, bare desperation Temmin heard in countless voices in the petitioning rooms—the young man begging for the release of a spanking, the muffled pleading of the woman tied to the couch—though he sensed Issak feared release as much as needed it. "Please…"

Temmin fisted the hand in Issak's hair, Issak, so composed and in control and now begging and needy. Temmin yanked him back and kissed him, a fierce, sloppy, imperfect kiss that brought Temmin more into the present, but took Issak further away.

"Keep hold of him," said Barik, kneeling on the floor. He took the last clamp, and fastened it to the skin of Issak's sac. The Embodiment jerked and howled, twisting this way and that to bite at Temmin, but he held on tight to Issak's hair.

"Soon," said Barik. "Soon. Senik, open the doors to Neya's chamber, and to the gardens." Cool nighttime air flowed in from the gardens, and with it, the excited murmur of worshippers. The large doors between the Gods' chambers opened, framing Allis: naked, bound and blindfolded like her brother, struggling against the restraints. From each nipple dangled the same clamps; two more hung from her labia. An older woman he recognized as Glaes Beloved, a woman as senior as Barik, knelt before Neya's Embodiment, gently tapping the clamps as they swung back and forth.

Anda stood behind Allis; she cupped the Embodiment's breasts, and let them fall. Allis let out an agonized growl, and Anda gave her the kiss she sought.

Temmin let go of Issak and stepped forward; Barik stayed him with a hand on his leg. "She's all right. They're both all right. It's hard the first time, watching them go through this. But every Spectacle we call the Gods, you will remember this, and wish you were in this room once more. Now go back to your station, Temmin Supplicant. Senik Postulant, it's time."

Temmin returned to his place behind Issak; he impulsively caressed the Embodiment's hair, only to draw back when Issak snarled and snapped at him. "Be careful," said Senik, handing him two of the heavy ruby pendants. "Issak's not there any more, but Nerr hasn't arrived yet. Watch Anda, and do as she does."

Allis was gone as well. A very young postulant Beloved Temmin knew as Evra gave Anda two diamond pendants, twins to the rubies; Anda slipped to the front, carefully avoiding gnashing teeth, and hung one from each nipple clamp. Allis screamed and threw her head back. "Go on, Temmin Supplicant," said Barik, and Temmin did as he was told; he fastened a ruby onto each nipple clamp. Issak stiffened and let out a strangled sound, quickly drowned out by keening from across the room. Two diamonds now dangled from the clamps on Allis's labia. She gasped and cried, settling into an almost-silent trembling; Issak trembled as well, as Barik added a ruby to the clamp between his legs.

One by one they fastened more gems to the clamps, until each one held four. Sweat poured down the twin's shuddering bodies. Their heads hung low, black hair rippling. Senik moved to one side, and put Temmin's hand on one clamp, his own on the other. "Do it quickly, Temmin. Follow my lead."

"On my mark," called Barik. "One—two—now!"

Senik and Barik whipped off the clamps; Temmin scrabbled at the grip, but was not far behind. "Press in," said Senik, and Temmin imitated him, pushing his thumb down hard and flat on the nipple. Panic rose in his throat as Issak screamed. He looked down and met Barik's eyes; the Lover nodded reassuringly as he molded Issak's balls. Allis sobbed, limp in her restraints, as Anda and Evra pressed down on her nipples, Glaes Beloved's head buried between her legs.

Abruptly, the sobbing stopped. Everyone pulled away from the Embodiments, Senik snagging Temmin by the collar and tugging him back. Smiles spread slowly across the twins' faces, and their heads rose. "They're here," said Barik. "Watch yourselves." He and Glaes removed the blindfolds. The eyes beneath glowed, a faint rose halo around the luminous green that grew to surround their entire bodies. Temmin wondered if it were a leftover from the incense he'd breathed in.

"Hello, Sister," said not-Issak.

"Hello, Brother," said not-Allis.

"Will You just let Me have you this time, or must I chase You down and prove Your desire yet again?"

An expression altogether unlike Allis—wanton, challenging—spread across Her borrowed face. "Perhaps this will be the year I outrun You."

"Liar," said the God, baring His borrowed teeth. "You let me catch You, year after year."

"Are you saying You're not as fleet of foot as I am?"

"I'm saying," said Nerr, pulling against His restraints, "that You want me, Neya. I can smell You. I can always smell You."

Neya licked Her lips. "You have to catch Me first. Let Me go, mortals, let Me go now!" Anda and Glaes worked at the straps, and once released, Neya-in-Allis gave a joyous whoop and bounded from the room into the garden, so quickly it seemed clear to Temmin She had no intention of letting anyone catch her.

"Now! Now!" howled the God. Temmin shook as he released the last strap around not-Issak's wrist. As soon as His hand was free, the God picked Temmin up by the chin, just enough to force him on tip-toe. "You, child," Nerr said in a voice that entered Temmin's bones. The God grinned, wild and frightening. "Clumsy boy. We've been waiting a long time for you." The last restraint slipped free. Nerr kissed Temmin quickly, biting his lower lip, and took off running after His Sister.

"Don't lose Him!" shouted Senik.

Temmin, Senik, Anda and Evra pelted after him, Barik and Glaes following behind at a more dignified pace. The gardens were packed with people on both sides of many wide paths lined with lanterns; Neya might have gone down any of them, but Nerr seemed to know Her path.

Through the flowers, the sculpture garden, almost into the Temple and out onto the street Neya-in-Allis led them, until they were far out onto the grassy lawns, where there were no people or lanterns; Temmin followed Senik's back, the only thing his still-unaccustomed eyes could clearly see.

Two screams came piercing from the darkness ahead, one triumphant, one enraged. "He's caught Her," said Senik. "Lights!"

A small fleet of clerics hurried from behind in a long stream, marking the Gods' trail with lanterns for the crowd to follow. They flowed forward, reaching the Gods at the same time as Temmin's group to form a circle of light and bodies around the struggling forms on the ground. "We provide protection during the Spectacle," said Senik, tugging him into a loose ring of Lovers and Beloveds surrounding the Gods.

"Who would hurt a God?" said Temmin.

"Oh, no," called Anda from a few paces away. "We're protecting the people. Fools sometimes try to join in. Instant death."

By now, the crowds had found them; they surged against the circle, held back from the ring of protectors by an outer ring of lantern-bearers who, now that Temmin had a moment to look around him, were of the Temple's Own. Inside the circle, Allis struggled to get away from Issak—no, it wasn't them, Temmin reminded himself—until Nerr pinned Neya so firmly she could not get away. She snarled and thrashed, strong even in Allis's small, soft body.

Warfare gave way to laughter. "I surrender!" cried Neya, weak with giggles. "I surrender!"

"You are once again Mine?" said Nerr, grinning down on Her.

"I am My own, Brother, this year and all years, forever and ever. But I share. Now kiss Me, before I change My mind!" Nerr leaned down and kissed Her, almost chastely. "Ah, Brother," She whispered in her borrowed voice, "how I miss You when We have no form! We were never meant to be two. Be One with Me tonight!"

"Be one with Me tonight, Sister!" Nerr and Neya's kiss turned from tender to voracious, almost a devouring. They were so very beautiful, a sight indeed, but the whole situation—the possession, the incest, the watching crowd—made Temmin more and more nervous. Neya climbed atop Her Brother, and Temmin turned away, cheeks hot against the night air. Allis's voice cried out in ecstasy, and the crowd matched it with an appreciative growl.

It would be different if he didn't know the twins. The avid faces coming and going in the lantern light didn't know them; Allis and Issak were almost abstractions, as real to most of the worshippers as a pair of statues.

The figures inside the circle shifted positions again and again—for Temmin had given up turning his head away and watched with a mixture of revulsion, desire and curiosity. The streams of people came and went, disappearing two by two and sometimes more into the dark; distant cries filled the air.

In time, a great deal of time, Nerr rolled off His Sister, and They lay side by side in the grass stroking one another's faces and crooning in a language only They understood, a musical, blissful, terrible crooning, the sounds of a voluptuous, erotic nightmare. The crowds began to thin; the blessing was over. Those who had received it had gone off to do their yearly duty, bestowing the blessing themselves among the leaves and grasses of the fields and forests. Those who had finished their duty were drifting back toward the dais near the Temple to witness Temmin's dedication and get one more glimpse of the Gods.

Nerr-in-Issak sat up. "This body is wonderful, very strong and responsive. It suits Me," He said in Tremontine. He stretched Issak's strong arms and legs, and patted the still-erect cock. "I'm almost tempted to keep it."

"Twice a year in a body is fun. Being trapped in a body, a crumbling, decaying thing however beautiful at first, is not. It's a bore. Better to borrow than to buy," said Neya-in-Allis. She stood up, pulling Her Brother to His feet after Her. Dirt and grass fell from Their bodies in a pittering rain around their feet, leaving Them clean and unsullied.

"Anda!" cried Nerr. He swept the round Supplicant into the air, swinging her high off her feet before putting her down and kissing her soundly. "Have you forgotten Me yet?"

For the first time since Temmin had known her, Anda blushed. "My Lord, You will forget me. I will never forget You."

"I never forget a maidenhead, sweetheart," He said, tweaking Anda's nipple.

"And this time, it's My turn," said Neya. She slid a finger inside Temmin's red linen shirt. "Adorable." She clapped Her hands together. "We have much to do, and while We have all the time in the world, you do not, little mortals." She strode off down the path arm in arm with Nerr, the lantern-bearers keeping a buffer around the informal procession as they walked back through the gradually thickening crowds near the Temple. Petals floated through the air, thrown in offering from the sidelines.

Temmin fell back to where Senik walked, one arm around a rugged blonde Lover and the other around Evra Postulant. "And how does the evening find you, Temmin Supplicant?" said Senik. "Wait, I know—it finds you terrified."

"I am not terrified," huffed Temmin.

"Don't worry. I don't think She'll hurt you. Nerr fucked someone to death once, but that was well over 500 years ago, and it was an accident."

"You're not helping!" Temmin stalked back to the front of the procession, hoping to find more sympathy from Anda.

"That was rather cruel," said the rugged blonde Lover.

Senik shrugged. "The world does not revolve around his navel. He'll be all right. Besides," he growled, biting at the other man's earlobe, "you like it when I'm cruel."

"True," sighed the rugged blonde Lover.

A few paces ahead, Temmin had fallen in step with Anda. "I don't know if I can do this," he muttered.

"You'll be all right," she said. "I survived it. You will, too."

"Be truthful with me. Do They scare you?"

"They're Gods, of course they scare me—did Senik tell you about the time 500 years ago? If he weren't so pretty, I'd kill that man," scowled Anda. "You'll be with Neya anyway. I don't think She's fucked anyone to death, ever. I hope if it ever happens it's Senik, but he'd probably die happy."

"Maybe She hasn't done it before, but there's always a first time," he muttered.

"You're a very quick study, Tem, but you're not going to inspire that level of passion your first time out," said Anda.

The two mounted the dais and joined the Most Highs; Ansella was nowhere to be seen. Before he could ask after her, High Beloved Malla said, "And how is your first Spectacle, Temmin Supplicant?"

"Where's my mother?"

Malla laughed. "I find it odd to discuss a man's mother on a night like this, my dear. The Queen felt that she'd done her duty, and went home. Not a surprise, considering her advisor. Now, watch."

The crowds had fallen to their knees as the Gods moved among them, stopping to give a kiss or caress a bowed head, favors that often led to the recipient fainting dead away or smothering under a pile of onlookers anxious to share the blessing. Neya and Nerr ascended the dais, and the murmured prayers of the multitude ceased. Temmin searched for even a shred of Allis and Issak as They approached, but there was none; the calm professionalism usually on their faces had been replaced with a radiance that gave off both light and heat, as if the Gods truly burned inside them. He feared that if his eyes met Theirs he might burn to ash and blow away. He dropped his gaze to the ground.

"You have brought us a gift?" They called out together.

"Temmin Supplicant," responded the Most Highs.

"Approach Us."

No turning back. Temmin rose on shaking legs, eyes still down; he cast a glance at the stairs leading downward and out into the night, to whatever else there might be for him in this life, turned and faced the Gods. Something compelled him to look into Neya's borrowed eyes. In their green depths, figures moved, coupling and uncoupling and recoupling with others, an endless dance of love and pleasure that expanded to encompass him and then the world, enveloping it all in the rose light that shone from Her. "Would you serve Us?"

"Yes," he said hoarsely.

"Would you learn from Us?" said Nerr.

"Yes," he replied, his voice strengthening.

"Would you share that knowledge with the world?"

"Yes," he said.

Neya kissed him then, filling him with a euphoric languor, an erotic pulse flowing from Her lips down his body and back up in a neverending coil, a joined spiral. He was completely alive, completely at home in his body, and afraid of nothing; whatever doubts he may have had dissolved. In that moment, whatever she asked of him he would have done. The elation stayed with him even when She stepped back, even when Nerr tore his shirt from his back and kissed him so hard he wondered in the back of his mind if his lips were pulped. Fingers at his waist untied the red linen trousers; they caught on his arousal, but he shifted and they fell to the floor, leaving him naked before the crowd of worshippers.

"We accept your supplication, Temmin," said Neya. They led him off the dais into the Gods' Chambers and shut the doors behind them.

SEVENTEEN

The chanting of Temmin's name glided under the Chambers' closed doors to the gardens; inside, it was still. Temmin floated lightheaded, as he had near the incense smoke. The idea that perhaps he'd been enchanted flitted through his mind until Neya took his hand and led him to the low, enormous bed in the middle of the room. His mind emptied into the shifting present of animals: no past, no future, only now, as it had been in that brief moment in the chapel, the now-wordless, soundless voice singing all around him, no longer small.

Beside the bed stood many ritual offerings of cakes and candies, stacked in towers of intricately patterned pink and white. "Sweets!" exclaimed Neya, seizing several delicate little crescent moon-shaped cakes, and popping a white chocolate bonbon into her mouth. "The best in years. Sweets of all kinds," she smiled at Temmin. She slipped a sticky pink confection between his lips. "One to stop your tongue, sweet Temmin. This is a night of secrets," She said. "You will not speak of this night ever, to anyone, you will share the blessings you receive in this bed in Our service for two years and two days, and you will use the wisdom We give you the rest of your life. Do you agree?"

"Yes, of course, Lady," he answered.

Neya smiled and kissed his hands. "There is no creature sweeter than a young mortal. So agreeable, so pliant. Now," she said, "show Me what you know about women." Temmin looked down into Her eyes. His mother appeared first, full of comfort and love. "She is important, certainly, but she is in the realm of Amma—mostly," murmured the Goddess. Then his sisters, Ellika at the forefront, so like their mother in her gold-and-cream looks, and Sedra behind her, so like their mother in her stormy temperament. "These women are mysteries for later," chuckled the Lady.

Next came Alvo. "He is not a woman. We are talking about women, not sex, Supplicant. In your time with My Brother, you will explore this one."

Mattie followed, her face tear-stained and frightened, and Temmin felt his stomach sink even through the euphoria. Then Emmae, spirited and strong even in her subjugation. Arta—a wrench at his heart—her innocence and tenderness turned against her, because of him. Anda, voluptuous and gleefully forthright. And finally Allis herself, knowing and wistful, the mystery.

He scrabbled for the commonalities, a joining thread, but found none. "I don't think I know anything about women. The women I know are all different." His eyes teared up; Senik was right, he knew nothing, he was a disappointment. "I'm sorry."

Neya smiled. "Wise little one, that's the first thing one must learn about women. Lie down. You will learn something else, a secret. Are you ready? Taste a Goddess." She straddled his head and lowered herself down until Her folds were the boundaries of the world.

At first, She tasted of the ocean, salty and clean, as if water swirled around him; he lapped at it, searching for its source. Then came earth, loam rich and dark, and green things growing. A bitterness arose, herbal and strong, but as he licked it turned to honey, thick on his tongue. He let out a muffled moan and drew every bit of Her he could into his mouth.

No time, no place, only Her, until a mouth slid down his length. Temmin had forgotten Nerr, but remembered now as His tongue worked on him. It was far too much, far too soon; he would never last. He tensed in panic.

Neya shifted, lifting him out of his fears and into the moment; once more, Her taste and smell were everywhere, and everything. How could he worry? He breathed in as deeply as he could: roses and sandalwood, and then the scent of the broom growing around Whithorse, the herbs that Jebby crushed under his hooves as they rode over the hills. His heart swelled with love for his home. He loved the Lady above him, he loved the Lord beside him, he loved his land, he loved his people, he loved the world. Love pulsed through him until it burst from every pore, a gushing of ecstasy leaving him blind and deaf but for the rushing of his blood.

Temmin's first thought when he returned to full consciousness was that he'd come too soon; They would be angry. And yet, a hand held his cock; he was still hard. He hadn't come at all, though he could swear he had. Two tongues licked his face, catlike, cleaning him. When he opened his eyes, They had finished and were kissing one another above him.

Neya sank down beside him on one elbow. "Now I shall reward you. Ask any question you'd like. Anything. I will answer you truly."

Temmin's brain struggled to string words together, let alone a question. "Did I please you?" he finally said in a thick voice.

Nerr burst out laughing. "A chance to ask a Goddess a question, and you ask that!"

"Did I say the wrong thing?" said Temmin, struggling to sit up.

"That's two questions," said Neya. "To answer the first, yes. Your eagerness to please made up for your lack of finesse. In time you will have a very talented tongue, little Prince."

"That's good," he said, shaking his head to clear it. "That's…what just happened? I came, but I didn't."

Nerr squeezed him at the root until his eyes fluttered. "You will always be ready when you are with Us. We'll give you many releases, but you will not spend, you will not shoot your seed unless we allow it. Your pleasure belongs to Us."

"Enough," said Neya. "I wish to enjoy this gift."

Nerr slipped behind Temmin and put His arms around him, stroking him until his head rolled back against His broad shoulder.

Neya pinched his nipple. "Pay attention." Temmin brought his head up with a start. "Better." She straddled his lap and brought his hands to her breasts. They were heavy and full, perfect as his hands had always known they would be. Every time he'd ever looked at Allis, he had imagined her breasts, just like this.

A knife cut through his arousal. This was not Allis. He touched Allis's body, but the Lady was not Allis. He had wanted his first to be her. "I am Allis," said Neya. "But then, I am every woman who desires a man. I know your thoughts. I am a Goddess. Allis is far away, but she feels this, and she will remember this. We are both your first, and you will have her many times before your service is through. Now, please *Me*."

She brought Her breasts closer to his face, and he ran his tongue around each nipple before taking one in his mouth. She tasted like no human woman—not Anda, nor his ancestor's memories of Emmae. She tasted of flowers: the honeysuckle he plucked off the walls of the stable and ate with Alvo back home on lazy summer evenings, the sunlight still slanting low among the trees. What an odd thing to come to mind.

"Everything you've ever loved, every person, every place," Neya whispered, "everyone and everything you've ever wanted, I am all of that. I am the fulfillment of desire."

All his yearnings converged into one. He kissed Her deeply, tongue searching Her mouth and finding each love there. Nerr's hand reached between them, guiding him inside Her. The head rested briefly at Her entrance, and then She was on him.

Hot and wet, yes, he knew women were hot and wet inside from his limited experience both real and inherited from the book, but this was a perfect wetness he would drown in, a perfect heat he would burn in, burn to ashes until all that was left was his smile. She fit around him as if he'd been made for Her, and he wondered if he had been. The ecstasy flooded him again, and when he returned from it, She still rode him in a long, slow rhythm. "You know nothing, Temmin, nothing at all," she murmured. "But you will learn." She threw her head back and let out a long sigh of pleasure. She pulsed all around him, always moving, riding him and coming over and over but never letting him spend, keeping him in a driven euphoria, driven to please Her no matter what. All he wanted was that, to stay sheathed inside Her, to laugh with each joyful ripple that moved through Her.

Neya rose up on Her knees; the warm air against his suddenly exposed cock felt icy cold. She lay back on the bed, her arms and legs open and appealing. "There is an old, old ritual, before the founding of your line, Prince Temmin, before your namesake was ever thought of. Your people don't remember it. But in the men of your line it still lives, buried deep in memory, and I have waited so long for you to remember—a thousand years I've been waiting for you to return to Me. Bring down the blessing on your land, on your people. I am the field, you are the plow."

Temmin fell on Her, sliding back inside with a grunt. The deep earthy smell came to him again; it sprouted into green tendrils that curled around him as he furrowed inside Her; they held him close and twined around his root. The green burst into bloom, simple, homelike flowers at first— honeysuckle, pinks, sweet peas, fields of daffodils, all flowers that made him think of Whithorse again. Then came white roses and gardenias, freesias and tuberose, the scent of the incense in Allis's ordeal, reminders of her suffering, and he wept as he kissed the Goddess inhabiting her. His tears ripened the blooms into fruits: apples striped in red, russeted pears, berries wild and cultivated, purple plums with their white-bloomed skins, peaches soft as a woman's thigh, and some he'd never seen before.

"Well done, my King, well done," She sighed.

"Lady, I am not King!"

"You will be. Look at Me, Temmin." He gazed into the green of Her eyes again. The fruit slowly rotted; the smell of decay and dry leaves filled his nose. Figures reappeared in Her eyes: his father on a battlefield; Sedra shielding a child; Ellika standing against Tremontine soldiers; Jenks galloping across the rolling hills of Whithorse, sword in hand; Ansella bloody-handed and sobbing; Teacher and the Traveler Queen, wreathed in flames.

"What's going to happen, Lady?" he cried.

"You. You will choose to be either Temmin the Liberator or Temmin the Magnificent. Tell Teacher: It's time. Take your blessing, Temmin—don't be afraid, take it! It's yours, take it!"

Temmin let out a long roar, lips snarling back from his teeth, and plunged into Her.

Temmin woke up, unsure whether he'd been dreaming or if the lovemaking really had gone on all night after the visions. He remembered slipping into Neya over and over, holding Her in his arms as Nerr took Her, kisses that left him blind, breasts and hands and mouths and cocks, but a film overlayed it all, turning it indistinct and hallucinatory: a terrifying, ecstatic fever dream. Again, there were no windows in the room, and he couldn't gauge the time.

He rose. Allis and Issak lay each to one side, clearly themselves again even in sleep. Their faces were drawn and exhausted; Anda hadn't told him the half of it. Allis turned in her sleep, clutching vaguely around her shoulders for sheets, but they lay heaped at the bottom of the bed. Temmin stooped to cover them both.

There on each twin's left hip was the silver sigil he'd seen and dismissed on Issak the night before—they both had one. Now that his head was clear of the incense, he recognized them instantly as the same sort of sigil the Traveler Queen had placed on Emmae. He hadn't seen one on Issak the week before. Were they new? Or had something else happened to him?

A prickling shiver passed over his scalp, and he decided to tell no one, just as he had said nothing about seeing Teacher in the mirror. Well—he'd told Teacher, but that was only logical.

Temmin was always hungry, but the night's exertions brought the word "starving" into clear, sharp focus. He cast about for the towers of sweets, but the plates were bare of everything, even crumbs. He found a towel to wrap around his nakedness, and shambled into the anteroom ruffling his hair, hoping for breakfast. The antechamber was deserted but for neatly laid-out clothing—Lover's red for him, undyed for the twins—a small tray of cold food he immediately began to ransack, and a note addressed to him from Anda, too late for the bread loaf's topknot: "LEAVE THIS FOR ALLIS AND ISSAK, GREEDY GUTS. Get dressed and come to the Supplicants Chamber for a proper breakfast."

This promised proper breakfast hurried him into his red Temple garb and through the door leading directly to the Supplicants Chamber. Only one of the beds was occupied, but it was occupied to capacity. Once the occupants untangled themselves, the bed proved to contain Anda, Senik, the rugged blonde Lover, Evra Postulant, and a very confused but happy apprentice chandler. Anda called for breakfast, and the rest carted the chandler off to the baths and thence to the dining hall.

"So?" said Anda once they were settled with the fragrance of coffee and toast all around them.

"So?" shrugged Temmin, slapping marmalade on his toast a little more firmly than necessary. "You've been with Them. I don't need to tell you."

"Was it what you hoped it would be?"

"Was yours?"

She shook her head impatiently. "Temmin, you're different. You're different from any other Supplicant this Temple has ever had, and that includes Finnia—you've heard of her, yes, the other royal Supplicant? You are one of a kind. I *cannot* believe your investiture deserves only 'so.'"

Temmin hesitated. The Lady had said he must never discuss it with anyone. But surely, talking to another Supplicant, someone who'd laid in that bed herself, would be all right. He opened his mouth, but his tongue stuck; his mouth filled with the sticky, pink taste of a Neya's Day sweet. No matter how hard he tried, not a word would come out. "Ah," said Anda. "She showed you something."

"Many somethings," Temmin blurted, tongue released. "Did She not show you anything?"

"He did. Not Her. I can't speak of them, either," she murmured, "and they were all personal, anyway. I just thought—since you're different—maybe that was different, too. Maybe She'd tell you something meant for everyone. The Most Highs hoped She would."

Allis and Issak staggered in. "Food," said Issak.

"Coffee," said his sister.

Anda went to the side door and called for more of both. "Are you all right?" said Temmin, pouring coffee into cups.

"The usual," said Allis in a haggard voice. "We'll be eating most of today, eating and sleeping."

"Mostly sleeping," said Issak, piling his plate high with the remaining bacon, sausages, eggs, fruit, as Allis gnawed on a chop. "But also eating."

"Is there anything I can do?" squeaked Temmin.

"Pass the jam."

The Embodiments devoured what food was left on the table, their usual sophistication and poise abandoned, and pounced on the reinforcements when the servants carried them in.

After a trip to the bath crowded with lethargic men and women, and a soak in the hot pool until they were all the color of well-done lobsters, Temmin and Anda helped put the twins to bed, each in their separate rooms with attendants nearby if needed. "Now what?" said Temmin.

"Now nothing," yawned Anda, plucking a candy off one of the huge piles of offering sweets distributed among the clergy. "I'm clean, I'm brushed, I've tucked the Holy Ones in, I'm done. No one who worked last night does anything today. The lay servants run the place, the petitioners' rooms are closed, and there's no real offering traffic the day after a Spectacle. I am going back to bed for a nap. Aren't you tired?" Temmin shook his head, still wet and shaggy from the bath. "Well, you may do whatever you like, but don't expect me to do it with you." She rose from the couch they were sharing, dropped into her bed, and was asleep in five minutes, her odd, musical snoring muffled in the crook of her arm.

Temmin nibbled in boredom at one of the traditional crescent moon cakes heaped on a nearby plate, eating first the delicate green icing leaves, then the pink icing rose, then the whole little white fondant-covered cake all in a bite. He pocketed a handful of candies intending to take them to Ellika, before he remembered that he couldn't go back to the Keep for at least a few days, if not a few spokes. He shuffled into the bathroom, past the giant mirror in the antechamber and around the modesty wall, and relieved himself, pensive and staring off into space as he pissed.

The full enormity of what he'd done weighed down on him. He wouldn't see Jenks, or Sedra, or Ellika, or his mother for some time. They might try to come here, but he was sure his father would discourage it with everything at his disposal. Perhaps the King might even sack Jenks—a horrifying thought he didn't let himself dwell on. He might see Teacher, if Harsin let anyone see Teacher ever again. How odd that a tutor would prove to be Temmin's greatest ally; he would never have imagined it. He actually wished he could see Teacher, if only to talk about the sigils he'd seen on the twins. Teacher knew about magic—everything Temmin knew about magic, he'd learned from Teacher.

He gave himself the shake, tucked himself back into his red trousers, and walked around the modesty wall, only to stop abruptly before the mirror. Reflected in it stood Teacher—sharp, visible, not the usual shadowy figure just beneath his own reflection, but Teacher standing in the Tower Library. Temmin could read the titles in reverse on the books stacked beneath Teacher's hand, until the hand emerged from the glass. Temmin took it and let himself be pulled through.

"I saw you," he began in a rush, "I saw you clear as anything, clear as through a window pane! What's happening? There's more, too, I saw marks on the twins! Hello, by the way! Are you all right? And before I forget—" he dumped his pocketful of candies on the table among the piles of books — "can you get these to Elly? I'd have brought some for Sedra, but she doesn't like them."

"With luck, I will be released from the Library before they grow stale," said Teacher. "But do calm down. Start over."

Temmin explained the silver sigils on the twins' hips. "They glowed!"

"Have you seen them before?" said Teacher, an intent, almost frightening look on the pale face.

"No, just since last night, though truthfully I hadn't seen Allis naked before." Temmin blushed furiously. "Still, I *have* seen Issak naked, and there was no mark before, I swear. And then there's this mirror thing. It used to be that when you watched me, I saw you as if you were a shadow, just under my reflection."

"And now?"

"Now it's as if I'm looking into the next room. I don't see myself at all, only you and wherever you're at. You don't think," Temmin gasped, "you don't think I can use reflections now, do you?"

"Try."

Temmin squared his shoulders before the mirror. For a brief moment, he examined his face for signs; did he look different now? Older? More experienced? No, just his same old self, as he had been when he first arrived less than a spoke ago, the increased fur on his chin the only difference. "Show me…show me…what do you say exactly?"

"The general formula is 'If this or that is within sight of a reflection, show me,' but it doesn't really matter as long as you have the skill and can say something."

"All right, then, show me Allis!" The mirror remained resolutely still. "Perhaps she isn't before a reflection—I didn't pay attention to her room. Show me...let's see, where would I know there'd be a reflection...oh! Show me Papa's study!" Nary a ripple. "That answers that question," Temmin sighed. He turned away from the mirror, secretly glad to be free of magic; it seemed more a burden than a blessing.

"You are growing more magically sensitive, the first Tremont in 358 years to do so," said Teacher.

"What do the sigils mean? Are they the same as Emmae's? They don't look exactly like hers, but very like."

"Charms against the getting of children, yes. Maeve—the Traveler Queen—bestows them on the Lovers' Embodiments—permanent ones— and temporary ones on the Supplicants. The next time you see Anda Supplicant, pay closer attention. You will see one almost exactly like Emmae's. If the other clerics can afford one, and she likes them, Maeve gives them marks as well."

"What happens if she doesn't like them?"

"She takes their money, and in time perhaps a child will come."

"Oof," said Temmin, ruffling his hair. "I'll be getting a sigil, too, then?"

"You will not. You are in the direct succession. Neither you nor your father may ever carry one. It is Pagg's Law."

"Pagg's Law!" Temmin exclaimed. "Who has time to read that thing but the Fathers? It's as thick as my thigh. So what—what happens if I get someone with child?"

"Then congratulations would be in order."

Temmin gawped, then shut his mouth in consternation. Fathering children at the Temple had never once entered into his considerations. "But what happens? Do I acknowledge him—or the mother? How would I even know? Wait—you'd know!"

"I would know the moment you became king about any sons you might have, but no sooner, and I would never know your daughters. Do not waste too much time on this. You will be taught many ways to avoid getting children. Now, more importantly," said Teacher, an avid, almost greedy expression stealing over the usually placid face, "what did you learn last night?"

"Oh," said Temmin at this abrupt shift. "I can't talk about it. I tried."

"She showed you nothing?"

"She showed me many things. I don't know what they mean, but every time I try to talk about them, I can't." He wilted in the face of Teacher's obvious disappointment, and then remembered. "But She did say to tell you something."

"Tell me something?" said Teacher. An unaccustomed flush came to the pale cheeks. "Tell me what? Please, Temmin, tell me."

"She said to tell you it's time."

"That is all?"

"That's all."

"That...that is enough," said Teacher, sinking down onto the one stool in the Library.

Temmin realized he'd never seen Teacher sit on anything other than a table top. "What does it mean?" he said. "Time for what?"

"Time for something I have waited for, waited a very long time. I have been waiting for you—or the one who would be you. I hoped you were the one, but I was not sure. You still might not be the one, but if it is time..."

"You make no sense. The one for what?" he said impatiently. "Please stop speaking in riddles!"

"In this matter, riddles are all I have," answered Teacher. "Just as you cannot speak of certain things now, so I cannot speak of certain things." The pale silver eyes, cold and powerful, looked through him; Temmin shuddered. "I am made of secrets, Temmin. And now, so are you."

In the days after his investiture, Temmin fetched and carried for Allis and Issak. To Temmin's relief, the bloom was creeping back into Allis's face, and Issak no longer looked as if someone had crumpled him up and thrown him away—though Someone had, thought Temmin.

Even so, Temmin saw little of them. He lived the unglamorous life of a Postulant. He got lost a lot. He joined a class of newly minted Postulants studying anatomy: not the obvious kind, but the kind in which one learned the names of the bones of the hand. He kissed an extraordinary number of people. Senik hadn't been joking: in the Temple, a kiss meant "Hello," "Goodbye," "Thank you," "You're welcome," and occasionally, "What are you doing after anatomy class?" He learned to sleep through Anda snuffling her tuneful little snore in the bed opposite, and, rarely, in his bed beside him.

Temmin did not miss the Keep, at all, but he did miss his mother and sisters, and especially Jenks. Temmin sent several messages to them and had given up ever hearing back, when one day Senik called Temmin to a receiving room. "A representative from your father, I believe," he said.

It was Winmer.

Temmin advanced into the room, his hands in fists. "What do you want?"

"Your father bid me bring you a message, along with your post, Your Highness," said Winmer with a bow; he held out a neat packet of letters.

Temmin folded his arms across his chest, and made no move to take the packet. "What is the message?"

Winmer inclined his head and withdrew the packet. "He bids me tell you that your two friends at Whithorse are now your responsibility. They may not return to the Keep as servants. He also adds that what he did, he did out of sincere concern for both you and the Kingdom."

"Balls to that," snapped Temmin. "The King has a great deal of nerve sending you of all people here. I know you're behind the blackmail, Winmer. Only the most loathsome of men would use Arta Dannikson like that."

Winmer sighed, and spread his arms in conciliation. "Your Highness, I am the King's man. It doesn't matter what I think is right. When the King comes to me, it's not for advice. I do what the King commands me to do— I find ways to make what the King wants, happen. In the matter of your Supplicancy, he wanted to find ways to stop it, and so I did. I was unsuccessful, but that is less a criticism of my dedication than it is a tribute to yours. Well done, sir."

"So it's some sort of game? Is that what you're saying? It's all right to be contemptible, as long as it's your job—or—or if you win?" said Temmin, unfolding his arms and taking a step forward.

Winmer stood his ground and smiled, the corners of his mouth curving up to touch the ends of his tidy mustache. "A King should always have clean hands, don't you think, sir? Perhaps also a Prince. Some day soon, you will have a man like me to keep yours clean as well." Winmer left the packet on the low table, bowed, and departed.

Temmin blinked after him. Never, never would he have a man like Winmer, he said to himself.

He plunked himself down on the wide, low couch and picked up the packet of mail. At the top of the stack, he found a small note addressed to him in Ellika's curlicued script and bearing her seal in bright blue wax. He broke the seal:

> *Dearest Temmy,*
>
> *You are a sly boots indeed & I am very proud of you even though you have made Papa very angry & I miss you! Seddy & I will see you at the Temple on Nerr's Day to give you your brother-gifts—Papa can't stop us from doing that, at least!*
>
> *Much, much love,*
> *Your sister E*

Temmin smiled. He took up the next letter; it bore the rearing stallion postmark of Whithorse Estate, and the pragmatic handwriting of his best friend.

He sat up straighter.

"Your Grace," it began:

> *I have done as you asked, but things are easier now that word has come to us about you and the Temple. I have to say I am surprised by that since I helped you skip lessons here. But I am sure things are different in the City.*

Miss Dannikson is getting along. She seems to like learning her letters at the school, but she is uncomfortable learning to be a gentlewoman.

Here the words, "Are you sure that's what she wants?" had been smudged out, but were still legible enough if Temmin squinted.

My mother likes her, and so do most of the women here. She is very sweet and pretty and I see why you might like her.

Wallek is all right, I suppose. He is very keen on fighting. He is good. We have had a couple of bouts for fun. Then he challenged the Guards Captain, and at the end there was more red on him than his hair, I will just say that. Wallek got a lot more serious about training after. You are right, he does not know much about horses. He says he is the third son and never paid attention much since he would not get the blacksmith shop and did not want it anyway. But he is learning because I told him you want him to, and you told him to do what I said. I could wish he took that last a little more serious sometimes.

Everyone here is well. They are all very excited about you and the Temple, and keep talking about Nerr getting the Heir. Sometimes I think they are expecting gold to rain down from the sky now. People are stupid.

About Mattie, I am very surprised to hear about that. You may wish to know that she has left the Estate and no one seems to know where she has gotten to. She and her mother do not seem to be in Reggiston any more.

As for the other thing. Forget it. It does not matter.

Your obedient servant,
Nollson

Temmin rattled the letter absently, mulling it over and over. Alvy never used his titles, ever, unless he was angry or important people were watching. He signed himself "Nollson." And "Forget it?" How was Temmin supposed to forget it?

At least Fen and Arta were all right. Temmin would have to take them into his service, but he had no clear idea what he might do with them; Fen would definitely make a good sparring partner, but what would he do with Arta?

And Mattie had disappeared. Well, his father had said she might. He hoped that wherever she'd gone, she didn't hate him too much, and that she was happy.

Neya's Day flower buntings no longer arched above the streets of Arren, but a soft, flowery mood still hung over the town, weeks after the festival. The winter's coal smoke had finally blown away with the snow, leaving the air clear and the sky a fragile but unbroken blue. Mattie Dunley, now Mattie Ambleson, walked through the streets toward Arren's market square, and saw none of it.

Mattie hated market day in Arren, even with the newly mild weather. She missed Reggiston's clean, wide boulevards, the squares with their pots of colorful flowers. The outdoor cafes would be open now; girls in bright dresses would be drinking coffee and eating little cakes with their young men on their day off, and she would not be among them. (She wouldn't have been among them were she still there, but in her homesickness, she glossed over that unfortunate fact.) The ancient, gnarled apple trees lining the sloping road toward the Mother's Temple on its little rise were probably in bloom now, she thought with an inward sigh.

Arren was gray by comparison, the high brick and stone houses piled on either side of her throwing the narrow street into shade. Even the windows looked funny here: tall and thin, topped with arches that made her feel like startled eyes looked down on her. Without its Paggday basket, Mattie's arm felt bare; her bored but attentive footman held a much larger one instead. Mattie was used to being a servant, not having one trailing behind her, and the liveried young man's presence at her back set apprehensive prickles at her nape, as if she were being followed. She *was* being followed she told herself, but it was just Pawl.

Just then, her new and unfamiliar bootheel caught in a chink in the paving stones. She abruptly teetered and tried to catch herself, but gravity was against her.

Hands caught Mattie firmly round the waist and checked her fall; even so, the world spun and sparks flew all around her vision. "Are you all right?" a man's voice said. "Can you stand?"

She put her foot down, and pain flowered in her badly twisted ankle. "No, Pawl, I can't. Let me lean on you...oh!" she cried, the sparks increasing. "Perhaps you might hail a cab."

"Most certainly, and I shall escort you home as well, miss, yes?" said the man in a musical, cultured Corrish accent not at all like her footman's rough monotone.

Now that she no longer feared for her skull, she realized a stranger's hands held her up, not Pawl's. They belonged to a Corrishman whose dark eyes tilted down at their outside corners. They would have given him a mournful, almost sinister, air, but for the rest of his handsome face, kind and attentive. "Oh, thank you, sir," she said, coloring, "but Pawl can see to me."

"Nonsense, I won't hear of it," said the man. His smile warmed the gray street; it went straight into her heart, a small ray of unexpected spring. The painful sparks in her vision receded, and Mattie suddenly saw the gilt work on the lamp posts, and the cheerful, molded plaster swags of fruit and leaves festooning the elegant, narrow windows of the building opposite. The hair at Mattie's nape prickled again, this time with sudden, inexplicable elation.

A quick gesture from the man, and a hackney cab appeared as if it had been waiting. Between the Corrishman and Pawl, they gently packed Mattie into the hackney; the Corrishman sat down on the seat opposite, and said to Pawl, "Run to your mistress, and tell her to expect us." Pawl nodded unquestioningly and trotted double-time down the street toward the Ambleson townhouse; the Corrishman tapped on the roof twice, and the cab followed the footman more slowly through the Paggday traffic. How easy everyone found it to obey this stranger, she thought somewhat drowsily.

"I'm afraid these are hardly the usual circumstances. May I introduce myself, miss?" said the Corrishman. His voice fell in velvet folds around her, silken and rich, and she wondered how she'd ever thought the Corrish accent sounded funny; in his mouth, it sounded lyrical, almost exotic.

"Oh, please do!" she said.

"I am Adrik Adrikov, and it is my honor to assist you, Miss...?"

"Dun—Ambleson, sir, Miss Ambleson." She became acutely aware that she was alone in a cab with a strange man. "Oh, dear," she said faintly. "I'm afraid I've behaved very improperly."

"Never say so, Miss Ambleson, never! No one would speak ill of you— why, what were you to have done, lie there in the street? But never worry, here we are at your own front door." He climbed down from the hackney and turned back, holding out his arms. "I shall carry you up the stairs and make sure you're safe, yes?"

"Oh, Mr Adrikov, that's far, far too much trouble—oh!"

The Corrishman scooped her up before she could object further or wonder how he knew her address, and she put her arms around his neck rather than be dumped into the street. As he carried her into the house she could smell his cologne, a golden, mossy scent that mixed with the fine wool of his suit, and something else far beneath, a lurking dark; it registered deep in her heart. She closed her eyes and let herself enjoy his closeness, his strong arms holding her as if she were a little package. "I'm so lucky you were there today, Mr Adrikov," she murmured. She felt as if he were carrying her into a new life, into some unexpected, exciting future; Reggiston and its enticing beauties began to fade.

"Oh," the Corrishman smiled, "the luck was all on my side entirely, Miss Ambleson."

APPENDIX I
TREMONTINE CALENDAR
AND MEASUREMENTS

The Tremontine "wheel of the year" begins on what we call Halloween. It contains eight "spokes," somewhat like our months; spokes are between 44 and 47 days long, and follow the seasons:

Fall's Ending: Begins on Harla's Day, the midpoint between the fall equinox and the winter solstice.

Winter's Beginning: Begins on Eddin's Day, the winter solstice.

Winter's Ending: Begins on Amma's Day, the midpoint between the winter solstice and the spring equinox.

Spring's Beginning: Begins on Pagg's Day, the spring equinox.

Spring's Ending: Begins on Neya's Day, the midpoint between the spring equinox and the summer solstice.

Summer's Beginning: Begins on Nerr's Day, the summer solstice.

Summer's Ending: Begins on Venna's Day, the midpoint between the summer solstice and the fall equinox.

Fall's Beginning: Begins on Farr's Day, the fall equinox.

Years are reckoned from the founding of the kingdom, held to be the death of Temmin the Great. Years since that date are "Kings' Year," "Year of Our Kings," or "KY" for short; years before that date are "Before the Kings," or "BK."

Otherwise, time and distance are named as they are in our world; neither you nor I have the time to keep referring back and forth to imaginary measurements. ("Just how many oomphlats are in a d'for'glon, again?") For instance, a Tremontine week has seven days; a day has 24 hours.

Money is in base ten:

1 gold = 100 silver = 10,000 copper

I don't care if this makes it sound like D&D. Neither you nor I have time for intricate money schemes, even if intricate money schemes are more plausible than the logic of base ten. Actually, Intricate Money Schemes is the name of my Pink Floyd cover band.

I have taken one other liberty, and that's with the names of the days of the week. They are:

Ammaday (Monday)

Farrday (Tuesday)

Eddinday (Wednesday)

Nerrday (Thursday)

Neyaday (Friday)

Vennaday (Saturday)

Paggday (Sunday)

There is much more world-building nonsense in the wiki at MeiLinMiranda.com, though it's going to have to be rebuilt; most of what's there is from the first draft of this series.

APPENDIX II
PRONUNCIATIONS

I hate it when I don't know what the heck names sound like, and so I assume you do too. Thus:

Allerach: ALL-er-ock (The "ock" is a German "ach" sound)
Alzeh: AL-zeh
Amma: AH-mah
Ansella: AN-sella
Barle: BARL
Bordigalle: BOR-DIH-GALL (equal emphasis)
Gian: JEE-AHN (run together in one syllable)
Inchar: in-CHAR
Issak: ISS-ak (*not* Isaac)
Leute: LOY-teh
Naister: NAY-ster
Ouve: OOV
Tremont: TREH-munt
Vakale'le: vah-kah-LAY-LAY
Valmouth: VAL-muth
Whithorse: WIT-horse (*not* white-horse)

If it's not here, it's pronounced as written (example: "Allis" is "Alice").

ACKNOWLEDGMENTS

I must first thank eumenides on LiveJournal. She was the first reader who made me believe I might actually be able to write my own stories.

The original version of this book was only the story of Warin and Emmae, and a very clunky, fairy-tale-like story it was. Until my dear old friend Manoki got hold of it, and started asking me question...after question...after question! That Darn Manoki (as she became known) wanted to know everything about the world these characters lived in—and I mean *everything*. As I answered her questions, I gradually got the first draft of this series. I'm *still* answering her questions! Manoki has been my most consistent supporter—I love you, kiddo. After fourteen years of online friendship, we've really got to meet!

My editor Annetta "Nettah the Edittah" Ribken has been my rock. Working with her has been one of the best educations I've ever received. She was the perfect editor for this story, and I have Twitter to thank for finding her. Now you've found her, and if you need an editor, you should contact her.

Karen Wehrstein has also added invaluable insights. Many of the final touches on the book were a result of some long, thoughtful, exhausting conversations. Thanks for sticking with it, Karen!

Alice Fox has brought my characters to visual life now for nearly two years. Her consistent ability to take the descriptions I give her and send me back the exact person I envisioned is uncanny.

MCM is Canadian. This annoys me, as Canadians get free health care AND free ISBNs. He also designed the book block. He is awesome. Go watch him write live some time.

My "non-existent beta group" suffered through this entire volume. I thank them for not dying of shock when the story took a different shape from the draft they expected, and for giving me critical feedback as we progressed.

All of the readers at MeiLinMiranda.com who have encouraged me for two years now—I love every single one of you crazy people.

Perfumer Elizabeth Barrial of Black Phoenix Alchemy Lab knows me from Adam. Well, she probably knows of me from the BPAL.org forum, but you know what I mean. Nevertheless, I have to thank both her and the wonderful, generous members of BPAL.org for leading me literally by the nose out of the long twilight of my illness and into my real, *fabulous* self that I've been hiding for far too many years.

My best friend A encouraged me and patiently listened as I "talked story." Thanks, sweetie.

Special thanks go to Daniel Gudlat for wiki duty above and beyond the call, and Northwoodsman for compiling the definitive Tremontine calendar. Eddin is proud of both of you.

My husband and children sat through two years of Mama scribbling at all hours of the day and night. I forgot to cook, I forgot to sleep, I forgot appointments. I obsessed and talked to myself. They loved me anyway. I love them more than they can ever guess.

But the biggest thanks go to those who made this book possible: the forty-eight people who bought special $25, $50 and $100 packages to fund the editing and production of this book. All these people expected in return was the story you've just read. I know ONE of these people in real life. I am humbled and so very honored by their trust. Here are their names—if some look unusual, it's because they've requested I use their "screen names" from MeiLinMiranda.com.

Listed in alphabetical order:

Andrea
Alyxe Barron
Bert Belknap
Brandon, aka V
button-nosed_turtle
Rebecca C.
Benjamin Dunn
TeKiesha Elliott

eric the girl

Lawrence Evalyn

Rachel Feldman, aka BCT

Gia Greenheart

giom

Goforbroke

Daniel Gudlat

Jo Guthrie

Nevin Hillegass

Jackie aka applejax

Katie

kawaiikune

Krey

Rebecca R. Kurth aka BekaShmeka

kwee the warrior

Heather Kittae Lee

Ashley MacDonald

Sean Manning

J. McIlwain

Megan aka the Which

MsGamgee

Northwoodsman

RandomTym

Samaris

sarianna

Saudadina

Scarth

Amanda Schloss

scrapper

Sarah Schumacher

James Sheppard

ShEriNik

Chris Shull

Leslie Sinak

Stormy (Our Official Spokesmodel)

temporaryglitter
Tolovana
Vandole
viruslife
Anna W aka the paradox

You have changed my life, and I will never forget you.